THE BLADE BEARER

BY

K.M.ASHMAN

D1568864

MEDIEVAL MAP OF WALES

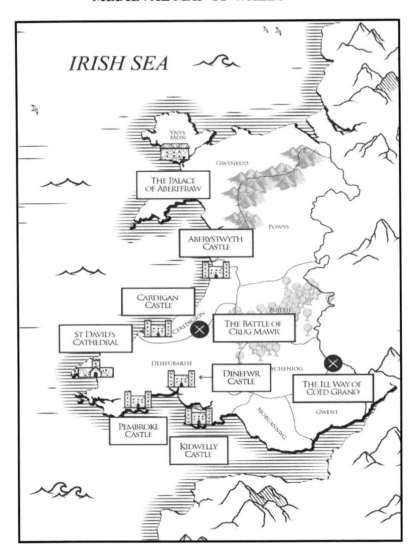

Though the borders and boundaries of early Wales were constantly changing, for the sake of our story, the above shows an approximation of where the relevant areas were at the time.

CHARACTER LIST

Although correct pronunciation is not really necessary to enjoy the story, for those who would rather experience the authentic way of saying the names, explanations are provided in italics.

The 'll' can be difficult to pronounce in Welsh, and is formed by placing the tongue on the roof of the mouth, while expelling air past the tongue on both sides. Non-Welsh speakers sometimes struggle with this – audible representations are available online.

THE HOUSE OF ABERFFRAW
Gruffydd ap Cynan: King of Gwynedd – *Gruff-ith ap Cun-nan*
Angharad ferch Owain: Queen of Gwynedd – *Ang-har-rad*
Owain: Son of Gruffydd - *Owe-ain*
Cadwaladwr: Son of Gruffydd – *Cad-wal–a-dwr* - (rhymes with shoe but roll the letter 'R')

THE HOUSE OF TEWDWR
Gruffydd ap Rhys: (known as Tarw) – *Tar-oo* (roll the letter 'R')
Nesta ferch Rhys: Tarw's Sister – *Nessa* or *Nest-Ah*

OTHER CHARACTERS
Stephen of Bloise: King of England

NORMAN/ENGLISH FORCES
Robert Fitzmartin: (Robert fitz Martin) Marcher Lord of Cemais - English leader
Maurice Fitzgerald: (Maurice fitz Gerald) Marcher Lord of Llansteffan
Stephen Demareis: (Stephen de Mareis) Castellan of Cardigan Castle
John of Salisbury: Castellan of Pembroke Castle
Maurice de Londres: Castellan of Kidwelly Castle

WELSH FORCES

Owain ap Gruffydd: Son of King Gruffydd - Welsh leader
Cadwaladwr ap Gruffydd: Son of King Gruffydd
Hywel ap Maredudd: Lord of Brycheniog – How-ell
Dog: Tarw's right hand man
Robert of Llandeilo: Tarw's trusted ally
Cynwrig the Tall: Priest

PLACE NAMES

Aberffraw: *Ab-er-frow*
Brycheniog: *Brick-eye-knee-og*
Deheubarth: *Du-hi-barrth* (roll the letter 'R')
Dinefwr: *Din-e-foorr* (roll the letter 'R')
Crug Mawr: *Creeg-Ma-oorr* (roll the letter 'R')
Gwynedd: *Gwin-eth*
Kidwelly: *Kid-well-ee*
Pembroke: *Pem-broke*
Carmarthen: *Car-mar-then*

Prologue

AD 1135

Gwenllian ferch Gruffydd, daughter of the king of Gwynedd and known as the Warrior Princess, was the wife of Gruffydd ap Rhys, the last prince of Deheubarth in Wales. Despite their royal heritage, they lived outside of the law and with only a small band of loyal men at their backs, became a serious problem to the English, rebelling against authority and raiding their interests in the pursuit of a free Deheubarth.

Despite the crown's concerted efforts, they remained at large for many years, operating from the forest-covered area in mid Wales called the Cantref Mawr. Eventually, the English king offered them both amnesty in return for the cessation of hostilities, and though they agreed in the short term, the peace was short lived and they soon returned to the struggle, pursuing their dream of returning Deheubarth to Welsh control.

With this in mind, in February 1136, Tarw rode north to seek reinforcements from Gwenllian's father but while he was away, the English, under the control of Maurice de Londres of Kidwelly Castle, organised an army to quell the potential uprising and in an effort to gain time for her husband, Gwenllian was forced to rise against the English with an army of her own. Unfortunately, she was betrayed by one of her own men and after being ambushed by the enemy, undertook a fierce battle where her forces were defeated.

Despite the code of chivalry demanding otherwise, Maurice de Londres beheaded Gwenllian on the battlefield in front of Kidwelly Castle. One of her sons was also killed while another was taken into captivity.

With the Welsh army destroyed, all remaining signs of revolt disappeared, and the English rulers set about crushing any lingering hopes of independence with a campaign of violence and brutality.

In the north, word reached Tarw and the rest of Gwenllian's family. King Gruffydd was old and almost blind so unable to react in any effective way and for a while, the death of the popular princess caused fear and despair right across the country. The English and their allies took advantage of the confusion and within months, any thought of freedom in Wales, especially in the south, had been extinguished, seemingly forever.

Without an army, Tarw returned to Deheubarth to avenge his wife but with so many still shocked by the terrible defeat, he found little support for a fresh campaign and the people resigned themselves to living under the brutal regime of the triumphant English castellans. Distraught, the Prince sought drunken solace in the halls of the few he still called friend.

However, in the west of Deheubarth, in the cathedral of Saint David, one lowly and pious old priest who had known Gwenllian since she was a child, knew he couldn't let her death go unavenged.

One spring morning, after praying to God for strength and guidance, he finally got to his feet and took a deep, painful breath. He knew the path was going to be hard and the chances of success limited, but with an iron resolve, and with nothing to lose except his life, Cynwrig the Tall left his cell in the bowels of the cathedral and set out to seek vengeance.

Chapter One

Kidwelly

April AD 1136

    'Molly,' shouted a voice from the tavern, 'are you done yet, there're plenty more out here need seeing to.'

    The penny whore in the back room sighed and leaned back against the wall at the end of the timber bed. It had been a long day and if she hadn't been on her feet serving jacks of frothing ale to drunken revellers in the tavern, she had been on her back seeing to their other needs. Neither occupation was a problem in itself for she was well aware of her station in life, it was just that sometimes, just sometimes, she would have liked a few moments to herself instead of constantly having to avoid the grasping paws of drunk men seeking sexual relief for a measly penny.

    She looked down at the sleeping man next to her on the bed. He was dirty and stank of ale. Most of her customers did but this one was different. He was a regular and one of the few who at least treated her with a semblance of respect. There was always some talk first, an unusual but welcome trait rarely requested by her other customers, and he was always gentle, another quality rare amongst the taverns of the poor. Not tonight, though. Tonight he had been angry, not at her but with life in general. He had obviously drunk far too much and though he had tried to undertake the act his penny had bought, he had failed miserably and had collapsed into a drunken sleep at her side.

    Presented with a rare opportunity, Molly had let him lay and helped herself to some of the ale he had brought through from the tavern. For what seemed like an age she just lay there, listening to the noise as the market traders squandered their hard-earned coins in games of chance and drank leather jacks of bitter ale. Finally, she picked up the remaining chunk of bread the man had brought in with him and dipped it into the tankard before finishing his ale in three swallows.

    'Macsen,' she said quietly shaking him by the shoulders, 'wake up it's time to leave.' When she had no reaction she shook him harder, this time receiving a drunken grunt of acknowledgement.

    'Macsen,' she said again, 'come on or you will raise the ire of the landlord and I can't afford to lose this job.'

Slowly the man came to his senses and finally sat up on the side of the bed. His head hung down and his tangled filthy hair reached way down past his face. Molly crawled over the sheepskin cover and placed her hands on his shoulders, rubbing them gently.

'Do you feel better?' she asked quietly.

'What do you mean?' he grunted without moving his position.

'You were very angry,' she said, resting her head on his shoulder, 'and I have never seen you like that before. I thought you were going to beat me.'

The man looked up over his shoulder and the whore tilted her head to meet his gaze.

'I would never do that, Molly,' he said, 'you alone are the only friend I have around here and besides, there are many others who I would lay my wrath upon should they ever cross my path.'

'Then what has brought you to such anger,' she said, 'has some knave dealt you ill?'

'God has dealt me ill,' said the man, 'and I curse him for it.'

'Don't say that,' gasped Molly, making the sign of the cross on her naked breasts. 'You will have us both burn in the fires of hell for even thinking such things.'

'And I would welcome it,' said the man, 'for it can inflict no more pain than that which I already bear.'

Molly fell silent for a moment before getting off the bed and donning a thin woollen shawl. She walked around and knelt before the man, taking both his hands in hers.

'Now you listen to me,' she said, 'I don't know where you have come from or indeed who you really are, but I know a good man when I see one, and you fit that title like a hand in a glove. Whatever the circumstance that dragged you into this pit of despair, surely it can be reversed?'

Macsen snorted as he stifled a laugh of derision.

'Molly,' he said lifting his head to stare into her eyes, 'I like you but let us not forget that you are a penny whore without knowledge of the world beyond this town.' He saw a brief look of pain in her eyes at his description and lifted one of his hands to brush a stray lock of hair away from her face. 'I mean no ill by the remark,' he continued, 'it is just a statement of fact. Whore or not, you are still a good friend but there are things that you don't understand.'

'Then tell me,' said Molly. 'Share your burden and I swear I shall tell not a soul.'

The man shook his head.

'I cannot, Molly,' he said, 'for to speak my shame aloud would surely crush my soul forever.'

'Then at least let me help.'

'How can you help; do you have riches or armies at your disposal?'

'Admittedly not,' said Molly, 'but I could wash your clothes for a start, you stink of the sty. Why don't you come back when the tavern is closed, and I will arrange a bucket of hot water for you to bathe while I wash your clothes?' She reached up and gently wiped his brow. 'You look done in, Macsen,' she continued, 'what you need is some hot food and a good night's sleep. Tomorrow the world will seem a better place.'

The man caught her stare and for a moment she thought he would agree but finally he released her hands before standing up and retrieving his clothes from the floor where he had thrown them in his drunken yet overly optimistic lust an hour earlier. He dressed quickly and pulled on his boots before walking over to the door that led back through to the tavern.

'Where are you going?' asked the whore. 'You have given me no answer.'

'My filth and wretchedness are the burdens I bear for being beneath the lowest of the low,' said Macsen, 'and though you honour me with your offer, it is one I cannot accept.'

'Why not?'

'Because this is who I have become. Now, I have a few pennies left for ale and a game of chance. Perhaps Satan will allow the dice to fall in my favour and I can start to rebuild my fortunes this very night.'

'Macsen,' snapped the girl again, 'if you continue to court acquaintance with the devil then our friendship will not survive even this night. Our Lord is watching over all of us and I promise he will not forsake you. He will show you the way.'

'Perhaps so,' said Macsen, 'but I doubt it. Now, I am going back out there. Are you coming?'

'Wait,' she said, and threw her shabby dress over her head before joining him at the door.

'About earlier,' said the man, nodding toward the bed, 'I don't recall…'

'That's because it didn't happen,' said Molly with a smile, 'but worry not, your secret is safe and as far as they are concerned out there, you were the best lover I ever had.'

'Thank you,' said Macsen and leaned down to place a kiss on her forehead. 'Now come on, there is ale to drink and dice to throw.'

He turned and walked through the door into the crowded tavern and after taking a deep breath, Molly followed him through.

'Here he is,' roared a giant of a man as Macsen walked into the packed room, 'my drinking partner and his virgin bride.'

The men in the tavern roared with laughter at the jest and some ushered Macsen over to the table where he had spent the last few hours drinking with the vagrants and thugs of the town.

'Landlord, bring ale for this smitten lover,' shouted the large man, 'and make sure you fill the cup to the brim this time or I swear on Satan's cock I shall drown you in your own barrel.'

'Can I take his place,' shouted a voice from the rear of the tavern, 'for surely I know no better way to die.'

Again, laughter filled the room as the landlord brought a carefully filled jack over to the table.

'Who is paying,' shouted the landlord over the noise, 'for there is neither charity nor credit in this house?'

'I have coin,' said Macsen quietly, 'and I pay my debts.' He reached into his pocket for his purse but the giant man grabbed his hand.

'Let it lay where it is, Sir Ram,' he said, 'for this ale is my gift to you. Besides, judging by the way you roll the dice I suspect that the few pennies you still possess will be in my own purse before this night is through.'

Macsen gave a thin-lipped smile and took the jack in his shaking hand before emptying half in a couple of gulps.

'You have a thirst about you,' said the giant with a grin, 'so am I correct in saying the virgin bride there worked the Ram hard?'

Macsen looked over at Molly, catching her eye for the fleetest of moments.

'Oh, he was no Ram, Master Geraint,' she said, looking up at the farm hand, 'for Rams are small in stature, short of service and ill to the eye. I would say he was more of a wild stallion fresh from the mountains and would have serviced a whole herd of fillies given the chance.'

Laughter abounded again, and the man known as Geraint slapped Macsen hard on the back in acknowledgement.

'Excellent,' he said, 'but now to more important things. Show me your pennies, good man, for there are dice to be thrown.'

On the other side of the town, another man sat in a tavern in the shadows of Kidwelly Castle, no less dishevelled but as sober as a priest. The ale on the trestle before him had lasted over an hour and he was in no hurry to get more, not because of cost but because he wanted his wits about him as he sought the information he required without raising too much attention to himself.

'You have nursed that jack a long time, my friend,' said the landlord coming over, 'is it not to your taste or are you as destitute as you look?'

'The ale is fine,' said the beggar, 'but my belly feels like there are rats fighting over who is to rule my innards.'

'Then let's hope there is a victor soon for there is a caravan due in this very afternoon and I need these seats full of thirsty drinking men, not knaves without a penny to their name.'

'I understand, my lord,' said the beggar, 'and I will be on my way soon enough.'

'See to it that you are, or I will have you thrown out, rats and all.'

'Of course, my lord,' said the man and nodded his head in deference as the landlord walked away.

The beggar lifted his jack and took another sip of the warm ale. His demeanour was small and subservient, but his eyes were as sharp as any lance and he took in everything about him, unnoticed by the rest of the customers. Men came and went without raising his interest but eventually two came in that he knew would be likely targets for his closer attention. Slowly, and as if carrying a lame leg, he started walking over to the door but feigned a stumble and fell crashing into the trestle where the two newcomers sat.

'Steady old man,' laughed one of the men, 'it seems the drink has gotten the better of you.'

'Alas, it is not the drink that aides my fall,' replied the beggar as he struggled to stand, 'but an English arrow taken just five hundred paces from this very tavern not two months since.'

'You fought in the battle where the Lady Gwenllian was defeated?' asked the second man, his interest piqued.

'I was there, yes and though I cursed the Norman archer who inflicted this upon me at the time, it turned out to be a blessing I should thank him for.'

'Why would you say that?' asked the first man helping the beggar to his feet.

'Because my wound was received just before the lady Gwenllian, may our lord rest her soul, was forced onto the plain where she was murdered by Maurice de Londres. I could not walk so stayed hidden amongst the trees. Had I not, I would surely have perished alongside all those good men out on the field.'

'Indeed, it was a terrible day,' said the man, 'and you have my respect for fighting alongside the lady Gwenllian.'

'My lord, I am afraid you misjudged me,' said the beggar, 'for I am no fighting man, I simply cooked the broth in the camps and collected the arrows for our archers between assaults.'

'Nevertheless, it was a role that needed to be filled and many would not have done so. Please, let me buy you a drink.' He turned to stare across the tavern. 'Master landlord, a tankard of ale for this fine man here, and with it a hand of bread, if you please.'

'Do not be taken in by his tales,' said the landlord, 'and let me throw him out into the gutter where the likes of him belong.'

'My tale is true,' said the beggar, 'and I have the scars to prove it should you wish to see.'

'That won't be necessary,' said the first man. 'My name is Gwyn, and my friend here is known as Skinner after his trade. It is rare to come across a survivor of the battle for any taken were banished or imprisoned. Would you share your tale with us in return for ale and food?'

'I will, my lords, though I saw little from my place hidden amongst the bushes.'

'Then perhaps you can recall what the lady Gwenllian was like to ride alongside prior to her fate?'

'Of course,' said the beggar, 'what do you want to know?'

'Anything,' replied Gwyn, 'for her tale intrigues us all, but first we should know your name. What should we call you?'

'Alas, the name given to me by my Christian parents has been lost in the mists of time, and the title bestowed on me by those who would jest about my place in this world has now become the only name I know.'

'And that is?'

'My lord,' said the beggar, 'in deference to my lowly position, I am known as Dog!'

Chapter Two

Gwynedd

April AD 1136

Angharad sat in her chambers before her fire with her favourite wolf hound at her feet. At seventy-one years of age, she was tired and very susceptible to the cold. Around her knees lay a blanket of finest wolf pelts and though she was advanced with age, she was certainly not infirm. A pitcher of warmed wine sat on the table near the fire, and a platter of sweetmeats lay almost untouched beside it.

Across the room near the window sat her personal servant Catrin, repairing part of a tapestry that had become damaged during a boisterous banquet in the main hall a few days earlier. Apart from the crackle of the logs in the flames the room was deathly quiet.

Catrin was only thirty and had recently been moved to Angharad's personal service following the death of the previous incumbent but already she was proving indispensable to Angharad and indeed, to Angharad's husband, Gruffydd ap Cynan, the king of Gwynedd.

Angharad groaned and sat upright as she reached for the sweetmeats.

'My lady,' said Catrin, getting up from her chair, 'please allow me.'

'I am not incapable quite yet, Catrin,' said Angharad as she fed some of the treats to the dog, 'and the day I cannot reach a platter from my own chair is the day they should dig my grave.'

Catrin approached her mistress and crouched down at her side.

'How are you feeling today?' she asked, touching Angharad's forehead, 'has the fever returned?'

'No,' said Angharad, 'it seems this delicate flower plucked from the fields of Englefield as a young girl has turned out to be tougher than boot leather in her advanced years.'

'You will outlive us all, that much is true,' replied Catrin with a smile.

'Bring my shawl,' said Angharad, getting slowly to her feet.

'Where are we going?' asked Catrin walking over to the pegs on the wall.

'I wish to visit the king,' said Angharad.

'My lady, is that wise? Only last night the ague still engulfed him, and he may pass the demons on to you.'

'Utter nonsense, girl,' said Angharad, 'when you have lived as long as me you will learn that once cured of any particular affliction it is often the case that you are not again infected quickly by an ailment already conquered. Besides, he is my husband and my place is by his side.'

'Of course, my lady,' said Catrin and picked up the shawl to drape it over Angharad's shoulders.

'I swear this thing gets heavier by the day,' said Angharad. 'Speak to the dressmaker and see if she can find something lighter but no less warm.'

'Of course, my lady,' said Catrin and retrieved her own shawl before following the queen out of the door.

A few minutes later they crossed the landing and climbed the stairs to the King's chamber at the top of the tower. The early spring winds crept through the gaps in the timber walls and Catrin considered returning to the queen's chambers to get their cloaks.

'I swear he only chose this room out of vanity,' mumbled Angharad as she laboured up the steps. 'Any other king would have chosen one near the great hall, but no, my husband deems it necessary that even in sleep his head should remain above all others.'

Catrin chuckled.

'I don't think the king has an ounce of vanity in his body,' she said, 'he just likes his peace and quiet.'

'Trust me,' said Angharad as she paused to catch her breath on the final landing, 'in his day this man could be as vain as the highest born princess.'

'That amuses me,' said Catrin, 'for I have always imagined the king as the most feared ruler Wales has ever seen.'

'And indeed he was,' said Angharad, 'but he had his moments. Anyway, enough of such frivolity for if he knew I had shared such things with you, that pretty head of yours would be atop a spike before the cock crows.'

Catrin composed herself and followed Angharad up to the king's chamber. Outside stood a man at arms guarding the door as well as a servant sitting on a nearby chair.

'My lady,' said the servant getting to his feet. 'Forgive me, we were not expecting you.'

'Evidently,' said Angharad. 'Please inform the king I am here.'

'He is in discussion with the Lord Owain,' said the servant, 'on matters of state.'

'My son is here? Why was I not informed?'

'My lady, I was equally un-informed and only became aware of his arrival when he appeared less than an hour ago.'

'Nevertheless, you should have sent a messenger. Now are you going to announce me or shall I just walk in?'

'Of course, my lady,' said the servant and walked past the guard to open the doors.

Inside the chamber, Gruffydd ap Cynan sat in an enormous bed covered with sumptuous sheepskin covers. The little white hair he had left lay wisplike on his bald head and his eyes were milky white, devoid of sight. An apothecary sat at a nearby table, quietly mixing a potion from a bag of collected herbs and powders.

At the bedside stood Owain, Gruffydd's oldest son and heir to the kingdom of Gwynedd and at the sound of the doors opening, both men turned their heads in annoyance.

'Who is it?' rasped Gruffydd, 'and why do you interrupt a private meeting?'

'My lord,' said the servant bowing his head, 'the Lady Angharad begs audience.'

'Who? asked the king, straining to hear.

'Your queen, my lord, the lady Angharad.'

'Tell her to wait,' mumbled the king, 'I am dealing with matters of state.'

'Of course, my lord.' said the servant but as he turned away, Angharad walked past him and strode toward the bed.

'I will do no such thing,' she announced as she walked over to greet her son, kissing him on the cheek before turning to face Gruffydd. 'And you, dear husband, should know by now that such instruction only adds gloom to the day of your servants when they will so obviously be ignored.'

'Damned woman,' mumbled the king, 'I should have taken your head years ago.'

'And then where would you have been?' asked Angharad, tidying up the covers around his legs, 'without me you would have been a pauper within months.'

'Or significantly richer,' mumbled the king.

Owain smiled at the banter and it brought back memories of how happy his life had been growing up at Aberffraw, the palace on Ynys Mon where the king had his seat of power.

'Hello mother,' he said, 'you look well.'

'As well as can be in the circumstances,' she said turning to face him, 'so why are you are here? To discuss options of retribution perchance?'

'Perhaps,' said Owain,' but if truth be told, we can do nothing without father's support. The task is too great.'

'Is this true?' asked Angharad turning to face her husband

'There are many matters to consider,' said Gruffydd.

'What matters?' asked Angharad. 'Surely the only matter that counts is that the head of the bastard who killed our daughter sits on a spike outside the gates of his own burning castle.'

'An ideal scenario I agree,' said Gruffydd, 'but to raise an army capable of doing such a thing takes time and money.'

'It has already been more than two months,' said Angharad, 'how much time do you need?'

'My love,' said the king, 'please don't challenge me on this. To raise an army and arrange the necessary support to keep them in the field for months, needs a great deal of thought and preparation, especially as it may include a siege.'

'Father,' said Owain, 'I have already told you that I can have over two thousand well-armed men in the field within days, each supported by your Cantref lords. Just say the word and we can be riding south before the month ends.'

Gruffydd turned his head toward the window.

'Is the physician still here?'

'I am, lord,' said the apothecary, 'and your medicine is ready.'

'Then leave it on the table and be gone,' said Gruffydd,' and take everyone with you. This conversation is for the ears of my family only.'

'Of course, my lord,' said the apothecary and placed all his ingredients back in the wooden box before leaving the room along with the servants.

'Are we alone,' asked the king when the door finally closed.

'We are,' said Owain.

'Good, then we can talk freely. You have to understand that it is not just a case of sending an army south to avenge your sister, there are other important matters to consider.'

'What is more important than killing the man who beheaded your daughter? That and that alone should be consuming your very soul.'

'First of all,' said Gruffydd, 'if you think that two thousand men are enough to ride through Ceredigion and into Deheubarth without challenge then you are sadly mistaken. Such a force would get no further than Cardigan before being put to the blade by the forces of Stephen Demareis.'

'I do not fear the constable of Cardigan,' said Owain, 'and welcome combat.'

'Spoken like a man with limited experience of warfare,' said Gruffydd. 'Demareis is reputed to have almost five hundred men, including experienced cavalry within a day's ride of Cardigan and when word reaches him about any force riding through Ceredigion then you can guarantee they will be encamped within the castle walls before the following dawn.'

'Five hundred?' said Owain. 'Less than a quarter of those I can field.'

'That does not include those he can summon from Cemais,' said Gruffydd. 'If there was to be a rally behind his calls for reinforcement you can increase that number tenfold and even if perchance you should reach Kidwelly castle, how long do you think you could last laying siege to the fortifications? In weeks your supplies would run out and you would be too far south to rely on any resupply from here. No, Owain, this plan as it is, has no chance of success.'

'Then tell me what we are to do, father,' said Owain, his voice rising in frustration, 'for I cannot just sit around and wait while my sister's murderer gets fat, regaling stories of her defeat in battle. Don't forget, she was trying to hold back the enemy in order to gain her husband time in recruiting our support when she died. If not for love, then we at least owe her memory a duty of honour.'

'I agree,' said Gruffydd, 'and I will put my mind to it, indeed there are some plans already afoot, but you need to be patient. Besides, if we were to march against Maurice de Londres now it could be seen as an assault on the crown of England, and the king could react against Gwynedd.'

'Surely not,' said Angharad, 'as he has his hands full defending his position against the attentions of Matilda. There will be a civil war between them and should the Empress claim her dead father's crown as rightfully hers, then who knows what will happen?'

'I believe that is unlikely,' said Gruffydd. 'England is not ready for its first queen. Stephen will emerge victorious, of that I am sure.'

'But surely, while they fight each other,' said Owain, 'there is no better time to strike. Stephen is unlikely to send more men at arms into Wales while he is at risk from Matilda's armies.'

'He wouldn't need to. A series of letters is all it could take and those loyal to the king would muster their men at arms at a moment's notice. Don't forget, Robert Fitzmartin holds a strong standing army in Cemais, as does Richard de Claire in Ceredigion. Combined with Demareis' men in Cardigan, they would create a formidable foe and could easily march against Gwynedd.'

'Fitzmartin is loyal to Matilda, not Stephen.'

'Nevertheless, any such loyalties would be put aside albeit temporarily if they saw a Welsh army as being a threat. No, leave this to me and I will consider all the options, but one thing is sure, we need a wedge to be driven between the English forces before we can even contemplate an action against Maurice de Londres.'

'And what form will this wedge take?' asked Owain.

'I know not at the moment,' said Gruffydd, 'but as soon as it makes itself known, we will be ready to act.'

Owain gave a deep sigh, realising that it was pointless arguing any further. When his father was in this sort of mood there was no budging him from any stance taken.

'In that case,' he said eventually, 'perhaps you will allow me to withdraw and get some refreshments. It has been a long ride and I am exhausted. When I have recovered, I will come to see you again, perhaps on the morrow.'

'If you come as my son, you will be welcome,' said Gruffydd, 'come as a warlord and you will be shown the door forthwith.'

'I understand,' said Owain with a smile and turned to Angharad. 'Mother, will you join me?'

'In a while,' said Angharad, 'first I will spend some time with my husband. Somewhere beneath all this bluster is the man I married, and I am determined to seek him out.'

'Then I wish you the best of luck,' said Owain. 'You will find me in the lesser hall.'

Angharad smiled and watched her son leave the king's chambers. When he was gone she turned again to her husband.

'He means well,' she said.

'I know,' said the king seeking her hand with his own, 'but if I was to bend to his whims then we could lose even more of our children. Trust me on this, the time will come for vengeance but now is not that time.'

'If you say so,' said Angharad, 'but anyway, enough talk of warfare, how is my man today?'

'Old, tired, blind, sick, bedridden,' he replied, 'but apart from that, full of the joys of spring. Can you not see?'

Angharad smiled.

'Well at least the wit is unaffected,' she said and leaned forward to kiss his forehead. 'Have you taken your potions today?'

'Aye, though they are as much use as donkey piss. How do you fare?'

Angharad paused and looked over to the window.

'If truth be told,' she said eventually, 'I cloak my pain with levity whilst inside I   ache to hold my little girl in my arms just for a moment more.'

'She was a grown woman with purpose of mind,' said Gruffydd, 'and I could not be prouder of her.'

'She had no right to be leading an army,' said Angharad, 'she should have been in a hall somewhere admonishing the servants.'

'She did what she had to do,' said Gruffydd.

'And it got her killed so what was the gain in such bravado?'

'I know it seems a waste,' said Gruffydd, 'but her name will live forever. Cry rivers when we are alone, my love, but outside of these walls, hold your head up high and speak her name with pride for she was as good as any man I ever knew.'

Angharad turned to face the king, grateful he could not see the silent tears streaming down her cheeks.

'I miss her so much,' she said eventually, 'my heart aches even to hear her name.'

'As does mine,' said Gruffydd, squeezing her hand, 'but I swear by all that is holy, her death will not go unavenged.'

Angharad wiped away the tears and forced a smile.

'So,' said Gruffydd eventually, 'are we done here?'

'No, we are not,' said Angharad. 'Move over you old goat for it is a long time since I laid alongside you, clothed or unclothed.'

'Remove your gown and you will see that there is yet life in this old goat,' he replied.

'Your optimism is as outrageous as your memory,' laughed Angharad as she climbed upon the bed, 'but I will settle for an embrace.'

'So be it,' said the king, and moved to one side as the queen lay beside him. He placed his arm around her and they lay in silence for an age, enjoying the closeness and memories of a lifetime together. Finally, as the king's snores floated gently around the room, Angharad gently extricated herself and pulled the covers up to his chin.

'Sleep well, my king,' she whispered and left the chambers, closing the door quietly behind her.

Down in the lesser hall Owain was talking to one of his Sergeants by the fire. Above them, the angled oak rafters bore the heavy thatched roof, each decorated with shields, weapons and the stuffed heads of the many animals killed in the hunts on Ynys Mon. Stags, boar, rabbits and even wolves stared down to the flag-stoned hall where many men had drunk and revelled until unconscious through ale and wine.

At the far end of the hall, racks of spears lined the walls and above them, the draped flags of those defeated by Gruffydd in a lifetime of battle.

Angharad walked in to the stink of ale and dried sweat, striding through it as if it was the sweetest smelling meadow.

'Mother,' said Owain as she approached, 'is he sleeping?'

'He is,' said Angharad and turned to the man at Owain's side. 'Master Michael, it is good to see you again. Is your family well?'

'They are,' said the Sergeant, 'and my wife sends her greetings.'

'Perhaps they should visit soon, it would be nice to see them again.'

'I will make the suggestion, my lady,' said Michael as he bowed his head.

Angharad turned to Owain.

'Tell me,' she said, 'this plan you presented to the king. Was it detailed?'

'I laid out only the facts,' said Owain. 'He gave me no chance to discuss strategies.'

'Then share them with me,' said Angharad, 'and we shall see what sense they make.

'Mother, war is a subject for men. You wouldn't understand much of it.'

'Owain, dearest,' said Angharad taking the cup of ale from her son's hand, 'I have been beside your father most of my life and have witnessed the planning and execution of more battles than you can imagine, both as victor and vanquished. You would be surprised at what this old woman knows about strategy.' She paused to drain the cup before placing it back on the table and looking up to her son. 'Now, are we going to talk or not?

Chapter Three

The Cantref Mawr

April AD 1136

    Robert of Llandeilo led his horse slowly along the path, his eyes glued to the ground. He had walked the forests for several days since leaving the Carmarthen road looking for the signs that would lead him to the man he sought but without much luck. His quarry was well used to the rebel held forests and if he had suspected there would be people looking for him, he would have taken every precaution to hide any trace of his presence.

    Despite this, one of the travellers on the path had assured him there was a stranger camped in a tiny side valley of one of the wooded hills that was rarely frequented by any rider and it was this path Robert had taken.

    Pausing for a rest he looked up at the mountains ahead. If this was indeed the place then there was nowhere for the man to run if he was discovered, at least not on horseback for the slopes were too steep. On either side of the track, the trees were thick and ended at the foot of rocky escarpments so there was no escape that way. If his man was there, then he would be caught in a trap of his own making.

    After tying his horse to a tree, he carried on walking up the path, this time, making every effort to keep as quiet as possible. He needed his man alive and the best way to achieve that was with complete surprise.

    Slowly he crept forward with one hand on the hilt of his sword until a slight change in the air made him stop dead in his tracks, the smell of a rabbit being cooked over a fire. With renewed resolve he continued until eventually the slope dropped away toward a tiny stream and beside it was the man he sought. Tomos Scar.

    Robert lowered himself slowly to the ground and peered through the undergrowth at the makeshift encampment. A small tent was tied between two trees and next to the stream, a horse and a pack-mule grazed quietly alongside each other. Scar had his back to Robert, totally engrossed in cooking his supper. A skin of ale hung from a lower branch and the remains of a butchered deer lay nearby.

Robert scanned the rest of the valley. When he was happy his quarry was alone, he checked the approaches to the camp before deciding to wait until dark. He looked up at the sky. Night was probably no more than a couple of hours away and as Scar was obviously settling down for the night, he could risk withdrawing without fear of his man escaping. Realising he could do no more, he crawled backward and headed back down the valley.

For the next hour or so he saw to his horse before eating some cold meat from his own food pouch. Finally, he sat back against a tree and though he closed his eyes, he did not sleep. There was too much at stake.

As he rested he thought back over the past winter and how his life had been turned upside down. Just a few months ago he had held a position of trust, serving the steward and his wife at Llandeilo Manor but all that security had been torn apart when the two had been exposed as no less than Gruffydd ap Tewdwr and his wife, Gwenllian ferch Gruffydd, having sought refuge from their lives as rebels for the sake of their sons.

Things moved quickly after that and once the subterfuge had been exposed, it wasn't long before the pair returned to the saddle and drew men to their cause in renewing the fight against the English occupancy of Deheubarth. For a while there had been a glimmer of hope in every man's chest across the south but while Gruffydd, or Tarw as he was known, was away seeking reinforcements, Gwenllian had been forced to lead an army against Maurice de Londres of Kidwelly Castle. Despite having a strong force at her command, she was ultimately defeated by the treachery of one of her own men who informed the enemy of her hidden position. That man was Tomos Scar.

Robert swallowed hard. He had been very close to Gwenllian and when he learned of the manner of her death, his heart felt like it would shatter with pain. Beheading was no way to die for any commander who had surrendered on promise of leniency, let alone a woman, especially as Robert had been elsewhere at the time, fooled by Tomos Scar in pursuing a futile plan to harry non-existent English reinforcements.

The pain was still palpable, and he had no idea what the future may hold so when an old priest had sought him out and asked him to undertake a quest to find the traitor and retrieve an item of value, he grabbed it with both hands.

Now, here he was, weeks later, just a few hundred paces away from the man he wanted to kill but had promised he wouldn't.

He looked skyward and saw the clouds gathering. It would be a dark night and he needed to get back up to the outskirts of Tomos Scar's camp. He popped the last of the meat into his mouth and removed his heavy cloak. It might be cold but if he had to fight, he did not want to be encumbered by its weight.

Just under an hour later, Robert once again peered down into the camp of the traitor responsible for Gwenllian's defeat. The fire still burned but it was getting low and there was no sign of Scar.

He waited as long as he could but as the cold started to seep into his bones, he knew could wait no longer. Slowly he got to his feet and made his way carefully down the slope. His heart raced for though he was adept with a sword, Tomas Scar was known as a fearsome warrior and would put up a good fight.

As he neared, he heard the sound of the man's light snoring and buoyed by his success drew his knife across the rope tying the tent to the tree.

The heavy waxed linen immediately collapsed causing Tomas Scar to cry out in confusion. Robert immediately pounced and pressed his blade hard against his victim's chest.

'Stop struggling, Tomas Scar,' he said, 'or I swear I will stick you where you lay.'

Immediately the tangled man lay still, and all Robert could hear was the sound of the man's heavy breathing.

'Who are you?' rasped the tangled man, 'and what is your purpose?'

'You have something I want,' said Robert, 'and if you do exactly what I say, I might be tempted to let you live. Now what is it to be?'

'I have nothing of value,' said the muffled voice, 'take a look around, I am as destitute as any beggar.'

'We will see,' said Robert. 'Now listen very carefully. That pressure you can feel in your belly is the point of my blade. Any sudden movements and I promise you I will skewer you like you did that rabbit. Understood?'

'Aye,' said Scar.

'Good. Now I am going to lift this cloth from your head so we can talk face to face. Remember, you move, you die it is as simple as that.'

'Understood,' said Scar.

Robert leaned over to grab one edge of the tent fabric and slowly peeled it back to reveal the dirty bearded face of the man he had been pursuing. Tomas Scar stared up at his tormentor with ill-disguised hate but as his sight became accustomed to the little light available, his eyes narrowed in recognition.

'I know you,' he said, 'you were an ally of that bitch Gwenllian.'

'Aye. I was,' said Robert, 'and you are the man responsible for her defeat at Kidwelly.'

'What do you want?' said the prisoner, realising the terrible predicament he was in. 'Like I said, I have nothing of value.'

'I will be the judge of that,' said Robert, 'and on the morrow we will talk, but now there is something I would share with you.'

'What?'

'This,' snarled Robert and with a swing of his fist, smashed Scar across the head.

Dawn was breaking when Scar finally awoke. He had been conscious several times through the freezing night but as he was sat against a tree with his hands tied securely around his back, and a much thinner cord wrapped around his neck lashing him to a branch above, there was no chance he could escape.

The cold ate into his bones and the ropes cut deep into his skin. Across the clearing, his aggressor had rekindled the fire and was sat huddled beneath a heavy blanket near the warming flames.

'You,' croaked Scar, 'can I have some water?'

Robert ignored the request and leaned forward to stir the embers of the fire.

'Please,' said Scar, 'I have a great thirst.'

Robert sighed and picked up the leather cup still containing the dregs of ale Scar had drunk the previous night. Standing up he emptied the cup and filled it with water from the stream before walking over to stand before his prisoner.

'Sleep well?' he asked.

Scar stared deep into Robert's eyes, getting the measure of the man.

'I know what you are thinking, 'said Robert, 'but trust me, there is no way you are getting out of these bonds alive unless you give me what I want.' He lifted up the cup and poured the water into his prisoner's mouth. 'So,' he continued, when the water had gone, 'are you ready to talk?'

'I have no idea what it is you want,' said Scar.

'First of all, I want to talk,' said Robert

'About what?'

'About why you betrayed Gwenllian?'

'I did what every man true to Deheubarth should have done.'

'Why do you say that?'

'She was Gwynedd born,' said Scar, 'and had no blood ties to Deheubarth. She had no right to march down here meddling in affairs that didn't concern her.'

'She was Tarw's wife. Surely that gave her every right?'

'As a wife, perhaps but not as a commander of men.'

'What do you mean?'

'We were doing fine until she appeared,' spat Scar. 'Everyone knew their place and we were feared throughout the Cantref Mawr.'

'Feared by who, farmers and travellers? What about the real foe, the English, the Normans and their mercenaries. I hear none of those slept poorly in fear of a visit by the few brigands who dared to call themselves rebels?'

'What do you know?' snarled Scar, 'you were safe in front of the kitchen fires in Llandeilo Manor while us real men fought for independence.'

'Oh, so you recognise me now?'

'Aye, I do. You are Tarw's man.'

'I was,' said Robert, 'but also avowed to the Princess, the one you had killed.'

'I had no idea they would execute her,' said Scar. 'I was as shocked as you but still have no regrets. She divided the camp and deemed to lead when there were men far better than her better suited.'

'Like who?'

'Like me.'

Robert paused and stared at Scar.

'Is that what this is all about, petty jealousy?'

'She had it coming,' said Scar with a scowl.

'Why?' said Robert. 'Explain in as few words as you can manage what urged you to betray your own people, condemning many of those you called comrade to death.'

'Because she humiliated me,' shouted Scar suddenly, 'the spittle raining on Robert's face. 'Happy now?'

Robert slowly wiped his face as realisation dawned.

'Of course,' he said eventually, 'she bettered you in a brawl in front of your comrades.'

'She was just lucky,' said Scar, 'and everyone knows it.'

'On the contrary,' said Robert, putting together the pieces of the puzzle he had pondered for weeks, 'she beat you fair and square and despite you appearing to then pledge allegiance, you secretly plotted to betray her and the rest of the rebels just to get some sort of revenge. What sort of man are you?'

'I never meant for the battle to happen. Maurice de Londres promised that it was Gwenllian he wanted, and any killing would be kept to a minimum.'

'Really. And how did that play out?'

'The man is a liar,' said Scar. 'He promised me protection but has cast me away like a leper.'

'Oh, you are worse than any leper,' said Tomas. 'You are hated by men of both sides for betraying your own.'

'Then why don't you kill me and be done with it?'

'Nothing would give me greater pleasure, I assure you, but I have given a promise that I would let you live.'

'To who?'

'A well-meaning but misguided priest. Now, let's get down to business. I am aware that you were present at Gwenllian's execution, is that so?'

'So what? I had no hand in it.'

'Nevertheless, you were there.'

'I was.'

'And after Maurice de Londres and his men returned to the castle, you stayed on the field of battle to relieve the fallen of any valuables.'

'Aye, as did other men. There is no law against it but there was hardly anything worth taking so if it is silver pennies you are after, you will be very disappointed.'

'It's not coin I seek, but a weapon. One that you stole from Gwenllian herself.'

Scar's eyes narrowed as he realised where the conversation was going.

'You mean her sword?' He said eventually.

'Aye, her sword. There are many who have sworn that you took her blade and carried it from the field.'

'What if I did? It was no different to any other sword. It has no value.'

'Perhaps not to you but to others it was wielded by someone they revered, and they want it back.'

'Who does?'

'Their identities are unimportant. Now, do you have it?'

'What if I do?'

'Think carefully, Tomos Scar,' said Robert, 'I can just as easily kill you and search your possessions, so it is in your interest to just answer honestly and save your own skin. So, do you have it and if so, where is it?'

Scar paused and stared at Robert, trying to judge if he was as good as his word.

'Aye I have it,' he said eventually, 'but if I hand it over, what is to stop you killing me anyway?'

'Nothing,' said Robert, 'but that is a risk you have to take. Now enough talk. Where is the sword and don't try to trick me with another weapon for I cleaned Gwenllian's blade on many occasions and I will know if it is hers.'

'So be it,' said Scar. 'It lies buried in a shepherd's hut not far from here. Untie me and I will take you there.'

'Why is it buried?'

'Because I guessed that one day it may have value to the right buyer and decided to hide it rather than risk losing it on the road. Don't worry, it is well protected.'

'Where is this shepherds hut?'

'You will never find it with directions alone. Like I said, untie me and I will take you there.'

Robert leaned forward and placed his blade against Scar's throat.

'I will do as you suggest,' he said, 'but I swear by all that is holy, one step out of place and I will spill your guts.'

'Understood,' said Scar.

Within the hour, Scar sat astride his horse with his hands tied securely behind his back. Robert had cut the reins and tied each length of leather to Scar's upper arms allowing him to guide the horse. Slowly the prisoner made his way out of the valley, closely followed by Robert on his own mount and the mule tethered behind.

'How far?' asked Robert as they went.

'About two hours,' said Scar, 'though we would be much quicker if you freed my hands.'

'That is not going to happen,' said Robert, 'now shut up and ride.'

As soon as they had left the heavy tree line, Scar led the way up the gentler slopes until they were headed into the higher hills and by the time the sun was at its highest, they could see a tiny stone shelter nestled at the foot of a crag.

'Is that it?' asked Robert as they neared the building.

'Aye,' said Scar. 'It lays unused for most of the year so is useful when someone needs to lie low.' They reined in their horses and Robert dismounted.

'Where's the sword?'

'Buried beneath the dirt at the right of the fireplace.'

'Show me,' said Robert.

'And how am I supposed to dismount when I am trussed like a pig?'

'Like this,' said Robert and lifted Scar's leg to send him toppling from the horse.

'In the name of God are you mad,' he shouted from the floor, 'I could have broken my neck.'

'If the sword is there,' replied Robert, 'then there would be no issue either way.'

'And if it isn't? What would you have done then?'

'For your sake I hope it is,' said Robert grabbing Scar's hair and dragging him to his feet, 'now get inside.'

The two men ducked under the low lintel of the door frame and walked into the tiny thatched building.

'There,' said Scar nodding toward the fireplace at the end of the room.

Robert forced his prisoner into the corner and tied his feet together.

'Just a precaution,' he said before turning back to the fire place. Using his dagger, he scraped away at the surface, loosening it enough so he could scoop away the spoil. Within minutes he felt the coarse feel of sacking beneath his hands and soon pulled a wrapped object clear of the earth.

'I told you I was speaking truly,' said Scar, 'now let me go.'

'Not yet,' said Robert, 'I need to see it for myself.'

He unwrapped the sacking and found a second layer, this time of waxed linen. He undid the ties and lifted the sword within, holding it up to the light streaming in through the shack door.

'Well?' said Scar

'Aye, it is hers true enough,' said Robert and replaced it in the wrappings before carrying it out through the door.

'What about me?' shouted Scar. 'You can't leave me here?'

'I will be back for you soon enough,' said Robert and walked over to his horse before tying the bundle across his saddle. When he was done, he pulled a short shovel from his pack and walked toward the tree line.

It was over an hour before he returned to the hut, and this time he was carrying his sword.

'There you are,' said Scar, 'I thought you had left me.'

Robert leaned forward and cut the binds around his prisoner's feet.

'Get up,' he said and waited as Scar scrambled to his feet.

'Out,' said Robert simply.

The prisoner ducked under the lintel and headed toward the horses.

'Not that way,' said Robert prodding Scar with his sword, 'up there.'

Scar looked up the slope, confused.

'Why, what's up there?'

'You'll see soon enough now start walking.'

The two men headed up the small hill and as they reached the top, Scar caught his breath in fear. For a moment he stared in disbelief as he realised why Robert had been gone so long, he had been digging a shallow grave.

'You no good son of a whore,' he snarled, spinning around to face his captor, 'I should have known you would go back on your word.'

'I gave you no promises,' said Robert, 'I only told you what I promised the priest.'

'And you are happy to break that bond with a man of God?'

'I answer to the Lord himself, and not his servants,' said Robert, 'besides, compared to what you did, I am almost a saint. Now get on your knees.'

'Why?' gasped Scar.

'Because justice demands you suffer the same fate as the woman you betrayed.'

'I am to be beheaded?'

'You are indeed a clever man,' said Robert, 'now kneel.'

'Don't do this,' gasped Scar, 'I can get money, as much as you want.'

'Keep talking and I will open your stomach and watch you die slowly over three days. That or beheading and a marked grave. Your choice.'

Scar looked around, desperately seeking help or a way out.

'You are wasting your time,' said Robert, 'and my patience wears thin. Kneel or I will gut you right now.'

Scar lowered himself to his knees, shaking his head in fear and shock.

'Please, don't do this,' he mumbled, 'I beg of you.'

'Did Gwenllian beg?' asked Robert as he walked behind his prisoner.

Scar shook his head in silence, absorbed in his own misery.

'Then take a lesson from her bravery,' said Robert, 'and shut your squealing mouth. You are going to die here today, Tomos Scar so I suggest you use your last few moments making your peace with God.'

Scar's eyes closed, and tears ran down his face as he tried to remember a prayer. He mumbled some familiar words but finally fell silent.

'Have you finished?' asked Robert.

'Yes,' whispered Scar, 'but promise me, you will mark my grave.'

'On that you have my word,' said Robert, 'now stretch forward so my cut is clean.'

'Your soul will rot in hell for this,' said Scar, bending over to expose his neck.

'My soul is already cursed,' said Robert and with an almighty swing, brought his sword down to sever Scar's head with a single blow.

The head rolled forward into the shallow grave, coming to rest at the far end, the blank stare looking up accusingly at the man responsible. Robert glanced down before rolling the rest of the body into the hole.

'It's not much, Gwenllian,' he said looking up toward the heavens, 'but at least it is a start.'

An hour later Robert rode away from the shepherd's hut leading Scar's horse and mule behind him. Up on the hill was a neat mound of earth covering the body of Tomos Scar and at the end of the grave was a cross with a piece of leather pinned to the timber. On the leather was scraped one word. Traitor!

Chapter Four

Kidwelly

April AD 1136

Dog walked quickly through the back streets, seeking a certain tavern. The ale he drank the previous night with the two Kidwelly men had proved fortuitous and though he had been at pains to hide his true reasons for engaging them in conversation, one of the men finally mentioned something that made Dog lift a brow in interest. The tale had been about a vagabond who drank to excess most nights, losing good money in games of chance and challenging any of the laughing onlookers to a fight when their mockery became too barbed.

In itself the description could have fitted many men but the single comment that had piqued Dog's interest was when they laughed about the wretch once being so drunk that when a group of men set about him in the back alley leaving him injured and curled in the filth of the street, he actually claimed to be the king of Deheubarth.

It wasn't much but having had no other leads, Dog had made his excuses and left the tavern before scouring the town for any sign of the beggar. The night had passed without success, and throughout the following day his luck continued to let him down before finally he sat against a horse trough outside a back-street tavern to wait.

As the night closed in again, men arrived from their day's graft and the place started to fill. Dog decided to try the same approach as the previous night to try to find out if anyone knew of the man he sought when his luck changed, and he was approached by a woman from the tavern.

'Good man,' she said crouching down before him, 'I have a penny for you if can give me your aid for a short while.'

'A task?' asked Dog, feigning interest in the coin.

'Indeed. I need you to deliver a message.'

Dog paused. His cover as a beggar meant he should need every coin he could get but it was also important that he stayed in front of the tavern to see if the man he sought turned up.

'My lady,' he said, 'the coin is tempting but my leg is sorely wounded, and I can hardly walk.'

'The place is not far from here,' said the woman, 'and if you are successful, there will be ale and bread for your trouble.'

Dog realised he would have to do as she asked. No beggar would turn down such a bounty, and besides, once out of sight he could move quickly and be back before it was dark.

'I will try,' he said eventually and got to his feet.

'Thank you,' she said and pressed a penny into his hand. 'I want you to go to the rear of the pigsties and find the corn store. Beside it is an empty sty, long unused and awaiting a new roof. Do you know of it?'

'I have passed it on occasion,' said Dog, 'but what of it?'

'Inside you will find a man sleeping off a heavy afternoon's drinking. It is he the message is for.'

'So, what is this message?' asked Dog.

'Tell him to stay away from The Lantern this night for the men who beat him are here again and they are in a foul mood.'

Dog swallowed silently. By the whore's description, this man could well be the one he sought.

'And who is this man?' he asked eventually.

'Just a nobody with a big heart,' said the woman. 'Now off you go and when you return, your ale will be hidden behind the trough.'

'So be it,' said Dog and turned to hobble away, hardly believing his luck. After ten days searching, it was possible, that due to being in the right place at the right time, he may just have found his man.

Macsen dragged himself out of the stinking straw bale he had used as a bed for the past few days and sat up, his eyes closed to try and ease the pain in his head. His mouth tasted like it held the filth of the pigs and his whole body still hurt from the beating he had received a few days earlier. He looked around for the goatskin flask he knew was still half full of ale and drank deeply, completely uncaring of the rats that scurried around him.

Wiping the dregs from his unkempt beard he got to his feet and started to stagger down the mud filled street, keen to get to the nearest tavern but had got no further than one row when a group of three men appeared from the shadows.

'Hello again,' said one blocking his way. 'Remember me?'

Macsen peered up at the taller man.

'No,' he said, 'let me pass.' He made to walk around the man, but his tormentor stepped sideways to block his way.

'You should do,' said the man, 'I am the one you cheated out of five silver pennies in the Lantern the night before last.'

Macsen looked up again and recognised the man he had beaten at a dice game.

'I did not cheat,' he said eventually, 'you play like a blind man now get out of the road.'

Again, the man blocked his way but this time there was anger on his face.

'Nobody speaks to me like that,' he growled, 'especially those who dwell in the filth of the street.' Without warning he punched Macsen hard sending him sprawling into the mud.

'Take his purse,' said the other man and while Macsen lay semi-conscious in the mud, his attacker reached inside his victim's filthy cloak to search the pocket.

'Anything?' asked the second man.

'Aye,' came the reply and he tossed a small leather pouch up to his comrade. 'See if he is worth anything.'

'Three copper coins and a silver penny,' said the second man, 'a princely haul for someone so destitute.'

'It still doesn't cover my losses,' said the attacker, looking down at the pathetic figure in the mud before him. 'But I guess we are lucky to get that. What shall we do with him now?'

For a few moments there was silence before the smaller man answered coldly.

'Kill him and throw him in with the pigs. There will be nothing left of him by morning.'

'So be it,' said his comrade and drew a blade from his belt before standing over his victim.

'Sorry about this, my stinking cheating friend.' he said as Macsen struggled to get to his feet, 'but worry not, I believe they play dice in hell.' He altered his grip on his knife and pulled back on Macsen's matted hair to expose the throat.

'Do it.' said his friend but as the would-be murderer moved the blade to make the cut, a knife came spinning through the air and thudded into his throat. For a few seconds he blinked in shock, not realising what had happened and as he looked up, he saw a man running toward him from a side alleyway. His hands went up to the blade in his neck and as he realised what had happened, fell to his knees against a wall.

'Stay away from me,' shouted the second man as Dog ran toward him, 'I'm warning you, I'll gut you like a fish.' He lifted his cloak and withdrew a sword, swinging it wildly to stop the onrushing stranger but his lack of skill was evident and Dog drove his own blade up through his victim's heart.

The man fell to the ground, dead almost instantly and Dog spun around, his eyes quickly checking there were no more attackers. The first man had managed to crawl a few more paces through the mud before collapsing as he choked on his own blood. Dog walked over and stamped on his victim's head, shattering his skull before retrieving his knife and wiping off the blood on the dead man's cloak. Finally, he made his way over to Macsen who was still laying in the mud oblivious to the fight that had just occurred in his name.

Dog grabbed him by the hair and tilted back his head. The half-conscious man was plastered with filth and Dog had to empty his water bottle over his face to see any recognisable features.

'I hope for your sake you are who I hope you are,' he growled as he wiped away the mud with his sleeve, 'for that pouch contained the finest wine. Open your eyes.'

The man blinked several times before looking up at his rescuer. For a second they both stared at each other until finally Macsen spoke.

'Dog,' he slurred, 'is that you?'

'Aye it is,' replied Dog, 'and I have to say that you, my lord Tarw, are the most wretched example of a man I have ever had the misfortune to lay eyes upon.'

Several hours later, Tarw and Dog were safe and warm in a side room of a farmhouse two leagues from Kidwelly. Tarw was fast asleep on the pallet bed while his rescuer sat at a table eating a steaming bowl of sheep's head stew. His scimitar and knife had been carefully cleaned and both lay on the table beside him.

Tarw groaned and turned over on his side before opening his eyes and staring at the back of Dog.

'Where are we he?' asked eventually.

'Ah,' said Dog turning to face him, 'the prince awakes. And how are you, my lord?'

'Nothing a draft of ale won't sort out,' said Tarw.

'Food we have a plenty,' said Dog, 'and we are awash with honeyed water but alas, ale there is none.'

'Then we have surely died and gone to hell,' groaned Tarw.

'It is good food and rest you need now,' said Dog, 'not ale and wine. We will stay here until nightfall and then we will move on.'

'To where?'

'I cannot say, but there are friends waiting for you.'

'I am going nowhere,' said Tarw turning over onto his back and staring at the ceiling, 'except for the nearest tavern.'

'Nope,' said Dog nonchalantly through a mouthful of bread, 'you are coming with me whether you like it or not.'

'And how do you propose to do that?' asked Tarw turning his head again to face Dog. 'By tying me up?'

'If necessary,' said Dog, 'or at the point of my blade if needs be. Either way you are coming with me.'

'You can't do that,' said Tarw, 'you know who I am.'

'I know who you were,' said Dog, 'you were the last prince of Deheubarth. A principled man who commanded respect and avowed to release his father's kingdom from the grip of the English. Alas, the man I knew is certainly not present in this room, for it is occupied only by me and some shameful wretch squealing for ale like a child does its mother's breast.'

'I suggest you curb your tongue, 'snarled Tarw, 'lest I rip it from your stinking mouth.'

'Go ahead and try,' said Dog, his attention on a particularly large piece of mutton he had found in his stew, 'though I have to warn you that if you do, the next time you awake your head will be hurting even more than it does now.'

Tarw bit his tongue knowing that Dog was a fearsome fighter and he had little chance of beating him, even if he had a weapon.

'So, do you want any stew or not?' continued Dog over his shoulder. 'For I think I could probably finish this myself.'

'Just leave me some,' said Tarw laying his head back on the straw filled pillow.

'Your loss,' said Dog, peering in to the pot the farmer's wife had left on the table. 'There is still some good meat left in there, the cheeks if I'm not mistaken, but I can't guarantee they will be there much longer.'

'Lord have mercy,' whispered Tarw and swung his legs across the bed, enabling him to sit upright. 'Whoa,' he mumbled as the room spun around him.

'That bad, huh?' said Dog.

'Just shut up and pour me a bowl of stew,' said Tarw. 'Where are my clothes?'

'Being washed by the farmer's wife. I suggest you do the same with your body because you stink like a shit pit. There's a pot just outside the door and fresh water over there in those two buckets. It's as cold as a nun's embrace but as clean as her conscience.'

Tarw got to his feet and walked over to the buckets. He dropped to his knees at the first one and immersed his whole head before tossing his head back to throw his hair from his face.

Dog threw him a piece of linen and Tarw proceeded to wash the mud from the rest of his body. Finally, he picked up the second bucket and after walking outside, poured the contents over his head.

'Better?' asked Dog when he returned.

'Much,' said Tarw and pulled the blanket from Dog's bed to wrap around himself.

'Oy, that's mine,' said Dog.

'Mine's covered with mud,' said Tarw joining Dog on the bench. 'Now where's that stew?'

An hour or so later both men sat fully clothed at the table. The farmer's wife had returned their clothing and though Dog still looked like a beggar, his clothes were at least clean.

'I have never seen you so fresh,' said Tarw.

'There was no choice,' said Dog, 'Even my senses balk at the smell of pig shit and trust me, there was plenty of that after trying to carry you from Kidwelly.'

'I have no recollection,' said Tarw.

'No, you were unconscious most of the way. I had to steal a horse to get you out here.'

'That is a hanging offence,' said Tarw.

'It is well hidden,' said Dog, 'and we were not followed.'

'So, what are you doing here?'

'I told you last night, I came for you.'

'Why?'

'You have friends who are concerned for your safety and just as well for if I had been a few moments later you would have been stuck like one of those pigs you slept amongst.'

'I remember,' said Tarw slowly. 'A man who I had apparently beaten at dice.'

'I have no knowledge of that,' said Dog, 'but he will be playing no more games, nor his comrades.'

'So, who sent you?'

'I am ordered not to say in case you should let slip their identities.'

'I would never do such a thing.'

'With respect, my lord, the state you were in, I don't think you were in control of anything that came out of your mouth apart from vomit.'

'I'm not coming with you,' said Tarw.

'Why not?'

'I have to stay here.'

'And the reason?'

'I need horses and well-armed men to help me avenge Gwenllian. For that I need money and my friends have turned their backs on me. My only chance is to win it from those who know no better.'

'Your friends have not turned their backs on you,' said Dog, 'they have turned their backs on the man you have become. A drunkard who feeds his addiction to games of chance in a desperate attempt to hide the true problem.'

'Which is?'

'Devastation at the death of the only woman he has ever loved.'

Tarw sighed and looked down.

'I am not going to argue,' he said, 'for there is a wealth of truth in what you say but the concern about the money is real enough. I need funds to raise an army but without recourse, what other option do I have?'

'There is another path,' said Dog. 'But first you need to regain your self-respect and once more become the figure head for those in Deheubarth who feel as you do. Finance is available but not to a drunk. The memory of Gwenllian and indeed the future of Deheubarth needs the man you were, not the man you have become.'

Tarw fell quiet for a few moments and looked around the room

'So where are we exactly?'

'In a farmhouse just outside Kidwelly. These people are loyal to you, but we will have to move soon. If we were to be found here, they would join us on the gallows.'

'And you won't say where we are going?'

'No,' said Dog, 'so I suggest you rest while we can. Tonight, we will be riding hard.'

Tarw stood and walked over to the bed. On the way he saw his ale skin hanging on a chair. He looked at it for a moment before glancing over to Dog.

'Don't even think about it,' said Dog, 'now get some sleep.'

Chapter Five

Pembroke Castle

April AD 1136

Maelgwyn ap Gruffydd, son of Gwenllian and Tarw lay huddled in foetal position in a hole sunk into the floor of the castle's dungeon. A few inches above him, an iron grill ensured there was hardly room to move and he lay in a pool of his own excrement and dried blood. His body was lacerated from the many beatings he had received since being captured after the battle and his mouth held only the broken remains of any teeth he once had.

The darkness was total and only the sounds of people walking on the wooden floors in the castle above gave him any indication he was still alive. That and the pain.

Up in one of the towers, a lonely woman sat at her window, staring out across the bailey and over the palisade walls to the rooftops of Pembroke. Her own face was freshly bruised, and one arm nestled in a sling to aid the healing of the broken bone she had received from a beating administered by John of Salisbury, the castellan of Pembroke castle.

Since the battle two months earlier, Nesta had seen an ugly side of Salisbury that not even she had imagined. The death of Gwenllian had encouraged him to vent his long pent up anger and spite against anyone who had ever dared to cross him and within days had set out on a campaign of brutal subjugation in revenge for the failed rebellion. Hardly a day passed without someone being executed for crimes, no matter how minor and he took great pleasure in lining the roads between villages with the heads of those killed atop wooden stakes as a warning to others.

And it was not only physical revenge that he wrought on the people of Deheubarth, he also doubled the taxes of everyone, irrespective of their ability to pay. Livestock, chattels, even winter stores were taken from the outlying villages leaving many with nothing. His men justified their actions by saying the farmers had the whole summer in front of them to replenish their stores and they should thank God that rebellion had now been quashed and they could live in peace without fear of war.

Nesta swallowed hard. Since the death of her husband, Gerald, the previous castellan of Pembroke, her life had changed for the worse and now that Salisbury had total control, it had become a living hell. Every night he came to her chambers and forced himself upon her. Often it came with a beating, though occasionally he proffered his version of affection, a sickening trait that made her almost prefer the violence.

If it wasn't the case that her nephew, Maelgwyn was being held in the castle dungeon and under threat of death if Nesta didn't comply with Salisbury's every whim, she would have thrown herself from her window a long time ago.

The door unlocked behind her and a large woman walked in unannounced.

'Lady Anwen,' said Nesta getting to her feet, 'I was not expecting you yet.'

Anwen was the surly woman installed as Nesta's personal maid after the previous incumbent, Emma, had been executed by Salisbury's men for colluding with the rebels. Anwen did not exhibit any kindness toward Nesta and was loyal to the castellan but at least she wasn't cruel.

'If you get dressed quickly,' said the woman curtly, 'you may walk the walls and get some air. Two circuits only and then you are to bathe and get dressed in the red gown.'

'Why?'

'Master Salisbury is hosting a banquet this evening and you are to sit alongside him as his betrothed. The castellan expects you to be radiant, friendly and project joy at the prospect of your forthcoming marriage.'

'Does he?' said Nesta with a grimace. 'I suspect that may be too hard a task to undertake.'

'I suggest you make every effort,' said the woman, 'you wouldn't want to raise his ire.'

'You don't need to remind me what is at risk,' said Nesta with a sigh, 'just give me a few moments.'

Half an hour later Nesta walked along the ramparts of Pembroke castle, enjoying the vigorous breeze that swept her hair around her face in a flurry. Below the palisade, the town of Pembroke stretched away as far as the dock and she could see at least three vessels waiting to be unloaded, one cargo ship and two that seemed to be military transport.

'More soldiers?' she said to the guard accompanying her.

'Aye,' he said, 'apparently they were promised to Lord Salisbury by the king weeks ago to help keep the peace.'

'To be honest, I see no further risk from the rebels,' said Nesta, 'the uprising died with Gwenllian.'

'On the contrary, my lady,' said the soldier, 'as long as that bastard Tarw is at large there will always be a risk.'

'That bastard, as you call him, is my brother,' said Nesta without averting her gaze.

'I am aware of that, my lady,' said the guard, 'but nevertheless we are adversaries and he has been responsible for the deaths of many a comrade. My ire is aimed at him, not you.'

Nesta nodded silently. It was a strange set of affairs that had saw her married into the English establishment while her brother had fought so hard against it.

Many years earlier she had enjoyed a passionate fling with the then Prince Henry, son of William the Conqueror, bearing him a bastard son but when Henry ascended the throne, politics demanded he married a princess of Scotland so Nesta was sent back to Wales and ordered to marry Gerald of Windsor, castellan of Pembroke castle.

At first the marriage had been cold as it was obviously an arrangement designed to appease the Welsh population in Deheubarth, but over the years they became close and had several children together.

Since then she had been an onlooker in her brother's struggle to wrest Deheubarth from the hands of the English and though she had grown to love Gerald, her heart still yearned for the land of her birth to be free.

Subsequently she had managed to help the Welsh cause by passing messages to the rebels regarding the English strengths and movements but ultimately it had all been for nought. The rebellion had failed, Gwenllian was dead and though Tarw's body hadn't been found, there was no news of his whereabouts and she feared he was long dead. She paused at the base of one of the watch towers.

'Can we go up?' she asked.

'There is a ladder only,' said the guard, 'can you manage with your arm in that sling?'

'The bones have healed', said Nesta, 'and though it aches, I can use it as normal for short periods.'

'If you are sure,' said the soldier, 'then I see no reason you cannot. I will follow you up lest you slip, but rest assured I will avert my gaze from your skirts.'

Nesta suppressed a laugh as she turned to the ladder. Bearing in mind her situation, modesty was the furthest thing from her mind.

Up on top of the watchtower, one sentry was focused on the cleared land to the front of the castle while a second sat against a wall enjoying a few minutes sleep.

'My lady,' said the first after spinning around to face her.

'Hello, Rowan,' said Nesta in recognition, 'it has been a while.'

'It has,' said the sentry, 'you are seldom seen outside your quarters these days.' He stared at the bruises on Nesta's face and neck. 'There was talk that he beats you. My lady, but I hoped there was no truth in the matter. I see I was wrong. The man is an animal.'

'Still yourself, Rowan,' she said interrupting him, 'there is nothing you can do. Besides, the situation gets easier by the day.'

Behind them, Nesta's guard reached the top of the ladder and walked over to join them.

'And what situation would that be?' he growled, staring at Rowan with suspicion written all over his face.

'We were talking about the peace,' said Nesta with a glance at Rowan. 'It seems all the fighting will soon be over.'

'Only when every rebel has his head upon a spike,' said the guard and walked over to kick the sleeping sentry. 'Wake up,' he shouted, 'or I'll have you whipped like a dog.'

The terrified man sprang to his feet.

'My lord, it was a momentary rest only as our relief failed to turn up. I have been on duty since dawn.'

'Stand to your position,' said the guard, 'and when I go back I will sort it out.'

'Thank you, my lord,' said the sentry, realising he had gotten off lightly. Usually, being found asleep on duty was a minimum of fifty lashes.

Nesta walked over to the castellations and peered out. From here she could see over the far tree line and toward the northern mountains bordering the Cantref Mawr, the wild and treacherous land that was often home to rebels and brigands alike.

'Are you out there, Tarw?' she asked quietly, 'are you raising an army as we speak?'

'What did you say?' asked the guard from a few paces away.

'Nothing that needs concern you,' said Nesta eventually, 'just talking to myself.'

'My lady,' called a voice, 'are you up there?'

Nesta sighed and walked to the wall overlooking the bailey. Down below stood Anwen, her long brown cloak blowing in the wind.

'I am,' shouted Nesta, 'what is it you want?'

'It is time to return,' said Anwen. 'Come down now for there are buckets of hot water in your chambers awaiting you.'

'I will be there shortly,' said Nesta and returned to the outer wall. For a few moments she stared at the distant forested hills where she and her brother had grown up, learning to fight and ride horses together. Her heart yearned for a return to those happy times but the aches in her body were a constant reminder of the reality of her situation. She looked down, seeing the jagged rocks at the base of the tower. All she had to do was lean forward and her misery would soon be over. The exhilarating feeling of flying like a bird, followed by a few moments of pain before her soul was free to wing its way to wherever the Lord intended to be her final rest. Heaven, hell or even somewhere in-between was surely better than the place she was now.

'My lady,' said a quiet voice snapping her out of her reverie, 'the lady Anwen grows agitated. You should go.'

Nesta realised her knuckles were almost white, such was the firmness of her grip on the palisade wall. Slowly she released her hold and turned to face the sentry.

'Thank you, Rowan,' she said. 'I shall join her immediately. '

Rowan looked over the palisade to the rocks below.

'Do you know?' he said as if reading her mind. 'I once contemplated hurling myself from these walls to seek everlasting peace.'

'You did?' asked Nesta hiding her shock. 'What stopped you?'

'The fact that another had done exactly that same thing many months earlier but instead of dying, the lord saw fit to spare his life even though his body was shattered. He screamed in agony for weeks before the physician instructed one of the men to put him out of his misery.' He looked up at the princess. 'It will get better, my lady,' he said quietly, 'I promise.'

Nesta didn't answer but after giving him a tight-lipped smile, returned to the ladder. To keep Salisbury waiting invited anger over and above that which he usually possessed. And that was the last thing she wanted.

Chapter Six

The Cathedral of Saint David

April AD 1136

The priest once known as Cynwrig the Tall knelt below a cross in his sparsely furnished cell in the bowels of the cathedral. His eyes were closed tight, and his hands clenched together as he begged God to grant him enough strength to carry out one last task in his name.

Cynwrig had grown up on a horse farm as a boy but after he had managed to release King Gruffydd of Gwynedd from captivity many years earlier, his family had been killed by the Earl of Chester in retribution. Cynwrig had subsequently killed the Earl and as a self-inflicted penance, had dedicated the rest of his life to the church. As a young priest he had known the young Gwenllian well and had even travelled south with her and her husband when they had initially fled Gwynedd.

She had been the closest thing to a daughter that he had ever known so when the news had come she had been killed, he had been overwhelmed with grief. Eventually the heartache turned to anger and as the fog cleared from his mind, he knew he had to do something. As a young man he had been adept with a sword but since turning to God, he had never wielded any weapon in anger, so violence was out of the question. His body was old, but his mind was as sharp as any blade. For the past few weeks, he had made his plans and if the message he had just received was correct, the first of those strategies was about to come to fruition. Slowly he got to his feet and left his cell.

Outside, the young boy who had brought him news of two visitors, stood quietly by the door, patiently waiting to undertake any task the priest would have him do.

'Where did you say they were boy?' asked Cynwrig.

'In in the gatehouse, my lord,' said the boy. 'Shall I accompany you?'

'No,' he said, retrieving his cloak from a peg behind the door, 'but bring wine and food. I suspect they will be hungry. '

'Yes, my lord,' said the boy and scurried away down the candlelit corridor.

Cynwrig climbed the stone stairs from the basement and through the magnificent entrance hall of the Cathedral. After leaving the building he walked up the steep path to the gatehouse, his breath forming small clouds of moisture in the near freezing temperatures. Up above the stars shone like beacons in the night sky and the full moon helped them light his way.

As he reached the top of the path, one of the guards in the employ of the cathedral stepped out of the shadows into his path.

'You made me jump,' said Cynwrig.

'Forgive me, father,' said the soldier. 'I just wanted to ask if you want me to accompany you into the gatehouse.'

'To what end?'

'The two men waiting look a dangerous sort. I would venture they are brigands or smugglers.'

'They are neither,' said Cynwrig resting his hand on the man's shoulder, 'and I promise I am safer with them than with any other man I know but thank you for your concern.'

'If you are sure.'

'I am,' said Cynwrig. He walked past the guard up to one of the two stone towers flanking the huge double gates breaching the encircling cathedral wall. He paused for breath and after opening the small door, ducked under the lintel and into the gloom within.

At the far end of the room, a small fire crackled in the hearth while half a dozen candles burned on a trestle table, illuminating the remains of somebody's frugal meal earlier in the evening. Next to the fire, two men talked quietly, each still wearing their cloaks after a long journey. As he entered, the conversation fell away and both turned to stare at the priest.

'Cynwrig,' said the taller man eventually, 'is it really you?'

'It is indeed,' said the priest,' and praise be to God that you have been found alive.' For a few seconds there was an awkward silence before the priest strode across the floor and embraced his visitor. 'My Lord Tarw,' he said at last, 'you have been in my prayers every day since I heard the tragic news. Thank God you are safe.'

'Thank God and your henchman here,' said Tarw. 'If it was not for him I suspect my corpse would have already been thrown to the pigs.'

'I knew it would be a difficult task to find you and bring you here,' said Cynwrig, 'so when I heard Dog was still alive after the battle and seeking employ, his engagement was an easy decision.'

'Convincing him to accompany me without divulging the destination was even harder than you said it would be,' said Dog. 'Were he not a prince he would have spent half the journey knocked out.'

'Yes,' said Cynwrig, 'he was always headstrong.' He turned back to Tarw. 'It is good to see you again,' he continued, 'I just wish it could be in different circumstances.'

'What is done, is done,' said Tarw. 'All that matters now is that she is avenged and though it is good to see you again, I must shortly return and continue my quest for funding to raise an army.'

Cynwrig glanced at Dog.

'You have told him nothing?'

'Only that which you said I could share. The detail I have left to you.'

'He has told me you may be able to help,' said Tarw, 'but little else. In truth I only came under duress but when the destination became clear, I was happy to continue, if only to set eyes on someone I knew still called me friend. So, what is all this about?'

'All in good time,' said Cynwrig, 'you must both be exhausted after your journey?'

'Tiredness is a constant bedfellow these days,' said Dog, 'but nothing that a full flask and groaning table won't cure.'

'I have arranged food and drink,' replied Cynwrig, 'simple but honest fayre.' As he spoke a knock came on the door and the boy entered carrying a tray covered with a linen sheet.

'Perfect timing,' said the priest, turning to the boy. 'Please place it on the table and then you may retire for the night.'

'I am happy to serve you, my lord,' replied the boy.

'I am fine,' said the priest, 'thank you. Now go and get some rest.'

The boy bowed and left the room as Cynwrig turned back to his guests.

'I have anticipated your arrival for days,' he said, 'so you will find two cots already prepared in the guards' quarters on the floor above. Please, eat your fill and perhaps we can talk in the morning when you are rested.'

'In all honesty, father,' replied Tarw, 'my thoughts are a tangled mess and I would probably not sleep a moment. So, if it is not too much trouble, I would ask that you share the reasons for which you had me brought here.'

'I understand,' said Cynwrig, 'in that case, help me build the fire and as you eat, I promise I will tell you everything. The two men stacked the fire with wood from the stockpile before walking over to the table where Dog had already started his supper.

'Ample food,' mumbled Dog through a mouthful of cheese, 'though my thirst would prefer ale to wine.'

'I'm sure the guards can accommodate you,' said Cynwrig with a smile. 'Please, eat your fill and I will see what I can arrange.'

Tarw joined Dog at the table and both men set to the food with relish. Chunks of cold ham and hunks of bread were accompanied by slabs of cheese and a pot of melted butter. Tarw retrieved a jack from his cloak and filled it with wine from the flask before pausing and returning Dog's stare.

'I suppose this is alright with you?' he sneered.

'Do what you want,' said Dog with a shrug, 'I have fulfilled my part of the bargain. You can drown yourself in the stuff for all I care.'

'I'm glad I have your blessing?' laughed Tarw as the priest returned with a leather skin full of ale,

'Probably not very good but it is wet and cold,' said the priest placing the ale-skin on the table.

'No such thing as bad ale,' said Dog and after removing the stopper, drank straight from the neck before belching loudly and returning his attention to the food.

Tarw glanced at the priest.

'My comrade may lack the manners of court, but I recall he is an honest man and as loyal as a wolfhound.'

'There is no ceremony demanded in my company,' laughed Cynwrig, 'and I will be forever grateful that he has brought you here. Please, fill your bellies.'

For the next few minutes, both travellers tore into the meal, surprised at how hungry they actually were. Finally, they finished and while Dog nursed the ale-skin in a chair next to the fire, Tarw turned to the priest.

'So,' he said, 'now we are done, there are things to discuss.'

'Indeed there are,' said Cynwrig, 'but first I would hear of your situation.'

'My situation?'

'Yes. How is it that you became the wretch that my informers have reported to me? What ever happened to the proud prince that swore to return Deheubarth to the Welsh?'

'You know what happened,' said Tarw, 'and it needs no spelling out. The English took away my reason for living. The mother of my children was executed like a brigand and I swear there will be retribution. I suppose you will now condemn me for the blackness of my soul?'

'No,' said Cynwrig, 'I will not. For I share the blackness.'

'You do?' asked Tarw looking up. 'But how can that be? You are a priest.'

'My lord,' said Cynwrig, 'as you know, I looked on the lady Gwenllian as a daughter and since her death, my body and soul has been consumed with an anger unbefitting my station. My faith preaches forgiveness, yet my heart demands revenge. I am a weak man, nothing more than a sinner serving penance for an evil deed I carried out many years ago. As God is my witness, I have tried to forgive those responsible for her death, but I am ashamed to say that I have failed.'

'There is no shame in hating the men who killed someone you loved,' said Tarw, 'indeed, it is the only thing that keeps me alive and I swear that there will be a reckoning.'

'A reckoning?'

'Aye. Every waking moment I plot the death of Maurice de Londres and when I sleep, I dream of the day his head is on a spike. Alas, the achievement of such a thing will be no easy matter, for he is safe from assassin's blade and I fear only an army can reach him. An army which I do not have.'

'I understand you have been seeking such a force?'

'I have.'

'And have you had any success?'

'There are a few dozen men still loyal to my claim to Deheubarth and the same number who wish to avenge my wife, but we need money to raise an army. The English keep the people under a heavy yoke and few men can leave the fields to fight for a cause they believe is already lost. Now my head is clearing from the effects of too much ale, the reality is hitting me that I may never achieve the retribution my heart craves.'

'I see the burden weighs you down.'

'It does, but I will never give up until the day I am laid in my grave.'

For a few moments there was silence before Cynwrig leaned across to touch the prince's arm.

'My lord,' he said, 'there are no easy answers to this dilemma but these past few weeks I have had a plan crashing in my mind like waves on a beach, ideas that will not only avenge Gwenllian but free Deheubarth from beneath the English heel. Each time I confront these ideas I am scared by the futility but excited by the audacity. At first, I wasn't sure whether to share them with you, but I now see your heart burns as much as mine, I think they should be laid bare.'

'Whatever they may be, Cynwrig, spit them out for my own mind is a tangled web that cannot be deciphered.'

'In that case, wait here,' said Cynwrig, 'for there is something you should see.' He got to his feet and walked outside to speak to one of the guards, sending him on an errand down to the cathedral before returning to join Dog and Tarw in the gate house.

Ten minutes later the guard returned and placed a roll of sack cloth on the table before leaving the room. When he had gone, all three men gathered around the table and Cynwrig looked up at Tarw.

'My lord,' he said, 'what I am about to reveal will bring you both heartache and hope. It is my wish that the latter will outweigh the former.'

'Get on with it, Cynwrig,' said Tarw, 'you have me intrigued though I have to admit it looks too light to be sacks of gold coins.'

'It is not coin of any sort,' said Cynwrig as he unwrapped the sacking, 'though it is my belief it has a value a hundred times more than any treasury.'

Dog and Tarw leaned forward as the last folds were laid back and both men's eyes frowned in confusion.

'It is nought but a sword,' said Dog. 'I have seen many of far greater worth.'

Cynwrig didn't answer but stared at Tarw, eventually seeing the recognition in his eyes.

'Do you recognise it?' asked Cynwrig eventually.

'I do,' replied Tarw. 'It is my wife's blade.'

'It is. Your good friend Robert of Llandeilo retrieved it for me.'

'Robert,' gasped Tarw looking up, 'he is alive?'

'He is, my lord and sleeps soundly in a room not far from here. I saw no need to wake him.'

Tarw reached out and ran his fingers over the leather-bound hilt that was once held by the woman he loved.

'It is a wonderful thing you have done, Cynwrig,' he said, 'but I don't understand how this will help me raise an army.'

'Oh, it will do more than that, my lord,' replied the priest, 'for this sword has a power greater than all the money in all the castles from here to London.'

'And what power is that?' asked Dog. 'Has it been bewitched?'

'Nothing so sinister, Master Dog,' said Cynwrig, 'for it needs no witchcraft. This blade, borne in the right hands has the power of unity. The power to settle arguments between father and son and unite warring kingdoms that have fought for generations. With this sword, I believe that we can win the hearts and minds of our fellow countrymen to stir an entire nation from its self-imposed slumber.' He turned to Tarw. 'If God is with us, my lord, I believe that with this blade in the vanguard, and Gwenllian's name as our battle cry, then not only can we avenge her death, but free our nation from the English yoke.'

'Free our nation?'

'Yes. Gwenllian's death was a tragedy but the example she showed throughout her life and the manner of her demise at the hands of the English has kindled a fire in the souls of almost every Welsh-born man who draws breath. If we can fan those flames then I believe that for the first time in generations, there is a mood for unity. With your permission, I believe we can use her sacrifice as the rallying call to unite our country.'

Tarw stared at the priest and then back at the sword before finally filling the silence that had fallen in the room.

'And you believe before God that such a thing is possible?'

'I do, my lord. All I need from you is your blessing and I will coordinate a message to be sent around every village from

Cardiff to Ynys Mon. A holy call to arms in the name of Gwenllian.'

'You talk of a peasant's army,' said Dog coldly. 'It won't last a day against the English army.'

'I know and that is why I needed Tarw. He too will have an important role to play if we proceed.'

'And that is?' asked Tarw

'You have standing, my lord, and it will fall to you to muster whatever nobles you can to our banner. If we are to succeed we will need trained soldiers and many of them. You have to use your influence and contacts to rally men of strength to our call.'

'And where will I find such men?'

'Everywhere,' said Cynwrig, 'but I suggest you focus on the Marches. The men of Gwent, Brycheniog and Powys hate the English with a passion and if they believe they have a chance of victory, I see no reason why they will not unite in memory of Gwenllian. Hywel ap Maredudd has already challenged and defeated the English in the Gower and his success has not gone unnoticed.'

'It still wouldn't be enough,' said Dog. 'The English have vast resources to call on.'

'I know,' said Cynwrig, 'and that is why I am going to Gwynedd.'

At the sound of Gwenllian's home kingdom, Tarw's head shot up and he stared at the priest.

'You intend asking Gruffydd for help?'

'I intend more than that. I aim to ask him for his army and his sponsorship. With his men at our back and his treasury in support we can match the English with both numbers and expertise.'

'Then you are wasting your time,' said Tarw. 'I was there when the news reached him about Gwenllian and I begged him to ride south to seek revenge, but he did not want to know. His heart is as cold as his eyes, Cynwrig, the man is dead to me.'

'I agree he is slow to action.' said Cynwrig,' but I know him well and he has long been a friend.'

'What makes you think friendship will succeed where blood ties have failed?'

'Two things,' said Cynwrig. 'First of all, by the time we speak, the news of Gwenllian's sword will fill every tavern and church across Wales. Don't forget, she was a child of Gwynedd and it would be a foolish king who ignored the strength of feeling a holy quest can raise.'

'And the second reason?'

'The king owes me a debt of honour and I have waited a lifetime to ask for repayment.'

'What does he owe you that could possibly change his mind?'

'His life,' said Cynwrig.

All three men fell silent as the implications sunk in. Cynwrig had indeed saved the king's life many years earlier and no man of honour could ignore such a debt. Tarw turned and looked at Dog.

'What do you think?' he asked eventually.

'I think,' said Dog looking between the two men, 'I had best start sharpening my blade.'

Chapter Seven

The Cathedral of Saint David

April AD 1136

The following morning, four men walked along the base of the stone wall surrounding the valley that had hidden the cathedral from the sea for centuries. Robert of Llandeilo had joined the other three to break his fast and they now walked along the sentry path, discussing their next actions.

'As I have already stated,' said Cynwrig, 'The strength of feeling throughout the parishes of Deheubarth is almost palpable. Never have I heard such angst, and the need to do something is evident from the highest level to the poorest beggar. Gwenllian touched the hearts of many and retribution for her death is a growing cause. Consequently, to add fuel to the fire I have already arranged messengers to spread the word to all places of worship throughout Wales. With Gwenllian's story being spread by the church and the recovery of her sword as an emblem of her struggle, I expect the fire to become a raging blaze within months.'

'What will that gain?' asked Dog, 'other than sharing a tale.'

'Once the knowledge is in the hands of the people, it will ferment like the strongest wine,' said Cynwrig. 'Unrest will grow, as will the hope in people's hearts.'

'Do we ask them to muster in her name?' asked Robert.

'No, not yet, for without an army, they will be little more than sport for Maurice de Londres' archers. For now, we will sow the seeds and wait until the right moment before harvesting the crop.'

'I have seen no such fervour these past few months,' said Tarw.

'Perhaps your sight was misted by too much ale,' said Cynwrig, 'and besides, such thoughts are not to be voiced in taverns and whorehouses. The anger is there, Tarw but hidden behind the toil of daily life. It is a hard truth but at the moment you are seen as a sad figure and not a man behind whom a whole nation can rally.'

'So, my presence here is worthless?' said Tarw.

'On the contrary, it is essential to the plan. You are the true prince of Deheubarth, Tarw and it is you who must lead us in this fight.'

'And how am I supposed to do that if my own people see me as no more than a worthless drunk?'

'By showing them that you command respect across the nation. Come back before them at the head of a great army and you will get the respect you crave.'

'I have tried to raise an army but it is hopeless.'

'To raise your own perhaps, but there are others you can use.'

'What do you mean?'

'You should ride east and court the Welsh nobles along the Marches. Tell them what is happening and ask them for their support. Appeal to their common pride. Remind them of the oppression they and their forefathers have suffered on a daily basis and offer them hope that there is a better way. Muster every man you can and when assembled, march back here at their head beneath the banner of Deheubarth.'

'And assuming they agree, who will pay for their support?'

'Tell them that when the time comes, there will be funds to help them maintain a campaign.'

'Gruffydd's coin?'

'Aye, but don't tell them that. Just say it will be confirmed when the time is right.'

'So, you are confident you can get Gruffydd to open his treasuries?' asked Robert.

'As sure as I can be but if you will, I would welcome your company on my journey north. On the way we will share the burden of garnering further support, but the focus has to be reaching Gruffydd with our proposal.'

'Of course,' said Robert. 'I suggest we all meet back here by the first day of September to decide our next move. That gives us three months to kindle the fire.'

'It is a short time to raise an army.' said Dog.

'Don't forget,' said Cynwrig, 'at this stage we are only raising awareness. The fighting will come later.' He stopped walking and turned to the other men. 'I know this is a huge ask,' he said, 'but believe me, I wouldn't be suggesting it if I didn't think great things were possible. Gwenllian's death has affected people like nothing else I have ever seen, and we would be doing her memory an injustice to let these days pass without action.'

'I am happy to do whatever it takes,' said Robert. 'Just give me direction as to what is expected of me and I will carry it out unto my last breath.'

'Thank you, Robert,' said Cynwrig and turned to Dog. 'And you, Master Dog, will you stay, or will you join us?'

'If I leave,' replied Dog, 'then Tarw will probably fall drunk from his horse and be dead within a week. I guess I am going to have to stick around.'

'I need no chaperone.' said Tarw curtly.

'Think of him as your second,' said Robert. 'The marches are a dangerous place and two swords are better than one.'

'So, what about you, my lord?' asked Cynwrig. 'The final say in this matter is yours and yours alone. If you think it a futile quest, then you only need speak your mind. Withdraw your support and this ends where we stand.'

Tarw looked around the three men before finally answering.

'My friends, I have no idea how this will end or if we will live to share the tale, but if we achieve nothing except immortalising my wife's name across the country that she loved, then it will be a task well done. Any man would be lucky to have such comrades and you all have my everlasting gratitude.'

'In that case,' said Cynwrig, 'let us talk about supplies and strategies. With luck we can begin our journeys tomorrow. Agreed?'

All three of his fellows nodded their agreement.

'Good,' said Cynwrig, 'for time is limited. May God help us on our path.'

'Amen,' said the three men and they all turned to walk down to the cathedral.

Twenty-five leagues away, the steward of Aberystwyth castle sat at a table in the vault at the base of the keep, outlining the state of the castle's finances to the temporary castellan, Stephen Demareis. The true castellan was away with the lord of Ceredigion, Richard Fitzgilbert, attending the new king in Windsor but was due back in the next few weeks and his temporary replacement wanted to ensure every penny was accounted for prior to his arrival.

'So,' said Demareis, 'once the payment for the latest shipment of beef to Gower has been received, the ledgers will balance?'

'There is a shortfall of two shillings, my lord,' replied the steward, 'which was caused by one of the farmers failing to pay his taxes, but his farm has been confiscated and will be absorbed into the estate. Once his chattels have been sold we will be showing a surplus.'

'Good,' said Demareis. 'So, on to our food stores. I am led to believe they are running low. Is there a problem?'

'No, my lord. It is normal for this time of year. However, I have arranged for an increase in our salted beef and pork, as well as corn and dried fish. I expect it here by the end of the month.'

'In that case,' said Demareis sitting back, 'I believe our business is done. You may continue with your day.'

'Thank you, my lord,' said the steward and left the vault just as a heavily built warrior entered.

'Peter,' said Demareis looking up at his captain of the guard, 'you are back earlier than expected.'

'I am, my lord and have our quarry in custody.'

'Excellent,' said Demareis, 'let us go and see what they have to say.'

The two men left the keep and headed down to the bailey where a group of ten armed soldiers stood in a circle around two brigands laying the mud. Their feet were cut to ribbons and what remained of their clothing in tatters after being dragged most of the way behind a horse from their hiding place in a forest two leagues away. Demareis walked up to the prisoners.

'So, you are the men responsible for the slaughter of one of the king's deer,' he said coldly.

'My lord,' gasped one of the men through a bloody mouth, 'it was already dead, I swear. It had fallen into a ravine and was already covered in flies. All we did was take some meat to fight our hunger.'

'Dead or alive is not the issue here,' said Demareis coldly, 'you took the king's meat without permission. That means you stole it.'

'My lord, please,' gasped the second man, 'we were starving and would surely have died. Please show mercy.'

'I am no stranger to mercy,' said Demareis, 'so will offer you a choice. If you both agree who is responsible for the first cut on the king's deer, then that man will be hung. The other will be freed. However, if you disagree who is at fault, you will both die at the hands of my torturer. So, what is it to be?'

The two poachers looked at each other as the stark choice before them sunk in, both afraid to speak.

'My lord,' said the older man eventually, 'we are brothers. You give us an impossible choice.'

'If you are brothers then surely it is good that one lives to seed your wretched line, or would you rather die screaming alongside each other?'

'My lord…' said the man again

'I will ask you once more,' interrupted Demareis, 'and if there is no agreement then the option is withdrawn. So, for the last time, who is to die?'

Before the older prisoner could answer, his sibling lifted his arm and pointed at his brother.

'It was him,' he sobbed, 'he made me do it. I did not want to eat the deer, but it was his idea. He should be the one to die.'

'The older man looked down in shock, knowing the opposite was true but by speaking a lie, his younger brother had condemned him to death no matter what the outcome.

'Well,' said Demareis, 'is he telling the truth?'

The two prisoners stared at each other and the older brother could see the fear in his sibling's eyes.

'Aye,' he said slowly, 'it is. My brother had nothing to do with it.'

'Really?' said Demareis. 'You surprise me.' He turned to the captain. 'Hang him from the tower and leave his body for the crows.'

'Aye, my lord,' said the captain. 'And the other one?'

'Cut off his hands. Seal the wounds with pitch and if he lives, set him free. He will steal no more of the King's deer in this life.'

'Aye, my lord,' said the captain and as the younger man was dragged away screaming, two of the guards led the older brother to the steps of the palisade.

'You have the better outcome, brigand,' said one as he retrieved a rope from a cart. 'Make this easy for me and I promise it will be quick. Struggle and I will hoist you up slowly like a pennant. Understood?'

The man nodded and allowed himself to be led away to meet his fate.

'Your men have done well, captain,' called Demareis over his shoulder as he walked back up the motte to the keep. 'Stand them down for the night but make sure the walls are well guarded. I suspect the sight of one of their own dangling from the palisade may upset some of the locals.'

'Aye, my lord,' said the captain and turned to his men. The day had been long, but any excitement was better than the constant monotony of serving in this God-forsaken place. He had spent most of his life fighting in the service of the king and this was by far the most boring posting he had ever had.

Unbeknownst to him, that was soon to change.

Chapter Eight

The Palace of Aberffraw

May AD 1136

Owain stood stripped to the waist, enjoying the surprising warmth of the midday sun as he rubbed down his favourite horse with handfuls of hay. The sweat glistened on his skin and two serving girls glanced discreetly from their place at the well. He was much older than them and was married, but they knew he had a taste for the ladies and both hoped to be his next conquest.

'Owain,' said a voice and he looked up to see Angharad walking toward him.

'Mother,' he said, standing up and pushing his shoulder length hair back from his face. 'I thought you had taken to your sick bed.'

'It will take more than an ague to end me,' said Angharad. 'Women are made of sterner stuff, it seems.'

'Aye, that may be true,' said Owain. 'How fares the king?'

'Not good but he is as stubborn as ever and I have no doubt he will die on his own terms, not God's.'

'Or the devil's,' laughed Owain.

Angharad smiled and nodded at her son. For a moment she recalled his childhood and how he, his brothers and his beautiful little sister used to run her, and her servants ragged around the palace. Now he had grey teasing at his temples and his face showed the lines of age. However, he was no less handsome than he had ever been and had a body hardened by the rigours of training and combat.

'So', said Owain grabbing a handful of fresh hay, 'is there something you wanted from me?'

'Yes,' said Angharad, 'well actually, it is the other way around. I have managed to retrieve some money from the treasury without the knowledge of the castle steward, and I want you to have it.'

'You stole from the king,' laughed Owain. 'He could have you tortured for that.'

'He wouldn't dare,' said Angharad. 'Anyway, I have a purse of silver and I would set you a task.'

'Which is?'

Angharad looked around to ensure she wasn't overheard.

'I want you to send a rider to every village in Gwynedd and seek men expert in the use of the longbow. Look for those who have grown up with the bow and can hit a quarry at over two hundred paces nine times out of ten. The money is to pay the wages of those who pass the test. Make them eager to join us.'

'To what end?'

'I know your father,' said Angharad. 'His grief is eating away at him, but I do not think that he will allow Gwenllian's death to go unpunished. He will come around eventually I am sure, but in the meantime, there is no reason we cannot prepare.'

'Prepare what?'

'Our forces.'

'I have already said I can field two thousand men within days and of them, over one hundred are archers.'

'Perhaps so, but recently I attended a tournament and those wielding longbows not only doubled the range of hunting bows but were able to pierce the thickest of targets. I think perhaps that it would only be a boon to have such men in our command.'

'Farmers and hunters are not soldiers; mother and they would probably run at the first charge. '

'Perhaps so, but how many of those charging would fall to their arrows before the line broke?'

'A fair argument,' said Owain.

'Good,' in that case, carry out my request and muster them somewhere distant from Aberffraw. There is no need for prying eyes to learn of our ruse and certainly no reason to concern your father.'

'You are a wicked woman, mother,' said Owain, 'and would make a formidable foe.'

'Your father has always said I am the one adversary he never bested,' replied Angharad tapping her son on the shoulder. 'You finish whatever it is you have to do, and I will have the money brought to your quarters.'

'I am almost done here,' said Owain, 'just give me a moment to don my tunic.'

'Oh, I wouldn't rush,' said Angharad over her shoulder, 'you wouldn't want to disappoint your audience, would you?'

Owain turned and saw the two giggling servant girls still at the well. One raised her hand and wiggled her fingers in a semblance of a wave before they both turned away and headed back to the kitchens.

'No,' said Owain quietly to himself, as he picked up his jerkin, 'there's no rush at all.'

Angharad made her way over to the hall but as she walked, one of the castle servants ran up with a leather bag.

'My lady,' he said, 'a rider arrived at the gates just a few moments ago. He said I was to give this to you, and to you alone.'

'Thank you, Simon,' said Angharad and took the satchel from the servant before heading into the hall, intrigued as to what it may contain. Inside she sat at a table and opened the buckle to see a sealed parchment within. Moments later she had cut the seal and read the contents to herself, letting out a gasp of surprise just as her hand maiden entered the hall.

'My lady,' said the servant, 'I have been looking for you. There is broth ready for your meal.' She paused, seeing the look of shock on her mistress' face. 'My lady, what is it? Have you received bad news?'

'Oh no, Catrin,' replied Angharad, 'quite the opposite. An old and dear friend is on his way here to visit us, someone who I haven't seen for many years.'

'Do I know him?'

'I think not, but he was once as much a part of this family as my sons. His name is Cynwrig and he will be here the day after tomorrow.'

'Then I will make sure there is clean linen and fresh water in the guest lodgings,' said Catrin.

'Yes,' said Angharad, 'and ask the steward to also supply a second cot as he is travelling with a comrade.'

'Of course, my lady,' said Catrin. 'Is there anything else?'

'Yes, ask him to send a rider to Cadwaladwr. Cynwrig states that he has important news and he wants to share it with us all.'

'I will do it straight away,' said Catrin, 'now, about this broth.'

'The broth will wait, Catrin, I have to share this wonderful news with the king. It will give him great heart.'

'Of course, my lady,' replied the servant, 'I will bring it to your room later.' She left the hall to seek the steward as Angharad made her way up the stairs to the king's chambers. She had no idea what it was that brought Cynwrig from the south but whatever it was, she knew it had to be important.

Chapter Nine

Monmouth Castle

May AD 1136

Richard Fitzgilbert was a very powerful man and he knew it. Since supporting Henry gain the throne after the suspicious death of his brother, William Rufus many years earlier he had been rewarded handsomely and now over eighty manors fell under his control across the middle belt of England and as far west as Ceredigion in Wales.

These past few weeks he had been paying homage to the new king in Westminster but now he and his wife were headed homeward to Ceredigion along with an armed guard of over a hundred men. The journey had been arduous, and he had stopped at many of the English castles along the way for safety. Monmouth had provided one of those refuges and he and his party had stayed the past two nights, taking the chance to rest the horses. Today was no different and though he was keen to continue as soon as possible, his wife was still tired from the journey. Consequently, as he knew the local forests were famous for the quality of the boar, he had taken the opportunity to hunt.

'Good morning, my lord,' said the castle steward as Richard Fitzgilbert walked towards his waiting men. 'Your horse is in fine fettle and keen to be away.'

'Thank you,' said Fitzgilbert, 'I look forward to seeing what game you have in these forests. Perchance we will dine on the king of pigs this evening.'

'I'm sure we will, my lord,' said the steward. 'I have taken the liberty of supplying my best huntsman. He knows every divot for a dozen leagues in all directions. If there is a boar to be had, he is the man to find it.'

'Thank you, master steward,' said Fitzgilbert, 'you have thought of everything as usual. Perhaps we will stay a few more days and enjoy your hospitality.'

'Your patronage is always appreciated, my lord,' said the steward, and you may stay as long as you wish.'

Despite the offer, inside, the steward could feel his heart fall at the prospect. Feeding and housing a force of over a hundred men was an expensive task and to ask for payment to cover the extra cost would be an unforgiveable slight. Fitzgilbert was one of the most powerful warlords in the west and one word from him could make or break a man.

The warlord looked around the busy bailey. Dozens of traders sold their wares from the backs of handcarts and the place was a hive of activity.

'Is this normal?' He asked.

'The local traders bring their wares on this day every week,' said the steward. 'They are harmless enough and my men know each one personally. You are at no risk within these walls.'

'I will take your word on it,' said Fitzgilbert. 'Make sure my wife gets everything she needs.'

'Of course, my lord, and I hope you have a very productive hunt.'

'Oh, one more thing,' said Fitzgilbert, 'does your man know the route to Brycheniog?'

'Of course, my lord, the road is straight and easy to follow.'

'No, I mean the path that goes past Llanthony Abbey. I have a mind to visit the Abbot on my way back to Ceredigion two days hence.'

'We all know the route, my lord, but it is rough ground and unsuitable for your lady's wagon. Can I suggest you stick to the main road?'

'The carts can continue as planned but I have important business with the Abbot. We will re-join the wagons before the day is out. Worry not, they will be well guarded.'

'Of course, my lord,' said the steward, 'in that case, my men will accompany you as far as you wish.'

'Good. In the meantime, there is boar to be killed. Look after my lady, master steward. I will return before nightfall.'

'Aye, my lord,' said the steward and waited as Fitzgilbert mounted his horse. The gates opened, and the hunting party left the safety of the castle, leaving him breathing in the dust from the horses' hooves.

'He is a difficult man,' said a voice quietly beside him.

'Aye, he is,' said the steward, recognising the bailiff's voice, 'but he knows his mind and it is not my place to tell him otherwise.'

'He will be safe enough,' said the bailiff. 'Now come, let us relax while the air is empty of his demands.'

The two men walked back up the steps of the motte, both oblivious of the solitary trader that was pushing his handcart of pots and pans back out through the gate. A closer inspection would have noticed that he had sold not a single item and to leave so early in the day was very unusual. Any suspicious man would have questioned his intentions, but there were no such men on duty this day, and the trader was soon well on his way. Within an hour a solitary rider galloped southward leaving a handcart of unsold pots and pans hidden in the undergrowth.

Ten leagues away, a hundred or so warriors sat around a hidden encampment deep in a sprawling forest. For the past few weeks they had patrolled the byways of the kingdom seeking English columns to raid but those they had found were so heavily guarded, the risk of defeat was too great.

The commander of these men was no brigand, on the contrary, he was a known Welsh prince by the name of Morgan ap Owen, grandson of Caradog ap Gruffydd, the feared king of Gwent who had died at the battle of Mynydd Carn over fifty years earlier. However, despite his lineage he enjoyed no permanent castle as a base and spent his time living amongst the many manors of Gwent that still showed him allegiance. He and his men were battle hardened, fearless and hated the English with a passion.

Morgan ap Owen sat on a fallen tree trunk, nonchalantly waxing the blade of his sword as he listened to the man standing opposite him plead his case. Behind the traveller, stood two heavily armed warriors, each with a hand on the hilt of their swords in case of any sudden attempt on Morgan's life.

Finally, the talking stopped and Morgan looked up. The man before him was another Welsh prince and though they were all but equals, Morgan had cause to hate him. That man was Tarw.

'Are you done?' asked Morgan.

'I am,' said Tarw. 'I know there was bad blood between our families but that was a lifetime away and this is no time to embrace age old grudges.'

'Your father killed my grandfather at Mynydd Carn,' said Morgan, 'and as a result of that, our house was scattered to the winds. I would hardly call that a mere grudge.'

'As I said,' replied Tarw, 'neither I or indeed you were involved. The dice of fate fall as they will and it is for subsequent generations to live with the consequences.'

Morgan nodded silently and got to his feet. Slowly he walked over and made his way around the prince, dragging the point of his sword gently in the soil.

'What if I was to disagree,' he said softly. 'What if my view was that the sons should always pay the price of their fathers. What if I believed that debts of honour can last generations until settled by blood. Would that be of concern to you?'

'I cannot dictate your thoughts,' said Tarw, 'but I would say that to pursue such an avenue only leads to more bloodshed between those who should be at each other's shoulders. This is an opportunity to heal old wounds and deal the English a terrible blow. I have come here with only one comrade, knowingly putting my life in your hands. Join me and I promise I will return your grandfather's lands to you as well as the manors and castles he once controlled.'

'Methinks you get ahead of yourself,' said Morgan from behind Tarw. 'First you have to defeat the English, not only in Ceredigion, but all across the south of this country. No man has come close to such a victory since William the Bastard first set foot on our shores.'

'I know, and that is why I am here,' said Tarw. 'I need your men and those of your brother to bolster the armies we are building. Your strength in battle is common conversation throughout the Cantrefs and though your swords will be a welcome addition, just the knowledge that we ride together will bolster the confidence of those already committed. With you and Iorwerth on our flanks I know we can more than match the enemy strength.'

'And you say that Gruffydd of Gwynedd will support the fight?'

'He will.'

'How do I know you tell the truth?'

'I can only promise what I believe to be true.'

'So, it is not yet guaranteed?'

'No, but there is someone pleading my case as we speak. Don't forget, Gwenllian was Gruffydd's daughter and he is a vengeful man. I know he will not let this rest.'

'He has been quiet so far,' said Morgan continuing his circuit around Tarw.

'Perhaps so, but I know his anger ferments.'

Morgan appeared in front of Tarw again and lifted his sword, pressing the point gently against the prince's throat.

'Tell me why I should not kill you right now and go down in history as the man who avenged Caradog.'

'Because history will judge you as a common murderer instead of the grandson of a great king.'

Morgan stared deep into Tarw's eyes.

'You speak a good fight, Tarw of Deheubarth,' he said, 'and I have heard fair tales of your prowess in battle yet when it came to the greatest of all, when your wife and two sons were in the vanguard, you were absent. Why does that not fill me with confidence?'

'You know the tale well,' said Tarw, 'and it gets no better with the retelling.'

'Humour me.'

'My absence was justified,' said Tarw with a sigh, 'and one day God will surely be my judge yet there is not a day that goes by without me wanting to die in their place. Now, only the thought of retribution stops me hurling myself from the nearest crag.'

Morgan took a deep breath and lowered his sword.

'You have spoken well,' he said, 'but there are still unanswered questions. I will think on these things and we will talk again on the morrow. Until then, you and your comrade will be provided food and shelter.'

Tarw nodded his head slightly in acceptance.

'Then that is all I can reasonably expect,' he replied, 'and I look forward to speaking again.'

'How did it go?' asked Dog when Tarw returned to the horses.

'It is hard to tell,' said Tarw, 'but at least we have a bed for the night. Come, let's see to the horses and then get something to eat.'

A few hours later they sat outside a tent heating up a pot of cold cawl supplied by the camp cooks. The two men who had guarded Tarw when he was addressing Morgan earlier, stood a few paces away, relaxed but observant.

Dog grabbed a handful of dried mutton strips from his saddle bag and stirred them in to the pot along with salt and a slab of cheese. Within minutes the air filled with the wonderful aroma of meat laden stew and more than a few heads turned their way from nearby tents as he filled his and Tarw's wooden bowls. The cheese melted forming a greasy film and the smell made their mouths water in anticipation.

After a moment, Tarw looked up at the two guards still on duty.

'Have you eaten?' he asked, seeing their hungry looks.

One of the men glanced at his comrade before replying.

'Not yet.'

'Then help yourself,' said Tarw, 'there is plenty.'

Dog gave him a scathing look but said nothing.

The guard glanced again at his comrade and after receiving a shrug of his shoulders in reply, walked over to the fire.

'We accept your offer,' he said, 'but warn that if this is a ruse and you try to escape, then you will be found wanting.'

'I had no idea we were prisoners,' said Tarw, 'but it matters not. We have no desire to leave and only offer to share our meal with two fellow warriors who are hungry. That is no crime no matter what side of an argument you stand.'

'I will trust you, Tarw of Deheubarth,' said the first man. 'I hope you live up to your reputation. '

Both guards sat on the ground while Dog lifted the pot from the fire with a stick and placed it on the floor in front of them.

'You have me at a disadvantage,' said Tarw as the men retrieved their wooden spoons from beneath their cloaks. 'You know my name, but I know not yours.'

'John Farmer,' said the first man, dipping into the stew, 'and my ugly comrade here is Perry.'

'A long day?' Asked Tarw as they ate.

'Longer for the lack of action,' said John Farmer through a mouthful of stew. 'Alas, the English are more attuned to our intentions these days and any quarry worth having is usually well guarded.'

'I hear the Marcher lords traverse the border at whim.'

'Aye they do, and in strength. Though recently it seems their eyes are turned toward London.'

'Because of the struggle for the English throne?'

'Aye. Stephen may be king, but Matilda has her own eye on the crown. It will all turn bloody, mark my words and when it does we will be around to take advantage.'

'So where is Morgan's brother? I thought he would be here.'

'He will arrive soon enough. He has been shadowing Fitzgilbert's caravan since they left Hereford, hoping to find a weakness.'

'Why?'

'Because both Morgan and his brother have been dealt ill by Fitzgilbert in the past, and opportunities of finding him outside the security of any of his castle walls come few and far between.'

'You mean to kill him?'

'That is the plan.'

'He is the king's man and I would guess he is well guarded.'

'He is, but no man can go through life without making a mistake. Hopefully, his will come soon enough.'

'Do you not fear retribution from the crown?'

'Like I said, they are too busy jostling for position against each other, so we have to make the most of any opportunity offered. '

Tarw glanced at Dog. If what he was hearing was true, then it added even more reason to unite. With King Stephen's mind on the possible challenge by Matilda, his attention would not be on Wales.

'Where are you from? 'asked Tarw dipping another biscuit into the remaining broth.

'Caerleon,' said the guard, 'both of us.'

'And is your background farming?' asked Tarw but before he received an answer, another two men appeared out of the trees to relieve the guards.

'Our gratitude for the cawl,' said John Farmer standing up, 'and I hope you get agreement on whatever it is you came for.'

'As do I,' said Tarw and watched them walk away to their own tents.

The new guards were more aloof and leaned on a couple of trees at the side of the clearing, rarely taking their eyes off the two men. Soon the night closed in and Tarw and Dog ducked into the tent to crawl beneath their waxed woollen blankets.

Both men were fast asleep when the sound of someone banging on the damp canvas tent dragged them back awake. Dog woke with a start and reached for the knife he kept at his side.

'Who's there?' he asked loudly.

'John Farmer,' replied the voice, 'your presence is required by Morgan. Get dressed and quick about it. There is no time to lose.'

Dog looked at Tarw who shrugged his shoulders in reply. He looked up toward the canvas over his head.

'I hear birdsong,' he said, 'it must be almost dawn.'

'Why do you think he wants us at this hour?' asked Tarw

'I don't know,' grumbled Dog, 'but I already hate him for waking me. That was the best sleep I have had for many a week.'

'Come on,' said Tarw throwing back his blanket, 'let's see what this is all about.'

Ten minutes later, they stood in front of a roaring fire in a clearing. All around them the trees were a hive of activity as men retrieved their equipment ready to strike camp. Horses pawed the ground, already caught up in the air of excitement.

'Tarw,' called a voice and both men turned to see Morgan striding out of the darkness.

'You summoned us?' replied Tarw.

'Aye, I did. There have been developments and we have no time to lose.'

'What is happening?' asked Dog. 'Are we at risk?'

'On the contrary,' said Morgan, 'for once fate is in our favour and we have an opportunity too good to waste.'

'A caravan perchance?' said Tarw.

'Oh no, Tarw,' said Morgan, 'a prize worth far more to me than any caravan. The life of Fitzgilbert.'

'But I thought he was safely within Monmouth Castle.'

'Aye, he is. But the day after tomorrow he is heading west to Ceredigion.'

'I have heard he is guarded by over a hundred experienced men at arms,' said Dog. 'Surely you don't intend to confront them?'

'Not all of them,' said Morgan and turned around to summon someone out of the shadows. 'Weasel, come here and tell these men what you told me.'

A slightly built man with a face weathered by wind and rain skulked forward and stared up at Tarw.

'My lord,' he said, 'Yesterday I was in the castle bailey at Monmouth selling my wares and overheard a conversation between the steward and the commander of the English column.'

'Fitzgilbert?' asked Dog

'Aye, that was his name. I heard him say he intended to head to Brycheniog via Llanthony Abbey in two days' time. That means he will be there tomorrow.'

'And?'

'That way can only be accessed via the 'Ill Way of Coed Grano,' a narrow path frequented by brigands and murderers. If he carries out his plan he is exposing himself to attack.'

'I know of this path,' said Dog, turning to Morgan, 'and it is indeed an ideal place for an ambush but even with surprise on your side, I cannot see you getting the better of them, not with your current numbers.'

'I agree,' said Morgan, 'but there is more. Continue your tale, Weasel.'

'My lord,' said the small man, 'I heard the man say that his lady is ill and will stay with the wagons on the road to Brycheniog while he visits the Abbot. He also said she will be well guarded.'

Morgan turned to Tarw with an evil smile on his face.

'That means,' he said, 'that his force will be split and, in my opinion, by far the greater number will be tasked with protecting his wife.'

'I agree,' said Tarw. 'He would not leave the caravan unprotected.'

'Which means,' said Morgan, 'Fitzgilbert has fallen straight into our laps. Not only will he be outnumbered but the land is in our favour as well as the element of surprise.'

'So, you intend to attack him?'

'Aye, I do,' said Morgan, 'and will take great pleasure in slitting his throat.'

Dog's eyes narrowed in suspicion as Morgan turned away.

'Wait,' he said, 'what has this to do with us?'

'Oh, didn't I say,' said Morgan, 'you will be coming with us.'

'You want me to ride at your side?' asked Tarw, shocked.

'Oh no, Tarw of Deheubarth, you will not be at my side, you will be leading the attack.'

'This is not our quarrel,' said Dog.

'Perhaps not,' said Morgan, 'but I'm sure we all agree that every dead Englishman is one less to worry about and besides, this is a chance for the prince to prove himself.'

'What do you mean?' asked Tarw.

'I still have my doubts about you,' replied Morgan, 'and don't know whether your reputation is true, or bluster spread by your fellows. Prove to me that you are worth fighting alongside and I will commit my men to your cause.'

'That is horse shit,' growled Dog but Tarw held up his hand to silence his comrade.

'If I do this,' he said, 'and we are successful, you will join us in our fight?'

'Aye, I will, but first I want to piss on Fitzgilbert's cold dead corpse.'

Tarw paused and glanced at Dog before looking back at the Gwent prince.

'In that case, I agree,' he said. 'What do you want me to do?'

'Prepare your horses, we have a hard ride ahead of us if we are going to get to the forest above the abbey before tonight. Once there we will make our plans and get into position before dawn.' He turned and walked away as Tarw and Dog returned to their own tent.

'Are you sure about this?' asked Dog as they walked.

'I am not,' said Tarw, 'but if this is the only way to get him and his men on side, then it is a risk worth taking.'

'But you are risking your life.'

'My life ended with Gwenllian's,' said Tarw. 'Now come, we must make ready.'

Chapter Ten

Aberffraw

May AD 1136

Catrin stood at the window in the king's bedchamber, relating everything that was happening to the bed ridden monarch.

'Is he here yet?' asked Gruffydd.

'Not yet, my lord but he must be near, for a rider is speaking to the queen and she has assembled the staff to greet him. He must be a very important man.'

'On the contrary, Catrin,' replied Gruffydd, 'he is amongst the most lowly and humble men I have ever met but to me, he is more welcome in my household than the greatest of kings.'

'I hear he once saved your life, my lord.'

'It could be said he saved my life on many occasions,' said Gruffydd,' such was the wisdom of his counsel, but I owe him so much more. He, more than any other person taught me that any man worthy of kingship should display humility as often as he picks up a sword. If it wasn't for him, I would wager Gwynedd would not enjoy the position of strength it does now.'

'I'm sure that is down to you my lord,' said Catrin glancing back at him, 'not some lowly priest born of a family of horse breeders.'

'You have not met him,' said the king, 'and yes. I have ruled Gwynedd to the best of my ability but in the background, it was his teachings that shone light on the paths that I chose.'

'Oh,' said Catrin suddenly, 'I think I see him. There are two riders on the path near fox wood, wait, no three. Two men and a boy. Would that be them?'

'We will soon find out,' said the king, 'help me to my chair. I will receive him here.'

As she did as she was told, the king started another coughing fit that drained him of all his strength and within moments he had collapsed on the bed, as weak as a new-born kitten.

'You have been awake for hours, my lord,' said Catrin, folding back the covers on the bed and helping him in, 'and visitors or not, you need to rest. There will be plenty of time to receive your friend.'

'Aye,' gasped the king. 'Perhaps I will be stronger on the morrow.'

'Then get some sleep. I will explain to the queen you are indisposed.'

Gruffydd didn't answer but just closed his eyes in exhaustion. Although he knew his life was coming to an end, the thought of dying worried him not. The thought of dying without avenging his daughter, however, burned at him like the hottest brand.

'I don't see what all the fuss is about,' stated Cadwaladwr down in the courtyard, 'I remember him as a well-meaning, but interfering priest. No more than that.'

'I will suffer no disrespect to Cynwrig or his companions,' said Angharad, chiding her son, 'when you were nought but a boy, he helped bring you up and made you the man you are today. He is as much a part of this family as you or I.'

'I remember him well,' said Owain. As boys he made us laugh and though he was a man of God, I recall him being something of an expert at sword play.'

'He fought alongside your father for many years before turning to the church,' said Angharad.

'Well we are boys no longer,' said Cadwaladwr, 'and after he has said what he wants to say, I will be returning to my manor. My time is better spent elsewhere.'

'We will hear him out,' said Angharad, 'and you will be pleasant.'

Cadwaladwr grunted something under his breath but though he was almost fourty years old, neither he nor his brothers ever risked their mother's scorn with disrespect.

'Here he is,' said Owain and watched as two of his own men escorted the road-weary travellers through the gates.

Angharad looked up at Cynwrig as he reined his horse to a halt. For a second, she was shocked by how much he had aged but soon recomposed herself and walked forward to welcome him. Cynwrig dismounted and turned to greet the queen.

'Cynwrig,' she said with a smile, 'I am so happy to see you. With no sign of ceremony Angharad stepped forward and embraced the ageing priest, holding him tightly for several moments.

'Surely this behaviour does not become a queen,' said Cynwrig with a smile, 'especially one who looks as young as she did half a century ago.'

'Stop your nonsense,' laughed Angharad, holding him at arm's length, and staring into his eyes, 'I am as wrinkled as an old walnut, as are you I may add.'

'True, but this old walnut has life in him yet and if your husband is willing to fight me I am still happy to whisk you away.'

Angharad smiled, enjoying the nature of the banter they had shared so many years earlier.

'Now that is a fight I would pay to see,' she said, 'and to the winner the spoils.'

'Now don't you go stirring by blood, my queen,' scorned Cynwrig playfully, 'for I know not how many beats this old heart has left.'

'You and the king will live forever,' laughed Angharad.

'Talking about the old devil,' replied Cynwrig looking around, 'where is he? In the wine cellar with some comely wench I would wager.'

'Alas his devilish days are over,' said Angharad, 'and he lays abed with an ague. I will take you to see him shortly but first I would meet your travelling companions.'

Cynwrig turned as his comrade and a boy walked over to join them.

'This is Robert of Llandeilo,' announced Cynwrig. 'A noble who lost everything in the southern rebellion yet was fiercely loyal to your daughter and her husband right up to the end.'

'I am very pleased to meet you, Robert,' said Angharad, 'and I will be forever grateful for whatever support and comfort you gave our daughter.'

Robert inclined his head in acknowledgement of her station and kissed her proffered hand.

'The lady Gwenllian was a very special woman,' he replied, 'and was loved by every person who ever met her. My heart will be forever broken.'

Angharad swallowed hard and forced herself to smile again before turning to the young boy at Robert's side.

'And who is this young chap?'

'This is um…' Cynwrig hesitated and looked at Robert who shrugged his shoulders in reply.

'What nonsense is this?' laughed Angharad. 'Have you forgotten his name?'

'I don't think I have ever known it,' said Cynwrig. 'He has been addressed as the boy ever since he came into my service two years ago and it seems to have stuck.'

'Well we can't be having that,' said Angharad, rubbing the boy's dark curls, 'you have to have a name. Do you remember what your mother called you, young man?'

'I don't remember my mother, my lady,' replied the boy, 'but I think someone once called me a rascal.'

'It is marginally better,' said the queen, 'and it certainly suits your appearance. If it is acceptable to you, then henceforth I will call you Rascal.'

'Of course, my lady,' said the boy and gave an extravagant bow, much to the amusement of all present.

'Worthy of any court,' laughed the queen and turned back to the priest.

'Cynwrig,' she said beckoning her sons, 'do you remember Owain and Cadwaladwr?'

'I do,' said Cynwrig, 'though these two are far too ugly to be your sons. Surely they are imposters?'

'Your attempts at humour are still as bad as I remember,' said Owain and held out his arms in welcome. Cynwrig returned the embrace and turned to Cadwaladwr.

'Ah, the baby of the family, I see you are as happy as ever.'

'I bid you welcome, Cynwrig,' said Cadwaladwr coldly, 'but he made no effort at physical contact.'

'What, no embrace?' roared Cynwrig. 'Come here.' He wrapped his arms around the reluctant man before releasing him and turning to the queen.

'So, wench, is there no wine for the prodigal son?'

'Of course,' laughed Angharad, there is a pitcher awaiting you in your quarters and we have arranged a feast in your honour tonight, but you will share no food or ale at our table while stinking of sweat and camp fires.'

'My aroma offends you?' asked Cynwrig with a contrived look of hurt on his face.

'Aye, you stink to high heaven. Leave your horses here and they will be well tended by the grooms. There is hot water waiting for you and once you are clean and rested, we will meet again in the main hall.'

'That sounds like a grand idea,' said Cynwrig and took the queen's arm as she led him to the visitors' quarters, closely followed by Robert and the boy.

'Well that was quite an entrance,' said Owain, watching them leave.

'Did you hear him?' asked Cadwaladwr, 'he called our mother, the queen of Gwynedd, a wench.'

'A term of endearment only he can get away with,' laughed Owain. 'He is a special man, Cadwaladwr, and this family owes him a lot. You would do well to remember that.'

'I am getting fed up of people extolling his virtues,' replied his brother, 'and am only interested in any news of justice for the murder of our sister. Anything other than that will mean no more to me than the chatter of the washer women.'

'Well, we will see soon enough. Come, let's relieve father's cellars of that fine wine he thinks he has hidden so well.'

'That's the best idea I have heard all day,' said Cadwaladwr and followed his brother to the house.

The main hall at dusk exuded a warmth that made Cynwrig feel he had come home. Not just because of the enormous fire in the far grate and the hundreds of candles around the walls, but because the space was filled with the chatter of smiling people and the sound of minstrels playing subtle tunes in the background. Rascal's eyes were as wide as the platters on the table, taking in the extravagance, and even Robert was pleasantly surprised.

'Your friends certainly know how to treat their guests,' he said as they walked through the hall.

'It is a bit much, admittedly,' said Cynwrig, 'but don't forget, Gruffydd is a very wealthy man, He controls almost the whole north of the country and while he is feared by many, he is respected by all, even the English. It has taken many years, but Gwynedd is now entirely in his control and he is probably the strongest king outside of London.'

'Is he here?' asked Robert looking around.

'Alas no. I am told his health took a downward turn a while ago and he is sleeping. Hopefully we can meet him on the morrow.'

'I hope so,' said Robert as he accepted a tankard of ale from a serving girl, 'every day that passes is another day wasted.'

'Cynwrig,' called a voice and both men turned to see Owain striding towards them across the hall. 'You are here at last,' he said,' mother is getting quite impatient to see you again. Please, join us at the top table.'

'An honour indeed,' said Cynwrig. 'And my friend here?'

'Your comrade is as welcome as you,' said Owain. 'Come, there is wine, mead, and enough ale to inebriate the whole of Christendom.'

'In that case, lead the way,' said Cynwrig and they made their way over to where Angharad was deep in conversation with Cadwaladwr.

'My lady,' said Cynwrig, as he approached, 'please accept my apologies for the delay but trying to get the boy to bathe was as difficult as doing the same to a cat.'

'You are here now,' said Angharad with a smile, 'please sit and help yourselves to food.'

For the next hour, Cynwrig and Robert enjoyed the meal, relishing in the atmosphere whilst engaging in small talk with those nearest to them. The food was wonderful and the company charming but when Rascal finally left the table for a closer look at the minstrels playing the music, Cadwaladwr turned to speak to Cynwrig.

'So,' he said, using a linen cloth to wipe his hands, 'this has all been very pleasant but surely you haven't come here just to be feasted like the king himself?'

'I have not,' said Cynwrig, 'and indeed there are important things to discuss.'

'Then let us waste no more of your time,' replied Cadwaladwr, 'for you have travelled far to have your say.'

'Cadwaladwr,' interrupted the queen, 'this is not the time nor the place.'

'On the contrary, mother,' said Cadwaladwr, 'our guests have been made more than welcome and I'm sure they would be only too happy to repay our hospitality by explaining exactly why it is they have travelled the length of the country to see you.'

'Brother,' interjected Owain, 'we can discuss this later.'

'I want to discuss it now,' said Cadwaladwr coldly.

Owain's face changed slightly and though the smile remained, the muscles in his face worked hard to disguise the anger that was rising in his heart and he placed his meat knife carefully on the table with a slow and deliberate motion.

Although it had been many years since Cynwrig had last seen Owain explode into the temper he was famed for, the priest recognised the warning signs and moved quickly to calm the situation.

'Gentlemen,' he said quickly, placing his goblet on the table, 'Cadwaladwr is right. We have accepted this wonderful hospitality yet have kept you wondering as to the reason for our visit and that is unforgiveable.' He turned to the queen. 'My lady, in the absence of the king, are you happy that we share our knowledge with you and the rest of your family.'

Angharad turned to look at Owain who nodded slightly.

'In my husband's absence, Owain runs the estate,' she said, 'and though all final decisions lay with the king, my eldest son can speak for all of us.'

'In that case,' said Cynwrig, 'perhaps there is a quieter room where we may talk.'

'There is,' said Cadwaladwr standing up. 'Follow me.'

'Mother,' said Owain after staring at his brother for a few moments, 'have you finished your meal?'

'I am done,' she said, 'and perhaps it would indeed be an opportune time to talk.' She turned to Cynwrig. 'Please, feel free to bring your drink and I will have the servants bring a platter of cold meats.'

The group stood and left the hall to enter the antechamber where the steward spent his days. A servant followed them in and banked up the fire with logs before leaving and closing the door.

'My apologies,' said the queen, lowering herself into the only comfortable chair near the fire, 'but my aged bones are forever cold and need the comfort and warmth a fire brings.'

Robert and Cadwaladwr carried over the two long benches from the table at the end of the room and set them on either side of the queen. Everyone sat down except Cynwrig who held out his hands toward the warming flames.

'So,' said Cadwaladwr, when they were ready, 'this is all very homely but perhaps you can now explain why you are here?'

Cynwrig bent to add another log on the fire before turning to face the queen.

'It seems my bones are just as cold as yours these days,' he said.

Cadwaladwr, swallowed hard, angry at the obvious snub from the priest but before he could say anything more, Cynwrig turned back towards him.

'You are correct, Master Cadwaladwr,' he said with a sigh, 'we do have an ulterior motive for being here and that motive has both financial and military implications.

'I knew it,' said Cadwaladwr, 'how is it that whenever I see a priest these days, he comes complete with a begging bowl.'

'Cadwaladwr, that's enough,' said the queen, 'let him speak.' She turned to Cynwrig. 'Please continue.'

'It is quite simple,' continued Cynwrig, 'there is a mood throughout the country that like none I have ever seen before. An up-swelling of fervour that demands an end to the tyranny of the English crown.'

'You talk of a rebellion,' said Owain, 'yet it is only months since the last one took the life of our dear sister.'

'I do, but this time it has the potential to be like no other.'

'Nothing more than the talk of small men in taverns in my experience,' said Cadwaladwr.

'This is different,' said Cynwrig, 'and for the first time in generations, the people of Deheubarth strain at the leash to fight back.'

'Then perhaps you should cut them loose,' said Owain, 'and let them fight for what they want as my father did for so many years. Now we kneel to no man, be they pauper or king.'

'I am sure they will fight,' said Cynwrig, 'but at the moment they are nought but peasants and unlike Gwynedd, do not have a great king to lead them. Your father was like the brightest beacon in the darkest night and he set the standard that all Welsh kings aspire to reach, but alas they have been too busy fighting amongst themselves to focus on the real enemy. Now, however, I believe that at last, they see the error of their ways and are willing to join in a common purpose.'

'And that is?'

'To rise against the English and take back what is rightfully theirs.'

'And this is where we come in?' asked Cadwaladwr scornfully.

'Aye. The people are ready to rise but they cannot do it alone. They need the strength of your armies and the wealth of your treasuries to make it happen.'

'Ha!' Laughed Cadwaladwr. Now we get to the heart of the matter. Petty kings and jumped up lords who for almost a hundred years have focused on filling their own coffers and fighting each other, suddenly realise they have got it wrong and want us to clean up their mess. Well it isn't going to happen, Cynwrig. You have had a wasted journey.'

'Cynwrig,' said the queen leaning forward in her chair, 'I may have chosen better words, but my son has a point. Why should we open out treasuries and send our young men to die for a cause not of our making?'

'Because, my lady, the reason the country is rising from their slumber is something we all share, the very thing that causes the endless pain within your heart.'

'And that is?' asked Angharad.

'The death of your daughter,' my lady. The country wants to rise against the English in the name of Gwenllian ferch Gruffydd.'

Chapter Eleven

The Ill Way of Coed Grano

May AD 1136

Tarw eased his horse quietly along the path on the inside edge of the wood. In front of him was a single line of ten horsemen led by Morgan whilst behind, came another hundred or so riders, the sum total of his command. Tarw looked up at the moon flickering between the branches knowing they had to be in position before the sun rose.

The men were tired, after riding almost all the previous day via the hidden paths leading through the forests, but Tarw knew that if and when they launched the attack, any tiredness would disappear like a bird taking flight as the lust of battle fell upon them.

Carefully they continued and as the path widened, Morgan slowed his horse to allow Tarw to ride up alongside him.

'Are you ready for this, Prince of Deheubarth?' he asked quietly.

'Worry not about me, Morgan,' said Tarw, 'you just ensure that when this is over, you keep your promise.'

'I am a man of my word, Tarw,' said Morgan, 'and if we should survive this day, I will ride alongside you in Deheubarth.'

'What about your brother?' Asked Tarw. 'Will he join us?'

'I cannot speak for him,' said Morgan, 'but if there are English to be killed, he is unlikely to miss the opportunity.'

'I hope so, said Tarw for this is bigger than all of us.'

'One battle at a time, Tarw,' said Morgan, 'and after that we will talk of freedom.' He dug his heels into his horse's flanks and trotted forward to the head of the men.

A few hours later, all the horses were tethered deep inside a forest while the warriors hid amongst the undergrowth. Tarw and Dog crawled to the front edge of a thicket and looked down on the muddy track below.

'That is the Ill Way of Coed Grano,' whispered Dog. 'Abergavenny is north while Llanthony Abbey lies half a league that way.' He pointed in the opposite direction. 'If Morgan's man is correct, then Fitzgilbert will be travelling along this path sometime today. There is no other route.'

'But why here?' asked Tarw. 'I can see the way is narrow and their only escape from the valley is at either end but what is to stop them retreating onto the open ground on the far side and reorganizing? If we allow them to do that then they can easily counter.'

'Either Morgan is a stupid man, or he knows more than he lets on,' said Dog. 'Where is he anyway, I have not seen him since we left the horses?'

'He is covering the right flank,' said Tarw, 'to stop anyone escaping down the valley.'

'For a man with so much hate for the enemy, he seems keen to avoid the main conflict,' said Dog.

'We will see how it plays out,' said Tarw, 'but what bothers me is our lack of archers. The few we have carry hunting bows only.'

'A shame,' said Dog looking down on the path. 'In the right hands, two dozen longbows would easily cut their forces in half before they have time to dismount. Where are the rest?'

'With his brother,' replied Tarw. 'Still, we have what we have and must make do with it.'

'We should pull back and get some food and sleep,' said Dog. 'The lookouts will warn us in plenty of time if our quarry approaches.'

'You go,' said Tarw, looking back down at the path, 'I need to plan the attack. I will join you shortly.'

Dog nodded and retreated into the forest.

An hour later, Tarw walked the fifty or so paces back into the trees where the men were getting what rest they could and joined Dog against a fallen oak.

'Well?' Asked Dog, as Tarw sat beside him, 'is the ground favourable or should I tell my God we will be joining him shortly.'

'It is a good position for an ambush,' said Tarw, 'though I am still uneasy about the open ground. That gives any cavalry a huge advantage should they get a chance to reorganise.'

'Then our attack must be swift and brutal,' said Dog. 'Do not give them chance to think.'

'I agree,' said Tarw, 'and have made our plans accordingly.' He looked up at the moon through the branches. 'We still have a few hours until dawn so let's get some rest.'

Dog picked up Tarw's blanket roll and threw it over to the prince.

'There's some dried mutton left,' he said. 'We have lit no fires, but meat is meat.'

'Not for me,' said Tarw. 'I can never eat on the eve of battle. '

'Then you are a strange man,' said Dog delving into the leather bag, 'it serves no purpose to die on an empty stomach.'

Tarw unwrapped his waxed blanket and draped it around his shoulders before laying down beside the log. It had been a long time since he had last killed a man and though he was confident in his own abilities, he had no idea how he would react when it came to the fight. Gradually his eyes grew heavy, and for just a few hours, he was once again with his wife and four sons.

The sun was just rising over the distant hills when Tarw finally briefed his men. At first they were sceptical especially when he explained that the first wave of the attack would be armed with nothing but knives but as he explained the strategy, they realised that it made perfect sense.

'I need volunteers for the first line,' said Tarw. 'It is by far the most dangerous role but also the most important. Only men stout of heart and fearless should step forward.'

'I will go,' said Dog, before anyone had chance to answer.

Tarw stared at his comrade in surprise. Though he knew Dog had no peer in skill or bravery, this was not his fight.

'As will I,' said the man known as John Farmer, and he stepped forward to join Dog.

Within seconds, almost every man had volunteered and Tarw was somewhat taken aback by the collective willingness to lead the attack. He turned to John Farmer.

'You will lead the first assault,' said Tarw. 'Pick out fifty good men and sharpen your knives. To you will fall the most important part of the attack. The rest of us will follow with swords and axes.'

Once separated into two groups, they went over and over the plan of attack until every man was sure of his role until finally, they each made their way to their positions.

A few minutes later, Dog dropped to the ground alongside Tarw and unhooked the water skin from his belt. He pulled the stopper with his teeth and took a long drink before offering it to the prince.

'What's in it?' asked Tarw.

'Ale,' said Dog, 'I stole it from one of Morgan's men.'

Tarw stared at the skin before shaking his head.

'You finish it,' he said, 'for if I die today it will be with a clear head.'

'Your loss.' said Dog and drained the skin before letting out a quiet belch and throwing it to one side. He drew his curved sword and laid it on the ground before settling down to stare through the bushes at the path.

'You never did say where you got that from,' said Tarw, staring at the scimitar. 'Is it true what they say?'

'I don't know, what do they say?'

'I have heard tell that you fought as a mercenary for the French and took it yourself from the hands of a dead Saracen king near Jerusalem.'

'It is as good a story as any,' said Dog.

'So, is it true?'

'The truth is even stranger, Tarw,' said Dog, 'and one day there will come a time for the telling of it. Today is not that day.'

Fitzgilbert led his column of fourty men down from the hill and into the valley. Beside him rode one of his best knights, Robin of Ceredigion. In the distance they could see a narrow plume of smoke rising into the early afternoon air.

'That must be coming from the abbey,' said Fitzgilbert. 'They have been told to expect us and the Abbot is an old friend of mine. We will rest and eat there before heading on to Brycheniog. With good weather we should be able to re-join the wagons by dark.'

'As long as the rain keeps off,' said Robin, 'for I swear I have been wetter than a fish these past few weeks.'

'Patience, Robin,' replied Fitzgilbert, 'a few more days and we will be sitting before the largest of fires drinking mead and gorging on the finest venison.'

'And the women,' said the knight, 'don't forget the women.'

'Aye the women,' laughed Fitzgilbert, 'though that is one luxury I cannot share.'

'So, what is it that takes us to the Abbey?' asked Robin.

'Let's just say there are certain financial matters that need settling,' said Fitzgilbert, 'and the Abbot has been neglecting his obligations recently.'

'He owes you money?' asked Robin.

'We must all pay our way,' replied Fitzgilbert, 'even those who serve God.'

'Ha,' laughed Robin, 'I should have guessed.'

'The politics of high office is a maze of obligations and opportunities, my friend, and each path must be explored to its fullest to reap the rewards.'

A few hundred paces in front, four riders rode ahead, each man checking the route for any sign of trouble. The forest above the banking to their right was a concern but there was no way to get the horses up the rocky slope and through the trees to check without causing hours of delay. Besides, no brigand in his right mind would dare attack a fully armed column of English cavalry.

Slowly the column snaked its way down the path and though Fitzgilbert hadn't finished talking, suddenly the knight at his side reined in his horse and held up his hand.

'Whoa,' he said and Fitzgilbert looked across at him as the column ground to a halt.

'What is it?' Asked Fitzgilbert.

'Look,' said the knight and pointed to a flock of frightened birds that had taken flight from the trees adjacent to the scouts ahead. 'Something has given them cause for alarm.'

'Could it not be they were startled by our own men?'

'Aye, it could,' said Robin, 'but let us wait and see.'

'You worry too much,' said Fitzgilbert, 'there is not a force this side of Gwynedd that would have the nerve to attack my banner. Come, the day will be long enough as it is, and we have no time to waste.' He kicked his horse and continued down the path, quickly followed by his men.

Tarw and his men lay hidden in the forest edge having been alerted by the sentries. His heart raced furiously as their quarry came closer and he knew he would have but one chance to get it right.

'Get ready,' he whispered to the archer at his side, 'release on my command but do not hit Fitzgilbert. Morgan wants him alive.'

The nervous man nodded silently and notched an arrow into his bow string. Tarw only had five archers under his command so he had to make every shaft count.

'Steady,' said Tarw as the line of riders came into view, 'steady...*Now!*

The archer released the bow string and watched with satisfaction as the arrow thudded into the throat of the flag bearer at the front of the column.

'Archers release,' roared Tarw and the rest of the bowmen unleashed their arrows on the surprised men below.

Down on the path, Sir Robin was the first to react and in one swift motion, he raised his shield from the hook on the side of his saddle just in time to stop an arrow smashing into his head. Another arrow thudded into his side but though it pierced his chainmail, the thick gambeson beneath stopped the iron bodkin piercing his flesh.

'It's a trap,' he roared, and as the arrows came thick and fast, the rest of his comrades reached for their own shields. Within seconds, Sir Robin took stock of the situation and realised there was no way they could ride up the steep bank to engage the hidden attackers. His men's armour along with their heavy shields meant they now had fairly good protection against the archers but he knew they couldn't just stay there and be picked off. If they were to protect Fitzgilbert, they had to act, and they had to act now.

'My lord,' he bellowed, 'take the first ten men and ride down the path as hard as you can. Stop for nobody and take shelter within the Abbey.'

'What about you?' shouted Fitzgilbert.

'The rest of us will teach these brigands a lesson,' shouted Sir Robin. 'Now get out of here, I'll bring you their heads before dusk.'

Without another word, Fitzgilbert kicked his horse into a gallop and headed down the path at full tilt, followed by ten of Sir Robin's best men.

'The rest of you, dismount,' roared the knight. 'Form a line on me.'

Within moments every heavily armed soldier lined up at the base of the bank, holding their shields up against the few remaining arrows still falling.

'On my command,' shouted Sir Robin, 'we are going to advance up this bank and show these cowards how real men fight. We take no prisoners. Make ready, *advaaance.'*

As the men started climbing the slope, crouching behind the safety of their shields, Tarw glanced across at the men either side of him. Every warrior stared back with baited breath, waiting for the signal.

Tarw stood up and looked down at the climbing enemy as the rest of the ambushers got to their feet.

'Here they come,' he shouted, 'we have the high ground so make it count. You know what to do. First line, advance.'

As one, the first rank of men stepped from the cover of the trees and wielding their knives only, ran to the edge of the bank. With battle cries roaring from each throat, they launched themselves from the slope and directly into the English line knocking the enemy backward down the hill. The ferocity of the attack took the English by surprise and Sir Robin himself received the full weight of a man into his head and chest, falling backward to land in the ditch at the bottom of the bank. Men of both sides fell together, and, in the confusion, it took several seconds for those not injured to come to their senses.

With both sides in such close proximity, swords were rendered useless and though the English were heavily armoured, the attackers were well prepared and aimed their knife thrusts at their enemy's throats and faces. Despite this, the English were experienced soldiers and over half of their number managed to crawl from the ditch uninjured, searching desperately for the swords dislodged in the assault. Up above, Tarw shouted to the rest of the men waiting on the top of the bank.

'Now is our chance,' he roared, *'follow me.'*

With his sword in his hand, he ran down the slope and led the rest of the ambushers into the fight. Though their numbers had been devastated, the English fought ferociously, knowing there would be no quarter. Their heavy chainmail protected them against the worst of the blows, but the attackers had prepared well and many wielded two-handed battle axes, using them to great effect as they smashed them into the English legs and dropping them like winter trees.

'Shield wall,' roared Sir Robin seeing the threat, but it was too late. The few men who were still uninjured were surrounded by the superior numbers of Welsh and within moments, all fell under the heavy assault to be finished off with axes or swords.

Sir Robin picked up his own sword and swung it up under the chin of the first man to reach him. Instantly he was spattered with his victim's blood as the arteries were severed, and the knight turned just in time to duck under the swing of a heavy battle axe. He dropped down and smashed his boot into the attacker's knee, sending him screaming to the floor before driving his sword into his chest. Desperately he looked around and was devastated to see most of his men dead or dying.

Instantly the blood rushed to his head. His rage knew no bounds and he fought like a wild man, his sword swinging as if it had a life of its own. Men fell all around but he knew it was only a matter of time before he was bettered.

Desperately he fought like a wild man and another Welsh warrior was all but beheaded by the force of his blade. A momentary lapse in the intensity of the fight gave him the opportunity he needed, and he turned to run toward the horses. Tarw anticipated the move and though he had been wounded in the fight himself, he ran across to head him off.

'Tarw,' roared Dog, turning to see the impending clash, 'leave him, he is too strong.'

Tarw ignored his comrade and carried on running, picking a spear up from a fallen man as he went.

Despite his head start, the weight of the knight's armour slowed him down and before he reached the horse, he found his way blocked by Tarw brandishing the spear. Both men panted heavily as they stared at each other in silence. Finally, Sir Robin spoke.

'Are you the leader of these men?' he asked.

'All you need to know, is I am the man whom is going to take your life,' answered Tarw coldly.

'Spoken from behind the safety of a spear like a true coward,' sneered the knight, 'yet I can see you are a man of breeding so why not settle this with honour. Fight me one on one and to the victor the spoils.'

'Honour? You don't know the meaning of the word,' said Tarw.

The rest of the Welsh ran over and gathered behind the Welsh prince.

'Just kill him,' said Dog, 'and be done with it.'

Sir Robin looked around the battlefield. All his men were dead, and he knew there was no way he could get away alive. He looked down at his sword and back up at Tarw before finally casting his weapon aside.

'I am now unarmed,' he said, 'and pose no threat. Ransom me back to Fitzgilbert and you will receive a fair price for my life.'

'That was a big mistake,' said Tarw and without warning stepped forward to thrust the spear as hard as he could into the knight's stomach.

The knight stared down at the shaft of the spear in shock before sinking slowly to his knees. His experience told him that the wound was fatal and there was no way he would survive, even if he had immediate help.

'You have killed me,' he gasped, his voice croaking with pain. 'I surrendered and was surely due mercy.'

'I have shown you the same mercy that was shown to my wife three months ago,' said Tarw and with another thrust, drove the spear harder to burst through the knight's back.

Sir Robin cried out in agony and fell to his side as blood bubbled from his throat. His eyes rolled into the back of his head and Tarw released the spear to watch coldly as his victim choked on his own blood.

'My lord,' said Dog behind him, 'come, we are not yet done.'

Tarw didn't answer and just stayed staring at the dead man. He felt no sense of euphoria over the killing and realised that even if he slew a hundred more men, the pain of Gwenllian's death would never be eased.

'Tarw,' said Dog again, 'we have to go. Fitzgilbert is still at large.'

'We will never catch him now,' said Tarw turning to his comrade.

'Perhaps not but Morgan was waiting for such a move and may need our help.'

Tarw nodded and after a last glance at the dead knight, followed Dog over to the enemy's horses.

'Everyone grab a mount,' he shouted as he ran, 'those without, return to our own horses and follow as quickly as you can.' He jumped up onto the dead knight's horse and followed by several of his men, galloped along the track toward Llanthony Abbey.

The path led over the brow of a slight hill but as they reached the top, Tarw reined in his horse. Before him, Morgan and his men stood on the track, each bloodied after a ferocious fight. The English who had fled with Fitzgilbert lay dead around them, but it was clear that they had given a good account of themselves before being overwhelmed.

'My lord,' said Dog, 'look.'

Tarw followed his gaze and saw a horse stuck in the soft mud out in the field on the far side of the track and its rider a few paces away, struggling to free himself from the bog.

'Tarw.' shouted Morgan as the prince rode up, 'you are just in time. Come and see a pathetic excuse of a man who ran rather than fight.'

'Who is it?' asked Tarw looking over at the mud-covered fugitive.

'None other than Fitzgilbert,' himself sneered Morgan, 'and though his men fought well, he thought he could escape with his life.'

'That's why you weren't worried about the open ground,' said Tarw, 'you knew it was a bog.'

'Indeed,' said Morgan, 'it's well known in these parts as impassable. All we need to do now is decide what to do with him.' He pointed at Fitzgilbert, now laying motionless in the mud.

'A few well place arrows perhaps?' said Tarw.

'No,' said Morgan, 'I want something more fitting.' He turned to one of the men. 'Get as close as you can and throw him a rope. Bring him to me.'

'Aye, my lord,' said the man.

'And save the horse,' added Morgan. 'It is a fine beast and will serve me well.'

Ten minutes later, Fitzgilbert knelt before Morgan with his hands tied behind his back. The stinking mud covered him from head to foot and he was exhausted.

'Well,' said Morgan quietly, 'here we are at last. I have waited a long time for this moment.'

'I don't even know who you are,' said Fitzgilbert, his eyes bright amongst the drying mud, 'but if you harm one hair on my head then the wrath of the English Crown will fall upon you like the worst storm you have ever seen.'

'My name is Morgan ap Owen,' came the reply, 'and I think you overestimate your importance. The king is more worried about Matilda than a self-obsessed, power hungry nobody from Ceredigion.'

'You are wrong,' said Fitzgilbert, 'and I warn you, release me or will face the consequences.'

'There is nothing you can threaten me with that I have not faced a hundred times or more,' said Morgan, 'and because of you and your ilk, these past few years have been a living hell. However, they were all worth it for these precious few seconds.' He nodded toward John Farmer who walked behind the kneeling prisoner and pulled back Fitzgilbert's head to expose his neck.

'I was going to do this myself,' said Morgan, 'but I now want to see your fear as you realise you are about to die.'

'No,' gasped Fitzgilbert, his eyes bulging, 'please, I beg you.'

'Do it,' said Morgan, without taking his eyes off his victim.

John Farmer drew his knife from his belt and dragged the blade slowly across Fitzgilbert's throat. The flesh opened wide and blood started to pour down his neck as the noble tried to beg for his life.

Morgan leaned forward staring deep into the dying man's eyes.

'I will see you in hell,' he said and as Fitzgilbert slipped into unconsciousness, the last thing he saw was the Welshman spitting in his face.

The following morning, Tarw and Dog sat outside a tent, ten leagues away from the site of the battle. Immediately after Fitzgilbert's death, they had ridden hard, knowing that as soon as word spread, every English castle in the area would be sending out patrols to find the attackers. Now they were well hidden deep within a Gwent forest along with Morgan and his men.

'Here,' said Dog, handing Tarw a pot from the fire.

'What is it?' asked Tarw, sniffing the steam from the hot water.

'Forest herbs,' said Dog, 'It will make you feel better.'

'Do I drink it or rub it on my wounds?' asked Tarw suspiciously.

'Drink it,' said Dog. 'It will warm your innards and give you a light head, but it is all good.'

'I have heard of such plants,' said Tarw, 'and I know men have gone mad from drinking such stuff.'

'No madder than we already are for being here,' said Dog. 'If you don't want it then try it on your wounds. Who knows, we may find another use for it.'

Tarw grimaced and sipped on the hot water, nodding in acknowledgement at the mild minty taste.

'Well it doesn't taste like you are trying to kill me,' he muttered.

'Tarw said a voice and both men turned to see Morgan walking over alongside another man.

'Morgan,' said Tarw. 'You are just in time to try Dog's potion, designed to kill or cure I believe.'

'Unless it contains ale or wine, I don't think I'll bother,' replied Morgan. He tilted his head to the man next to him. 'This is my brother Iorwerth. He arrived a few hours ago.'

'Iorwerth,' said Tarw standing up, 'I have heard a lot about you these past few days.'

'Whereas your story precedes you by months,' replied Iorwerth, 'and I am sorry to hear about your wife. It seems she was a good woman, true to her heritage. Something lacking in many these days.'

'You have heard of her death?'

'How can I not? It seems her name is being spoken in every village I pass through these days. There are even whispers of an uprising in her name.'

Tarw looked at Morgan who nodded silently in acknowledgement.

'Anyway,' said Iorwerth, 'there will be time enough to talk about tomorrows. I am here to talk about yesterday. It is said you acquitted yourself well.'

'We lost over a dozen men,' said Tarw, 'but yes, we achieved what we set out to do. Though I expect this will not be the last we hear of it for Fitzgilbert was a powerful man.'

'Let us worry about that,' said Iorwerth, 'I just came to pass on my gratitude. When my brother's messenger reached me, and I found out Fitzgilbert was vulnerable, we rode hard to get back in time but alas, missed the battle.'

'It is true your extra numbers would have made it easier,' said Tarw, 'but what is done is done.'

'Nevertheless, you have my gratitude, along with my brother's. Fitzgilbert caused our family a lot of trouble these past few years and his demise is a portent of greater things for our line.'

'I agree,' interjected Morgan, 'but first there is a debt to be paid.'

'A debt?' Asked Tarw.

'Aye, I promised you my support if Fitzgilbert was killed and you have kept your side of the bargain. I am a man of my word, Tarw, and pledge my men to your struggle. When you are ready, name the place and the time and I swear I will be there.'

'As will I,' said Iorwerth.

Tarw paused before walking over to grasp both men's wrists in turn.

'It is I who should be grateful,' he said, 'and I swear, that should this thing happen, and we are victorious, it will be the beginning of a great new alliance between Gwent and Deheubarth.'

'I look forward to that day,' said Morgan, 'but now we have to leave. Once you have finished being tended by your wet nurse there, I suggest you leave this place as soon as possible.

'The man exhibits humour of sorts,' mumbled Dog without turning his face away from the fire.

'This place will be crawling with English within hours,' said Iorwerth, 'so waste no time.'

'In that case, I will bid you fare well,' said Tarw, 'and with God's grace, I will see you alongside me again within the next few months.'

'Aye,' said Morgan and without another word both brothers turned to return to their camp.

'So,' said Dog as Tarw re-joined him at the fire, 'you have your army.'

'I have one army,' said Tarw, 'of five hundred men. I will need a lot more.'

'Then I suggest we finish here and saddle our horses,' said Dog. 'There is much to do.'

'Aye,' said Tarw, sipping the hot drink, 'there is.'

Chapter Twelve

Pembroke Castle

May AD 1136

Nesta stood at the window of her quarters, watching the sun come up over the town of Pembroke. Behind her, John of Salisbury snored quietly in her bed having spent the night with the woman he was due to marry in a few weeks. Recently he had become calmer toward Nesta but though it could never be said there was any sort of mutual affection, at least the violence had stopped. On top of that, Salisbury enjoyed using his privileged position to great advantage, especially when it came to bedding women and many of the castle wives found themselves the focus of his attention when their husbands were away, usually at Salisbury's command. Many of the men affected knew what was happening in their absence but with his powerful allies and network of spies and assassins, he had the power of life and death at his fingertips.

Despite her disgust with Salisbury's habits, Nesta soon grew to accept the situation and now welcomed the nights when he stayed away from her chamber, for though the beatings were fewer, his passionless, selfish attentions combined with his overpowering body smell caused her to lose all interest in what had once been a very important part of her life.

Down in the bailey, the castle was coming to life. The large gates were pushed open and the many servants who helped run the place filtered in, ready to join those who had already been working for hours.

Horses that had not been exercised for days, were led out by the grooms for a quick gallop around the fields at the rear of the castle and the sounds of the sergeants waking up their commands to start the day's duties echoed around the castle walls. The smell of freshly baked bread wafted up to the window and Nesta felt her mouth-watering, having not eaten anything since the previous morning.

'Why is the window open?' asked Salisbury from the bed and Nesta swallowed hard, her body tensing as she waited for the admonishment that would surely follow.

'My lord,' she said without turning, 'I thought you were fast asleep.'

'I was,' said Salisbury, 'until some fool opened the window and let in all that damned noise.'

'My apologies,' said Nesta and reached for the shutters.

'Leave it,' said Salisbury, swinging his legs over the side of the bed and standing up. 'The damage is already done and this room stinks. Fresh air will be a boon.' He walked over to the window and stared down into the bailey, his flabby body naked in the morning light. 'The bread smells good,' he said scratching under his arms, 'bring me some with eggs and a pitcher of watered wine.'

'I will send someone straight away,' said Nesta and walked quickly to the door to summon a servant.

'No, you go and get it,' said Salisbury, 'and make sure it is still hot by the time you return.'

'My lord,' said Nesta, 'is that not a role for a servant and not the lady of the castle?'

'It is a job for whoever I say it is for,' said Salisbury, 'and today I want you to bring me my fayre.'

Nesta bit her lip, knowing that to argue invited a beating.

'Of course,' she said, 'but can I at least get dressed first?'

'Why, you are wearing a night gown are you not?'

'Indeed,' said Nesta, thinking quickly, 'but as you can see it is sheer and would you want the servants, especially the men seeing the secrets of the woman you will soon be calling your wife?'

Salisbury thought for a moment before replying.

'Your point is well made,' he replied eventually, 'you may don your cloak.'

'My lord,' said Nesta, 'if you allow me just a few moments I can get dressed properly and brush my hair. Once done I can...'

'Shut your mouth,' roared Salisbury, causing Nesta to jump in fright. 'When will you learn that I am your lord and master and will not countenance your continued stubbornness? Now get out and bring me my food before I have you paraded naked around the whole town like a common whore.'

'Of course, my lord,' she said and after grabbing her cloak from a peg on the wall, left the room and ran down the stairs.

Outside in the bailey, several people looked up at the shouting from the window high in the keep walls.

'He's started on her early this morning,' said one of two women walking across to the well. 'I feel for the lady Nesta, I really do.'

'Hush your words,' hissed the second woman quietly, 'he has eyes and ears everywhere and if he thinks you have dared to criticise him, he'll have you thrown from the castle walls.'

'It is so wrong,' said the first woman again, 'though this time, her words no more than a whisper. 'When Master Gerald was alive, it was almost a pleasure to work here but these days not a day goes by that I don't fear a beating.'

'It puts food in our bellies,' said her friend, 'so I suggest you keep your counsel, lest your future could end up in the whorehouses of the docks.'

The two women continued to the well as Nesta appeared at the top of the motte, holding her cloak tightly around her. The morning breeze was fresh, and she made her way down the steps toward the kitchens built into one side of the castle walls. As she crossed the bailey, several people passed her, each tipping their head slightly in deference of her station though none stopped to offer any conversation. John of Salisbury was clearly visible in the window of the keep above and none wanted to draw attention to themselves.

Nesta reached the kitchens and walked inside. After the freshness of the morning air outside, the kitchen was oppressively hot and already the staff were bathed in sweat as they prepared the food for the garrison. The place was a hive of activity with two giant cauldrons of potage hanging from iron frames above the fires and a pile of freshly baked loaves stacked in an alcove to one side. At the far end of the kitchen, a man was butchering a pig carcass, ready to be cooked for Salisbury and his chosen favourites later that evening.

At first nobody saw Nesta enter and for a few moments she stood at the door, watching the intense activity unfold. It had been a long time since she used to come down and chat to the kitchen staff, and these days, any free time she had was always under the watchful eye of an accompanying guard.

One of the women looked over, her eye caught by the fur collared cloak around Nesta's shoulders. She nudged the woman at her side.

'Look,' she said, 'it's one of the officer's wives. I wonder what she wants?'

The second woman glanced up from cutting the parsnips in the bucket between her knees before taking a second look and dropping her knife in shock.

'By the grace of God,' she gasped, 'it is the lady Nesta herself.' She jumped to her feet and waddled across the stone slabs as fast as her squat body would allow.

'My lady,' she said, as she reached Nesta, 'I am so sorry. We weren't expecting you.'

'Hello, Clara,' said Nesta, 'there is no need for concern. I have just come down for some food, so the master can break his fast.'

'Oh heavens,' said the lady, 'you go back up before you catch a chill and I'll send something up immediately.'

'No, you don't understand,' said Nesta, 'he made it painfully clear it is I who must take him his fayre.'

'Oh,' said the woman as realisation dawned. 'I am sorry.'

'There is no need to hide your thoughts from me. Clara,' said Nesta, 'you have always been like a favoured aunt to me and I see you as a friend but we all know what he is like. If he doesn't get his way, people will suffer so if you don't mind, if you could just get me some bread, some boiled eggs and a pitcher of wine, I will be on my way. But ensure the food is as hot as it can be lest he decides to take out his frustration with his fists.'

'Of course, my lady' said the cook and as she scuttled away, Nesta took the opportunity to wander around the kitchen, remembering the times when such an activity brought her immense pleasure. Now, it was no more than a distraction from the hell she endured on a daily basis.

She walked through the cold stores, seeing the row upon row of pheasant and duck, hanging from racks on the wall and the carcasses of two whole cows hanging from hooks in the ceiling. Slatted shelves were filled with dried vegetables and beneath, were barrels of oats and ground flour. As cruel as he may be, one thing was certain, John of Salisbury liked to eat the best food that was available, and his staff always kept a well-stocked kitchen.

On the far side of the cold stores she heard the sound of laughter emanating from a small side room and she wandered in, interested to see who could possibly find time for mirth in such difficult times. As she entered, she saw four soldiers sitting around a box, each helping themselves from a pot of hot oats. They looked up and she recognised one of them as the sentry she had spoken to on the ramparts weeks earlier.

'My lady,' he said as the men all stood up.

'Good morning, Rowan,' she replied, 'it is good to see you again.'

'And you, my lady. Will you join us? It's just some honeyed oats, but they are hot and sweet.'

'Thank you but I have to be away. Please don't let me disturb your meal.'

'I have had my fill anyway,' said Rowan, 'and was off to my cot.'

'At dawn?'

'Aye. We have just finished the night duty and have the morning to catch up on some sleep. If I may, will you allow me to walk you back to the keep.'

'Alas I cannot but you can walk with me back through the kitchen if you like.'

'Then that is what I will do,' said Rowan and the two made their way back through the cold store as the rest of the men returned to their food. Once they were out of earshot, the soldier stopped and looked at Nesta.

'Dare I ask if you are well, my lady?' he asked quietly. 'The last time we spoke you bore the marks of a beating.'

'I am as well as can be expected in the circumstances,' said Nesta, 'thank you for your concern.'

'Your late husband was always good to me,' said Rowan, 'and if I could do anything to help your situation, you know I gladly would.'

'There is nothing you can do, Rowan. Worry not for me for my situation is better than many. As long as I jump to his every call then my life is just about bearable.'

'Why not leave, my lady?' said Rowan, looking over his shoulder. 'Just name the day and I can have a horse and provisions hidden in the town for your escape.'

'And where would I go?' asked Nesta. 'His spies are everywhere and besides, I cannot leave Maelgwyn.'

'Your nephew?'

'Yes, though I haven't seen him since he was taken prisoner. Salisbury tells me he has him in captivity, but I have no way of knowing if he tells the truth.'

'He does,' said Rowan, 'Maelgwyn is still alive, if life is what you call the miserable existence that he currently suffers.'

'You have seen him?' asked Nesta, shocked at the revelation.

'Aye. On occasion we are tasked to guard the prison tower and once I took the food down to the dungeons. I saw Maelgwyn in one of the cells and I have to say, my lady, he is a sorry sight.'

'What do you mean?'

'He has been beaten badly,' said Rowan looking around again, 'and his wounds have been left untreated. Despite that he maintains his defiance.'

'Oh, the poor child,' said Nesta. 'Is there anything we can do to ease his pain?'

'I can probably manage to swop a duty and get a message to him,' said Rowan, 'but more than that would be impossible. The tower is guarded by men loyal to Salisbury.'

'I understand,' said Nesta. 'I have to go but will give it some thought. I will get back to you but in the meantime, if you see him again, tell him not to give up hope. If I get a chance I will try to get him out, I swear.'

'I will, my lady,' said Rowan.

'Good, now I must return. Go back to your comrades and I will be in touch soon.' She turned away and walked to the main kitchen where the fat cook was busy putting a loaf into a hessian sack.

'My lady,' she said, 'we are almost ready. The bread is still hot from the oven and I have placed a hot stone in the bottom of the sack wrapped in linen to keep the food warm. There are also a dozen boiled eggs straight from the pan. I only hope the master burns his mouth on them.'

'Thank you, Clara,' said Nesta.

The cook handed her the sack along with another linen bag.

'That one has a pot of butter, some salt and a skin of best wine,' said the cook, 'along with an empty pitcher. Just pour the wine into the pitcher before you enter the bedroom.'

'Thank you,' Clara said Nesta again, 'you have thought of everything.'

'Everything except how to poison the bastard without getting caught,' mumbled the cook.'

'Our day will come, Clara,' said Nesta, 'but until then, just keep doing what it is you do so well.' She leaned down to kiss the cook on her cheek and turned to leave the kitchen.

'Thank you, my lady,' said the cook as Nesta left the kitchen, 'and be careful.'

'Always,' said Nesta over her shoulder and stepped out through the door.

Glancing upwards she saw the castellan still staring down into the bailey and she quickened her pace. The slightest of complaints could tip his mood from aggressive to violent and she couldn't face that today.

By the time she re-entered her quarters, Salisbury was already dressed and donning his cloak.

'Where are you going?' she asked.

'I have business to attend,' he said.

'But what about the...' She left the sentence unanswered, realising he was taking great pleasure in taunting her. 'Will you be returning?' she asked.

'I may, or I may not,' said Salisbury. 'Either way you are to stay in this room until I do. The lady Anwen will keep you company.'

Nesta sighed. The thought of being locked in the tower for yet another day was frustrating, but at least it meant she wouldn't have Salisbury for company.

The castellan left the room just as the Lady Anwen entered. She turned and locked the door with a key from a belt around her waist before walking over to sit on one of the hard chairs.

'Good morning, my lady,' she said as she sat, 'what would you like to do today?'

Nesta stared at the woman but said nothing. Murder was probably not the answer the woman wanted to hear.

Chapter Thirteen

Aberffraw

May AD 1136

Cynwrig sat at the side of the king's bed. Gruffydd had been ill for days and hardly recognised anyone who came in but despite this, the priest had visited him every day, taking the time to chat quietly as he recalled their exploits as younger men. On occasion, the king would smile, and his head would turn toward Cynwrig at a particular recollection but most of the time, he just dozed as his weak body tried its best to fight off the infection.

On the other side of the bed, Angharad dabbed a wet cloth on her husband's brow until finally, Gruffydd fell into an exhausted sleep.

'He seems to be getting worse,' said Cynwrig, staring at the sleeping king. 'I will pray that God gives him the strength he needs.'

'I have never seen him give up on a fight in all the years I have been with him,' said Angharad. 'Do not give up on him yet.'

'I would never do that,' said Cynwrig with a sigh. 'But he has always been like a great oak to me, steadfast even in the strongest storms.'

'Even oaks fall eventually,' said Angharad, 'but I think this one has a few more days in him yet.'

Behind them a knock came on the door and one of the servants entered.

'My lady,' she said, 'there is a messenger downstairs with urgent news. He begs audience.'

'Is Owain around?' asked the queen.

'No, my lady,' he is out on a hunt, 'as is my lord Cadwaladwr.'

'I will be down momentarily,' said Angharad with a sigh and turned to the priest. 'It seems my days at court are not yet over. Perhaps you care to join me?'

'Of course,' said Cynwrig. 'Let the king sleep and I will return to see if there is any improvement on the morrow.'

Angharad kissed her sleeping husband's head and turned to the physician sat at the table near the window.

'Let me know if there is any change,' she said.

'Of course, my lady,' said the physician and followed them over to quietly close the door behind them.

'So,' said Cynwrig as they walked down the tower steps, 'have you had a chance to consider my proposals?'

'I have,' said Angharad, 'and I am indeed in favour of action of some sort.'

'But?' said Cynwrig anticipating her next sentence.

'But as long as the king is alive it is he who must give agreement, not I nor his sons.'

'But surely if he is incapacitated, it falls upon his nominated heir to make decisions in his place?'

'If it was in matters of justice, or the day to day running of our estates then I would agree,' said Angharad, 'but we are talking about sending the entire kingdom into a war with the English, one that could escalate beyond all reason. Don't forget, he fought all his life to achieve what he has built here in Gwynedd, so it would be incomprehensible for his family to risk it all without his input. I'm sorry, Cynwrig but we must just be patient.'

'Of course,' replied the priest and followed her in to the lesser hall. At the far end, still dressed in his riding cloak was a messenger, talking to the steward.

'My lady,' said the steward as they approached, 'this man has ridden here from Powys with important dispatches. Alas he will give them to the king only.'

'Thank you, master steward,' said Angharad and turned to the messenger. 'Welcome to Aberffraw,' she said. 'Unfortunately, the king is abed with a severe ague, but I am his queen, and, in his absence, I rule Gwynedd. You can leave the dispatches with me.'

'Of course, my lady,' said the messenger with a slight bow of the head. He delved into his satchel and retrieved a rolled parchment sealed with the stamp of Powys.

'The message is from King Madoc ap Maredudd,' said the messenger, 'and he has requested sealed confirmation that it has been delivered.'

'And he shall have it,' said Angharad, turning to the steward. 'Please draft a reply of receipt and I will personally sign and seal it.'

'Of course, my lady,' said the steward and turned to the messenger.

'Come, I will see you are fed and rested. You can leave for Powys first thing in the morning.'

'Thank you,' said the messenger and followed the steward from the hall.

'Well,' said Angharad walking over to the fireplace, 'let's see what we have here, shall we?'

She took a proffered knife from Cynwrig and cut the seal before unfolding the parchment. Cynwrig waited patiently and saw the colour drain from her face.

'My lady,' he said eventually, 'you look shocked.'

'I am,' said Angharad looking up at the priest. 'Madog reports something of great importance that could have huge implications for Gwynedd.'

'Are you able to share the content?' asked Cynwrig.

'I will,' said the queen, 'but first I need to send for my sons. This changes everything.'

Night time had already fallen by the time Owain and Cadwaladwr returned and as they walked into the lesser hall, both men threw their heavy cloaks to a couple of waiting servants.

'Bring a flask of ale,' said Cadwaladwr, 'and tell the kitchens we are hungry. It has been a long ride.'

'I have already arranged food,' said Angharad from a table the far end of the room. 'It will be with us shortly. Please, join us.'

Both men looked up and was surprised to see their mother sat with the priest. An unfolded parchment lay on the table before them.

'I was told this was to be a family meeting,' said the younger brother, pulling out a stool at the table, 'what is he doing here?'

'This concerns us all,' said Angharad, 'especially Cynwrig. There is still wine in the pitcher so slake your thirst and forget whatever petty arguments that may still cloud your mind. What we are here to discuss needs your full attention.'

'Is father still not well enough to join us?' asked Owain.

'Unfortunately, no, but this will not wait for his recovery.'

'It had better be important,' said Cadwaladwr, 'I was closing in on a stag worthy of father himself.'

'Oh, it is,' said Cynwrig quietly, 'and don't worry about blooding your spears, for I believe there will be plenty of opportunity for that.'

'You talk in riddles,' said Owain and turned to his mother. 'Right, we are here as you requested, what is it that is so important?'

'Today,' said Angharad picking up the parchment, 'I received this document from the king of Gwent. In it he reports that Robert Fitzgilbert and over fourty of his men were killed near Abergavenny a few days ago.'

Both men stared in astonishment. Under the command of Fitzgilbert, Ceredigion had for years given them great cause for concern along their southern border. Often, they had spoken of attacking the kingdom but as Fitzgilbert enjoyed the favour of the English crown, their father had always stepped back from the brink.

'Who killed him?' asked Owain eventually.

'It would seem they were ambushed by Morgan ap Owain and none other than Gwenllian's husband, Gruffydd ap Rhys.'

'Tarw was involved?' gasped Cadwaladwr. 'Why in God's name would he be anywhere near the marches? He should be busy raising an army to avenge our sister's death.'

'And that is exactly what he was doing,' said Cynwrig, 'but as I explained to you a few days ago, if we are to be successful in any fight against the English, we will need many experienced soldiers. Tarw was recruiting men in the east and I can only assume he got caught up in something not of his making.'

'Did they survive the battle?' asked Owain, reaching over and picking up the parchment.

'They did,' replied Angharad, though not without casualties. Morgan ap Owain has retreated with his men to the forests of Gwent while Tarw, it seems has now turned up on the doorstep of Madoc in Powys.'

Cynwrig smiled to himself as Owain read the document silently to himself. It seemed Tarw was certainly treating his task with the seriousness it deserved.

'In essence, this dispatch actually tells us nothing of importance,' said Cadwaladwr. 'All it says is that an English nobleman has been killed. It says little about whether Tarw has had any success in raising an army so apart from the interest value, it is meaningless.'

'On the contrary,' said Owain quietly as he looked up from the parchment, 'it means everything.'

'In what way?' asked his brother.

'Think about it,' said Owain, 'for years we have had trouble with Ceredigion. They prey on our southern villages with impunity whilst their Lord enjoys the protection of the English crown. Well Robert Fitzgilbert is no more and with King Stephen's attention elsewhere, Ceredigion will be in a state of chaos.'

'Leaving them open to attack,' said Cadwaladwr as realisation dawned. 'We could take advantage of the situation and launch an attack before they have a chance to reorganise.'

'My thoughts exactly,' said Owain and turned to Angharad. 'Mother, is father aware of this?'

'No, he is still too ill to be weighed down with such information. But in his absence, I would venture he would be taking a similar stance if he were here.'

'So, are we at leave to pursue such an action?'

'Ceredigion is not an ally,' said Angharad, 'indeed it has been a constant threat to our borders. To pre-empt a war with the whole English nation is a decision for your father only, however, to take immediate action to secure our kingdom against an enemy threat falls to his sons. I see this situation as the latter and will leave the decision making to you.'

Owain looked at his brother.

'What do you think?'

'I need to consult with my advisors,' said Cadwaladwr standing up, 'but I think it is too good an opportunity to miss.'

'As do I,' said Owain and got up from his chair. 'I will return to my castle immediately and make the necessary preparations. Let us meet back here in two days to discuss our plans.'

'You are not staying to eat?' asked Angharad.

'I will eat on the hoof,' said Owain over his shoulder as he strode toward the door, 'there is much to do.'

The two brothers left the building and a momentary silence settled in the hall. Eventually Cynwrig sighed and picked up his goblet.

'Well, it took them long enough,' he said quietly, 'but they got there in the end.'

'They did,' said Angharad glancing at her co-conspirator, 'they are both good men, but their skills are more suited to the battlefield rather than the politics of court. Their father, on the other hand is a master at both.'

'He certainly is,' said Cynwrig, 'and I can only pray he will be well enough to join us soon.'

'Worry not about Gruffydd, Cynwrig,' said Angharad picking up her own goblet, 'for in his own words, there is still life in the old dog yet.'

'Tell me something,' said Cynwrig, 'I know Ceredigion has always been a thorn in the side of Gwynedd, and that Fitzgilbert was a loathsome man but does his death really warrant an invasion?'

'There is undoubtedly a chance to strengthen Gwynedd's interests with such an action,' said Angharad, 'and as we have a very large army impatient to put their skills to the test, this is an ideal opportunity in the kingdom's interests.'

'And that is the only reason?'

'Well, it doesn't hurt that the quickest path to Deheubarth lies directly through Ceredigion, but it would be wrong of me to even consider that fact. Wouldn't you agree?'

She raised her goblet in a silent toast as Cynwrig stared back at her in admiration, realising that soft and gentle woman he had known so many years ago had become a formidable and calculating queen.

Chapter Fourteen

Aberffraw

June AD 1136

Cynwrig stood on the walkway high on the palisade surrounding the palace of Aberffraw. Beside him stood Robert and Rascal, each staring out at the impressive sight on the grassy plains below them. Row upon row of fully armed men stood patiently waiting for their commanders to come out through the gates, thousands of foot soldiers, each fully trained in the ways of war and experts with their weapons. Their polished leather armour gleamed in the early morning sun and the morning light glistened off the tips of thousands of lethal spear heads.

Another two thousand men stood behind them, each holding the reins of a war horse and waiting for the command to mount up.

In the distance, the road to Ceredigion was already shrouded in dust, raised from the wheels of the hundreds of supply wagons that had started the journey south many hours earlier.

'It's impressive isn't it?' said Angharad walking along the ramparts toward Cynwrig.

'It is,' said the priest quietly, 'and I feel a pang of sympathy for the men of Ceredigion for they know not what is about to fall upon them. When did your army become so structured and well equipped?'

'When you have fought as long as we have,' said Angharad, 'you learn that peace is the best time to prepare for war. Too many times our men have been found wanting. That will never happen again.'

'I have never seen so many men,' said Rascal peering over the palisade. 'Every man in the kingdom must be out there.'

'It is a big army,' replied the queen, 'almost five thousand souls, but what you see before you are just the warriors under the command of my sons.'

Robert turned to stare at the queen.

'There are more?'

'At least twice as many, but they are deployed elsewhere across the kingdom undertaking other duties. What sort of queen would I be if we sent every available man in one direction leaving us with little protection on the opposite flanks?'

'You fear the English may come from the East?'

'We fear nobody,' said Angharad, 'but it goes against everything I learned from Gruffydd to leave ourselves exposed. Owain and Cadwaladwr's commands are more than enough for the task in hand.'

'Which is?' asked Cynwrig turning to face the queen.

'Did I not say?'

'I know your sons are riding to Ceredigion but as to the extent of the engagement, you have said nothing.'

'My apologies,' said the queen, 'but I'm sure you understand that during the planning phase, as few people as possible are told of the strategies. However, at the moment they are very simple. Our armies will ride into Ceredigion, laying waste to any village or fortified manor house still in the hands of the English. We will work our way southward, clearing a swathe right across the kingdom to provide a belt of military free land between us and the south. The engagement will last for a limited time only and my sons will return here before the autumn leaves fall.'

'How far do you intend to go?'

'That depends on the strength of the opposition,' said Angharad, 'but at the moment we see Aberystwyth Castle as the furthermost target.'

'You intend to take Aberystwyth Castle?' asked Robert in surprise.

'Again, we will evaluate as we go,' said Angharad, 'but at the very least we want the fortress to see our men on their horizon. It is important for those who would do us harm to also know the extent of our own reach.'

Before Cynwrig could answer, a voice echoed across the palace grounds behind them.

'Open the gates.'

Everyone turned to stare into the courtyard. A hundred fully armed men were already mounted on impatient horses and the steam rose into the early morning air. Those at the front wore full leather chest plates each emblazoned with the crest of Gwynedd and at their head, Cadwaladwr and Owain sat upon two magnificent steeds.

The gates creaked open and Owain looked up to the ramparts.

'The time has come, my queen,' he shouted. 'When father awakes, tell him we rode with his name on our lips.'

'Fare ye well, my sons,' replied Angharad, 'and return to me as the victors you were born to be.'

Owain turned in his saddle and faced the rest of the riders in the courtyard.

'In the name of the king,' he shouted, 'advance.'

The riders spurred their horses on to trot through the gates and as they wheeled left along the base of the palisade, the thousands of men in the waiting army roared their approval.

'Look,' said Angharad as the banner man split from the column to ride up onto a ridge so every man could ride past. 'It stirs the blood to see it carried by men with pride in their hearts again.'

'Aye, it does,' said Cynwrig, 'and for a moment I forgot I am a man of the church.'

'What do you mean?' asked Angharad.

'Don't forget,' said the priest, 'I fought under that banner many times and my heart races again at the memory.'

'Your days of fighting are over, Cynwrig,' said Angharad, 'it is time for the younger men to prove their mettle.'

'Aye, it is,' said the priest with a sigh, 'though my younger self eyes this day with a stirring of jealousy.'

'Come,' said Angharad, 'let us see if the king is awake and if he is feeling better, perhaps we can break our fast together while the two of you bore me senseless with tales of battles long thought forgotten.'

Cynwrig nodded and left the palisade to walk back across the courtyard. Behind them, Robert and Rascal watched in awe as hundreds upon hundreds of men filed by.

Many leagues to the east, Tarw and Dog sat upon their own horses high on a ridge overlooking a valley. Alongside them sat the King of Powys, Madoc ap Maredudd and two of his falconers.

'There,' said Tarw, pointing down to an open field.

'I see them,' said the king and nodded to one of the men at his side.

The falconer removed the hood from the bird on his wrist and within seconds, it had focused on the several rabbits eating at the edge of the field. He released the ties, and everyone watched as the magnificent predator swooped down into the valley before catching an updraft to gather some height.

'Do you fly birds in Deheubarth?' asked Madoc as he watched the hawk circling.

'It was something I loved dearly,' said Tarw, 'but it has been a long time since I enjoyed such sport.'

'There should always be time for falconry,' said the king. 'It combines the majestic with the brutal, yet the outcome is to the benefit of all, king, falconer and bird alike.'

'It's not to the benefit of the rabbit,' said Dog.

'The hunt mirrors life,' said Madoc, 'there will always be rabbits and there will always be falcons.' He turned to look at the dirty soldier. 'Which would you rather be?'

'I do not criticise your thinking, my lord,' said Dog, 'just pointing out the two sides of the argument.'

'My lord,' said the falconer suddenly, 'she swoops.'

Everyone turned to watch the bird plunge from the sky to thump into its unsuspecting prey.

'She makes it look too easy,' laughed the king. 'Let's collect her and take her sister to find some ducks. They will give more sport.'

'Of course, my lord,' said the falconer and led the hunting party down the slope.

'So,' said Madoc to Tarw as he rode, 'have you heard from your man in Gwynedd?'

'Not in the past few weeks,' replied Tarw. Though I suspect that he will be aware by now of what happened in Abergavenny.'

'Oh, he is certainly aware,' said Madoc, 'and since then there have been very interesting developments.'

'What's happened?' asked Tarw reining in his horse.

The king followed suit and turned to face Tarw.

'It seems that your exploits near Abergavenny have had far more consequences than either you or Morgan anticipated,' he said, 'and as a consequence, the kingdom of Gwynedd is marching upon Ceredigion.'

Tarw stared at Madoc in disbelief. After the ambush, he and Dog had headed north to speak to the king of Powys regarding his potential support for a campaign in Deheubarth, and though he had enjoyed the protection and hospitality of the king's household, this was the first he had heard of any offensive by Gwynedd against Ceredigion.

'Are you sure?' he asked eventually. 'To what end?'

'I am told that they see the death of Fitzgilbert as the perfect opportunity to right some wrongs,' said Madoc, 'and as we speak, Gruffydd's sons are leading an army down to Aberystwyth.'

'How long have you known?'

'A few days, no more. I would have told you sooner but had other business to attend to and besides, that sort of information needs to be kept between as few people as possible to maintain secrecy, don't you agree?'

Tarw allowed the veiled insult to pass without comment but his mind raced. If what Madoc was saying was true, then the feeling of resistance in the country would swell even more and needed to be harnessed.

'This is news indeed,' said Tarw, 'and could have bearing on my plans to fight back against the English.'

'In what way?' asked the king.

'Ceredigion provides the best route down to Deheubarth from Gwynedd. If Gruffydd is considering my request for aid, he could be using this opportunity to clear the path.'

'Perhaps he has just decided to strike Ceredigion while the iron is hot and take whatever spoils he can for himself.'

'That is a possibility,' said Tarw, 'but I can't see even Gruffydd's armies being strong enough to invade the whole western coast. He will need aid.'

'I agree,' said the king, and that is why I have been absent these past few days.'

'What do you mean?' asked Tarw.

'Fitzgilbert was no friend of mine,' said Madoc, 'and though we never met in conflict, the constant pressure from his allies in the Marches meant our borders were always under pressure. Now he has gone, his treasuries have become very tempting targets to prince and pauper alike and I see no reason to let Gruffydd hog all the spoils to himself.'

'What do you intend to do? Surely you are not going to engage Gwynedd in a quarrel over who is to benefit?'

'Not at all, for I suspect there is plenty to go around. Gruffydd appears to be on his death bed but from what I can ascertain from my communications with his son Owain, they only intend ranging as far south as Aberystwyth. That being the case, it leaves the English interests in the far south of Ceredigion as fair game.'

'You intend to march into Ceredigion?' asked Tarw in shock.

'Aye, and my men have already crossed the border under the command of my son.'

Tarw fell silent, stunned at the revelation.

'So, as we speak,' he said eventually, 'there are at least two armies descending on Ceredigion. Gwynedd's from the north and yours from the east.'

'There are, but don't build up your hopes, Tarw, these are invasions aimed at capital gain only, not of conquest.'

'It is irrelevant,' said Tarw. 'The fact that there is confidence growing across the kingdoms of Wales to even contemplate such a thing adds weight to our argument of a nationwide uprising. If these forays are successful, then there is no reason why the whole country cannot rise up in anger.'

'You get ahead of yourself,' said Madoc. 'Gold and silver is one thing, to ask a man to fight and die in the name of a woman who was not even a kinsman is a completely different matter altogether.'

'Her name may be the rallying call,' said Tarw, 'but it is freedom that is the ultimate goal.'

'Acknowledged, but you are preaching to the converted. The average man is more concerned about food for his children and feed for his horse and as long as he has access to both, then it is irrelevant to whom he pays his taxes.'

'I beg to differ,' said Tarw, 'but I have not come to argue.'

No, you have come for military support,' said Madoc, 'and at this moment in time, I am undecided whether your cause is justified. Come, we are here to hunt, not talk of politics. This conversation can be continued tonight over a pitcher of mead.' He kicked his horse to trot after his falconers further down the slope.

'What are you thinking?' asked Dog riding up beside Tarw.

'I am thinking,' replied Tarw as he looked at the back of the departing king, 'that perhaps we have the beginning of a snowball at the top of a winter hill and all we need now is someone to start it rolling.'

Chapter Fifteen

Aberystwyth

June AD 1136

Stephen Demareis walked briskly down the steps into the bailey of Aberystwyth Castle. Alongside him was the servant who had brought him news of a messenger with urgent information. Down below he could see the castle steward talking earnestly to the dust-covered man.

A horn sounded repeatedly from the gate tower above, recalling any of the garrison who may be on duty in the town below and men ran everywhere throughout the castle, berated by the sergeants as they raced to their stations.

'What is happening?' demanded Demareis as he fastened his sword belt, 'and who sounded the alarm?'

'I did, my lord,' said the guard commander next to the steward, 'this man has news that warranted alerting the garrison.'

'Well?' said Demareis turning to the messenger. 'Spit it out.'

'My lord,' said the man, 'I am a woodsman and I work in one of our masters' commotes to the north. Yesterday I was heading out for the day's work and I saw clouds of smoke coming from behind a hill. I went to check and found one of the manor houses had been burned to the ground. Men were laying dead everywhere and all the livestock had gone.'

'Do you know who were responsible?'

'At first I thought brigands,' said the woodsman, 'but the tracks in the mud were many so I followed the trail. By afternoon I could see them in the distance, but I had to fall back lest I was seen.'

'How many were there?'

'In the raiding party about fifty but that is not the problem, my lord. When I saw them, they were re-joining a much larger column that stretched as far as I could see.'

'What?' gasped Demareis. 'And where was this column?'

'On the coastal road,' said the man, 'and they ride under the banner of Gwynedd. They are coming this way, my lord, so I rode through the night to warn you.'

Demareis turned to the steward.

'Are we in receipt of any communications regarding a state of war between us and Gwynedd?'

'No, my lord, I am just as surprised as you.'

Demareis thought furiously. An army of men heading south could only mean one thing, they were taking advantage of the death of Fitzgilbert and intended to attack the town. He turned to the castle steward.

'Send a patrol out to see what we are up against. Tell our men to waste no time and report back here as soon as they can, stopping for neither food nor drink. Once you have done that, report back immediately with the state of our armouries. I need to know our strengths and whether we can defend this place or not.'

'Yes, my lord,' said the steward.

'You,' continued Demareis, turning to the garrison captain, 'get every man onto the palisades and ensure they are supplied with everything they need to repel an attack. In the meantime, I will send messengers south to Dinerth to seek reinforcements.'

'Yes, my lord,' said the soldier and spun away to his duties.

Demareis turned to the messenger.

'You stay at my side for now and try to recall all that you saw. I want to know every tiny detail, everything you remember. Do this, and when we are done you can be on your way with a purse of silver as a reward.'

'Thank you, my lord,' said the man as he followed the castellan across the bailey. He hoped fervently that he would not be kept long, for if there was an army on its way, Aberystwyth Castle was the last place he wanted to be.

By early evening, all the available men under the command of Demareis had returned to the castle but even then, they numbered only a hundred in total. The rest had been sent to Abergavenny to help with the search for Fitzgilbert's murderers and would be unlikely to return for many days.

Demareis called a briefing for his sergeants and the guard commander.

'So,' he said when the five men had gathered along with the castle steward. 'How do we stand?'

'My lord,' said the guard commander, 'the scouts have not yet returned but there are already people arriving from the north who have been forced from their farms. It seems that the column claims the coastal road and are sending patrols far and wide, driving many existing land holders from their homes and replacing them with allies.'

'So, they are throwing out anyone English born, no matter if they have a legal claim on the properties?'

'It seems so. English, Normans or Flemish, it matters not. They see them all as usurpers and claim they are repatriating Welsh land to Welsh people.'

'We will deal with that in the coming months,' said Demareis. 'In the meantime, what about their strengths?'

'Until our scouts return with the detail it is hard to say but from what I understand so far, they number in the thousands.'

Demareis swallowed hard and turned to the steward.

'Tell me about our stores?'

'Food and water is not a problem, my lord,' replied the steward, 'we could withstand a siege for a month or more.'

'And if they decide to attack?'

'We have ten barrels of arrows and about five hundred spears.'

Both the guard commander and Demareis stared at the steward in disbelief. For a castle as formidable as Aberystwyth, the numbers were pathetic.

'What do you mean ten barrels?' asked Demareis eventually, 'we should have ten times that number.'

'I know my lord,' said the steward nervously, 'but we were so pre-occupied ensuring the food stores were full the arrows were overlooked.'

'The state of the armouries is your responsibility, master steward. Why were they allowed to run so low?'

'My lord, I agree there should be more, but many have been used and damaged on the practise fields and the column you sent to Abergavenny took fifty barrels with them.'

'That does not excuse you from allowing the armoury to run low. You should have allowed for that.'

'I did my lord, and there are a hundred barrels on their way here, but the resupply is not due for another two weeks.'

'This is unbelievable,' said Demareis. 'We hold a castle in the middle of Welsh territory, about to face an army of overwhelming strength and it seems we are powerless to defend ourselves.'

'My lord,' said the captain of the guard. 'We are not powerless. The men are well trained, and our walls are formidable. There is plenty of food and water so if we are indeed attacked, perhaps we can hold them back until the reinforcements you sent for get here.'

'Against thousands of attackers?'

'They cannot all attack at once and our position is favourable. We will need to hold out for just a few days.'

'I hope you are right, captain,' said Demareis, 'for at this moment in time, that is the only hope we have.'

A few leagues away, Owain ap Gruffydd called a halt to his army's march on the coastal road.

'It's nearly dark,' he said, 'we will stop here. '

'How far is Aberystwyth?' asked his brother at his side.

'A few hours, no more. Tell our men to get hot food inside them but make sure there are sentries posted in all directions. I don't want to deal with any surprises before tomorrow morning.'

'Our scouts tell us the enemy number in the dozens only,' said Cadwaladwr, 'we are at no risk.'

'Perhaps so but let us not be foolish before the real fight has even begun.'

A few hours later, Cadwaladwr entered his brother's campaign tent and helped himself to a flask of ale from a trestle table.

'Are the men in good heart?' asked Owain turning to face him.

'As well as any man who is about to face a battle,' said Cadwaladwr, 'but they are well trained and will not flinch from their duty.'

'I have no doubts about their bravery,' said Owain, 'and anyway, if the castellan has any sense, he will surrender before an arrow is fired.'

'It would be a good outcome,' replied Cadwaladwr, 'but one I think is very unlikely.'

The following morning, the sun had still not risen above the forests when Demareis ran across the bailey to climb a ladder to the ramparts on the palisade.

'I had a message to come straight away,' he said as he climbed, 'what is it?'

'See for yourself.' said the captain of the guard as the castellan reached the top and turned to stare over the palisade walls.

Demareis joined him and as his eyes became accustomed to the early morning gloom, he gasped in astonishment.

'May the lord have mercy on our souls.'

As was normal with all such fortifications, Aberystwyth castle was built on a small hill with a clear view of all sides. The open ground below had long ago been stripped of vegetation to deny any enemy cover to approach the palisades and the nearest dwellings were at least five hundred paces away.

Three sides of the castle were protected by steep slopes and any enemy coming that way would be hugely disadvantaged by the climb, but the eastern approach was far more level and joined to the higher ground by a spur of ground. Knowing this route would always be the preferred option for attackers, the garrison had dug a deep trench across the whole width of the spur filling it with sharpened stakes and the carcasses of long dead animals. Every soldier worth their salt knew that any scratch infected with rotting flesh probably meant a long and painful death sentence.

The small wooden bridge that crossed the ditch could be easily withdrawn and taken back into the castle should they come under attack and despite Demareis' doubts, it would take a well-prepared army to better the defences. Unfortunately for the castellan, from what he could see high up on his vantage point, that was exactly what the enemy had.

Down in the valley, row after row of fully armed men marched onto the plain between the town and the hill. To either flank, hundreds of horsemen gathered in their own massed ranks, the steam from their horses rising into the morning air. The breeze brought the sound of the horns and the bellowing sergeants arranging the army, and in the distance, Demareis could see a column of carts and wagons forming a defensive position.

'My lord,' said the captain, pointing to one side, 'look.'

The castellan turned to see several mounted men atop a small rise on the far side of the valley floor and above them flew the banner of Gwynedd, confirming his worst fears.

'Have they sent word of their intentions?' asked Demareis.

'Not as far as I am aware, but judging by the strength of that army, whatever it is, they are not going to take no for an answer.'

'We will send a messenger,' said Demareis. 'However this plays out, we need to know what we are dealing with.' He stared at the manoeuvers for a few more moments before turning away and descending the ladder. 'Keep me informed,' he said as he descended, 'and ensure the garrison stays alert. I suspect they will not attack yet but we should take nothing for granted.'

'Aye, my lord,' said the captain and returned his gaze to the thousands of men below.

'Why are we deploying our forces down here?' asked Cadwaladwr, watching the impressive display of might on the plain to his front. 'The slopes would result in us losing far too many men.'

'This is for their benefit only,' said Owain, nodding up toward the castle. 'They need to see what they are up against.'

'Shouldn't we be cutting off their escape routes to the east?'

'Let them go, should they so wish,' said Owain, 'a few dozen men worry me not.'

'So, when are we going to attack?'

'Possibly tomorrow,' said Owain, 'but first there are some things I need to know.'

Chapter Sixteen

Aberffraw

June AD 1136

'Cynwrig,' said Angharad turning to face the door in the king's chambers. 'Please, come in.'

'Thank you,' said the priest and walked over to the side of the bed as a servant closed the door behind him. Gruffydd was sat up against a pile of feather pillows and the queen was spoon feeding him a weak chicken broth.

'Cynwrig, my friend,' said the king pushing his wife's hand gently away, 'is it really you?'

'Aye, my lord,' said the priest, 'though to be truthful I was going to leave such was my impatience for your recovery.'

'Nonsense,' replied Gruffydd, 'I was well days ago, I just wanted to keep you waiting.' He turned to his wife and spoke quietly. 'Tell me,' he said, 'is he just as ugly or even more ugly than I recall?'

'Oh, he is not ugly at all,' said Angharad smiling up at Cynwrig, 'the years have been kind.'

'But not as handsome as me, right?'

'No man walking this country is as handsome as you, my king,' said Angharad, 'except of course that new groom we appointed a few weeks ago. I would leave you for him at the wink of an eye.'

'Cynwrig,' said the king sharply, 'have that man executed immediately.'

Cynwrig smiled broadly and went across to sit in a chair at the king's side. To see him getting better was wonderful and to hear him engage in the banter that they all used to share so frequently brought joy to his heart. However, there was no hiding the fact that Gruffydd was fading away and in all probability, the bed upon which he lay would become his death bed within months.

'You are looking well, my king,' he said kissing the Gruffydd's hand, 'and I thank the Lord himself that he has seen fit to lead my path here after all these years.'

'And I am glad you came,' said the king. 'It has been a long time.'

'It has.'

'So, my wife tells me you are here to raise an army?'

The bluntness caught Cynwrig out momentarily but then he remembered it had always been a trait of Gruffydd to skip niceties when it came to matters of court.

'Well, today I am here to see my old friend,' said Cynwrig, 'and to reminisce about the times when I was better than him in most things. Talk of other matters can wait until you are on your feet.'

'Nonsense,' replied the king, 'my body may be weak, and my eyes are useless, but my mind is as sharp as an executioner's blade. Besides, even blind I am a better shot than you ever were with a hunting bow. Now tell me, what is it that you want of the house of Aberffraw?'

Cynwrig looked up at Angharad, receiving a shrug of the shoulders in return.

'Well I'm not sure how much you already know,' said Cynwrig, 'but in essence, I believe a desire for rebellion sweeps the country like never before. People talk of it in the streets from here to Gower, but we need your help to make it happen.'

'Talkative people do not win wars, Cynwrig, warriors do.'

'Aye and that is why I am here, to beg resources in support of our quest. We need cavalry and foot soldiers, as many as possible with all the support they may need to execute a prolonged campaign. We also need money to convince potential allies that this is a quest worth joining.'

'Who are these allies you speak of?'

'I cannot name them at the moment, my lord but Tarw is negotiating with them as we speak.'

'Tarw?'

'Aye. He rides the eastern borders seeking the support of the Welsh kingdoms bordering the marches. We feel that there lies the highest probability of enlisting suitable men at arms. Especially in Powys and Gwent.'

'There is no love lost between the eastern kings and the Marcher lords admittedly,' said Gruffydd, 'but to commit to conflict when they share a border with the English could be a folly that comes back to haunt them.'

'Usually I would agree,' said Cynwrig, 'and it shames me to be promoting war but this country, and all the individual kingdoms within it cannot continue as we are. Gwynedd is the only one within Wales that prospers. Surely it would be a good thing for the others to enjoy a similar state of affairs?'

'Indeed,' said the king, 'but why should I put the prosperity of this kingdom at risk to help those who may one day ride against my sons?'

'I know that is always a risk,' said Cynwrig, 'and ordinarily I would not ask such a thing but this time it is different. Your daughter's name is on the lips of every welsh born person, man or woman and it could be the unifying factor we need. History would judge us ill if we failed to grasp this chance with both hands.'

Gruffydd took a deep breath and thought for a few moments before replying.

'Tell me,' he said, 'how strong are the English forces?'

'I can't be sure,' said Cynwrig, 'but we estimate that combined they could number up to ten thousand or more.'

'Ten thousand,' said Gruffydd slowly. 'You expect us to stand against an army of that size?'

'Not alone,' said Cynwrig, 'and that is why Tarw is garnering support in the east. If the kings and princes of the kingdoms of Wales can manage to just put aside their arguments for a few weeks, we can more than match the enemy's numbers.'

'Even if we did,' said Gruffydd, 'and even if we could then better them on the field which is not guaranteed, then all they need do is retreat behind their castle walls and wait for reinforcements.'

'I know,' said Cynwrig, 'but if we have the support of the people then they will be hard pushed to withstand the pressure. A whole country in uprising cannot be ignored.'

Gruffydd turned to face his wife.

'What do you think?'

'I think you should eat some more soup,' said Angharad, 'and let this matter be for today.'

Gruffydd nodded and turned back to face the priest.

'I hear you have my daughter's blade,'he said, 'and you wish to use it as a banner with which to rally the country?'

'That is my intention,' said Cynwrig, 'but I wanted to ask your permission first.' He looked at Angharad. 'Yours and the queen's. '

'Do you have it here?'

'It is in my quarters,' said Cynwrig. 'If you wish, I will bring it forthwith.'

'No,' said Gruffydd after a few moments. 'Let me gather my strength and we will discuss this matter again. For now, just accept my gratitude that you are here.' He leaned back against his pillows and closed his eyes as the tiredness came flooding back.

'Perhaps we can continue this another day?' said Angharad looking earnestly at the priest.

'Of course,' said Cynwrig standing up. 'Let me know when I may visit again.

'We will,' said Angharad, 'now the king must rest.'

'I understand,' said the priest and with a bow of the head, left the room.

Angharad turned back to the king to see a single tear running down his cheek.

'Gruffydd,' she said quietly, 'are you in pain?'

'I am,' he replied with a sigh, 'but only in my soul.'

'Have his words opened old wounds?'

'Not his words, but the fact that he bears her sword cuts deeper than any knife.'

'Why? He means well.'

'I know, but that blade was probably the last thing she ever touched and that truly breaks my heart.'

At the other end of the country, Nesta strolled along the inside of the palisades at Pembroke castle for her evening walk. Alongside her was the lady Anwen and though the air was pleasantly warm, she still wore a cloak.

'In a few months,' said Anwen, 'this place will ring with the sound of laughter and merrymaking.'

'If you are referring to my forthcoming marriage,' said Nesta, 'then I can only imagine who you are referring to for there will be little celebration from me.'

'Oh come,' said Anwen, 'you exaggerate the situation. I know that Master Salisbury can be a little short tempered, but he is a very powerful man and rumour has it that even King Stephen watches his success with interest. I would wager you could be walking the walls of Windsor within a few years.'

'I have lived in London,' said Nesta, 'and did not care for it. It is a dirty place and cannot hold a torch to the clean air of Deheubarth. No, if I am to be his wife, then it will be here in the land of my birth.'

'I would suggest, my lady, that your place will be wherever the Lord Salisbury dictates it will be.'

Nesta held her counsel and looked around the bailey. The evening was getting darker and she knew they would soon have to go and join Salisbury for their evening meal.

'Let's go this way,' said Nesta, turning away from their normal route.

'Past the stables?' asked Anwen, 'but the ground is muddy that way. Surely you don't want to get any on your dress.'

'Oh, come on,' said Nesta, 'I saw a new foal outside earlier and I would love to see it close up.'

Before Anwen could answer, Nesta walked across the bailey.

'My lady, it is getting dark,' sighed Anwen but when Nesta continued walking, she hoisted her skirts and followed her through the mud.

Moments later they reached the stables and Nesta stopped, her face a picture of disappointment as she looked into the small paddock.

'Oh, it's gone,' she said.

'It's probably just put away for the night,' said Anwen.

Nesta looked over to the double door on the far end of the stable block.

'You have a look in there,' she said, 'I'll check the side paddock.'

'My lady, we really have to go,' said Anwen.

'Another few moments won't hurt,' said Angharad, 'just see if it's there and we'll come back tomorrow.'

'If you insist,' sighed Anwen and turned away as Nesta stepped around the side of the building.

'I thought she would never leave,' said a voice and a man stepped out of the shadows causing Nesta to jump.

'Rowan,' she said, 'you are here. I didn't know if you would come. '

'The cook passed on your message,' said the soldier, looking around furtively. 'What is it I can do for you?'

'A simple task,' said Nesta. 'I want you to get a message to Maelgwyn and tell him to take heart and stay strong for there are things afoot.'

'What things?'

'I cannot say just yet,' said Nesta, 'and it is best Maelgwyn doesn't know in case he is forced to talk but Clara has shared some gossip that the people are saying in the town.'

'Gossip means nothing, my lady,' said Rowan, 'be careful who you heed.'

'I know but it is all I have at the moment. Do you think you can get the message to him?'

'Probably but not for few days or it will arouse suspicion. '

'I understand,' said Nesta,' but give him this also.' She pressed some dried beef into Rowan's hand. 'Clara will give you more when she can. It's not much but it may keep him alive.'

'It is a dangerous game you play, my lady,' said the soldier, pocketing the meat, 'and I will hang if caught.'

'I know,' said Nesta, 'and if you refuse, I will understand.'

Rowan paused for a moment before nodding.

'I will do it, but we can't meet again like this. If you have a message, just pass it through Clara. It seems she is a trustworthy ally.'

'She is,' said Nesta. 'Thank you, Rowan, I will see you are rewarded should I ever get the chance.'

'Your favour is enough,' said the soldier.

'I should go,' said Nesta, 'before Anwen returns.'

'Be careful, my lady.'

Nesta tip toed up to kiss the soldier on the cheek before turning away and walking briskly along the front of the stables just as Anwen was returning.

'There you are,' said the woman.

'Did you find the foal?' asked Nesta, leading Anwen away from the paddock.

'No, it seems it was a fool's errand for it was taken to be sold earlier today. Now we must make haste. The last thing you want is to be late for Master Salisbury.'

'You are right,' said Nesta as they walked quickly across the bailey, 'that would not be good at all.'

Chapter Seventeen

Aberystwyth Castle

June AD 1136

It had been three days since Owain's army had first paraded in front of the castle. Three days since the plain had rung out with the sounds of drums, horns and the unmistakable clamour of a vast army manoeuvering for position. Clouds of dust had hung in the air and the sound of cart masters berating their animals to go in directions they didn't want to go had echoed across the open ground below the castle.

Today was different for apart from the sounds of the odd horse snorting its impatience, the air was still. Surprisingly so, for there were over four thousand fully armed warriors lined up ready to commit to the assault and up above, the silence sent shivers down the spine of those watching from the castle walls.

'What are they doing?' asked Demareis.

'Preparing to attack,' said the captain.

'Are we ready?'

'As ready as we can be. I suspect they will come from the east. The ditch will be easier to cross than attacking up this slope.'

Demareis fell quiet and watched as a lone rider trotted along the front of the massed infantry. Obviously, he was addressing his troops, but his words did not carry up to the battlements.

'Ready the men,' he said eventually,' and pray that God is with us.'

Down below, Owain reined his horse to a halt in front of the massed ranks. For a moment he looked slowly along the front lines of men. Every set of eyes was upon him and he knew he had good warriors, but it took more than good men to take a castle, it took strength, bravery, sacrifice and not a little bit of luck.

'Men of Gwynedd,' he announced loudly. 'We have waited long for this day. For many years we have been untroubled by the English, for they knew they would lose as many as us in any war. However, to our south there has always been a wolf disguised as a sheep. Ceredigion under the lordship of Robert Fitzgilbert has been a constant drain on our resources, testing our borders and raiding our villages with impunity. For years we have ignored his indiscretions in the name of peace, but those days have come to an end.'

He paused as a mumble of anger swept through the ranks.

'Today,' he continued, his voice getting louder, 'we send a message across Ceredigion that no longer will we allow her armies to ravage our lands.'

Again, there was a reaction.

'The days of Ceredigion men raping Gwynedd women then racing back across the border to hide behind palisades are no more,' he shouted, 'for today we fight back.'

This time there was a roar of agreement from the soldiers and Owain allowed it to continue unabated for several moments before continuing.

'Once that pathetic pig pen they deem to call a castle has fallen,' he shouted, pointing up at the fortress, 'everyone will know that Gwynedd's soil will never again be trodden without invitation. Take this castle and I swear that every man here will share the spoils of anything we take in bounty and your names will still be on the lips of your grandsons' grandsons long after we have rotted in our graves. Are you ready for this day?'

'Aye,' roared the army in response and every man waved their weapons in the air or banged them against their shields as the battle lust rose.

Owain turned to the many sergeants at arms and cavalry officers at the front of each unit.

'You know your tasks,' he shouted, 'and the time for waiting is done. Upon the signal,' he paused and looked up at the castle walls, 'we burn that place to the ground.'

To the sound of cheering men, he spurred his horse to gallop along the front of the army and took his place beneath the banner of Gwynedd atop a small rise. He turned and looked back at the massed ranks of his army.

'Are we ready,' asked Cadwaladwr.

'Aye,' said Owain. 'We are. Give the signal.'

A man at his side lifted a horn to his mouth and a long haunting tone resonated across the plain. Immediately the sound of battle drums reverberated through the air and in response to the sergeants' commands, the first ranks of soldiers advanced toward the hill.

'Here they come,' shouted a sentry up in the castle, 'stand to the palisades.'

'Surely, they are not going to come up the hill,' said Demareis as the defenders rushed across the level ground toward the slope, 'they will be cut down by stone and arrow in equal number.'

'Perhaps they see it as an acceptable sacrifice,' said the captain. 'They have more men than we have arrows.'

'No son of Gruffydd will sacrifice men so easily,' said Demareis, 'this is surely a ruse.'

'Ruse or not,' said the captain watching as the nearest men laboured up the slope, 'we cannot ignore them.' He turned to shout across the castle. 'Archers to the west wall, every third man stay at your posts.'

The sound of men running across the timber platform caused the ramparts to shudder and within a minute the western palisade was full of archers.

'Select your targets carefully,' shouted the captain, 'and make every arrow count.'

'Aye, my lord,' came a united response and every archer loaded their bows as the remaining men collected boulders from the many piles stacked along the ramparts.

'Rocks first,' shouted the captain as the first of the attackers neared the top of the slope, ready...*now!*

The defenders pushed the boulders from the palisade to fall straight down to the ground below. Earthen banks ramped at an angle at the bottom of the wall caused each rock to bounce forward and roll over the lip of the hill and within seconds, the ranks of attacking Welshmen were torn apart under the onslaught.

'Again,' shouted the captain and more rocks followed the first.

Man after man was knocked down with broken limbs and several heads were smashed in by the crude but effective missiles but still the attackers came.

'Archers,' shouted the captain, 'get ready, release!'

A volley of arrows sped through the air and slammed into the nearest rank of attackers Most found their target and the cries of the wounded echoed above the beating drums down on the valley floor.

'Again,' roared the captain, *'cut them down.'*

Volley after volley flew at the climbing men and within moments, the well-drilled enemy ranks broke apart and started to retreat down the slope beyond the reach of the English bowmen.

Up above, the defenders broke out into a bout of cheering and hurled insults at the waiting army below.

'First blood to us,' shouted Demareis, 'looking at the bodies on the slope. I see over thirty men dead or wounded whilst we have received not a single injury.'

'My lord,' said a lone voice from along the palisade, 'I am injured. I tore a finger nail whilst carrying a boulder.'

Every man on the western palisade burst into laughter at the jest and even Demareis smiled. The captain, however, did not. He knew that the attack had been nought but an opening gambit and the worst was yet to come.

An hour later, Owain stood in his campaign tent with his officers. On the table was a charcoaled line diagram of the castle drawn on a large piece of linen. Along the western wall, crosses indicated the positions of every man identified as an archer during the attack and circles for any others who had been hurling the rocks.

On the far side of the table, one of Owain's trusted commanders held a slate covered with markings.

'Paulus,' said Owain, 'we have recorded the positions on the west wall, what can you add?'

The man leaned over and picked up a piece of charcoal.

'As you know, my lords,' he said, 'I was positioned on the higher ground above the eastern ramparts during the attack.' He put a mark on the opposite side of the castle. 'At first the palisade was well defended but when our men committed against the western wall, it was reinforced with archers from the rest of the castle. During the assault I counted no more than ten men left here.' He put several crosses indicating the positions on the drawings.

'Anything else?'

'Aye, there is a deep ditch on the approach to the castle gate up on the flat ground. The bridge has been destroyed and they have filled the trench full of spikes.'

'Can they be removed under cover of darkness?'

'Perhaps but I suspect they are well dug in and poisoned with filth. We would need time and will take a toll on our men.

Even then, any assault would be held up by the steep sides of the ditch and our men would be sitting ducks for the enemy archers.'

'Can it be bested by our cavalry?'

'No, my lord, the leap is too far for any horse and anyway, if we are to breach the walls, we will need our foot soldiers and their ladders. Cavalry will be of no use.'

Owain looked at the plan and counted the marks.

'So, we estimate no more than fifty archers in total and the same amount of men at arms. Not a small force but one we should easily dispatch given our numbers.'

'If we can breach the walls,' said Paulus.

'Agreed,' interjected Cadwaladwr, 'but unless we can get a ram across that ditch we will be limited to ladders only.'

'And that is not an option,' said Owain looking up at the gathered officers. 'There is a wealth of experience within this tent so set your minds to it and we will gather again in the morning to discuss what tactics are available to us.' He turned to his brother. 'Cadwaladwr, can you ensure there is a secure cordon around the castle overnight. I want nothing getting out or getting in.'

'Of course,' said Cadwaladwr and left the tent.

'Paulus,' said Owain, 'see to it that those who fought today have extra rations of ale and pay each of them a penny. Two for those with wounds.'

'What about the dead?' my lord.

'Have the priest bury them near the village. Record their names and put aside a silver penny for each of their families.'

'And the ones still on the hill?'

'Send out men under the cover of darkness to recover their bodies but take no risks. They are going nowhere.'

'Aye, my lord,' said the officer.

'Good,' said Owain, 'everyone, be back here at dawn and I want to see answers to the questions raised today. Those men died so we could garner useful information. We owe it to them to use it well.'

The men voiced their agreement and left the tent, leaving Owain to stare at the plans alone. The castle was undoubtedly in a formidable position and it seemed impossible to actually reach the walls without incurring heavy casualties, but he had known from the start it would not be easy and if he was going to earn the respect of his men as his father's heir, then he needed to succeed.

He picked up a tankard of ale and took a draft as he stared at the drawing. It was going to be a long night.

The following morning, Owain's commanders met again and several options discussed. Owain listened to everyone intently before dismissing them to give himself time to think. As his head cleared, he finally settled on a plan he thought would work and summoned his brother.

'Cadwaladwr,' he said, 'there is a way to do this, but we will only have one chance to get it right.'

'What do you mean?' asked his brother.

'The plan is audacious and will involve a heavy attack but if we are unsuccessful, those in the castle will not fall for it twice. Fail and we will either have to withdraw or settle down for a long siege.'

'We agreed we would not do that,' said Cadwaladwr, 'for it would only be a matter of time before the castle is reinforced from the south.'

'I agree, so we need to be successful and we need to do it quickly.'

'So, what is this plan, brother?' said Cadwaladwr. 'Speak it and I will let you know if you are heading along a foolish path.'

'It is not a foolish path I lay before you, Cadwaladwr,' replied Owain, 'but it could be a very bloody one.'

In the north, Gruffydd had recovered enough to leave his bed and sit in the chair alongside the fire in his quarters. A servant added another log to the flames before turning and bowing to the king and leaving the room.

'Do you want another blanket for your knees?' asked Angharad walking over from the table where she had been reading a letter.

'This one will suffice,' said Gruffydd, 'and the fire will soon warm my bones. Without your assurance otherwise, I would swear we were still mid-winter.'

'A mixture of old age and illness thins your blood,' said his wife, 'and besides, these mornings are surprisingly chilly. I've asked the kitchens to send up some hot oats.'

'Oats,' mumbled Gruffydd, 'can you not see I am a king and as such demand the finest venison?'

Angharad smiled and touched her husband's hand. Even though he was ill, and had been for a long time, he always engaged in humour whenever the situation allowed, and she loved him for it.

'So,' he continued, tilting his head toward her, 'did you read the letter?'

'I did. Owain says they arrived at Aberystwyth in good time and have already amassed a goodly amount of wealth for our treasuries from the manors they seized in your name as they travelled. Apparently, there is a column of well-guarded wagons on their way back here as we speak.'

'Manors are one thing,' said the king, 'castles are a different matter altogether. If I had been well, I would have counselled a more cautious approach before committing our men.'

'Owain knows what he is doing, Gruffydd,' said Angharad, 'and if he is going wear the crown of Gwynedd one day then he needs to be flexing his sword arm to garner allegiances. What better opportunity than the death of Fitzgilbert to do so?'

'I understand,' said the king, 'but there is a chain of castles all along the western coast from Aberystwyth right down to Gower. He needs be careful they do not react quicker than he anticipates. What is the date on the letter?'

Angharad looked at the parchment and then back at her blind husband.

'It is dated three days ago.'

'Then it is pointless worrying about what may happen.'

'Why?'

'Because, if those boys have any sense, the battle will already be over.'

Angharad was about to continue the conversation when a servant knocked and entered the king's chambers.

'My lord,' she said with a bow, 'my lady, Master Cynwrig begs audience.'

'Let him come,' said the king before his wife could answer, 'there are manly things to discuss.'

'As you wish, my lord,' said the servant and left the room.

A few moments later, Cynwrig entered and placed a package on the table before walking over to kiss the king's hand.

'My lord,' he said, 'you look like a different man. Shall I tell the grave digger his services will not be required this day?'

'I will outlive you yet, priest,' grumbled the king, 'and I will have no talk of graves. I want a mausoleum as big as a mountain. Sit and tell me what happens out in the world of men.'

'Please,' said the queen standing up, 'take my seat, Cynwrig, I have matters to attend to.'

'Thank you, my lady,' said the priest and waited until Angharad had left before sinking into the chair.

'Do you have any mead about you?' asked the king when she had gone, 'the wench refuses me anything stronger than watered wine.'

Alas no, but next time I come I will bring something that just might kill you off.'

'And a good way to go it would be,' said the king. 'So, have you robbed me of all my jewels yet?'

'Your wife is the only jewel I covet, my king,' said Cynwrig, 'but alas she has been tricked by an old devil into everlasting love.'

'Yes, she is far too good for me,' said Gruffydd with a smile. 'Anyway, what brings you here?'

'I came to see if you are well,' said Cynwrig, 'and to press you for a decision on that which brought me here in the first place.'

'Military support?'

'That and the weight of your treasuries,' said Cynwrig.

'I will say this to you, Cynwrig,' said Gruffydd, 'you are an outspoken man and you do not honey your words.'

'We have known each other too long, my lord,' said Cynwrig, 'and it would demean both of us if I was less than honest.'

'And for that you have my gratitude,' said the king. 'What is it exactly that you need, Cynwrig, for up until now there has been talk aplenty but little in the way of detail.'

'An army first and foremost,' said Cynwrig, 'the biggest you can raise, fully equipped and furnished with enough supplies to sustain a three-month campaign. On top of that, access to your treasuries to provide payment to others that may make up the shortfall.'

'Mercenaries?'

'Possibly, but hopefully fellow Welshmen who see the benefit of rallying to our call.'

'It is a huge ask,' said Gruffydd, 'and one that could bankrupt this kingdom.'

'There is that risk,' said Cynwrig, 'but there is also the possibility the cost could be repaid a hundred times over.'

'How?'

'The English treasuries are known to be healthy right across Wales. They take the taxes from our countrymen as regularly as the cock crows and then allow any monetary gain to gather dust in their castles. If we are able to better them on the field of battle, then those treasuries become the spoils of war.'

'Yet if we fail and our army is defeated, Gwynedd is left open to any man with half a mind to ride in and take what I have fought all my life to regain.'

'Then we must not fail,' said Cynwrig simply.

'And will God be on our side?' asked the king.

Cynwrig paused and stared at his friend. The king was a pious man and if he was told it was God's wish, then he would probably commit there and then.

'My lord,' he said eventually. 'I cannot claim God as a guiding light in this matter, but I do know this. Your daughter fought all her adult life for the betterment of her people. She died trying to free the impoverished from a reign of brutality and it is her death that rallies the kingdoms to unite under a common banner. If we are successful, then it will be in her name and if God doesn't shine his blessing on such a cause, then he is not the God I thought he was.'

'Is that not heresy?' asked the king.

'Call it what you will, my lord. All I know is that I have an ache in my heart like the heaviest rock and if I go to my grave without avenging one of the most beautiful souls who ever walked this land then my life will surely have been lived in vain.'

The two men fell silent and Cynwrig stared into the fire, surprised at the strength of his emotion.

'Do you have it with you?' asked the king quietly.

'My lord?'

'Her sword, have you brought it with you?'

'I have.'

'Bring it to me.'

Cynwrig walked over to the table and carefully unwrapped the package before carrying the sword over to the king and placing it on his lap.

Gruffydd's eyes stared unseeingly toward the fire as his hands gently moved up the leather scabbard and slowly drawing the blade.

'And this was definitely hers?' he asked gently.

'It was, my lord.'

The king ran his fingers down each side, examining every inch as if searching for a memory. Finally, he lifted it up and kissed the blade gently before replacing it in the scabbard and handing it back to the priest. Cynwrig placed it on the hearth before the fire.

'My friend,' said the king eventually. 'We have come a long way, you and I. Oft times we have disagreed, yet never have we allowed it to weaken our bond. You speak of my daughter as if she was your own and I love you for that. There is nothing I would wish more than to unite this country in her name, and the resources you ask for are indeed within my reach, yet I do not know if they are capable of achieving the outcome we seek.'

'Your sons are formidable warriors, my lord.'

'In reputation only. They have never led a quest of this magnitude.'

'Are they not laying siege to Aberystwyth castle as we speak?'

'They are, but I do not know if they will return victorious. Even if they do, the number of casualties will have a bearing.'

'So, are you saying no?'

'I'll tell you what I will do,' said the king. 'Let Aberystwyth play out as it will. When my sons return, I will see what they have achieved and at what cost. If it is acceptable, you will have your wish.'

'My lord,' said Cynwrig, 'your offer is indeed gracious, but their return could be months away and even if they do so as heroes, the moment may be lost to garner support throughout Wales. The mood is at its highest now and I need to ride south, spreading the word.'

'Then do it,' said Gruffydd. 'Prepare the way for the people's uprising you proclaim lays in waiting, and if God sees the merit in your cause, then I will send our armies south with my heartfelt blessing. I can do no more than that.'

'Then that is all I can ask,' said Cynwrig. He knelt at the side of the king's chair and kissed his hand. 'I know not how this will end or if I will ever see you again but whatever lays before us,

I will go to my rest knowing that I was once friends with one of the greatest men who ever lived.'

'Now you are speaking like a washer woman,' said Gruffydd pulling away his hand sharply. 'Get out of here and do whatever it is you priests do.'

Cynwrig got to his feet and stared at his friend for a moment in silence.

'Are you still here,' snapped the king angrily, 'go and take that cursed blade with you before I change my mind.'

The king's manner was abrupt, but Cynwrig was not fooled and as he retrieved Gwenllian's sword, he could see the tears welling in Gruffydd's eyes.

'I am leaving,' he said and turned toward the door.

'Cynwrig,' said the king as he walked across the room.

'Yes, my lord.'

'Don't you forget my mausoleum.'

'I won't, my lord,' said Cynwrig with a smile and left the king's chambers, not knowing if he would ever see his lifelong friend again.

The following morning, Cynwrig and Robert were in the courtyard, checking the tightness of their horses' girth straps. A pack mule was tethered close by, fully loaded with provisions as a gift from Angharad to help them on their journey.

'My lord,' said a voice and they turned to see Rascal running across the courtyard towards them. Behind him came the queen.

'Rascal,' said Cynwrig turning to greet the boy. 'I was hoping you would be back before we left.'

'I have been at my Lord Owain's manor,' said the boy looking between the two men. 'His groom has been teaching me how to ride a destrier. Where are you going?'

'We have to go and see if we can persuade the people to help us in the fight,' said Cynwrig.

'Are you coming back?'

Cynwrig looked down at the boy and hesitated before answering. He did not want to hurt him with the truth but knew he couldn't lie.

'Rascal,' he said eventually, 'I am an old man and probably don't have many years ahead of me. You on the other hand are a brave young man and King Gruffydd needs boys like you to keep this kingdom running. I want you to stay here and help him do that.'

'But have I not served you well?'

'As good as anyone could have dreamed but now it is time to say goodbye.'

'But father,' said the boy, 'I want to come with you. Who will make your soup when you are hungry or chew the meat when your teeth fall out?'

Behind Rascal, the queen's hand lifted to her mouth to stifle a laugh.

'I will have Robert here do any chewing I need,' said Cynwrig with a smile. 'You have been a boon to me, Rascal, but now it is time for you to make a life of your own. The lady Angharad here has promised to teach you reading and writing and how to behave in the home of a king. Isn't that true?' he said, looking over at the queen.

'It is,' said Angharad, 'and besides, if you leave, who is going to ride that destrier?'

'But you are also very old,' said Rascal, 'what about when you die?'

'My lady,' said the priest, stifling his own laugh, 'my apologies but the boy has always been taught to speak the truth of his thoughts.'

'A trait every man could learn from,' laughed the queen and turned to the boy. 'When it is time for me to go, you will be brought up in the new king's household.'

'Owain?' asked the boy.

'Yes, he is the heir and he will one day be king of Gwynedd.'

'I like Owain,' said Rascal, 'he lets me play with the swords.'

'Then it is settled,' said Angharad. 'Say your goodbyes and let these two fine men go on their way.'

Rascal turned and threw his arms around the priest's waist.

'Thank you, father,' he said, 'I will pray for you.'

'And I will pray for you,' said Cynwrig.

The boy turned to hug Robert who ruffled his curly hair.

'Be good, Rascal,' said Robert and make sure that one day you marry a very pretty girl.'

'Rascal,' said the queen, 'why don't you go up the watch tower. From there you will be able to see them ride away.'

Rascal's eyes opened wide in excitement for he was usually forbidden from climbing anywhere on the palisade.

'I will wave until you are no bigger than an ant,' he said and ran across the courtyard.

Cynwrig turned to face the queen.

'So,' he said with a sigh, 'you do know this will probably be our last goodbye.'

'I do,' said the queen looking deep into his eyes, 'but even if I lived a thousand more lives I would still not be able to thank you enough for what you have done for this family.'

'I did what I could,' said Cynwrig, 'but I did not do enough.'

'What do you mean?'

'I sometimes lie awake at night and wonder if she would still be alive if I had stayed at her side through all her years in Deheubarth.'

'God has a purpose for us all,' said Angharad, 'and you have more than fulfilled yours.'

'Well,' said Cynwrig, 'I have to go and see if I can stir this hornet's nest into life but if there is anything you ever need of me, you know that as long as I have a breath in my body, it will be yours to command.'

'Actually,' said Angharad, 'there are three things you could do for me.'

'Name them,' said Cynwrig.

Angharad glanced at Robert before replying.

'I will wait over here,' said Robert, taking the hint and walked over to talk to one of the guards. When he was out of earshot, Angharad turned back to Cynwrig.

'The first,' she said, 'is a command. Whatever conflicts lay on your path, you are to survive them all and die in your bed at a ripe old age.'

'I'm not sure that decision will be in my hands,' said Cynwrig.

'It has to be,' said Angharad, 'because when all this is over, and if your quest proves victorious, then I charge you with your second task, that of taking Gwenllian's two remaining sons to the place of her death for them to pay their respects and erect a memorial. Will you do that?'

Cynwrig stared at the queen and his eyes filled up.

'Don't you dare cry,' said the queen, 'for we will both make fools of ourselves. Just say you will do it.'

'Of course I will,' said Cynwrig, 'and it will make me the proudest man in Christendom.'

'Good,' said Angharad. 'They will be here when you return or if the king and I have passed on, then they will be with Owain.'

'I understand,' said Cynwrig. And the third thing?

'Sorry?'

'You said there were three things you would have me do.'

'Oh yes, I want you to stand still.'

'Stand still? But Why?'

'So I can do this,' she said and without warning she tiptoed up and kissed the priest firmly on the lips, pausing the briefest of moments longer than what would be considered decent.

'My lady,' said Cynwrig as she stepped back. 'I'm not sure that was appropriate. There are many eyes in this courtyard.'

'I'll tell you what it was, Cynwrig,' she said, 'it was long overdue. I love my husband dearly and I know he loves me but even he would not deny us both this briefest of moments as we near the end of our lives.'

'The old devil may chop off your head.'

'He has threatened many times,' laughed Angharad, 'yet here it is, still attached to my wrinkly neck.

They both fell silent for a few moments.

'Well,' said Angharad eventually, 'you had better be on your way.'

'I should,' said Cynwrig and turned to beckon Robert back to the horses. Both men mounted and after saying their goodbyes headed toward the gate. Angharad followed them across the courtyard and as Robert rode out of the palace gates, Cynwrig reined in and turned his head back to the queen.

'Before I go,' he said, 'may I ask you to answer one question honestly?'

'You may,' said the queen.

'If there is a life after this one, and if by God's grace we should meet there, would there be any chance...' He paused as he struggled for the right words. 'I mean, do you think that we ...' He stopped again and looked down at the queen.

Angharad placed her hand reassuringly on his knee.

'Cynwrig,' she said, 'I believe it is fate that we will meet again, not only in the next life but in the thousands of lives that lay waiting after that. Make of that what you will, but surely, somewhere in the mists of eternity there is a place for all things to play out differently.'

Cynwrig smiled and nodded silently at her.

'Travel well my old friend,' she added, 'and may God go with you.'

'And with you, my lady.' he said and without another word, kicked his horse to follow Robert out of the gates.

Chapter Eighteen

Aberystwyth Castle

June AD 1136

Paulus lay as still as a corpse on the hill leading up to the western palisade waiting for the quarter moon to disappear behind the heavy grey clouds. Spread across the hillside, two dozen other men did likewise, their faces blackened to avoid reflecting whatever light there was. For many, this was their third or fourth trip up the hill that night, each one a painstakingly slow crawl to avoid being seen or heard by the sentries above and though many got within twenty paces of the palisade, their purpose was not attack, but preparation. Each man had a package to be left on the slopes of the hill in anticipation of the following day's attack and it was imperative that they were not seen.

The clouds slid across the sky obscuring the moon and once again the hill was plunged into pitch black darkness.

'Now,' whispered Paulus and the man at his side joined him as he scrambled upward toward the lip of the hill, dragging his load behind him.

'This will do,' gasped Paulus dropping to the ground again, 'wedge them in here.' The two men stuffed the filled sacks between two boulders and weighed them down with smaller rocks. The last thing they wanted was them rolling back down the hill when the fighting started.

'That's it,' said Paulus, 'that's the last one.' The two men crawled backwards down the hill until they reached level ground before running back to the camp and joining their comrades.

'Are we all back?' asked Paulus looking around.

'Aye, you were the last, my lord,' said one of the other men.

'Good,' replied Paulus, grabbing a piece of linen cloth and dipping it in a nearby bucket of water, 'in that case let's get this muck of our faces and get some sleep. Refresh the sentries and change them every hour. Tomorrow we take the castle.'

The following morning Owain's army was once more formed up on the plain below Aberystwyth castle. Again, there was silence but this time, ranks of archers stood to the fore. Before each man was a bucket crammed with dozens of arrows along with a clay fire pot containing the smouldering embers of the previous night's camp fires.

'Is everything in place?' asked Owain to Paulus quietly.

'It is,' said Paulus. 'The wind is in our favour so all we need now is the signal from Cadwaladwr.'

On the other side of the castle, Owain's brother walked amongst his foot soldiers. Each had divested themselves of their weapons for the task before them involved no fighting. Nevertheless, they knew it was dangerous and many had borrowed extra gambesons from those comrades who were not taking part in the first wave of attack.

'Remember,' said Cadwaladwr, 'when we go, we stop for nothing. If a man falls, the one behind takes his place. Understood?'

'Aye,' shouted the men.

'Right,' said Cadwaladwr, 'take your places and I will make ready the archers.'

Up on the palisade, Stephen Demareis watched the comings and goings with concern. Down in the valley the main bulk of Owain's army was waiting, motionless in the morning chill but over on the east side there seemed to be far more activity. Overnight, the enemy had moved a dozen carts up onto the approach road, each holding half a dozen barrels. In addition, all the oxen used to pull the carts had been withdrawn, leaving the carts empty and useless.

'What are they doing?' he asked quietly.

'I have never seen such a tactic,' said the captain. 'Perhaps they are going to use them as a defensive position.'

'I don't like this,' said Demareis, 'it all looks too pre-meditated to be just a whim.'

The captain turned to walk away.

'Where are you going?' asked the castellan.

'To check the western approach. Don't forget, the main army is still down there and somehow I do not believe Owain will leave them idle for long.'

He walked around the palisade and stared down into the valley.

'What are you up to, Welshman?' he said quietly. 'What subterfuge do you engage?'

'My lord,' said one of the Welsh sergeants on the eastern approach to the castle, 'we are ready.'

'In that case,' said Cadwaladwr, 'give the signal.'

The sergeant nodded to one of his archers who dipped an arrow into a fire pot and blew on the embers gently, nursing them into life. The pitch covered cloth wrapped around the arrow head burst into flame and the archer notched the shaft into his bowstring before aiming it high above the castle.

'Do it,' said Cadwaladwr and seconds later, the arrow soared through the air leaving a dirty black line of oily smoke in its trail.

'The dice have been cast,' said Cadwaladwr, 'there is no turning back.'

'There it is,' shouted Owain down on the plain, 'archers, fire your arrows. '

Each of the hundred archers at Owain's disposal set light to an arrow and notched it into their bows.

'Target the palisades first,' shouted Owain, 'I will give the command when to switch. Ready, loose!'

A hundred arrows flew up through the air leaving a trail of smoke behind them. A few landed inside the bailey while most thudded into the castle walls, sending flames licking up the timber palisade.

'Again,' shouted Owain, 'and keep firing. Each man to empty a full bucket before they rest their arms.'

Over and over again the sky was filled with willow and as the fire arrows slammed into the wooden castle. The battle began in earnest.

'Every second man to the western wall,' shouted the captain as he ducked the arrows flying over his head. 'Fire party, ignore the thatched buildings, there will be no saving them. Concentrate on keeping any flames away from the keep and stables.'

Defenders ran from the far corners of the castle to the walls under attack. Many of the arrows embedded into the outside walls had already extinguished without causing any damage but some of the flames had started to take hold.

'Get water on those,' shouted the captain, 'and prepare to defend the walls.'

'But there's nobody on the hill, my lord,' shouted a voice and the captain looked down in confusion. 'Why waste arrows on a wall if there was to be no follow up?'

Down below, Owain turned to his archers.

'We have their attention,' he called, 'switch targets.'

Every archer peered up the slope and lowered their aims to the sacks of pitch-soaked straw that had been left in place the previous night.

Make them count, roared Owain and again the skies filled with fiery arrows. The sacks instantly burst into flames sending plumes of black smoke swirling around the hill and as the wind fanned the sacks into fiery life, billowing clouds of acrid smoke drifted up toward the castle walls.

'What's happening?' shouted one of the defenders between coughs, 'what are they burning?'

'Pitch,' shouted the captain, 'they intend using the smoke as cover. Look to your fronts.'

For a few seconds, the defenders could see nothing but then came the roar of hundreds of men charging up the hill.

'Here they come,' shouted the captain, 'archers, fire at will. Men at arms, look to your weapons.'

Within moments, dozens of men appeared out of the smoke, each screaming a battle cry to exaggerate their bravery. Many carried ladders and as they thudded against the walls, the defenders dropped rocks onto those unlucky enough to be first up. Those hit, fell backward and the defenders pushed the ladders sideways to fall into others nearby, sending the rest of the attackers hurtling to the ground. Those few who managed to get to the top were quickly dispatched with spears or swords to fall back onto their comrades.

Keep them out, roared the captain, *at all costs.*

Down on the plain, Owain could just about see the assault on the wall through the smoke and turned to the man at his side.

'Sound the signal,' he said and immediately, a horn echoed around the valley.

On the eastern side of the castle, Cadwaladwr heard the horn and turned to his men.

'There's the signal,' he shouted, 'you know what to do.'

Immediately the men on the carts smashed their heavy axes into the barrels, releasing hundreds of gallons of water onto each one. When every barrel was empty, they jumped down and lifted the hitching rails of the sodden carts, waiting for the next command.

'What are they doing?' asked a soldier besides the castellan up on the palisade. 'There is no way they can get over the ditch.'

'I don't know,' said the Demareis, 'unless...'

His eyes widened in horror as he realised what the tactic was and turned to his own men.

'Those carts are not intended to get over the ditches,' he shouted, 'they are to go in them.

The few archers atop the eastern palisade suddenly realised the danger and reached for their own arrows.

'Bring the fire pots,' shouted a voice but Demareis held up his hand.

'Don't bother,' he shouted, 'that's why they've soaked them in water. We would waste too many arrows before any caught alight. Aim for the men instead.'

Each archer notched their bows and waited as the first of the carts neared the ditch.

Down below, Cadwaladwr turned to his own men.

'Upon my command,' he shouted, 'I want to see this sky darkened by willow. Any Englishman who dares shows his head above the palisade I want dead before he has chance to pray. Archers, advance.'

The hundreds of Welsh archers marched forward and formed a position three men deep. Behind them came dozens of young boys each struggling with two buckets of arrows each.

'This will do,' shouted the sergeant in charge, 'go firm here. Notch your bows.'

Cadwaladwr looked at the waiting men behind each cart.

'Take heart,' he shouted, 'and stop for nothing. Archers, loose!'

Hundreds of arrows flew through the air from the first rank and as soon as they had left the bows, the second and third ranks released their own volleys.

'Keep them going,' shouted Cadwaladwr and turned to the carts. 'Now is your chance, *advance!*'

Each group of men holding a hitching rail propelled the carts toward the castle. Within moments the first flew over the lip of the defensive ditch, landing on top of the filth covered spikes.

'Next,' shouted the sergeant and the second crew pushed their cart over to land alongside the first.

'Keep them coming,' shouted the sergeant, 'you are too slow.'

The men increased the pace and soon all ten carts were spread along the bottom forming a rudimentary bridge, but it was still too low.

'*Logs,*' roared the sergeant and as he did, an arrow from the castle walls thudded into the neck of the man next to him, killing him instantly.

'*Archers,*' roared Cadwaladwr in a fury, 'keep their heads down or I swear we will use your bodies to cover the carts.'

A column of men ran through the massed ranks of men at arms, each carrying a sack of logs. Without slowing they continued to the trench and hurled the sacks on top of the carts, filling up any gaps and building up the level.

'Keep them coming,' shouted Cadwaladwr again, 'we're almost there.'

The stream of men carrying the sacks was relentless and as each discarded their load into the ditch, they returned for another from the many fully laden wagons in the rear.

More men fell to the arrows from the few archers on the palisade brave enough to show their heads but within ten minutes, every Welshman had withdrawn back to their positions and Cadwaladwr looked at their handiwork with satisfaction. The ditch that had been such an obstacle earlier in the day now contained a rudimentary walkway wide enough for ten men to cross side by side. It wasn't perfect and would be unstable underfoot, but it was good enough for what he intended.

'A job well done, sergeant,' he shouted, '*bring up the ram!*'

'This is hopeless,' shouted Demareis from his position behind the palisade, 'they do whatever they want, and we cannot reply.'

'Their archers outnumber us tenfold,' replied one of his men as dozens of arrows flew over their heads. 'To show ourselves invites certain death.'

Demareis looked up to see the captain running along the ramparts to join him at his position.

'What are we to do? asked the castellan as the captain dropped down beside him. 'We cannot even fire back such is their strength.'

'They will follow up soon enough with an assault,' said the captain, 'and when they do, their archers will be withdrawn. We have to be ready for that so do not lose any more men to their arrows, we will need them to defend the walls.'

'How fares the western palisade?'

'We have driven them back for now, but they will come again.' He got to his feet and peered carefully over the wall while creating as small a target as possible.

'What's happening?' said Demareis.

'My lord,' said the captain slowly, 'the situation just got a whole lot worse.'

'Take it easy,' shouted Cadwaladwr on the far side of the ditch, 'do not damage the wheels.'

The freshly felled oak trunk sat in a wooden cradle atop six cart wheels and as they manoeuvred it over the makeshift bridge, rows of men steadied it on either side.

'My lord,' shouted the sergeant at arms from behind him, 'we are running out of arrows.'

'Keep them coming,' replied Cadwaladwr, 'we are almost there.'

A few moments later the ram was successfully positioned on the castle side of the ditch and Cadwaladwr recalled his men back out of arrow range.

'Cease fire,' he shouted, and the sweat soaked archers lowered their bows.

'Casualties?' asked Cadwaladwr to the sergeant at his side.

'Three dead, four wounded,' said the sergeant, 'a small price to pay.'

'The tally will rise,' said Cadwaladwr, 'but the archers have done well. Withdraw them and prepare our men at arms. We will attack at last light.'

'And fight in the dark?'

'Aye, we want the enemy to be as confused as possible.'

'Of course, my lord,' said the sergeant and turned away to address the men as Cadwaladwr looked across at the giant ram. It had been a complicated task to get it over the ditch and was probably not big enough to breech the fortified gates, but he was not worried. If his brother's plan went as well as they hoped, it may not even be needed.

On the western approach, Owain's men made their way back across the flat ground to their staging area. Many carried wounds and they had left several comrades dead on the hill yet still, Owain was confident.

'With one more push we could have bested that palisade, my lord,' said Paulus, 'some of my men got onto the ramparts but were repelled. Next time we should mount a full-scale assault and not limit it to a selected few men.'

'There is method in my judgement, Paulus,' said Owain, 'and you will indeed get the full assault you crave but these past days have been nought but tests to judge the strength of the enemy positions.'

'So, our dead lost their lives for nothing?'

'Not at all. Their deaths have ensured that many more will live, and their families will be well looked after, but tonight, I promise that the castle will fall to us with minimum casualties on our side.'

'Of course, my lord,' said Paulus, 'and if my doubting manner gives you cause for concern, please accept it is only in the interests of a Gwynedd victory.'

'It is the role of a good captain to question his leaders in times of war, Paulus and I, your opinion. But the time for questions is over and the time for serious action is upon us. Inform the men that we will assault the wall again at last light.'

'And fight in the dark?'

'Aye, as will Cadwaladwr and his men on the eastern approach but this time there will be no withdrawal.'

'Do I lead the centre or one of the flanks?' asked Paulus.

'Neither, my friend,' replied Owain, 'you and your men have a far more critical role to play.'

Several hours later, as the setting sun lit up the western wall with a burnt orange light, many of the defenders stared over the castle walls in silence, most secretly afraid of what was about to happen. Others took the opportunity to sit against the palisades and grab what rest they could or quietly sip on the hot broth provided by what was left of the burnt-out kitchens. Those who had been wounded in the first assault but could still walk had been bandaged up and sat alongside the piles of rocks situated along the ramparts. Ready to do whatever they could to repel the impending assault.

On the eastern side of the castle, Cadwaladwr stood ready with a thousand fully armed men at arms and a hundred ladders. Another two hundred archers stood ready to provide cover and fifty soldiers had been tasked with assaulting the gates with the giant wheeled ram.

Down in the western valley, another four thousand men stood waiting for the signal, each fully aware that this time there would be no withdrawal. It was either take the castle or admit defeat.

Owain nodded to a waiting archer and as a flaming arrow soared through the sky, the battle drums once again pounded out their heart stirring beat.

'Men of Gwynedd,' shouted Owain drawing his sword, *'advaaance!'*

'Here they come,' shouted one of the men in the castle, 'stand to the palisades.'

Dozens of defenders stood up and swallowed hard as they looked out at the approaching armies. The superior number of men in the Welsh ranks was obvious and every Englishman knew that should they breach the walls, the castle would be overwhelmed in moments.

'Take heart,' shouted the captain, 'they can only use a certain amount of ladders at any one time. Deny them the wall and we can still win this fight. Archers, as soon as they are in range, use whatever you have left to cut them down and then pick up a sword. We need every arm wielding a blade if we are to survive this day.'

As he spoke the first of many arrows thudded into the palisade and the battle cries of the attackers roared through the evening air.

The final battle for Aberystwyth castle had begun.

Chapter Nineteen

Aberystwyth Castle

June AD 1136

'*Hold them out,*' roared the captain above the deafening sounds of the brutal fight and smashed his sword across the head of an attacker about to climb over the palisade. The Welshman fell back onto his comrades below as the captain dragged the top of the ladder sideways sending it crashing to the ground. 'Keep going,' he shouted as he retrieved his sword and ran along the ramparts, 'deny them this wall and the day can still be ours.'

He looked around, his heart beating as loud as the reverberating battle drums outside the castle, shocked that despite the disparity of numbers, the defenders were more than holding their own against the attackers. On the eastern wall the situation was much the same and though the ram hammered against the gates, the heavy strutting his men had put in place was working well and the gates were holding out.

He looked down into the bailey. Most of the buildings were ablaze from the relentless hail of fire arrows.

'*You,*' he roared at a wounded man limping across the bailey, '*get yourself back up here or I'll kill you myself.*'

The man looked up in horror. His arm hung useless at his side and his ankle was obviously badly injured where he had been knocked from the defensive wall. Groaning in pain he headed back toward the palisade as another soldier ran past the captain on the ramparts.

'Where are you going?' demanded the captain, grabbing him by the throat and pushing him up against the wall. 'Return to your post.'

'My lord,' gasped the soldier, 'I seek the castellan. The gates are creaking, and we need more men in case they are breached.'

'What do you mean, find the castellan? Is he not on the eastern wall?'

'No, my lord, we have not seen him since the ram first beat against the gate. We thought he was with you.'

The captain released the soldier and stared over to the far side of the castle as his mind raced. He hadn't seen Demareis since the latest assault had started and someone would have told him if he had been killed. He looked around the burning buildings and then up the slope of the motte. The keep would be their last position of defence but surely Demareis would not have sought refuge so quickly before the walls had even fallen? He turned to the soldier.

'Get back to your station,' he said, 'I will send men to the gate.'

'Aye, my lord,' replied the man and ran back the way he had come.

Outside the castle, Paulus lay motionless on the hill, all but invisible in the darkness. Beside him lay a hundred men, equally still as they waited for the signal to move. The noise of the battle echoed through the air, yet they could see nothing of it for they were hidden amongst the rocks of the southern slope. Slowly they got to their feet and advanced as quietly as they could toward the looming palisade. Up above they could see two sentries but apart for the occasional glance over the palisade onto the dark hill below, the English soldiers' attention was taken by the ferocious battle being fought on the far side of the castle.

Gently, Paulus and four of his men raised the first ladder against the wall. Others soon followed, and Paulus led the climb as stealthily as he could. As he reached the top, one of the sentries turned and saw the blackened face of the experienced warrior but before he could cry out, Paulus used his momentum to swing his sword across the Englishman's neck, cutting deep into his throat and sending him hurtling into the bailey below. The second sentry heard the muffled cry but as he turned, a spear flew through the air and thudded into his chest, sending him backward to join his comrade in the bailey.

Paulus looked around for more guards, but everyone was involved in the fight. For a few seconds he couldn't believe his luck for they had anticipated a fight as soon as they had breached the walls. More ladders joined the first and within a few moments, all his warriors were in the castle, crouching low to hide amongst the shadows along the inside of the palisade. Without speaking, twenty men split from the main group and after descending to the bailey, raced across to the motte and up the steps to the keep. Paulus and his men stayed hidden, holding their breath in anticipation. If they were going to take the castle without the need of a long siege, they needed to secure the inner fortress.

Up on the motte, the group reached the keep without being seen and though Paulus saw a short struggle with the two sentries on duty, they were quickly overcome and his men disappeared inside.

'Wait,' he hissed, to his remaining men, 'they remain undiscovered, so we'll give them a few more moments to take advantage.'

They waited for what seemed like an age until finally Paulus knew he could wait no more.

'Come,' he said to the rest of his command, 'it seems the keep is ours, now it is for us to make the final move.'

His men followed him down to the bailey and raced towards the gate with weapons drawn. The few defenders caught out in the open were slow to react and cut down without quarter. Their screams echoed around the courtyard, but it was too late, Paulus and his men reached the defenders still fortifying the inside of the barricade and mercilessly fell amongst them with untethered brutality.

'My lord,' shouted a soldier from up above, 'behind you.'

Up on the ramparts, the captain turned away from the palisade and as he looked down into the bailey, his heart sunk. At least fifty of the enemy had managed to breach the walls and there was fierce fighting at the gate. Immediately he knew the day was lost for if he moved men from either of the walls, the palisades would be bettered. He turned to the last chance anyone of them had and looked up at the keep but was aghast to see smoke beginning to come from the shutters. Up on the top he could see a man waving the flag of Gwynedd and he knew there was nothing he could do; the day was lost.

'Withdraw,' he shouted across the castle, 'yield the walls, form up at the base of the motte.'

Men looked around in confusion. The momentary distraction allowed more of Owain's men to better the walls on the western palisade and within moment, the Welsh were pouring onto the ramparts.

'Withdraw,' shouted the captain again, 'the walls have fallen.'

All around the castle men rushed to the ladders while others, desperate to escape the rampaging attackers jumped from the palisade to land heavily in the bailey. Those still able to walk quickly reformed around the captain, wielding whatever weapons they still had to hand.

Any hope they still had evaporated as the gates finally gave way and hundreds of men poured through to rampage into the castle grounds while others made a beeline for the remaining defenders huddled together in the bailey.

'Hold,' roared a voice as they moved in for the kill and the Welsh lines stuttered to a halt. Gradually the noise of battle eased off and Cadwaladwr made his way to the front of his men, his face bloodied from an enemy blade.

'Who speaks for you?' he shouted.

Every one of the English defenders looked around but Demareis was nowhere to be seen.

'I do,' said the captain eventually and stepped forward from the group of terrified men.

'In that case,' said Cadwaladwr, 'do you cede the castle?'

The captain looked around at the men at his side. Everyone looked back at him with fear in their eyes and he knew there was little point in fighting on.

'Do I have your word my men will be treated well?' he asked eventually.

'What does it matter?' asked Cadwaladwr. 'If I decide to kill you, you will die either way.'

'Yes, but if that is your intention, we would rather die with swords in hand,' said the captain with a cold look in his eyes. His fingers moved slightly on the hilt of his sword as he prepared to defend himself from the men to his front.

Cadwaladwr stared at the captain, pondering his decision.

'You have my word,' boomed a different voice and all eyes turned to see Owain riding his horse into the bailey. 'Throw down your arms and you will be treated fairly.'

The captain looked back at Cadwaladwr who paused before nodding his agreement.

'Lower your weapons,' shouted the captain and tossed his sword to one side. His men followed suit and they waited with bated breath to see if the Welshman was good to his word.

'Take them away,' said Owain as he dismounted, 'I will decide what to do with them on the morrow.'

'What about this one?' asked one of his men, pointing his sword at the English captain.

'Leave him,' said Owain 'he stays with me.'

The defeated English soldiers were led away as Owain turned to the captain.

'So, you are the castellan?'

'I am not,' replied the captain. 'The castellan is Robert-Demareis.'

'And is he here?'

'He was,' said the captain, 'but he hasn't been seen since the battle started.'

'Hiding perhaps?' suggested Cadwaladwr with a sneer.

'If he is, it is without my knowledge,' said the captain.

Owain turned to a sergeant at his side.

'Search this place from top to bottom,' he said, 'and bring the castellan to me. Take one of the prisoners with you to identify him.'

'Aye, my lord,' said the soldier.

'So,' said Owain turning back to face the captain, 'you are the one responsible for holding us out these past few days.'

'I was responsible for the strategy, said the captain, and the men fought under my command. If there is retribution to be had it must be on my head alone, not on those who followed orders.'

'For such a small force, you caused us a lot of problems,' said Owain, 'and many of my kinsmen are dead because of you.'

'It is you who was the aggressor,' said the captain, 'all we did was defended what was ours by right. You would have done the same.'

Owain nodded and stared at the captain.

'Your voice sounds Welsh,' he said eventually, 'yet you serve an English master.'

'I know no other way than the ways of war,' said the captain. 'My mother took me and my brothers to follow the army when my father was a lancer under King Henry and I grew up learning how to fight. I go where I am ordered to go.'

'Do you not have allegiance to the land of your fathers?'

'There is no combined land of my fathers, only kingdoms where a man is often pitted against his own kin. Even you know the truth of it, Owain ap Gruffydd.'

'You know of me?'

'Your father casts a long shadow and you fight under the banner of Gwynedd. You can be no other.'

'What you say is true,' said Owain, 'and we are indeed a divided country, but what if there was another way. One where there was only one banner covering all kingdoms?'

'A united Wales'

'Aye.'

'There will be no such thing in my lifetime.'

'We will see, captain,' said Owain and turned to Cadwaladwr. 'Take him away but treat him well. There could be a place for such men in our armies should we march south.'

'Do you think he would switch sides?'

'I know not, but I will talk to him again soon. In the meantime, we have a victory to celebrate.'

'My lord,' shouted a voice and they turned to see one of the sergeants dragging a young man across the bailey.

'Who is this?' asked Owain.

'I found him hiding in the stables,' said the sergeant, 'and was about to relieve him of his head but he offered information in return for his life.'

'Information?' said Owain, staring at the terrified young man. 'It had better be good, boy.'

'My lord,' stuttered the prisoner, 'I am a mere stable hand and I admit I hid away when the fighting started but the castellan found me and ordered me to prepare his horse.'

'Why did he need a horse?' asked Cadwaladwr,' There was no way he could have gotten past us on the eastern approach.

'My lord,' said the boy, 'he left through the postern gate behind the stables as soon as it was dark.'

'There is a postern?' asked Owain, his face turning red with rage as he turned to face his brother, 'why was I not informed?'

'The northern wall was never seen as a route of attack or escape,' said Cadwaladwr, 'such is its steepness. Our scouts were never tasked with close scrutiny.'

'Yet he managed to take a horse that way,' snapped Owain and turned to the captain.

'Did you know about this?'

'About the castellan's escape, no. About the postern, yes, but it has been nailed up for years and never used. It was never an option.'

'Where does it lead?' asked Owain sharply.

'Out onto the northern face of the cliff,' said the captain. 'The path is narrow but passable if I recall but like I said, it has been years since anyone has used it.'

'Send out a party of riders,' said Owain turning to Cadwaladwr, 'and see if we can run him down.'

'We do not know which way he went,' said Cadwaladwr.

'Oh, yes we do,' said Owain, 'the only direction where he would find allies. *South.*'

A few days later, the Gwynedd army were once again formed up on the plain below Aberystwyth castle. To the front stood every archer under Owain's command, each one furnished with a single arrow and a fire pot. Behind them the main bulk of the army waited patiently. Some were wounded, many more were hung over but every single one was thankful they had survived the battle.

The little used cavalry had split into two groups, each flanking the massed soldiers and before them all, wrapped in sewn linen shrouds lay a line of over a hundred dead bodies.

Owain rode his impressive mount slowly along the front rank before turning to address the men.

'We are here,' he said, 'to pay our respects to our comrades. These men before you paid the ultimate price and we should never forget that they died so others may walk free. The house of Aberffraw will see that their families are looked after, but it is the duty of every man here to ensure their names are never forgotten. In days to come, when you drink your ale with friends and kin, take a moment to toast their names, for they paid dearly for that privilege.' He paused and looked across the massed ranks. 'Before we leave this place,' he continued, 'it is important that we send them on their way with a fitting tribute.' He turned his horse and looked up at the castle.

'*Archers ready,*' he roared, and every bowman set light to their single arrow. He drew his sword and held it high in the morning air, 'In honour of our glorious dead, we dedicate this victory to their memory. May God bless their souls.' He brought his sword sharply down and within seconds, every flaming arrow soared through the sky toward the empty fortification above. The bailey had been packed with hundreds of bales of hay, each soaked in pitch and as the rain of fiery arrows fell amongst them, the flames reached up to consume what was left of the castle.

On the eastern side, more archers did the same and as the army watched, the walls rapidly succumbed to the fires and the castle became a raging inferno.

Owain watched the castle burn for an age, seeing the clouds of black smoke bellowing into the sky before riding back to the rest of his fellow officers.

'A fitting tribute,' said Cadwaladwr.

'There will be other such monstrosities that will soon suffer a similar fate,' said Paulus. 'And each one will be a tribute to the greatness of Gwynedd.'

'You are wrong,' said Owain looking up at the burning castle. 'This was the first and the last of this campaign. Our advance ends here.'

Paulus stared at Owain and then at Cadwaladwr in confusion.

'But why?' he asked eventually. 'Ceredigion is on her knees and her castles are there for the taking.'

'Tell him,' said Owain and kicked his heels into his horse to ride back to his campaign tent.

'Last night,' said Cadwaladwr, turning to face the officer, 'our scouts returned with important information. It seems we have been beaten to the next prize by Rees ap Madoc.'

'Rees ap Madoc? asked Paulus. 'Why would a prince of Powys be on the west coast?'

'It seems that King Madoc also saw the opportunity and wanted some of the prize for himself. He sent his army under the command of his son to combine with his brother, Hywel and rode west. Our victory here will go down in history, but our advance has been halted. It ends here Paulus, we cannot venture any further.'

'But surely we can continue south. Our men are strong and well trained. We fear nothing, and as such we should take advantage while Ceredigion is on its knees.'

'I agree but with at least two other armies seeking similar targets we are at risk of starting another war between the kingdoms of Wales and that we cannot risk.'

'So, what are we to do now? '

'Today we will bury our dead and tend our wounded,' said Cadwaladwr. 'Tomorrow we go home.'

Just over ten leagues away to the south, one of the sentries on top of the gate tower of Cardigan Castle looked across at a rider approaching from the town a few hundred paces distant. The horse was obviously lame but despite this, it carried a man slumped across its neck.

'Look at him,' said the sentry, to his comrade. 'What sort of man still rides when his horse is lame?'

'Whoever he is,' said the second man, 'it looks like he intends coming in here. Should I tell the gate guards to let him in.'

'Of course not,' said the first guard, 'you know the situation, until we get a new castellan we are to stay secured until further notice. '

'Fitzgilbert has been dead for weeks,' said his comrade, 'when is the king going to get off his fat arse and nominate a replacement?'

'Such things are not for the likes of us', said the first man.' He'll be here soon enough I'm sure. Until then, the steward said the gates stay locked until we have a new master and whatever he wants, he gets.' He looked down as the horse neared the bridge across the defensive ditch.

'Hold there, stranger,' he shouted, 'state your business or head back the way you came.'

The rider looked up weakly and they could see it was the face of a filthy, exhausted man.

'I need to see your master,' he croaked. 'Let me in and I will explain everything.'

'I can't hear you,' replied the guard raising his voice, 'speak up. Tell me where you come from or I'll have our archers cut you down where you stand.'

The man sighed and gathered his strength before looking up again.

'I cannot speak any louder,' he said his throat raspy, 'I am sick and need help. Please, open this gate.'

'It seems we have an idiot on our hands,' said one of the guards, 'what shall we do?'

'He might be an assassin,' came the reply. 'If we let him in he could kill us in our beds.'

Both men laughed and looked down at the rider. As they did he fell from his horse and landed on the wooden bridge with a heavy thud. Even from their position high on the wall they could see he was sick.

'Now what are we going to do?' asked the first guard. 'He can't go back if he can't stand.'

'We could arrest him and throw him in the gaol,' said his comrade, 'for wasting the time of the king's men.'

'But what if he is plagued? We could infect the whole castle and be on sentry duty for a month.'

'That's if we don't get sick and die,' said the second man.

'What goes on up there?' shouted a voice from below and one of the guards walked over to the inner wall to stare down into the bailey.

'We have an imbecile outside who seeks entrance,' said the sentry. 'I think he may be a brigand.'

'Is he alone?'

'Aye, and he just fell off his horse.'

The sergeant walked over to the gate and slid back a hatch to look out. When he saw there was no threat he ordered the gates open and walked over.

'Wake up,' he said kicking the man in his side, 'who are you?'

The victim just groaned in reply and the sergeant leaned down to turn him over. For a few seconds he stared in confusion, wondering where he had seen him before, but his eyes widened as he realised who he was. He turned his head toward the castle.

'*Get me some help,*' he roared, 'and send for the steward.'

Men started running everywhere and within moments the sick rider was laying on the floor of the bailey, his sodden clothing being loosened by the sergeant.

'What's happening?' shouted a voice and the sergeant looked up to see the steward running towards him.

'My lord,' replied the sergeant, 'this man collapsed outside the gate. He is barely alive.'

'He looks ill,' said the steward, 'why have you brought him in?'

'I had no other option.'

'Why not?'

'Because, my lord,' said the sergeant, 'this man is Stephen Demareis, the castellan of Aberystwyth castle.'

Chapter Twenty

Brycheniog

July AD 1136

Tarw waited patiently in a hunting lodge hidden amongst the wild hills of western Brycheniog. By the door, two warriors watched him constantly, each heavily armed and obviously more than capable of cutting him down should he give them cause.

This was the fourth day running he had come to the lodge to talk to the man he sought but each time he had met with little success. Ordinarily he would have left but this was far too important a meeting and if it meant swallowing his pride, then that was what he would do.

'I grow tired of this game,' said Dog at his side. 'Let us seek aid elsewhere before I die of boredom.'

'We will wait,' said Tarw quietly. 'This man is too important not to be involved.'

'He is a good warlord admittedly,' said Dog, 'but there are many other similar men, each as good.'

'There is none as capable as he,' said Tarw, 'don't forget, he defeated a much bigger English army at the beginning of the year at Gower. That sort of experience is invaluable.'

'I hear he suffered heavy casualties.'

'Indeed he did, yet he still emerged victorious. Since then men have flocked to his banner and apart from Gwynedd, he has probably the largest Welsh army under his command.'

'So, where is he?'

Tarw shrugged his shoulders.

'They said he would be here today so all we can do is wait.'

He looked around the lodge, seeing a line of empty sleeping spaces, each with a wolf skin blanket and a straw pillow. The skulls of all sorts of animals hung from the rafters but pride of place belonged to the many wolves that had been taken, an impressive testament to the skill and bravery of the hunters.

An old man methodically swept the wooden floor with a straw broom, clearing away the debris of the previous night's celebrations while another fed wood into the fire.

'Old man,' said Dog eventually. 'Why do you keep a fire going? It is as hot as hell in here.'

'In readiness for whatever the hunt brings back, my lord,' said the slave. 'The master will have his meat hot.'

'Impressive,' said Dog looking at the head of the boar impaled on a spear near the fire. 'Was that taken recently?'

'A few days ago, my lord. It is the biggest of the year and taken by Master Hywel himself.'

'I wonder if there is any meat left,' mused Dog, 'it has been a while since I enjoyed a chunk of King Pig.'

The man didn't answer but turned his head toward the door. Outside he could hear the unmistakable noise of a large group of horsemen riding into the camp and the speed of his fellow slave's sweeping noticeably increased.

'At last,' said Tarw and stood up to walk to the door alongside Dog.

The two guards each lowered their spears to point toward his body.

'You will stay here,' one said, 'until told otherwise.'

Dog 's eyes narrowed, and his hand went to the hilt of his sword, but he kept his counsel.

'Is your master with them?' asked Tarw.

'He may be,' came the reply, 'you will find out soon enough.'

Tarw and Dog returned to sit on the bench alongside the table, both quiet as the noise of the returned hunting party echoed around the camp outside. After what seemed like an age, the door burst open and several warriors walked in, each in good humour and retelling the tales of the day's hunt. Some stared at Tarw as they passed but others pointedly ignored the two strangers and walked to their bunks to remove their tunics. Behind them came two more men and though Tarw had never met Hywel ap Maredudd, he instantly knew which one was the self-claimed Lord of Brycheniog.

Tarw and Dog stood up as Hywel entered but the giant warrior made his way directly to the table and finished off half a jug of ale in one go.

'You,' he growled turning to the slave, 'make sure this table groans under the weight of ale pots before I throw you on that fire.'

'Yes, my lord,' said the man and shuffled towards the ale barrels stacked in the corner.

Hywel turned to face Tarw and stared directly into his eyes without flinching. For a few moments there was an awkward silence and even Dog, who was usually unimpressed by most men had to admit there was something about Hywel that demanded respect.

'My lord,' said Dog eventually, 'this is…'

'I know who he is,' said Hywel. 'Tarw, the bull of Deheubarth.'

Tarw nodded slightly in acknowledgement.

'And you are the famed Lord Hywel ap Maredudd, Lord of Brycheniog and defeater of the English at Gower.'

'Amongst other places,' said Hywel walking around the table. 'I hear you have come seeking aid?'

'I have,' said Tarw. 'There is fight coming, and we need men of your ilk to ride alongside us to ensure victory.'

'I am always up for a fight,' said Hywel looking between Tarw and Dog, 'but I choose my battles carefully.'

'As should all men,' said Tarw, 'but I think this will be of interest and I request only to plead my case. If you decline, then I will ride away and bother you no more.'

'I heard about your wife, said Hywel, 'and you have my condolences. Even up here, her name is spoken in awe around the camp fires. It is said she was a fine woman.'

'She was,' said Tarw, 'thank you.'

'Do I guess correctly that your mission is to recruit men to your banner to seek retribution?'

'You do,' said Tarw. 'There is a rising anger across the kingdoms at the manner of her death and I hope to harness it to turn it against the English.'

'A noble quest,' said Hywel, 'but one that has failed many times before.'

'I know,' said Tarw, 'and I hear that argument often but that is no reason to hold back. It takes many blows of an axe to fell an oak.'

Hywel Nodded and turned to Dog.

'I see you carry a heathen blade.'

'It depends on your definition of heathen,' replied Dog. 'May I see it?'

Dog paused before drawing his weapon from its scabbard and offered it hilt first to the warrior.

'It's light,' said Hywel swinging the blade back and forth, 'does that not cause a problem?'

'It is a blade not a cudgel,' said Dog, 'and as sharp as a crone's tongue.'

'So, the man who wields it needs to be an expert in his craft to better his opponent?'

'He does,' said Dog.

'And are you such a man?' asked Hywel bringing the blade down to rest gently on Dog's shoulder. His eyes narrowed as he stared coldly into the smaller man's eyes.

'I do well enough,' said Dog, returning his stare.

'My friend,' said Tarw, watching the exchange. 'That blade is truly the sharpest I have ever seen so I suggest you take it away from Dog's neck.'

'If it is as keen as your master says it is,' said Hywel, addressing Dog, 'then a simple swipe would drop you right now.'

'It would,' said Dog, 'but I suspect you would be dead before your arm tensed enough to draw the blade.'

'And how would that work?'

In a flash of movement, Dog brought his stiletto dagger from his belt to point upward beneath the man's chin.

'It depends on who is quicker,' said Dog coldly, 'and I fancy my chances.'

The men nearby stopped what they were doing and walked over, some drawing their own blades.

'Hold,' shouted Hywel raising his hand but not taking his eyes off Dog. The pressure of the knife under his chin had already drawn a tiny droplet of blood and he knew that one thrust would send the blade into his skull. Silence fell around the lodge as both men weighed each other up.

'I like you, strange man,' said Hywel eventually, 'and think you would be a valued ally. For that reason, I will let you live.' He removed the scimitar from Dog's shoulder and offered it back, hilt first.

Dog lowered his knife and placed it back in his belt as the tension eased in the lodge. Hywel sat back onto the table top and looked the two men up and down.

'I suspect you have heard about Aberarth?' he asked as one of the slaves walked over to offer him a tankard of ale.

'We have,' said Tarw, also accepting one of the tankards, 'they say your army burned Dinerth Castle to the ground.'

'Aye, it is now no more than ashes blowing in the wind.'

'Did you lose many men?' asked Dog, replacing his scimitar into its sheath.

'A few but the gains were huge. Copper, slaves, coin and even a casket of gold. More importantly we have denied the English a safe haven in west Ceredigion.'

'And that is the part that interests me the most,' said Tarw. 'With those two castles gone, as well as Aberystwyth further north, the path to Deheubarth via the western coast road lies wide open and it would be remiss of us not to take advantage.'

'To do what, exactly?'

'To ride against the English as a united army,' said Tarw. 'They will be shocked at the extent of their defeats and will be confused as to what to do next. King Stephen still hides away in his London palace and sees us as no more than an irritating itch. All around us the dice fall favourably, and we have to take advantage.'

'There are still many Englishmen stationed across the south,' said Hywel, 'and dozens more castles. It will take an army ten times the size of mine to stand up to them.'

'And we will have that army,' said Tarw,' but it is yours that is the most important.'

'Why?'

'Because the blood of war still stains your warriors' blades and the embers of victory still burn in their bellies. If we can reignite that fire and with you in the vanguard, I believe it will encourage every man that follows to fight like they have never fought before.'

'And how far do you want us to go, Dinefwr?'

'As far as we can', said Tarw, 'but why stop at Dinefwr? If God is with us I don't see why we cannot grow in strength and sweep across the south to drive the invaders completely out of Wales.'

'I'll say this for you, Tarw,' said Hywel. 'Your ambition is untethered.'

'Is that bad thing?'

'Not at all. You remind me of myself as a younger man.'

'So, will you consider our proposal?'

'I'll tell you what I will do,' said Hywel. 'I have things to attend to, but tonight my men and I will feast on one of the deer we killed today. Join us and we will discuss your request over ale as all such things should be. There are spare wolf pelts and as long as you can find a space to lay down, you can share our roof.'

'I cannot ask for more,' said Tarw.

'Then it is settled. Get one of these good-for-nothing slaves to find you a space and see what is in the pot to allay your hunger. Tonight, we will talk.'

Without waiting for an answer, he stood and walked out of the lodge leaving the rest of his men to divest themselves of their riding gear.

Later that night, Tarw and Hywel sat next to the fire in the lodge talking between themselves. At the giant table, Dog ate with the rest of the warriors, exchanging exaggerated stories of valour in battle. Several slaves kept the warriors supplied with ale, often receiving slaps across the head for poor service.

What was left of a deer carcass lay in the centre of the table and each man cut off chunks of venison as he saw fit before using his hands and teeth to tear it into bite size pieces.

'So,' said Hywel, throwing a stripped deer rib into the fireplace, 'you really believe you can raise an army big enough to challenge the English?'

'Aye, I do,' said Tarw. 'All we need is the commitment from men such as you and there is nothing that can stop us.'

'Even if you achieve what you say you can,' said Hywel, 'and we march south with ten thousand men, the English can more than match our number.'

'Perhaps so, but they are little better than mercenaries on foreign soil while we will be fighting for freedom.'

'Many have fallen in the same quest.'

'Aye, but this time it is different. Everywhere I go across the kingdoms I see armies manned by those who once fought under the English banner. Those same men have now returned home and brought the skills of war back with them, skills that they pass on to others of a same ilk. Owain's army in particular have well drilled cavalry and a standing force of over two thousand warriors who train day in and day out. Combine those with men such as you who are no stranger to battle, and it is a potent mix.

'Even if we are victorious, what is to stop the English king sending a reinforcing army ten times our number to reclaim that which he has lost?'

'I have it on good authority that he is too concerned with the threat from Matilda to risk his main troops in Wales. If he was to direct his strength here, Matilda's army could land on the east coast of England and be in London within days. He would never risk it.'

'Perhaps in the short term but once his argument with Matilda is settled, he could turn his attention here.'

'Probably but that may be many years from now. We could use that time to consolidate as a united nation and by the time he or she turns to face us, they will realise we are a force to be reckoned with. They would be compelled to negotiate.'

Hywel fell silent for a few moments and leaned forward to stir the fire with an iron poker laying by the hearth.

'And what about payment?' he asked eventually. 'War is an expensive pastime.'

'There will be no payment,' said Tarw, 'but if everything falls into place, we will arrange to feed your men while on the march. Once battle commences, every man may keep whatever they take as bounty except from the churches or castle treasuries. That will be shared equally between those leaders who bring their armies to the field after Gwynedd's expenses have been deducted.'

'An attractive proposal,' said Hywel, 'for we found a very healthy treasury at Dinerth Castle.'

'The walls of the English treasuries bulge from their contents,' said Tarw, 'a wealth earned by Welsh blood to be spent by English royalty.'

Hywel took another draft of his ale before sighing and turning to face Tarw.

'I will sleep on it,' he said, 'and you will have my answer at sunrise. Until then, the time for such talk is done. Now we will get drunk and remember fallen friends.'

'To the fallen,' said Tarw and lifting up his tankard, sunk the contents in one.

At the main table, Dog got to his feet and staggered out of the lodge. His head was light from the ale, but he still had his wits about him. Outside he relieved himself against the wall and turned his head to see one of the warriors leaving the hut and heading toward the stable. The nervousness of the man's manner made Dog wonder what he was up to and he considered following him but soon returned to his senses. This was strange territory and it was none of his concern as to what Hywel's men got up to. He finished his business and returned to the stifling warmth of the lodge.

A few hundred paces away, the nervous man headed into the forest and waited near a tree marked with an x carved into the bark. Ten minutes later a hand grabbed his head from behind and he felt a blade against his neck.

'Keep still,' hissed a quiet voice, 'or you die right here.'

'I have something that you may want to know,' said the warrior without moving.

'It had better be good,' said the hidden man, 'I risked a lot coming here. What is it?'

'First the payment,' said the warrior, swallowing hard.

For a few moments there was silence until a leather purse of coins landed at the feet of the Welshman.

'Ten silver pennies as agreed,' said the voice, 'but if your information is poor, you get nothing.'

'There is a prince of Deheubarth in the lodge,' said the warrior, 'a man who goes by the name of Tarw. He is here to recruit an army against the English of Deheubarth.'

'An interesting development,' said the voice, 'but not one that worries me unduly. Why should I pay good money for this?'

'Because I have overheard him say that he has many of the Welsh kingdoms under his banner including Gwynedd and Powys. If this is true, then he could present a serious risk to the south.'

Again there was silence as the man considered the information.

'And you are sure about this?'

'I heard it myself.'

'Do you know the target of the campaign?'

'Down through Ceredigion and into Deheubarth via the western road.'

'When does he intend to march?'

'The date is unclear, but it will no doubt be before the winter snows.'

'Anything else?'

'No. He leaves here tomorrow so I thought I should let you know as soon as I could.'

'Why?'

'In case you need to cut him down on the trail.'

'No,' said the man eventually, 'that will alert his conspirators. We will let him make his plans and react accordingly. This may be the opportunity we need to wipe out any resistance once and for all. You have done well, my friend but know this. If this is a ruse, you will pay a price that no man should ever have to endure. Do you understand?'

'Aye,' said the warrior, 'I do.'

'Good. Now return to the lodge and keep your eyes and ears open. If you hear anything more that may be of interest, leave a message in the usual place.'

The pressure of the blade on the warrior's throat eased and a few moments later, he returned to the lodge, the weight of the purse a pleasing feeling in the inner pocket of his jerkin.

'Who's he?' asked Dog as the man sat down again at one end of the table.

'That's Edwin Crab,' said the half drunken warrior at his side. 'A strange one and no mistake. Why do you ask?'

'No reason,' said Dog, 'there is an unease about him that I find odd.'

'Like I said,' replied the warrior, 'he is a strange one and has few friends but enough about him, how about a game of dice?'

'Aye,' said Dog turning back to the table, 'but drink your fill while you can for by the time I have finished, you will be poorer than the lowliest of beggars.'

'We will see, master Dog,' replied the warrior with a laugh, 'we will see.'

Chapter Twenty-One

Cardigan

August AD 1136

Stephen Demareis walked the ramparts of Cardigan Castle with the steward and a scribe. Since his arrival after his flight from Aberystwyth he had become obsessed with the ensuring defences at Cardigan were as strong as they could be and in the absence of anyone senior, had taken it upon himself to ensure the same mistakes would never happen again. He looked down from the palisade to the river Teifi arcing along the rear of the castle and then over to the far bank.

'Master steward,' he said eventually, 'I understand this part of the river is tidal.'

'It is, my lord,' said the steward.

'At low tide, is it passable by a man?'

'No, my lord. The only way to approach this way is on a boat.'

Demareis looked down at the wooden wharf beneath the palisade.

'And that is the only place a boat can dock?'

'Yes, my lord.'

'Place bales of hay beneath it and have it guarded day and night by two men with fire pots. If we are attacked, I want it burned immediately.'

'My lord, that wouldn't make sense. Nobody in their right mind would attack across the river. Their ships would be easy targets for our fire arrows and besides, the wharf is needed for our own resupply ships.'

'If we are besieged, master steward, there will be no resupply from that direction. Have the preparations made immediately.'

'Of course,' said the steward and nodded to the scribe who noted the request on a sheet of parchment.

'Is the far bank in arrow range?' continued Demareis.

'To longbows, yes but we are well protected behind the palisade.'

Demareis looked along the ramparts.

'I want barrels of water every ten paces along this wall,' he said. 'In fact, place them around the whole perimeter and throughout the bailey.'

'To what end?' asked the steward.

'Fire arrows are terrible weapons, master steward,' said the new castellan, 'and we will be prepared should they be used against us. Now, how many arrows do we have?'

'The armouries are fully stocked, my lord. At least fifty barrels.'

'Get me a hundred more barrels,' said Demareis, 'and have them placed along the ramparts alongside the water. I don't want our own archers having to go and find them if needed. What about food?'

'Again, my lord, our granary is full, and our cellars hang with salt beef.'

'Livestock?'

'A hundred sheep on a nearby hill and a local farm tends fifty cows on our behalf.'

'I want half of them killed and butchered,' said Demareis. 'Preserve the meat in barrels of salt if needs be but I want this place able to withstand a long siege.'

'My lord,' said the Steward, 'please forgive me but do you not think we are perhaps preparing too much for a situation that may never happen? I mean, bearing in mind the strength of our forces across Deheubarth, it would be a foolish man who besieges a castle so able to summon reinforcements.'

'Perhaps so,' said the castellan, 'but I will take no chances. I was lucky to escape with my life in Aberystwyth, master steward and I know that if we were to face the same foe that we did there, I am unlikely to do so again. Have my orders carried out and gather whatever dried goods you can from the markets. I want to see every available space stacked high with barrels of food and fresh water. Sharpen every blade and drill the men in their defensive strategies until they can do them in their sleep.' He looked out over the palisade. 'If they come, master steward, I swear that this time we will be ready.'

Fourteen leagues from Cardigan, two riders made their way through the forests of Dinefwr. Their destination was the remains of the wooden castle that had once stood proudly on a hill above the plains but was now only charred shell of what it had once been. As the tree line came to an end, the first man reined in his horse and looked up at the damaged fortress, the place his family had once called home.

'It is worse than I remember,' said Tarw, 'and will take a lot of work to rebuild it to its former glory.'

'A problem for another day,' said Dog at his side. 'All we need to do at the moment is find somewhere safe to camp before any of the English spies recognise your face.'

'The forest trails are lightly trodden,' said Tarw. 'I doubt we were seen.'

'Even the trees have eyes,' said Dog. Come, 'we should go.'

The two men kicked their horses and followed the winding path up the hill towards the fire-blackened towers that had once held the impressive gate.

'Did you live here long?' asked Dog as they neared.

'Hardly at all,' said Tarw. 'When I was a boy my mother sent me to Ireland away from the attentions of the English. It was only when I was with Gwenllian that we lived here and even then, for only months at a time. We had to keep moving or feel the weight of the crown's wrath.'

'It looks like it was an impressive place,' said Dog.

'It was,' said Tarw. 'My sister often told me the tales of how it was growing up here and I am tainted with envy at the stories.'

'Perhaps it will be great again.'

'As long as I have breath left in my body,' said Tarw, 'then that is my goal.'

They stopped before the gateway into the castle and dismounted. The path was covered in deadfall and a stream had recently overflowed, leaving a residue of dried mud.

Tarw started to lead his horse carefully into the castle but stopped suddenly when Dog spoke quietly behind him.

'Wait.'

Tarw recognised the tone of his comrade's voice and froze where he stood. He turned around to see Dog kneeling on the ground running his fingers gently over an indent on the path.

'What is it?' asked Tarw.

'A footprint,' said Dog looking up, 'made less than a few hours ago.'

Both men stared at each other and as Dog got to his feet, Tarw started to withdraw his sword.

'Leave it where it is, stranger,' said a voice from the trees, 'else you will have a dozen arrows in your back before it clears the scabbard.'

Again, Tarw froze and stared at Dog, hardly daring to breathe. Slowly he eased the sword back into the scabbard.

'Now turn around,' said the voice.'

Tarw did as he was told and peered into the treeline a few paces to his front.

'Who are you?' asked the voice, 'state your business here.'

For a few seconds Tarw hesitated. If he told his true name and the ambushers were English, then he was a dead man.

'Speak truly, my lord,' said Dog quietly behind him, realising the dilemma, 'the English would have no need to hide amongst the trees.'

'My name,' said Tarw, 'is Gruffydd ap Rhys, prince of Deheubarth and I come seeking shelter in the castle of my ancestors.'

For a few moments there was silence until a man stepped out from behind a bush.

'A bold claim for one so bedraggled,' he said lowering his bow, 'can you prove it.'

'I will vouch for him,' said a voice and another man stepped out of the undergrowth a few paces away bearing a spear. 'I rode under his banner many years ago.'

Tarw turned to face the second man and recognised the face of one of his most loyal followers from when he and Gwenllian rode as rebels.

'John Hayman,' he said, realising he was amongst friends, 'I remember you well.'

'And I you, my lord,' said Hayman, walking over to the prince. 'I knew you would return here eventually.' The two men embraced roughly as the rest of the hidden warriors emerged from the trees. Amongst them were many faces Tarw recognised and they gathered around the prince, excited to be in his presence once again.

'What are you doing here, my lord?' asked Hayman, 'Deheubarth is crawling with English patrols. You could have been caught at any moment.'

'Indeed, we saw many,' said Tarw, 'but used the hidden paths of our fathers. I have come to seek those still loyal to the colours of Deheubarth to ride at my side against the English.'

The man glanced down the path and then back at the prince.

'Do you have an army?'

'I have enlisted many armies,' said Tarw, 'each willing to fight and die to release this country from beneath the English heel, but the one that is most important to me is the one not yet mustered.'

'And what army is that?'

'The one made up of men who have the blood of Deheubarth running in their veins,' replied Tarw. 'The one made up of the kin of those who died at Gwenllian's side in the shadow of Kidwelly Castle and the uncounted others whose bones creak under the weight of the English yoke. That is why I am here, John Hayman, to enlist those who will run no more.'

'Then you have come to the right place, my lord, for right here in the place your father called home there are men loyal and true already waiting to fill the front ranks.'

Tarw looked around the clearing estimating no more than thirty men.

'Is this your total number?'

'Some are out hunting, about twenty men in total but there are other places like this all across Deheubarth, each with bands of like-minded men waiting for the right time to show their arm.'

'You are scattered across the kingdom?'

'Aye. To gather in large numbers invites the attention of the castellans so we keep our bands small but make no mistake, each is as keen as the other to strike against the hand that felled Gwenllian.'

'Do you know where these men are?' asked Dog.

'Aye, we do. The English burn our manors and farms thinking they are denying us refuge, but it is there that those with revenge in their heart muster, amongst the ashes of the places they once called home. There is no better rallying call.'

'How many men in total?' asked Tarw.

'It is hard to be sure, but I would estimate over five hundred. Some are nothing more than farm hands, but others are seasoned warriors. All you have to do is send word and they will rally to your banner within days.'

Tarw turned to Dog.

'I told you this journey would not be in vain,' he said.

'Aye, you did,' said Dog. 'There is much to do but it is a good start.'

'Come,' said Hayman, stepping aside, 'we have shelter within the palisades and the approach roads are well guarded. Should any English patrols head this way we will be long gone before they even set eyes upon the castle.'

Tarw nodded and led his horse between the damaged gate towers. Inside the bailey, the remains of the castle buildings were almost totally destroyed and the keep that once stood proud atop the motte was nothing more than a pile of ashes but amongst the remains, he could see many tents and temporary shelters.

'The kitchens are relatively intact, my lord,' said Hayman, 'you can lay your bedroll there.'

'We have our own tent,' said Tarw. 'All we need is a space to pitch it.'

'With all due respect,' replied Hayman, 'we have waited a long time for you to return. Now you are here, please allow us to show the respect due to you as our leader and prince. The kitchens are no palace, but they are warm and dry.'

Tarw looked at Dog who shrugged his shoulders in return.

'Then I accept your offer,' said Tarw turning to Hayman, 'but only if there is space. I will take the place of no man already settled there.'

'I'm sure we can all budge up a little,' said Hayman. 'Come, leave your horses here and we will see what food we can find.'

'Not for me,' said Dog. 'I prefer more spacious quarters so will sleep elsewhere.'

Tarw nodded and turned away to follow Hayman to the kitchens built alongside one of the palisade walls.

'There's space for your tent near the northern wall,' said another man to Dog. 'Shall I take you there?'

'I can find my own way,' said Dog, 'but there is something you can get for me.'

'Food?' asked the man.

'Aye,' said Dog. 'That and ale.'

In central Wales, Cynwrig the Tall stood beside a lidded water barrel in the market square of Builth. All around him, people started to gather, all keen to hear the words of the strange priest who had been travelling between the villages of Wales preaching his message of unification. Eventually more than a hundred men and women assembled and Cynwrig turned to see Robert of Llandeilo walking toward him.

'Is this it?' asked Cynwrig nodding to the crowd.

'I've spread the word through every tavern and side street I could find.' said Robert. 'There may be a few more on their way but I would not recommend waiting any longer.'

Cynwrig nodded and climbed up on to the barrel. The noise from the crowd died away and the priest held out his arms in a welcoming gesture.

'Thank you for coming,' he said eventually as he looked around the crowd. 'I expect you are wondering why I have asked you to gather here today.'

'We know why,' said one of the men in the front of the crowd, 'you want us to fight and die in retribution for Gwenllian's death. She may have been a great woman but why should our sons also die?'

'That is not entirely correct,' said Cynwrig, 'though I understand that the rumours that precede my arrival can often get confused. I confirm that my crusade was instigated by the death of the princess for I have never met a godlier person. She spent most of her life fighting for freedom and the manner of her death underlined the contempt in which we are held by the English. However, my personal hurt is nothing compared to the upwelling I have seen across the breadth of this country. A trickle of anger has become a flowing river and that needs to be turned into a torrent.'

'Surely you do not expect to come to these villages and expect us to follow you?' said the man again. 'Who would feed our families while we are gone?'

'I expect no such thing,' said Cynwrig, 'in fact I expect nothing. All I ask is that you hear me out.'

'Go ahead, father,' said a woman from the back, 'you are here now so say your piece.'

'My friends,' said Cynwrig, 'you all know the story of Gwenllian and how she was beheaded after surrendering to save the lives of her men but perhaps we have lost sight of the woman she was.' He paused and looked around, knowing that the mere mention of the princess's name engendered fascination to all in earshot. 'Gwenllian ferch Gruffydd,' he continued, 'was a princess from one of the greatest houses of Wales yet she chose to forgo the trappings her birthright offered, choosing instead foliage for her roof and potage for her fayre.'

'For over twenty years,' he continued, 'she and her husband rode the hidden tracks of Wales putting pressure on the English supply lines and causing them to commit more resources to protect their interests. Many a supply caravan found themselves ambushed on the road and though they were made to pay a heavy toll to continue, few were killed unless they fought back. And what did she do with the toll? She gave it to the poor. That's right, after taking what little they needed for food, Gwenllian and Tarw redistributed any goods or money amongst the villages closest to the ambush.'

A murmur flowed around the crowd as the priest talked and more people gathered as the meeting went on.

'They did not kill for killing's sake but to help the needy and then only when circumstances demanded it. Yet such was the effect of her actions the king of England himself put a bounty on her head, one that was never claimed. Many men went willingly to the gallows rather than give up her whereabouts, such was the love in which she was held but alas, her life was ended when she was cruelly executed by Maurice de Londres on the field of battle after they had agreed terms of surrender.'

Cynwrig sensed the mood of the crowd changing to anger as he reminded them of the circumstances in which the warrior princess had died.

'And so,' he continued, 'it is for that reason that even as we speak, like minded men are traversing the Welsh kingdoms seeking support for what is nothing less, than a holy quest. Not only to revenge her death but to free us from the English heel once and for all.'

The crowd was visibly angry now, as he knew they would be. Even in the most peaceful of men, a yearning for freedom was only ever just beneath the skin and all he had to do was harness the passion.

'We haven't come here to take you away from your families,' he continued, his voice rising even higher, 'all we ask is ten men, strong and true to join with those from other villages who have already committed to our cause.'

'What difference can ten make?' asked a voice.

'Ten men from a hundred villages is a thousand in total,' said the priest, 'and there are countless villages across Wales. If each matches that commitment, we will be like the tide upon the shore. All we ask is for ten volunteers to commit and be willing to fight in Gwenllian's name. However, there is a part in this for you all to play.'

'Here it comes,' shouted a voice, 'he wants our money.'

'On the contrary,' said the priest, 'I will leave here today as poor as I rode in. What is yours is yours, but should ten men commit, then I would ask that the village supports their own by providing them with horses, food, weapons and enough coin to sustain them for a three-month campaign. If we can achieve that, then the rigours of the path to war will be eased for those taking up the call. Are you godly people willing to share that burden?'

'Aye,' came the reply from almost a hundred voices.

'When do you want us to ride,' shouted a young man in the crowd, 'for I swear I will be amongst those to bear arms.'

'In a few weeks,' said Cynwrig. 'When the time is ready, we will send riders to spread the word amongst the villages and when it comes, those who answer the call will muster in a given place under Tarw's banner.'

The crowd burst into chatter and Cynwrig nodded to Robert knowing that the moment was opportune.

'One more thing, my friends,' shouted Cynwrig as Robert removed a package from his horse, 'we would ask those willing to join us to register so we know what numbers to expect. Your names will be recorded by my comrade Robert of Llandeilo.'

'Where is the parchment,' asked the eager young man in the crowd, 'for I will make my mark forthwith.'

Cynwrig turned to face Robert at a nearby trestle table, knowing that the next few moments were the most important of all. Robert nodded slightly, confirming he was ready.

'Right there,' cried Cynwrig, 'beneath the blade of Gwenllian.'

Robert raised the sword and drove it down into the wooden planks of the table.

The crowd gasped in awe before falling silent as the weapon swayed from the impact. Many crossed themselves, conscious that the hilt formed the same shape as a cross and some fell to their knees, overcome by the emotion and symbolism.

'Well,' said Cynwrig, cutting through the silence, 'in the name of God and Gwenllian, who is with us?'

In the north, Gruffydd had recovered well from his illness and though he was still weak, he was able to leave his quarters for the first time in months. Today he had even dressed in his finery and on his head, he bore the crown of Gwynedd, the first time he had worn it in years.

Arm in arm with Angharad he walked slowly through the door into the great hall and made his way to the ornate wooden throne at one end before turning to face the many men who had been invited to one of the most important days Gwynedd had seen in a generation. Before him stood row after row of his finest warlords and at their head, his two eldest sons Owain and Cadwaladwr. Angharad helped Gruffydd into his seat and nodded to the steward, giving him authority to proceed.

The steward unfurled a parchment and cleared his throat.

'On behalf of Gruffydd ap Cynan, undisputed king of Gwynedd, I welcome you all to this house and pray you bear witness to all that is about to befall.' He lowered the parchment and turned to face the king.

'My lord,' he said, 'your subjects await your address.'

'You can speak from where you are,' said Angharad quietly as her husband struggled to his feet.

'Nonsense,' said Gruffydd, 'I am king and will act as one.' He stood as straight as he was able and although he could see nothing, everyone in the room felt he was looking directly at them.

'I have summoned you here today,' said Gruffydd, 'to share with you a choice that will change the world in which we live. As you know, my sons Owain and Cadwaladwr have recently returned from Aberystwyth after besieging and destroying one of the strongest castles in Ceredigion.'

A murmur of approval rippled around the hall.

'I have fought all my life to make Gwynedd what it is,' continued Gruffydd, 'and though we are as strong as any of the kingdoms across Wales, yet it has taken a lifetime to get where we are. We are safe, our people are well fed, and few go cold when the winter snows fall. Now, as I grow old, I often think that my work is done and we should enjoy what we have gained, but these past few months, many things have happened to make me reconsider my stance, not least the death of my daughter.' He paused as the significance of his loss sunk in and Angharad reached up to discreetly squeeze his hand. 'As we speak,' he continued, 'there are good men recruiting armies from across Wales, from Powys to Deheubarth, to ride against the English and they have petitioned me to join their campaign. I admit that I had my doubts but after the success of my sons, I am of a mind to join them. There is a feeling sweeping through Wales that I have not seen in my lifetime, one of anger fed by the need for justice and freedom. My sons have shown us that there is nothing to fear by marching south and with the new English king fighting off civil war even in his own corridors, I have to ask myself, if not now, then when?'

'My friends,' he said, his head turning as if he was looking around the hall, 'after taking advice from my most trusted warlords and my two sons, I hereby proclaim that Gwynedd will once more take up the sword and march against those that would do us harm. You are hereby ordered to muster your men and sharpen your axes for before the winds of autumn cross our fields, my sons, Owain and Cadwaladwr will lead the armies of Gwynedd to war.'

The roar of approval took the king by surprise and as their cheers echoed around the hall, Owain walked up to take his father's hand.

'My lord,' he said above the cheering, 'you know you have made the right decision and I swear we will do you proud.'

'Pride is not something I need,' said Gruffydd, 'but the grave looms and before I am laid to rest I need a settled mind.'

'You speak of retribution for Gwenllian?' asked Owain.

'Aye, I do. Carry her name before you as a banner, my son. Send a message up to heaven that we have not and will not ever forget her.'

Owain dropped to one knee and kissed his father's hand.

'I swear by God Almighty,' he said, 'that every drop of blood spilt will be in her memory.'

'Then go,' said Gruffydd quietly, 'and free this great land from the oppression of generations.'

Owain stood up and kissed his mother's cheek before turning to the still cheering men.

'Well,' he roared, *'there is a war to be fought, what are you waiting for?'*

In Pembroke, one of the stable hands ran across the bailey of Pembroke castle and up the steps of the motte to the keep. One of the two permanent guards stepped forward and stopped him as he approached the door.

'What do you want, boy?' he asked, his manner surly.

'I have an important message for the castellan,' said the boy.

'From who?'

'I know not but the pigeon that carried it was one of a batch we sent to Powys.'

'Give it here,' said the guard, 'I will pass it on.'

The boy handed the message over and returned to his duties as the guard entered the keep and walked up the stairs to knock on the door of Salisbury's quarters

'My lord,' he said after the castellan had bid him enter, 'a message arrived for you a few moments ago.'

Salisbury took the pouch and carefully unwrapped it before walking over to the window to benefit from the extra light. His eyes scanned the tiny writing before discarding it on a side table and turning to face the waiting guard.

'Find the steward,' he said, 'and tell him to attend me immediately.'

'Aye, my lord,' said the guard and left the room.

'What is it?' asked Nesta from his bed.

'Nothing that is any concern of yours,' snapped Salisbury, 'and would do well to mind your own business. Get dressed and return to your quarters. You will wait there until summoned.'

'Of course,' said Nesta and got out of the bed to retrieve her clothes.

Twenty minutes later, Salisbury and the steward sat at a table in the castellan's quarters discussing the message.

'So, who sent it?' asked the steward.

'The name of the man is not important,' said Salisbury. 'Suffice to say it is someone I trust.'

'One of your spies?'

'Aye. He is riding here as we speak with important information but in the meantime, he has sent us this warning.'

'What does it say?'

'Basically,' said Salisbury throwing the tiny parchment across the table, 'it says we need to prepare for war.'

Chapter Twenty-Two

Mid Ceredigion

September AD 1136

Owain and Cadwaladwr looked down into the valley from their viewpoint high upon a hill. Spread out below them was an enormous military camp, stretching as far as the eye could see. Their army had left Gwynedd over ten days earlier yet was still only a few day's ride from Abefraw. A frustrating situation but one born out of necessity.

Hundreds of tents lay dotted across the landscape and many campfires sent swirling columns of smoke high into the evening air. In the distance, well drilled cavalry carried out their never ending manoeuvres, practising every situation they could think of in anticipation of the battles to come. Archers fired arrow after arrow into targets on the slopes of the hill before retrieving them and starting all over again while men at arms practiced their spear lunges and shield walls under the belligerent eyes of the experienced sergeants.

'I have to admit,' said Cadwaladwr, 'our strength surpasses that which I had anticipated.'

'Father has been true to his word,' said Owain, 'and there is only a small force left to defend Gwynedd if there should be a need.'

'Nobody will be looking at Gwynedd any time soon,' said Cadwaladwr, 'all eyes will be on Ceredigion and Deheubarth.'

'I hope so,' said Owain. 'Anyway, what news of our allies?'

'The Powys army is on the move,' said Cadwaladwr, 'as are the men of Gwent. They should be here in a few days.'

'And Brycheniog?'

'Hywel ap Maredudd has not replied as yet but he is hard to find. The messages from Tarw swear that Maredudd has sworn his commitment but we have heard nothing.'

'We need to know soon,' said Owain, 'for we cannot wait much longer.'

'The men are not idle and train hard,' said Cadwaladwr, 'and the supply caravans stretch from here to Ynys Mon.'

'Aye, but they cannot continue like that indefinitely. We have calculated we need enough food for three months and that includes anything that we can scavenge en route.'

'Once we start moving,' said Cadwaladwr, 'there will be no stopping us and the Ceredigion farms in the south will yield whatever crops or livestock they have. Until then, we should finalise our tactics.'

'Aye,' said Owain, 'we should but before then, there is something I want you to see.'

He turned his horse and rode along the ridge to a small copse near the top of the valley. On the far side of the trees, they dismounted and walked over to a line of over five hundred archers, each aiming their arrows at distant targets. Behind them were hundreds more, waiting their turn.

'I heard about these men,' said Cadwaladwr, 'they have been practising in the fields across Ynys Mon.'

'Aye, they have,' said Owain, 'they arrived last night and there are more on the way. It was the idea of our mother many months ago, they have been selected for their expertise with a longbow.'

'We already have many archers,' said Cadwaladwr, 'each well trained in the ways of war and able to react at a moment's notice. These men are nothing more than farmers and hunters.'

'They are exactly that,' said Owain, 'but the power and accuracy their longbows bring to the battle will stand us in good stead.'

'Perhaps so,' said Cadwaladwr, 'but once the enemy closes in, there is no place for untrained men. Our forebears learned that the hard way over many generations.'

'Warfare changes all the time, brother,' said Owain. 'Perhaps there is a place in all armies for such men.'

'Well we will see soon enough,' said Cadwaladwr, 'and I hope you are right. For their sakes if nothing else.'

In Dinefwr, Tarw had received the message about Gruffydd's decision to march south weeks earlier and had spent the time mustering whatever men he could to his banner. Riders had been sent far and wide to issue the call and as men started to turn up at the castle ruins Tarw had withdrawn his forces further into the dense forests that made up the majority of the Cantref Mawr.

The camp was busy as men continued to trickle in and though his force was growing daily, he had nowhere near the numbers enjoyed by Owain and Cadwaladwr.

'What do you think?' Tarw asked Dog as his men trained hard amongst the trees of a hidden valley.

'I'd like to say their passion will overcome their inexperience,' said Dog, 'but I fear it would be a misleading statement.'

'Time is not on our side,' said Tarw, 'and we must do the best we can with what we have.'

'When do we march?'

'Owain will send riders a full day before they break camp and by my reckoning, we can be with him within two days somewhere north of Cardigan. In the meantime, we need to keep doing what we can to make these men as good as they can be.'

'Suddenly it gets real,' said Dog, 'and if truth be told, it forms a spark of doubt in my heart.'

'In what way?' asked Tarw.

'I have killed many men, my lord, and am no stranger to death but when I look down there and see boys trying to be men, then I have to admit a darkness clouds my soul.'

'The price is outweighed by the rewards,' said Tarw, 'you know that.'

'Aye I do. But it does not mean I have to enjoy it.'

Tarw fell silent and before drawing his sword and walking towards the nearest group of sweating young men.

'Where are you going?' asked Dog.

'To help with the training,' said Tarw. 'Like you said, most are only boys bearing men's weapons so if I can teach even one of them a useful parry, then perhaps a life can be lengthened. Come, let's see what we can do.'

In mid-Wales, a column of five hundred men at arms and over two hundred cavalry wound its way past a motte and bailey castle high on a hill. Though the castle was in English hands, Hywel ap Maredudd feared no interference from the occupants for he knew his force was far too strong to be attacked.

'My lord,' said the officer at his side, 'we are being watched from the treeline. Do you want my men to cut them down?'

'No,' said Hywel, 'by now every Englishman within twenty leagues will already know we are on the march so we will waste no more time. We have to rendezvous with the Gwynedd army before the moon is full.'

'Do you know where?'

'At the moment all I know is it will be somewhere north of Cardigan. Owain will send details in the next day or so. In the meantime, we press on.'

'Aye, my lord,' said the officer and kicked his heels into his horse.

'Well, Tarw,' said Hywel quietly to himself, 'you have truly stirred up a hornet's nest in your late wife's name, I just hope you know what you are doing.'

Chapter Twenty-Three

Cardigan Castle

October 6th AD 1136

Stephen Demareis stood atop one of the towers and stared out in awe at the vast English camp that had materialised outside the castle walls over the last few days. Tents filled every available space and he knew that hundreds more were pitched in the fields on either side of the river. Armed men marched everywhere, and the ground was already a quagmire beneath their feet.

News of the Welsh threat had spread like wildfire and every spare man had been sent to bolster the army assembling in Cardigan under the command of Robert Fitzmartin, the Lord of Cemais.

'My lord,' said a voice behind the castellan, 'your presence is required in the main hall.'

Demareis turned and climbed down the ladder before heading up the motte and into the keep. Although he was now essentially the castellan of Cardigan Castle, Lord Fitzmartin was in overall charge and assumed total control of every decision regarding the forthcoming battle.

He entered the hall and saw two trestle tables had been pushed together and covered with a large linen map showing the local landscape. Around the table stood a group of English knights and other nobles who had joined them to defend Cardigan from the Welsh aggressors.

The talk was subdued as Demareis took his place at the table. The map was impressive and surprisingly detailed. Their scouts had been busy for days and the information they brought was as accurate as it could be in the circumstances.

'Gentlemen,' said a voice from one end of the room and everyone turned to see Lord Fitzmartin entering the hall along with two other men. 'I apologise for keeping you waiting but I was being briefed by these two men, John of Salisbury and Maurice de Londres. You may know that they were responsible for defeating a strong Welsh army earlier this year and their experience will be invaluable.' He walked up to the table and looked around the gathered nobles.

'Most of us already know each other,' he said, 'so we will skip introductions and I will explain as we go if needs be but first of all, let me summarise the situation as I see it.'

'As you know, a few months ago our comrade Robert Fitzgilbert was brutally murdered in Powys, the victim of a cowardly ambush by Morgan ap Owen, a brigand who lays spurious claim to the throne of Gwent. Unfortunately, our friend's untimely death left Ceredigion rudderless and it seems that Gruffydd ap Cynan, another Welshman with claims above his station, saw it as an opportunity to ignore any treaties previously agreed and march southward to ravage territories belonging to the English crown.' He looked around the room, the anger and disgust clear upon his face. 'It is apparent,' he continued, 'that so far they have managed to destroy the castles at Aberystwyth, Dinerth and Caerwedros as well as laying waste to much of north Ceredigion and now, having sampled the taste of victory, think they are strong enough to bring their campaign south. Well I have been sent here, my friends, to tell you and the rest of Wales that this is not going to happen.'

A murmur of approval rippled around the room as Lord Fitzmartin continued.

'King Stephen himself is fully aware of the threat and has empowered me to commit whatever resources necessary to put a stop to this madness once and for all. As far as we are aware, the enemy numbers about seven thousand in total including some brigand from the east. Now that is indeed an impressive number, but these men are mostly farmers who have been called up to fill their ranks, or rebels more used to hiding in the forests than fighting on a field of battle.'

'My lord,' said Demareis, 'please forgive me, but may I make an observation?'

'Of course,' said Fitzmartin.

'My lord, I was at Aberystwyth when Owain besieged the castle, and barely escaped with my life. I can assure you the men who attacked that day were not simply conscripted farmers or unorganised brigands, they were well trained and well equipped. We should not take them lightly.'

'Thank you,' said Fitzmartin, 'and of course you are correct. Any army capable of felling a castle should be taken seriously but consider this. Outside these walls, we are assembling the largest army ever seen in Wales. Already there are almost five thousand Norman levies, drafted in from across Wales and the south of England. Another nine hundred are on their way along with another thousand, battle-hardened Flemish mercenaries. Add to that the cavalry that myself and Maurice Fitzgerald bring to the field and we have a well-balanced army of over ten thousand men, all experienced in the ways of war. With respect, my friend, I would suggest that even half that number is well able to defeat those who deem to challenge us.' He turned to one of the men at his side. 'Wouldn't you agree, John?'

John of Salisbury looked around. Every eye was upon him and despite his meteoric rise to power in Deheubarth, he knew it meant nothing to the men in this room. So far, he had proved nothing and most of the others present were either of noble birth or had worked their way through the ranks to achieve a level of respect he could only dream of. Some, like Fitzmartin had the ear of the king himself.

'My lords,' he said eventually, 'as you are aware, a combined force of my own men and those under the command of Maurice de Londres defeated a Welsh army in the shadows of Kidwelly Castle a few months ago. An army led by none other than the witch Gwenllian herself. As usual, their tactics were to fight from the shadows like cowards and it has to be said, in such circumstances they have no peers. However, once we managed to flush them out onto the open field, they were almost infantile in their tactics.'

'Explain,' said one of the men on the opposite side of the table.

'For a start, there were no cavalry,' said Salisbury turning to face him, 'and many wore no chain mail or gambesons. Those who did were ill practiced in the ways of war and were slow in their movement. Their tactics were poor, as was the discipline. A few passes by our cavalry left them scattered like leaves in a wind and though they were brave in their manner, they were easy targets for our archers.'

'I heard Gwenllian yielded,' said the man, 'yet she was executed on the field of battle. Was that wise?'

'It was necessary,' said Salisbury, 'Deheubarth has suffered from years of rebellion and brigandry at the hands of that woman and her followers. At the time, she and her husband were planning an assault on the castles of Pembroke and Kidwelly so

when we finally cornered her on the field of battle, it was an
opportune moment to end her reign of brigandry once and for all.'

'But did she not surrender?'

'With respect, my lord,' interjected Maurice de Londres,
'you were not subject to the years of fear that woman wrought
upon Deheubarth. Perhaps if you had, then your perception of the
morality of such an action may have been different.'

'Gentlemen,' said Fitzmartin, 'what is done is done and we
are not here to argue amongst ourselves. Our role is to stop this
Welsh uprising in its tracks and ensure they will never again see fit
to challenge the crown. Every man in this room has skills or
information that will bring about that situation so to that end, we
are all charged with planning the coming confrontation.' He turned
and nodded to one of his younger captains who emptied a bag of
white chess pieces on the table and started placing them around the
drawing of Cardigan Castle.

'As you know,' said the captain as he arranged the pawns,
'within the next few days we will be at full strength and our forces
are mustered here. Each figure represents a hundred men or a
hundred horses and as you can see, our numbers are impressive.'
He moved along the table and emptied another bag, this time of red
pieces. 'According to our scouts,' he continued as he placed the
red pawns tightly together, the bulk of the enemy are here, camped
in a valley somewhere in the centre of Ceredigion. However, we
also have intelligence that there are others on their way to join
them.' He spread out some of the figures to the east of Cardigan
and more to the south. 'Again, our scouts are busy providing
information and though these columns in themselves are not a
threat directly, they open up two further fronts where we may have
to commit large numbers. Using this map, it is our intention to plan
our strategies accordingly.'

When all the figures were in place he stepped back, and all
the men manoeuvred to get a better view. The white pieces were
more numerous, but it was the three different red positions that
gave most cause for concern.

'So,' said Fitzmartin. 'The situation is this. At first we
thought the enemy was going to launch a three-pronged attack on
Cardigan and made our plans accordingly. However, it soon
became apparent that Owain's army in the north was waiting for
something. We now believe it was for those other two columns to
reinforce their number.'

'So, they are going to attack as one?' asked Salisbury.

'We think so. Our scouts have reported both columns have changed direction and are on course to rendezvous with Owain in the next day or so.'

'We should intercept the smaller columns now,' said one of the men, 'while their numbers are few and victory is assured.'

'I disagree,' said Salisbury looking at the map. 'I know these routes, and both are heavily wooded. If we attack them there they will be in their element and any numerical superiority on our part will be nullified. The sort of numbers needed to ensure an advantage would severely weaken our defences here at Cardigan and invite an immediate assault by Owain's main army in the north.'

'My thoughts exactly,' said Fitzmartin, 'so we need to face them on open ground. My suggestion is this.' He leaned over and moved the two separate groups of red pawns to join the larger group in the north. 'We allow them free passage to join with Owain but in the meantime, reconnoitre a suitable open place to meet them on the field of battle away from Cardigan itself. By doing so, we will deny them the cover of the forests they appear to favour.'

'My lord,' said Demareis, 'if I may, I know of such a place.'

'Show me,' said Fitzmartin.

The castellan leaned over and pointed at a thick black line already drawn on the linen map.

'This is the main road south from Gwynedd to Cardigan,' he said. 'There are others, but they are impassable for an army the size of Owain's.' He pointed at a position three quarters along the line toward Cardigan. 'This place here,' he continued, 'is a hill called Crug Mawr. It is situated at the lower end of a shallow valley and lies directly on the road southward. If we deployed there, we would have the advantage of higher ground and clear views of anyone approaching from the north. If Owain is determined to reach Cardigan, then he has to come that way.'

'Is it forested?'

'No, my lord. The area was cleared for grazing many years ago.'

'Is the lower ground suitable for horses?'

'Aye, it is flat and hard with no streams or fences as I recall. A defeated foe would have nowhere to hide and would be forced to retreat northward.'

'Pursued by our cavalry,' said one of the men quietly. 'It would be a slaughter.'

'Assuming we are victorious,' said another.

'Victory is not in doubt here,' said Fitzmartin, 'we have over ten thousand fully trained men at arms under our command and face a foe less than two thirds that number made up of rebels and farmers. Our cavalry will tear their lines apart and when they do, our Flemish mercenaries will be upon them like wolves on sheep. This is our opportunity to subjugate this country once and for all.' He looked around the gathered commanders. 'Are there any naysayers?'

The men looked at each other in silence, finally turning to face their commander.

'In that case,' said Fitzmartin, 'it seems like we have found our position. Send word to the sergeants to prepare the army. Tomorrow, we march on Crug Mawr.'

Chapter Twenty-Four

Ceredigion

October 8th AD 1136

Owain sat astride his horse talking to one of his advance patrols alongside his brother. The scouts had ridden several leagues forward, backed by over a hundred cavalry to ensure there were no ambushes along the road and had returned to give their reports.

Behind them the Welsh army stretched out as far as the eye could see, columns of armed men interspersed with heavily laden wagons as they made their way south. On the flanks, more cavalry rode the slopes of the ridges and far to the rear came the herders, driving the cattle that were so important in maintaining a campaign this far away from home.

'Well,' said Owain, 'is the way clear?'

'Aye it is,' said the scout, 'for the next five leagues or so.'

'And after that?'

'We are not sure yet. Our spies inform us that the English army are on the move and have headed out of Cardigan toward Crug Mawr. If that is the case, they will have their own patrols out and you said to hold back from any engagement.'

Owain glanced at his brother with concern.

'Did you not say that Crug Mawr was an important landmark on our march?'

'Aye it is. From the crest you can see as far as Cardigan and it would have made a good staging post from which to launch our attack on the castle.'

Owain turned back to face the scout.

'When will they get there?'

'I am told their vanguard will be there by dark tonight and the rest of the army sometime tomorrow.'

'Then it is denied to us?'

'Aye.'

Owain fell silent, considering his options. Though battle was inevitable, the fact that he would now have to engage an enemy that held the vital high ground made it all the harder.

'Any news of Hywel ap Maredudd?' he asked.

'He will be here within two days,' said the Scout.

'And Tarw?'

'No word for several days, my lord, but I know he is on his way. It may be advantageous to hold back until they both get here.'

'No,' interjected Cadwaladwr, 'we have waited long enough. Our advance has momentum and to delay even longer would allow the enemy time to fortify their defences on Crug Mawr. I say we press on and set up camp in full view of the English. When they see what they are up against it may send fear into their souls.'

'I agree,' said Owain looking toward the mass of men filing past their position. 'To hesitate may put doubt in the minds of our own forces and that is a risk we cannot afford. Keep your men on alert and let me know the moment anything changes.'

'Aye, my lord,' said the scout and turned his horse away to ride southward.

'It is the right decision,' said Cadwaladwr watching as the man rode away. 'This war is now inevitable, and anything less than full commitment would be seen as a weakness by friend and foe alike.'

Owain looked up at the sky.

'Another few hours until dark,' he said, 'but now we know that Crug Mawr is unattainable as a position, I think we should set up camp early and let the men rest. Tomorrow night, some of them may not have that luxury.'

Ten leagues away, the hill called Crug Mawr was a hive of activity. On the southern slopes and in the fields to either side of the road leading into Cardigan, thousands of men had set up camp and were busy preparing for the battle they knew was coming. The mood was light-hearted for though the eve of battle was always a tense time for any man of war, the knowledge of their superior number and quality of forces instilled a sense of confidence seldom felt on any field of conflict.

Fitzmartin and John of Salisbury walked along the track leading up to the top of the hill. Men sat on both sides as far as the eye could see, most sitting at their camp fires, cooking the hunks of salted beef or fish supplied by the store wagons of the English army.

'Good food?' asked Fitzmartin as he passed one group.

'Aye, my lord,' said the soldier, 'we have no complaints.'

'Good,' said Fitzmartin. 'We need you as strong as possible over the next few days.' He walked on, exchanging small talk with many of his men, a trait he was well known for and his men loved him for it.

'You are very personal with your men,' said Salisbury as they walked.

'It costs nothing,' said Fitzmartin nodding to a familiar face. 'And it engenders comradeship amongst the men.'

'I don't understand,' said Salisbury.

'We are normally the faceless commanders who stay to the rear while these men face the steel of the enemy,' said Fitzmartin. 'They die in our name and yet many would not recognise us if we knocked upon the doors of their houses. The least we can do is to let them put a face to a name.'

'I disagree, my lord,' said Salisbury as they neared the top of the path. 'Such men will do as they are ordered and no more. Do you not think that they would be elsewhere if they did not fear the gallows?'

'Some perhaps,' said Fitzmartin, 'but many are here through loyalty, if not to me, then to their comrades. My presence is no more than a banner but nevertheless, it sends out a message that we are all in this together.'

The conversation ended as they neared the crest of the hill. All along the crest, dozens of sentries stood ten paces apart, each holding a spear and wrapped in heavy cloaks against the chill of the evening air as they stared north, alert for any sign of the Welsh army.

'My lord,' said a voice as a man walked out of the gloom towards Fitzmartin. 'I was not expecting you.'

'Are you the guard commander?' asked Fitzmartin.

'Aye, my lord. I have almost a hundred men on guard up here and a hundred more at base of the hill with the same number sleeping back in the tents. They are rotated regularly so no man gets tired.'

'What about further north?'

'We have scouts out,' said the guard commander, 'and they will give us plenty of notice should there be any movement, but we do not expect anything before tomorrow at the earliest.'

'Why do you say that?' asked Salisbury.

'Look there,' said the commander pointing northward, 'beyond that far hill.'

'I see nothing,' said Salisbury screwing up his eyes. 'What am I looking for?'

'As it becomes darker,' said the guard commander, 'it will become more obvious. There is an unnatural glow from behind the ridge line. That is the light from the hundreds of enemy camp fires. They are at least a full day's march away.'

'Could it not be a ruse?' asked Salisbury, 'a distraction while they advance under the cover of darkness?'

'Our scouts inform us differently,' said Fitz- Martin, 'and I agree with our guard commander here. We have no more than a day to prepare.'

In Pembroke Castle to the south, Nesta walked briskly across the bailey. This time she was alone as the Lady Anwen was laid up with an ague and as most of the garrison had been called up to the army in Cardigan, it was relatively simple to get out of the keep without raising any undue concerns. Rowan was one of those still stationed in the castle and at last, after several days trying she had managed to get a message to him. Quickly she headed into the stable and walked carefully through the gloom toward the furthest stall.

'Is anyone in here?' she whispered nervously.

'Aye,' came a voice, 'over here.'

Nesta made her way into the darker shadows to find Rowan waiting for her.

'Rowan,' she said, touching his arm, 'thank you for coming. I thought you may have left with the rest.'

'I have been laid up with a fever,' said the soldier, 'and only today was I able to stand for the first time in over a week. I suspect I will be sent up to Cardigan soon enough.'

'Then we have little time. I have a plan and I need your help.'

'To do what?' asked Rowan.

'To help Maelgwyn escape from his cell.'

The soldier stared at Nesta in shock.

'My lady,' he said, 'you know not what you ask! If I do this I will be hung as a traitor, we both will.'

'Only if we are caught,' said Nesta.

'My lady, it's not possible.

'There has to be a way,' said Nesta, 'the castellan is in Cardigan as are most of his men. This is an opportunity to be grasped with both hands for when he comes back, I suspect he will wed me within days and kill Maelgwyn.'

'Even if I could get him out,' said Rowan, 'where would he go?'

'Leave that to me,' said Nesta. 'I have people waiting to spirit him away. Once he is clear of Pembroke, Salisbury will never find him.'

'And what about you?'

'What about me?'

'You can't stay here with Salisbury, especially if Maelgwyn escapes. He will take his frustrations out on you.'

'I care not about myself, Rowan,' said Nesta. 'I have seen enough tragedy to last ten lifetimes and if truth be told, I am tired of it all. Once Maelgwyn is free, Salisbury can do to me what he will and if that includes a hangman's noose then so be it.'

'No,' said Rowan eventually, 'I will not do it.'

'You have to, Rowan,' replied Nesta, 'this may be his only chance.'

'I cannot, my lady. By doing so it will be as if I am signing your death warrant myself and that is a burden I will not bear.'

'Rowan,' said Nesta, 'I am begging you. Please, that boy has lost his mother and his brother in terrible circumstances. If it was not for me, Salisbury may never have found out about Gwenllian's plans in the first place and she could still be alive. He has been tortured to within an inch of his life because of me and he knows that the best he can hope for is a swift death. Please don't let him suffer anymore.'

'What do you mean, because of you?' asked Rowan. 'What has Gwenllian's death to do with you?'

Nesta hung her head for a few moments and when she looked up, there were tears in her eyes.

'I knew of Tarw and Gwenllian's plans,' said Nesta,' and was helping them from inside the castle.'

'Helping them, how?'

'By passing on information via my maid. I would find out what I could and send messages to the Cantref Mawr. Alas, Salisbury found out and fed me false information. Gwenllian marched to her death because of my failure to establish the facts. Her death and that of all those poor men who died alongside her weighs heavy upon my soul, so if I can do the slightest thing to make amends, even if it should cost me my life, then it is a path I am willing to take.'

'My lady,' started Rowan but his voice fell away as she stared pleadingly into his eyes.

'Rowan, I am already in hell. Please grant me this tiniest of hopes. I know God will never forgive me for what I did but if I can gain the life of Gwenllian's son, then perhaps at least her soul may rest a little easier.' As she finished, the tears started to flow, and she flung herself forward to bury her face in the soldier's shoulder.

The soldier was momentarily taken aback. The chance to even talk to someone like Nesta was out of reach to most men but to have her bare her soul and seek comfort was a situation he could never have envisaged. For a few moments he froze but eventually lifted his arms to hold her to him. As he did, her body shuddered with anguish and as she cried in his arms, he knew he could not decline her request.

'My lady,' he said, pushing her gently away, 'please, compose yourself.'

Nesta wiped her eyes with the loose sleeve of her dress.

'I'm sorry,' she said eventually, 'I don't know what came over me. Please forgive me my moment of indiscretion.'

'There is nothing to forgive,' he said. Not for your request or the fact that soulless men used you to gain advantage. You thought you were doing right before God and it was Salisbury that turned that situation into the deaths of so many men. The guilt is his, not yours.'

'Whatever way you look at it,' said Nesta, 'it does not change the fact that people have died and are still dying because of my input. Even this impending war can be traced back to me as it was I that caused Gwenllian's death. If I had not done what I did, then she would still be alive and her brothers would not be seeking revenge.'

'You take on too much responsibility,' said Rowan. 'This war has been a long time coming and even if Gwenllian still lived, how long do you think it would have been before the yoke of the English became too heavy?' Do not increase your burden, my lady, for much of it lays elsewhere.'

Gwenllian looked at the soldier, realising he was one of the very few friends she had left in the castle.

'Thank you,' she said eventually, 'and of course, you are correct. I cannot ask you to risk your life for Maelgwyn, the responsibility is mine and mine alone. Please forgive my plea.'

She turned to walk away but Rowan reached out and grabbed her arm.

'Wait,' he said, 'I will help you but on one condition.'

Nesta turned around and looked at the soldier.

'Anything,' she said.

'My lady,' continued Rowan, 'I think there may be a way, but it is very dangerous. I will probably fail but if God is on our side and I can release him, my condition is that you also leave this place and ride to safety beside him.'

'I cannot leave,' said Nesta, 'I have responsibilities.'

'To who?' asked Rowan, 'not to Salisbury, that's for sure.'

'The people of Deheubarth need me,' said Nesta, 'I am the last link back to the time when my father ruled this kingdom. Without me they would have nothing.'

'That may be true,' said Rowan, 'but they need you alive not dead. If I manage to free Maelgwyn, it would be your neck in the noose and that helps no one. Make the escape arrangements for you as well as Maelgwyn and I will do what you ask. That is the best I can offer.'

'And what about you?' asked Nesta. 'Will you come with us?'

'If God spares me in this venture then I will also run,' said Rowan, 'but it is a task I will not contemplate unless you give me your assurance you will flee this place alongside your nephew.'

For a few moments Nesta stared at the guard again.

'In that case,' she said eventually, 'I agree. If you can get Maelgwyn out, I will arrange safe passage for three into the Cantref Mawr and from there to a place of safety.'

'Thank you, my lady,' said the soldier. 'Now you should leave before your absence is noticed. I will send a message via the cook when I have news.'

Nesta threw her arms around the soldier, this time in gratitude rather than upset.

'Thank you,' she whispered, 'and I swear that if we are successful then you will be suitably rewarded.'

'Your life and happiness are all the reward I need,' said Rowan. Now be gone, there are things to prepare.'

Nesta turned and disappeared into the evening darkness. Behind her, Rowan 's hand crept to the handle of his knife as he thought of what lay before him. One way or the other, his time at Pembroke castle would soon be at an end.

Chapter Twenty-Five

Crug Mawr

October 10th AD 1136

Despite the numbers of men on the field, the dawning day held a reverential silence, as if knowing that before the sun set, thousands would lie dead or dying in the autumn mud. Mist rolled gently across the valley, reluctant to lift its deathly veil on the men shivering in the morning air as they waited for the battle to start. Row after row of men at arms stood patiently side by side, their fingers flexing around spear shafts or caressing the hilts of their swords to keep the blood flowing in chilled fingers. Most were clad in high quality chainmail or closely packed gambesons and every single man bore a shield displaying the colours of their allegiance.

The Gwynedd infantry made up the vanguard backed up by the men brought by Morgan ap Owain from Gwent. Behind them came the massed ranks of the civilian longbowmen, everyone nervous about the forthcoming battle.

As was usual in such formations, the cavalry deployed on either flank, having been reinforced the previous evening by the arrival of Hywel ap Maredudd and his men from Brycheniog and though their horses were smaller than the magnificent destriers preferred by the English, their smaller stature and stocky frames meant they were far more suited to the rugged Welsh terrain.

Further back, hundreds of supply wagons lay scattered randomly across the valley as even the cart-masters had abandoned their roles to join their comrades. Untended camp fires sent the last of their smoke skyward and flocks of crows hopped hopefully between the tents seeking any titbits the men had left the previous night. This was a day when every blade counted and there was nowhere for anyone to hide.

In all, the Welsh army was made up of over eight thousand men including the cavalry and though such numbers were not unknown on the field of battle, this time it was different for unlike the ragtag forces of their predecessors, the assembled men were fully equipped, well trained and had a common purpose. To rid Ceredigion and Deheubarth of their English overlords.

At the head of the army, Owain sat motionless upon his horse, his heavy cloak wrapped tightly around him. On his right was his brother Cadwaladwr and on his left Hywel ap Maredudd. All were silent as they waited for the mist to reveal what lay before them.

'Are your men ready for this?' asked Owain to Hywel. 'You have been here hours only.'

'Worry about your own men,' said Hywel, 'mine are well used to war and are keen to dull their blades on English bone.'

'Your victory at Gower is celebrated across the kingdoms,' said Owain. 'We are lucky to have you at our side.'

'Tarw is a persuasive man,' said Hywel, 'though I am surprised that he is not here alongside us.'

'He is on his way,' said Cadwaladwr, 'I just hope he can join us before we engage.'

'Whether he is or not,' said Owain, 'we cannot rely on his numbers and must use what we have.' He looked up at the sun. 'A few more minutes and this mist will be gone and when it does, we will see the size of the task before us.'

'So, what are you expecting?' asked Hywel, straining his eyes to see as far as he could down the valley.

'Crug Mawr lies directly ahead,' said Cadwaladwr. 'Our scouts tell us the English have left Cardigan and assembled on and around the hill.'

'So, they have the advantage of the high ground?'

'They do.'

'Is there no other way around?'

'No,' said Owain. 'The other routes invite ambush. This is the only road that lets us deploy our full strength.'

'And you intend to face them on an open field?'

'I do. My father's army is well versed in the tactics used by the English. Many fought for their king in France and we have taken many lessons on board.'

'Still,' said Hywel, 'to face an English army in the open is a risk that may demand a heavy price.'

'Any death is a heavy price,' said Owain, 'whether it be one man or a thousand. Today, many will die on both sides but with God's grace, they will pave the way for a free Wales.'

Again, the three men fell silent but as the last of the mist spiralled away, a solitary dog started barking in the abandoned camp behind them as if in shock at the strength of the foe being unveiled.

'Oh, sweet Jesus,' murmured a voice from one side, 'they've brought the whole damned English army with them.'

Owain ignored the remark and focused his attention on the scene unfolding before him. As expected the size of the enemy forces was huge and it was obvious that they had taken advantage of the night to deploy their troops across the whole width of the hill.

On the lower slopes they could see the massed ranks of Flemish mercenaries, famed for their ferocity in battle and as the ground rose immediately behind them, more than five hundred archers. Seven thousand Norman levies filled the rest of the hill and on each flank stood a thousand cavalry, the steam from their mounts replacing the disappearing mist. On the top of the hill stood another hundred horses, each ridden by the elite cavalry, the knights and officers of the English Army including the overall commander Robert Fitzmartin and the lord of Llanstephan, Maurice Fitzgerald.

'The advantage is indeed theirs,' said Hywel quietly, 'both in position and numbers. If what you say is true and this is the only road south, then they have it effectively blocked and the only way to advance is to remove them from that hill.'

'I agree,' said Owain, 'and that is what we are here to do but the steepness of that slope worries me. I am confident our men are equal to any the English can field but to fight uphill and against prepared lines is exhausting. We need them to come down and face us in the valley.'

'Why would they do that?' asked Hywel. 'If I was them, I would simply wait where they are. Any fool could see that the advantage of the high ground is not one to surrender unless absolutely necessary.'

'Perhaps not,' said Owain, 'but if we can lure them down it will be a completely different matter.'

'And how are you going to do that?' asked Hywel.

Owain turned to Hywel.

'By using the advice of a very great tactician,' he said. He turned to Cadwaladwr. 'Ready the men brother, we will waste no more time in posturing. Prepare to advance.'

Cadwaladwr turned his horse and rode away to issue the necessary orders as Owain and Hywel both discarded their cloaks.

'So,' said Hywel, untying the leather ties that secured his battle axe across his saddle, 'who is this great tactician you speak of? Do I know of him?'

'It was not a man who shared long evenings discussing tactics these past few months, Hywel,' said Owain glancing at his fellow warrior, 'but a woman who has lived a lifetime at the side of one of our country's greatest warriors.'

'You have taken advice from a woman?' asked Hywel, the surprise clearly evident on his face.

'Aye,' said Owain, 'but fret not, friend, for though she has never wielded a blade in anger, her counsel has won many a battle.'

The ground between the two armies was bare and as the last wisps of mist finally disappeared, the commanders of both armies tried to calculate what the best tactics would be to gain whatever advantage they could. As had been noted by one of his opponents at the far end of the valley, Fitzmartin was confident he had gained a huge advantage by securing the high ground, not just because it was easier to defend but because of the advantageous viewpoint it afforded on the enemy position.

At his side sat John of Salisbury astride his own destrier, an animal whose elegant lines suggested it was more suited to the gentler sport of hunting than the blood and terror of a full-scale battle. The other commanders deployed to the cavalry on either flank but as Salisbury had been present at the battle of Kidwelly only months earlier, he had been instructed to stay at Fitzmartin's side to offer an insight into the enemy tactics. An order he was more than happy to obey bearing in mind its position of relative safety.

Fitzmartin gazed down the slopes before him, comfortable in the knowledge that not only did he have numerical superiority but every single one of his men were experienced in warfare and knew what to expect. He looked up and across the valley floor to the gathered enemy less than a few thousand paces northward.

'Well,' he said quietly, 'there they are at last, assembled in all their glory.'

'Glory,' sneered John of Salisbury, 'I seen no such thing nor opportunity for them to achieve anything near that outcome. All I see are rows of peasants lined neatly up for the slaughter.'

'Really?' said Fitzmartin, 'for I see a vast army, one that is hell bent on removing us from this hill.'

'Ambition is useless if it isn't matched with ability,' said Salisbury, 'and in my experience, these people are poorly trained and quick to flight. Once you unleash the cavalry they will scatter like autumn leaves.'

'Possibly,' said Fitzmartin, 'but let us wait a while and see what transpires.'

'Actually,' said Salisbury, 'I think the wait will be shorter than you anticipate. It looks like they are manoeuvering for an advance.'

'It does,' said the commander as the massed ranks spread out across the field, 'why would that be, I wonder?'

'Possibly lack of experience places undue expectations in their leader's minds.'

'I'm not so sure,' said Fitzmartin, 'I have heard it said that Owain is a very astute commander of men and is no fool. If he thinks that there is something to gain by assaulting a foe who has the advantage in number, experience and position then there must be merit in his thoughts.'

'Let him come,' said Salisbury, 'we will swat them away like flies.'

Both men fell silent as they watched the Welsh manoeuvers. Slowly but efficiently, the many lines of men at arms spread out until they reached right across the valley, stretching the body of their main army very thin.

'A curious deployment,' said Salisbury, 'they weaken their core and open up the centre to a direct cavalry charge.'

'Perhaps that is what they want,' said Fitzmartin, 'and intend to fall upon our horsemen as soon as their lines are breached.'

'But that doesn't make sense,' said Salisbury, 'all we would have to do is reorganise further up the valley and turn to charge their rear. They would be forced to face us on two fronts, especially if our infantry was to advance immediately behind the cavalry charge.'

'I think that is exactly what he wants,' said Fitzmartin, 'because by doing so we would be surrendering the advantage of the high ground. A costly move but one that he may be willing to pay to get us off the hill.'

'If that is the case,' said Salisbury, 'then so be it. There is no way they can defeat us in open warfare especially if our cavalry is attacking their rear.'

'No,' replied Fitzmartin, 'I think we will stick to our plan and let them bring the fight to us. Let them advance to within arrow range and we will see what damage our archers can do. After that if they manage to reach the slopes, which I very much doubt, we will maintain our positions and let them fight uphill for every step. When exhaustion kicks in from fighting our mercenaries, then and only then will we unleash our levies to pour upon them like a deluge. They will be overrun within moments.'

'And the cavalry?'

'To be honest, I can't see them being needed such is the strength of our position but once the Welsh army has been turned, we will mop up the remainder with no quarter given.' He turned to Salisbury. 'How does that sound to you?'

'That sounds,' replied the castellan, 'like the perfect way to wipe out the Welsh menace once and for all.'

Chapter Twenty-Six

The Welsh lines

October 10th AD 1136

Cadwaladwr stood up in his stirrups and looked left and right along the length of the Welsh vanguard. Each flank now stretched to the valley sides and though it proved an impressive sight, the lines were only six men deep, not strong enough to withstand a cavalry charge. He looked across at his brother and raised his sword in the air, signalling that the army was ready. Owain raised his own sword in acknowledgement before bringing it down swiftly to order the advance.

'*Drummers,*' roared Cadwaladwr, 'beat out the pace, men of Wales, *advaaance!*'

The air reverberated as the slow marching beat echoed through the morning air and every man stepped forward as one. Birds flew into the air at the sudden change from eerie morning silence to the hypnotic rhythm of seven thousand men on the move.

'Maintain your lines.' shouted Cadwaladwr glancing in either direction, 'keep tight.'

Sergeants echoed his orders across the advancing army and within moments, the throng had settled into a deliberate pace.

'Shields,' shouted Cadwaladwr and every man lifted their shield to chest level without breaking their monotonous pace.

'Why are you presenting shields?' shouted Hywel to Owain as they rode their horse at the front of the army. 'We are well out of arrow range.'

'The battle starts first with the minds,' said Owain, 'long before the first drop of blood has been spilled.'

'What do you mean?' asked Hywel.

'You will see,' said Owain.

The army continued their relentless pace forward and had only gone another thousand paces or so before Cadwaladwr roared out a second command.

'*Draw blades.*'

Again, Hywel looked over his shoulder, confused that every man now had a weapon in their hands even though they were still nowhere near the enemy.

'On my command,' shouted Cadwaladwr... *'now.'*

'As one, every man in the welsh army smashed their weapon into their shields as another fifty drums added to the relentless beat, sending a wall of sound toward the hill. On every second pace, the beat rang through the air and irrespective of any effect it had on the waiting enemy, it lifted the hearts and spirits of every Welshman marching to battle.

Cadwaladwr raised his sword again and this time the battle cries of seven thousand men filled the air. Foot soldiers, lancers, archers and cavalry all added their screams of defiance toward the enemy and even the civilians to the rear joined in the cacophony. Horns echoed around the valley and within moments the noise was deafening. The Welsh army was marching into battle.

Up on the hill, the waiting English stared in shock. Everyone experienced in battle was used to the sounds of warfare, but such a thing was usually reserved for the final charge, not when the enemy was several hundred paces away.

'What are they doing?' asked Fitzmartin, 'they waste precious breath in meaningless gestures.'

'False bravado,' said Salisbury, 'and like I said, inexperience. I say we charge them now and end this farce.'

'No,' said Fitzmartin. 'This will play out as it will.'

Both men stared as the approaching army got within five hundred paces, the noise not diminishing for a second.

'My lord,' shouted one of the younger officers at Fitzmartin's side, 'look.'

Both men stared upward and saw a single fire arrow sweeping across the sky, trailing black smoke behind it.

'What are they up to?' shouted Fitzmartin but before Salisbury could answer, the whole valley fell into a sudden silence as the Welsh army came to a sudden halt. The cacophony ended instantly, and the air was deathly still. Up above the arrow continued its arc across the valley before plummeting back to earth to embed itself harmlessly in the soil between the two armies.

Down on the flat ground, Cadwaladwr's voice echoed again across the valley.

'Men at arms,' he roared, *'stand aside.'*

Immediately the Welsh ranks opened as every other man stepped behind the one on his left in a well-practised manoeuver, leaving hundreds of channels through to the rear.

'Rear ranks advance,' shouted Cadwaladwr and as Fitzmartin and Salisbury watched in confusion, over two thousand cloaked men ran through the channels of the vanguard to form their own ranks at the front of the army, each carrying what appeared to be a staff and a heavy pack.

'What are they doing,' said Fitzmartin again, 'who are those men?'

'I have no idea,' said Salisbury, 'but they look harmless enough to me.' Despite his arrogance his voice was not as confident as before. Whatever Owain had in mind, it was certainly a tactic none of the English officers had seen before.

Within moments the Welsh army again fell still and Owain rode forward until he was within two hundred paces of the hill. He reined in his horse and looked upward.

'Robert Fitzmartin,' he shouted, 'I know you can hear me. On behalf of the combined kingdoms of Wales I demand you cede this hill and lead your men back to England. Do this and I give you my word that your men will not be harried in anyway and no blood will be spilled. Refuse and I swear that this ground will be knee deep in English blood before this day is done. I offer this concession once and once only.'

Up on the hill, Fitzmartin and Salisbury stared in astonishment. Despite the noise and impressive advance, the fact was that the army below them was still much smaller than theirs and were disadvantaged regarding ground.

'That man has the nerve of the devil himself,' said Salisbury, 'and I look forward to seeing his arrogant head on a spike.'

Fitzmartin didn't answer but rode his horse a few paces forward to identify himself to the prince below.

'Owain ap Gruffydd,' he shouted over the heads of his men, 'you certainly know how to put on a spectacle, I grant you that, but it is nothing but show. This hill is ours and will remain ours. As will Ceredigion, Deheubarth and all other kingdoms in the south. Indeed, it is only a matter of time until even Gwynedd bends a knee to England so do your worst, Welshman, for this will be your last battle.'

Down below Owain took a deep breath.

'And is that your final word?'

Fitzmartin didn't answer. Instead he turned to one of the archers at his side.

'One only,' he said, 'and make it good.'

The archer notched an arrow and after taking careful aim sent it skyward.

Down below, Owain saw the approaching arrow plummet from the sky and at the last moment, lifted his shield.

The arrow thudded into the painted wood and though the first few inches emerged on the reverse side, all impetus had been stopped and Owain was unhurt. The Welshman used his sword to swipe away the arrow and looked up at the English commander again.

'You have had my decision,' shouted Fitzmartin, 'now return to your peasant army before I forget my manners and unleash another five hundred arrows down upon you.'

'You had your chance, Fitzmartin,' shouted Owain as his horse reared up, 'there will be no quarter asked or given this day. Let history show that I offered you terms.' He turned away and rode back to the waiting lines of cloaked men as the jeers of the English echoed behind him.

'You know what to do,' he shouted as he neared the front lines, 'prepare bows.'

Every one of the men discarded their packs and long cloaks before taking hold of their staffs on the top end and using their full body weight to bend them inward. The strain was evident on everyman's face such was the tension in the timber but as they notched looped strings over the end, it became clear that what had originally looked like staffs from a distance, were in fact longbows.

'Longbows,' said Salisbury up on the hill, 'why would he bring hunting bows to a battle?'

'An arrow is an arrow,' said Fitzmartin thoughtfully, 'perhaps he has no skilled archers to call upon so uses what he can.'

'Yes, but they will have no discipline or tactical knowledge. One charge from our men and they will flee like the wind.'

For a few moments, they watched as each of Owain's archers unwrapped their packs and stuck dozens of arrows in the ground before them.

'What is the range of a longbow?' asked Fitzmartin, his gaze transfixed on the men across the valley.

'Who cares?' said Salisbury, 'our men can loose three arrows to every one from a longbow.'

'*What is the range?*' roared Fitzmartin suddenly, his whole manner changing. 'And how powerful are they compared to ours. *Somebody tell me!*'

'My lord,' said the archer who had loosed the single arrow at Owain minutes earlier, 'a skilled hunter with a longbow can bring down a stag at five hundred paces.'

'And ours?'

'Less than half that,' said the archer. 'Our arrows cannot reach them from here, but our front ranks are well within range of theirs.'

Fitzmartin looked across the valley as realisation finally dawned. The Welsh archers had already loaded their bows and were taking aim high into the morning air.

'*Shields,*' he roared, but it was too late. Owain had already given the order to loose and as Fitzmartin looked on in horror, the sky darkened from the flight of two thousand arrows.

Seconds later the first volley smashed into the Flemish lines, bursting through gambeson and chainmail alike. Men cried out at the impact and hundreds fell dead or severely wounded. For a few moments, their comrades failed to react, shocked at the sudden devastation amongst them.

'*Get those shields up,*' roared one of the sergeants, '*or die where you stand.*'

Those lucky enough to survive the first few volleys managed to muster together and overlap their shields above their heads, creating a semblance of protection against the deadly hail but there was no let up from the barrage and when the next volley arrived it became evident that it would not be enough. The immense power of the longbows meant that many of the heavy arrows smashed right through the shields and as the deluge of death continued, the ranks of Flemish mercenaries were torn apart.

On the other side of the field, Owain watched the battle unfold from the back of his horse. At his side, Hywel watched in amazement as the lethal barrage continued. Though experienced in war, he had never considered the longbow as a weapon until now, but the effect of the volley fire was devastating, and he knew that this day, whatever the outcome would change warfare forever. Behind him, a line of drums beat out a steady rhythm and on every tenth beat, a new volley soared through the air towards the hill.

'*Keep it up,*' roared Cadwaladwr, riding back and forth along the front of the archers as arrows sailed over his head, 'there will be no let up until you hear the signal.'

'Why volley fire?' shouted Hywel to Owain, 'would it not be better to let them fire at will?'

'Single arrows can be avoided,' replied Owain loudly, 'whilst volleys offer a man no place to hide. Fitzmartin will recover soon enough but until then we have to maximize the effect.' Both men fell silent again and watched as thousands of arrows soared toward the enemy lines.

'My lord,' shouted one of Fitzmartin's officers, 'the Flemish are being slaughtered, what are your commands?'

Fitzmartin stared down the hill in shock. Even as he watched, good men were dying throughout his vanguard and he knew they could not sit back and watch his front lines get slaughtered with no chance of retaliation.

'My lord,' shouted the officer again, 'shall we sound the withdrawal?'

'To where?' said Fitzmartin. 'There are seven thousand more men behind the Flemish. There is nowhere for them to go.'

'Then they must advance,' said Salisbury, 'while they still have a chance to have some effect.'

'They will be slaughtered,' said Fitzmartin. 'I need time to think.'

'There is no time,' said Salisbury, 'surely it is better to die in battle than waiting on a hill for the inevitable?'

Fitzmartin's mind worked furiously. He knew he had to do something quickly and he still had a massive advantage but that would soon be whittled away if he hesitated much longer.'

'My lord,' shouted Salisbury again, 'we have to advance, to stay here invites death without a single drop of Welsh blood being spilled. All they have to do is advance and we will all be within range of their bows.'

'You are right,' said Fitzmartin, 'this hill is no longer the advantageous position we thought it was.' He turned to the officer at his side. 'Sound the signal for the first advance.'

'Aye, my lord,' said the officer, 'and the cavalry?'

'Tell them to also prepare, I want the whole army ready to advance at a moment's notice.'

The officer turned his horse and galloped away as Salisbury rode closer to Fitzmartin.

'What are you thinking?' he asked.

'We will use the Flemish mercenaries whilst they still have value,' said the commander, 'and draw the strength of the enemy. As soon as they are engaged we will follow up with cavalry and levies.' He turned to one of his signallers. 'Give the signal to advance,' he said, 'one blast only.'

The young man raised a horn to his lips and after taking a deep breath, sent a solitary note around the hill.

Down below, the Flemish infantry heard the signal and though they were experienced men, many looked at each other in disbelief. To advance under this rain of arrows was certain death.

'Come on,' shouted a sergeant from behind the shield wall, 'what are we waiting for? If we stay, we die, if we advance, there is a chance we live. Follow me!' He burst out from behind the shield wall and ran forward a few paces before turning to face what was left of his force.

'On me,' he shouted, 'and heaven help any man who turns from the fight.' The roar of defiance from the remaining five hundred mercenaries echoed across the field and as the sergeant turned to lead the advance, his remaining men charged down the slope to join him, leaping over their dead and dying comrades as they ran. Within moments they were racing across the field toward the Welsh lines, every man screaming with rage and fear.

'Archers,' roared Cadwaladwr, seeing the threat, 'change targets.'

The archers lowered their longbows to take aim at the charging mercenaries and awaited the command.

'First volley on my command,' shouted Cadwaladwr, 'ready...*loose!*'

Another two thousand arrows cut through the air though this time, as the range was shorter, the power was much greater and many smashed into the attackers with unprecedented force. Well targeted arrows not only pieced the chain mail worn by most of the Flemish but burst right through their bodies, killing them on the spot. Volley after volley followed, but though their impetus was slowed, the Flemish kept coming.

'Archers retire,' shouted Cadwaladwr, 'Men of Gwent, present shields.'

Immediately, the archers turned and ran back through the channels of the infantry to the safety of the rear. Owain, Cadwaladwr and Hywel followed them through and took their position immediately behind the Gwynedd army. The lines closed and every foot soldier in the front rank dug the bottom of their kite shaped shields in the mud at their feet for extra stability and leaned their shoulders against them to brace for the impact they knew was coming.

The men in the second rank lifted their own shields over the ones in front, adding to the height while the third rank presented their long spears over the shoulders of those before them, forming a lethal wall of spikes toward the onrushing enemy.

'Owain,' shouted Cadwaladwr over the noise. 'Look to the hill, the main army is on the move.'

The Welsh prince looked up and saw thousands of English infantry making their way down the slope to follow the Flemish into the assault.

'Take up your positions,' he shouted to Cadwaladwr and Hywel, 'and await my command.'

Both men wheeled their horses away, Hywel riding to join the cavalry on the left flank, while Cadwaladwr joined those on the right. Owain turned back to face the imminent battle to his front. All thoughts of gaining any tactical advantage were gone, now it was down to the fight and though he knew he commanded one of the best trained and equipped armies seen in Wales for generations, the sight of the massed ranks of levies pouring down the hill made him question whether he could be victorious.

'Dear God,' he said quietly drawing his sword, 'grant me strength this day.'

'Here they come,' roared a grizzled sergeant in the front rank, 'brace.'

The screaming hoard of Flemish mercenaries headed toward the centre of the Welsh lines, covering the last few yards with renewed energy and a fury drawn from seeing so many of their comrades cut down by arrows. The first to arrive ducked under the spears and hurled themselves at the shield wall with all the force they could muster, driving the defensive line backward.

The Welsh held firm but before they could reorganise, more warriors reached the wall and taking advantage of the momentary confusion, used their own comrades' backs as a step to hurl themselves over the shields and into the midst of the Welsh army. Most were cut down as they landed but many managed to regain their feet and lash out with whatever weapons they carried with them. Panic ensued as the more inexperienced men in the rear ranks witnessed the brutal reality of hand to hand fighting for the first time. Flemish axes smashed clean through chain mail and jets of blood showered over shocked men as blades hacked through flesh and bone alike.

The impact was immediate and as panicking defenders turned to protect themselves from the enemy at their backs, more attackers ploughed into the weakened wall to force a breach the width of twenty men in the Welsh lines. Within moments, the Flemish had divided the lines and though there were now no more than a hundred or so left alive, the effect on the Welsh was devastating.

'Don't just stand there,' roared Owain, 'cut them down.'

Men momentarily shocked at the savagery of the assault came to their senses and poured to the aid of their comrades. More experienced warriors waded into the fray, matching the Flemish in both skill and ferocity.

'Watch your front,' shouted Owain, 'the main battle is still to come.' Every eye turned to see the huge English army forming up a few hundred paces distant and many men recited whatever prayers they could. 'Now you know what to expect,' shouted Owain, riding along the rear of the lines, 'do not get caught out again.'

On the hill, Fitzmartin and Salisbury followed the main English army down onto the flat ground and waited as their forces quickly formed up.

'My lord,' gasped one of his officers, 'the Flemish have broken through.'

Fitzmartin looked across the field and saw that over a hundred of his mercenaries were now behind the enemy lines and fighting man to man with the Welsh reserves.

'They have no chance,' said the officer, 'they are vastly outnumbered.'

'That is irrelevant,' said Salisbury, 'their advance has proven a point, that those lines are too stretched to be of any use. If a few hundred can break through, think what our massed ranks can achieve.'

'My lord,' said the officer again, his voice agitated, 'we should send men immediately to aid the Flemish. They are being cut down like hay.'

'Not yet,' said Fitzmartin.

'But my lord…'

'They are mercenaries, Master Oswald,' snapped Fitzmartin, 'and know what they signed up for. Salisbury is right, their deaths are unfortunate, but their actions have shown us the way. Their lines are so thin, a focused charge at the centre will plough right through them. Give the signal, prepare to advance.'

Behind the Welsh lines the few remaining mercenaries had been forced into a group standing in an outward facing circle, each wielding his weapon defiantly while scowling at the Welsh archers who had them surrounded. At their feet lay dozens of men, both Flemish and Welsh who had died during the brutal fight.

Owain galloped across and reined in his horse. He glanced toward the hill, knowing the main English army could advance at any moment and he had no time to waste.

'My lord,' shouted one of the mercenaries as he approached, 'we yield and seek quarter. Let us go and we swear we will leave this field immediately, never to return.'

Owain thought furiously. He knew that he could not spare any of his own men to guard them if he took them prisoner yet if he allowed them to go, they could break their word and return to the fray at any time. The Mercenary who had spoken threw down his huge battle axe.

'My lord,' he said again, 'we are done here. Let us go and you will never see us again.'

The rest of his comrades followed suit and threw down their weapons. Owain hesitated. To kill unarmed men, especially warriors as brave as these went against everything he stood for but there was a battle to be won and these men had just killed many of his own.

'I vowed no quarter,' he said eventually, 'and I will keep to my word. You took the English coin, now you must pay the ultimate price.' He turned to the waiting archers. 'Cut them down.'

'Wait,' gasped the mercenary but the word had hardly left his mouth when three arrows embedded themselves deep into his chest. Slowly he sank to his knees and as blood started to pour from his mouth, he spluttered the last words he would ever say.

'May God forgive you.'

Within seconds, the last of the Flemish vanguard were all dead, cut down by a hail of arrows and Owain turned to the more urgent matter in hand.

'Paulus,' he shouted, summoning one of the officers who had fought at his side at Aberystwyth, 'take command of our archers. Have them reform and prepared to fire over our heads on my command.'

'What about our wounded, my lord?'

'After the civilians have brought the last of the arrows, have them retrieve those men who can be saved and take them to the wagons.'

'Aye, my lord,' replied Paulus and turned away to his task. 'You heard him,' he shouted, 'regain your positions and face the front.'

Owain dismounted from his horse and looked toward a group of boys carrying buckets of arrows from the wagons at the rear. A mop of curly black hair caught his eye and for a moment he stared in surprise as he recognised the boy.

'Rascal,' he shouted as he led his horse over, 'what are you doing here? I sent you to Aberffraw.'

'My lord,' said Rascal, his dirty face shocked at the reality of war, 'I ran away and joined the supply caravan to help. Please don't be angry with me.'

'You should have stayed at home,' shouted Owain, 'this is no place for young boys such as you.' Even as he spoke the words he realised his own hypocrisy for all around him, boys of a similar age to Rascal were carrying buckets of arrows or helping to drag the wounded to the rear. He swallowed hard, realising there was not much he could do. He had grown fond of the boy but to send him away now could display favouritism.

'Listen,' he said, 'I have a very important job for you, one that I would entrust to no other.'

'Just say it, my lord,' said Rascal, 'and it shall be done.

'Good. Give those arrows to one of the archers and then take my horse to the rear. Make sure she is taken far from here away from all this fighting. Can you do that?'

'Of course, my lord.'

'Look after her well, Rascal and you will be suitably rewarded when this day is done.'

'What if you die, my lord?' asked the boy bluntly.

Owain smiled and ruffled the boy's hair.

'Then in that case, she is yours to keep. Now be gone and make sure you give her some water.'

Without another word he turned and forced his way through the tight lines to the front of his army. A few hundred paces away stood the English forces, now down from the hill and forming up ready to advance. Again, he paused for to fire upon an army not yet ready was considered dishonourable but there was a battle to be won and he knew he had to employ every means possible. Honourable or not.

'*Archers,*' he roared lifting his sword high in the air, 'make ready, *loose*'

Behind the army, Paulus relayed the order and once again the skies were darkened by thousands of arrows.

'Volley fire,' shouted Paulus, 'sound drums.'

Again, the beat of the Welsh drums rang out and volley after volley of arrows ripped through the air, slamming into the English ranks. Owain knew that there was no way he could stop the advance with arrows only but he had to kill as many as he could while he still had the chance.

'Reform,' he shouted, 'deepen the ranks, cavalry to the flanks.'

On both ends of the waiting army, thousands of men turned inward and ran behind the first three ranks to add strength to their position. The cavalry led by Hywel and Cadwaladwr took their place, leaving no gap unfilled.

'Come on, Fitzmartin,' he said under his breath, 'let's get this done.'

'Prepare to move,' shouted Fitzmartin as the Welsh arrows continued to smash into his men, 'on my command, advaaance.'

The massed ranks of the English army started their march forward, most holding their shields high before them as defence against the arrows. Despite this, the power of the longbows once again proved crucial and as the army was so densely packed together, almost all of the arrows found a target and hundreds more fell at every volley.

'My lord,' shouted one of Fitzmartin's officers, 'the enemy has reorganised and now their ranks are ten deep.'

'What is he playing at?' shouted Salisbury. 'Why has he reversed his tactics?'

'Because by thinning out his lines initially,' replied Fitzmartin,' he has lured us into an attack across a narrow front. A very clever move for he now has strength in depth and our men are easy targets for his archers.'

'Then we have to retreat,' shouted Salisbury, his face ashen, 'their arrows are devastating our ranks.'

Fitzmartin stared across the battlefield. To reorganise his men during an advance would invite confusion and he would lose far too many to the Welsh archers. The rain of arrows was taking its toll, but he knew the only chance they would have would be to engage them at close quarter.

'There will be no retreat,' shouted Fitzmartin from his horse,' we came here to win a battle and we have not yet drawn blood. Increase the pace, sound the charge.'

The sound of three long blasts filled the air and as one, the massed ranks of the English army broke into a run across the open field.

'Here they come,' roared Owain. *'Front ranks present shields, spear men, make ready.'*

'Archers, fire at will,' shouted Paulus, 'drop as many as you can before they are upon us.'

Released from the constraints of volley fire, the longbow men increased their pace and hundreds of heavy arrows thudded into the enemy all over the field. In the front ranks of the Welsh army, the shield wall went up again but this time, those in the rear prepared to throw their spears as soon as the enemy came into range.

'Make sure you repel the first charge,' roared Owain above the noise of screaming men, *'hold the line and await my signal. When it comes, you know what to do.'*

Again, every man braced and as the enemy raced toward them, many realised that today was the day they would die.

Chapter Twenty-Seven

Pembroke Castle

October 10th AD 1136

Nesta lay in her bed, sleeping fitfully. Over in the fireplace, the embers of last night's fire glowed dimly in the darkness of the shuttered room and her evening meal lay uneaten on a wooden platter on a table near the window. As usual she had been alone when the food had come from the kitchens, but the thought of eating made her feel ill and the bowl of meaty stew now had a thin layer of solidified fat over the untouched contents.

A knock came on the door and Nesta's eyes opened slowly, lifting her from the dream where she had once more been a happy girl playing in the valley below Dinefwr castle.

'Who is it?' she asked quietly.

'My lady,' came a voice, 'it is Anna Greentrees from the kitchens. I have been sent to retrieve the platters from last night. Is it a suitable time?'

'Just a moment,' said Nesta yawning and she got out of bed to don a heavy velvet robe. She walked over to the door and slid back the bolt, allowing a young girl not much older than fourteen to come in to her quarters.

'Good morning, my lady,' said Anna Greentrees, 'please forgive me if I woke you.'

'Not at all,' said Nesta, 'I have stayed abed far too long anyway. What time of day is it?'

'Mid-morning, my lady,' said the servant. 'Can I collect your tray?'

'Please, go ahead,' said Nesta, walking over to the window to open the shutters. She peered out into the fresh morning air. 'It looks quiet down there.'

'It is,' said Anna placing the platters on the tray. 'Since the garrison left to join the army in Cardigan the castle is like a graveyard. Still, it makes our work easier in the kitchens.'

Nesta smiled and turned to Anna, looking at her thoughtfully.

'Anna, do you have the ear of Carla, the main cook?'

'Indeed I do, my lady,' said Anna. 'She is my aunt's sister and it was she who gave me employment as a kitchen servant. I will be forever in her debt.'

'In that case,' said Nesta, 'I want you to give her a message on my behalf.'

'Of course, my lady.'

Nesta looked at the full bowl of stew still untouched on the tray in the girl's hands,

'Tell, her,' said Nesta, 'that the food was disgusting, and I summon her to my presence immediately to explain herself.'

'My lady,' gasped Anna horrified at the revelation, 'my sincerest apologies.' She looked down at the cold stew and back up at the princess. 'Mistress Carla will be distraught and will surely be punished by the castellan for her error.'

'There is no need for anyone else to know, Anna,' said Nesta, 'this can stay between us. Any punishment to be administered will be by me and me alone. Do you understand?'

'Of course, my lady,' said Anna.

'Good, now be gone and remember, say nothing to anyone else or her punishment may be worse than it needs be.'

'Yes, my lady,' said Anna and after a brief curtsey, hurried from the room.

In the dungeons of the castle, Rowan carried a bucket of water and a leather bag along a short corridor. At the far end one of the permanent jailers sat at a table, his head resting on his arms as he snored gently in the candlelit gloom. Rowan new that he could probably overcome the jailer and release Maelgwyn should he be so inclined, but he also knew that this was not the time. The final preparations were not yet in place.

'Sleeping again,' said Rowan, and the jailer sat suddenly upright, momentarily confused by his surroundings. His hand reached out and picked up a rusty sword from against the wall.

'Who's there? he asked, his eyes squinting to make out the shape in the darkness.

'It's me,' said Rowan, 'one of the soldiers who has shared guard duty down here these past few weeks.'

'What do you want?' asked the jailer, 'and why are you not in Cardigan with the rest of them?'

'I was sick,' said Rowan, 'but am getting well. I leave in a few days but have a task to do given by the castellan himself.'

'What task?'

'I have brought food and drink for the prisoner. I am also to bathe his wounds.' He held up the bucket as if to prove his intentions.

'He was fed yesterday,' said the jailer, 'the castellan said he was to have food every other day and then only enough to keep him alive. Why would that change?'

'Who knows?' said Rowan with a shrug. 'Perhaps Salisbury aims to fatten him up ready for the gallows.'

'A waste of good food if you ask me,' said the jailer, 'and I have received no such instruction. I should check with the castellan himself.'

'He is not here, remember?' said Rowan. 'He is in Cardigan with the rest of the men but as I will shortly be joining them, perhaps I can relay a message.'

'You do that,' said the jailer.

'I will,' said Rowan, 'but to be honest, the last time I saw this prisoner he seemed at death's door and if he should die before you get your confirmation then I suspect both you and I would be held accountable and trust me, I can think of better ways to spend my time than hanging by the neck from the castle walls. Just let me give him some food and I will be on my way.'

The jailer stared at Rowan suspiciously.

'Let me see what you have in that bag.'

'Some rags and a piece of stale bread,' said Rowan. 'Why are you so suspicious?'

'This man is valuable,' said the jailer, 'and if he was to escape, the castellan's wrath would fall on my shoulders.'

'You can lock me in there with him if you like,' said Rowan, 'but to be honest, your suspicions anger me. I am as much a part of this garrison as you are.'

'You were loyal to Gerald,' said the jailer, 'and I was warned not to trust any who served under him. Sometimes, old loyalties never die.'

Both men stared at each other in a stand-off until finally Rowan put the bucket down and threw the bag over to the jailer.

'Here,' he said, 'you do it. I have dice to play.' He turned away but breathed a silent sigh of relief when the jailer called out behind him.

'Wait.'

He tipped the bag upside down and allowed the contents to fall on the floor before rummaging through them to ensure there were no hidden weapons.

'Happy now?' asked Rowan as the jailer saw he had been telling the truth.

'Pass me the bucket,' said the jailer, ignoring the jibe.

Rowan did as he was asked, and the jailer plunged his hand into the warm water, searching for anything that may be concealed beneath.

'Now you are being ridiculous,' said Rowan 'If I had wanted to help him escape, I could have killed you while you slept.'

'I was not sleeping,' grumbled the guard, 'I was resting my eyes and knew you were there all along.'

'If you say so,' said Rowan.

Eventually the jailer was satisfied and reached inside his jerkin to retrieve a key on a long piece of cord.

'Be quick,' he said as he unlocked the cell, 'or I may just lock you in there permanently.'

'I need light,' said Rowan and waited as the jailer lit a second candle.

'I want it back,' he mumbled and watched as the soldier ducked into the cell before locking the door behind him.

Inside the cell, the stench was overwhelming, and Rowan could see the overflowing filth bucket in the corner.

'Maelgwyn,' he said holding up the candle, 'where are you?'

A noise came from the corner and the soldier peered into the shadows.

'Maelgwyn,' he said again, 'it's me, Rowan. We talked a while ago.'

'I remember,' said a voice. 'You are the one who is loyal to my aunt.'

'Keep your voice down,' hissed Rowan. 'I am here to help but that jailer is loyal to Salisbury only. If he suspects anything then we are both doomed.'

'You said you were going to help weeks ago,' said Maelgwyn, 'but I have seen neither hide nor hair of you.'

'It was difficult,' said Rowan, 'but I did what I could. Did you not receive the food?'

'Only the slop they give me every few days. Apart from that there has been nothing.'

'I promise I sent food when I could,' said Rowan, 'it must have been taken by that rat of a man outside the door.'

Maelgwyn shuffled forward into the circle of candlelight and Rowan was shocked at how thin the young prince had become. He was hardly more than a skeleton with grimy tangled hair hanging down to his shoulders. His face was filthy, and his skin covered with infected wounds that lay untreated after his many beatings at the hands of his captors.

'What's the matter?' asked Maelgwyn seeing the look of horror on the soldier's face. 'Do you not like what you see?'

'What have they done to you?' asked Rowan quietly.

Maelgwyn retreated out of the light and sat against the wall.

'I waited, Rowan,' he said, 'just like you said I should. But nobody came. It would have been better if I had opened my own veins.'

'I am sorry we made no better effort,' said Rowan, 'but this place is well guarded, and I could not get near without raising suspicion, but I am here now.'

'What's the point?' asked Maelgwyn, 'I am too weak to walk let alone run.'

'Leave that to me,' said Rowan, 'but first we need to get you out of here.' He walked over and kneeling before him, gave him the bread. 'Here, eat this.'

Maelgwyn ate as quickly as his broken teeth would allow as Rowan dipped a rag into the warm water.

'Right,' said Rowan as he bathed Maelgwyn's face, 'listen carefully. 'I have more food with me, but you must not let the jailer know. If he finds out, I won't be allowed back in and you need as much strength as you can muster. Look over my shoulder and tell me if we are being watched.'

'I don't think so,' said Maelgwyn eventually 'but it is dark.'

Rowan continued to bathe Maelgwyn's wounds, his stomach turning at the stench from the pus but as he dipped the rag into the bucket again, his hand went to the bottom and sought a tiny notch where it met the sides. Quickly he lifted the false bottom and retrieved the piece of cooked pork hidden there.

'Here,' he said, glancing over his shoulder to check they were not being watched, 'eat as quickly as you can but keep me between you and the door.'

Maelgwyn rammed the meat into his mouth and chewed as best he could in the circumstances. When he was done, Rowan gave him a second piece but grabbed Maelgwyn's wrist before he could continue.

'Not yet,' he said, 'you have hardly eaten anything lately, so your stomach is not used to it. Wait until I have gone, and you hear the guard snoring. The last thing you want is to be sick.'

Maelgwyn nodded and placed the wet meat beneath him before staring at Rowan in the gloom.

'So, when do I get out?' he asked eventually.

'Soon,' said Rowan. 'Now the jailer thinks this will be a regular thing I can bring you good food every day.'

'Don't wait too long, soldier,' said Maelgwyn, 'for even with a belly full of meat I fear I will not last much longer.'

'Stay strong,' hissed Rowan as the key rattled in the door behind him, 'a few more days, no more.'

'Enough,' shouted the jailer as the door opened, 'he's had his bread so tip that bucket out and get out of there. Remember he is a treasonous Welsh rebel and deserves everything he gets.'

'I'm done,' said Rowan over his shoulder and stood up, leaving the prisoner in the darkness behind him. He ducked through the low door and back into the corridor, closely followed by the jailer.

'Will you be here tomorrow?' asked Rowan as the jailer locked the door.

'Aye, why what is it to you?'

'I think we started out on the wrong foot,' said Rowan, 'so perhaps tomorrow I will bring some ale to make amends.'

The jailer stared at Rowan with suspicion but finally nodded.

'I accept ale from any man,' he said, 'friend or foe.'

'In that case, I will see what I can do,' said Rowan and turned away to leave the dungeon.

'Don't forget the ale,' said the jailer behind him and at that moment, Rowan knew he had the man exactly where he wanted him.

Nesta was already dressed by the time Carla came from the kitchens. Normally the cook would have been denied entry to the keep but the princess had sent word to the guards that she was expected and was to be shown to Nesta's quarters immediately.

'My lady,' gasped Carla as she was shown to the princess's room, 'you summoned me.' The fat woman was red faced and out of breath from the climb.

'I did,' said Nesta sternly, 'for these past few days the standard of food you have served me, and this castle's garrison has been nothing short of pig's swill. What have you to say for yourself?'

'My lady,' said Carla wringing her hands, 'I don't understand. I have prepared your meals the same way as I always have and there has never been a complaint before.'

'Well there has now,' shouted Nesta, 'sit down and be quiet.'

The cook did as she was told, shocked at the tone of the princess' admonishment as Nesta walked over to the guard still standing in the doorway.

'Thank you,' she said, taking hold of the door, 'I will take it from here.'

'My lady, I should stay in case she attacks you.'

'There is no need for that,' said Nesta, 'I know the woman from old, I am perfectly safe.'

The guard looked at the still panting cook and nodded his agreement.

'If you need me, just call,' he said and walked out into the corridor. Nesta shut the door behind him and placed her ear to the wood. His footsteps receded as he descended the stairs and Nesta turned to face the cook.

'My lady,' said Carla, 'please, I am so sorry, but am at a loss to explain what happened...'

'Carla,' said Nesta rushing over and crouching down to give the cook a hug, 'fret not for it was all a ruse to get you up here without raising any suspicions.'

'A ruse, said Carla, 'but I thought...'

'I know what you thought,' said Nesta, 'and I am sorry for the upset I really am, but I could think of no other way to get you here.'

'But why?'

'Because I need your help.'

'For what?'

'To get my nephew out of the castle.'

'My lady,' said Carla, 'I don't understand. Maelgwyn is still in the gaol and even if you can get him out, how can I possibly be of help?'

'Carla,' said Nesta, 'listen to me. In the next day or so, Rowan will free Maelgwyn from the dungeon while Salisbury is still in Cardigan. If we can get him out of the castle, I have friends waiting to spirit both him and me away to a place of safety but therein lies the problem. Until now I could not see how we could escape these walls without raising the alarm but last night an idea came to me and I need your help to make it happen.

'Anything my lady,' said Carla, 'for if you were to stay here I see nothing for you but misery and an early grave.'

'So, you will help me?'

'Of course I will,' said Carla, 'just tell me what you want me to do.'

Chapter Twenty-Eight

Crug Mawr

October 10th AD 1136

'*Hold the line,*' roared Owain again as the enemy closed in and as every man in the Welsh ranks rammed their shoulders against the rear of the shield wall, the horde of English levies smashed into them like a tidal wave. The impact was enormous and all along the centre of the defensive lines, men were driven backward under the force. Attackers poured through any gaps and axes smashed into the heads and shoulders of anyone exposed. Defenders fought desperately to fill the breaches and men from the rear ranks desperately stepped over their dead or wounded comrades to replace them in the front ranks.

Owain was knocked backward and found himself at the feet of his own men as they tried desperately to repel the charge. For a few seconds it seemed he would be trampled into the mud, but a huge hand reached down and hauled him to his feet before handing him back his dislodged sword. The Welsh commander looked into the face of the giant man and nodded his gratitude before turning and adding his weight again to the rear of the shield wall.

The front lines of both armies fought desperately to gain advantage but the solid row of shields between them meant neither gained any immediate ground as they struggled for breath in the crush.

Fitzmartin sat astride his horse behind the first wave watching the battle unfold. He knew that such an impasse was often the case in these circumstances but was still disappointed that his committed assault of two thousand men had gained little in the way of penetration. Before him, another five thousand levies waited nervously, knowing that no matter which side won the initial struggle, the battle would eventually open up and it would end with man to man fighting.

Up above the rain of lethal arrows continued to fall and though men still fell to their deadly power, the Welsh archers were now in range of the English army's smaller bows and the volleys were more sporadic as the longbow men came under fire themselves.

'Give the signal,' shouted Fitzmartin and as the sound of a horn again ripped through the air, the pressure on the Welsh defensive lines eased as the English unexpectedly stepped backward. The men at the shield wall gasped in relief, glad to be able to catch their breath and for a few moments watched as the English retreated but they had gone no further than ten paces or so when their ranks opened and the front line was replaced with hundreds of men bearing huge, double bladed battle axes.

Before Owain could react, the English horn sounded again and the attackers surged forward for the second assault, determined to destroy the shield wall. Wood splintered everywhere under the force of the impacts and few men hit directly by such force managed to stay on their feet. Breaches appeared right across the lines and the English took advantage to pour through wherever they had an opportunity. Iron and steel tore apart flesh and bone and within moments, men on both sides were covered in the blood and guts of hand to hand combat. Men considered strong and invincible only moments earlier screamed in pain as their limbs were cleft in two, their bodies torn apart by devastating blows from axe or pike. Those closer in had to resort to knives and clubs as the fight was too crowded to wield swords effectively, and the mud at their feet quickly turned to scarlet as it was fed from the veins of the wounded. Terrified men desperate to stay alive amongst the carnage lost control of any humanity they once had, tearing at their enemy with anything they had to hand, including weapons, bare hands or even their teeth.

Despite the enemy gains, Owain's men knew it was essential to hold the wall as long as possible and all across the Welsh position, sergeants demanded those alongside them hold the lines, whilst hoping their reserves would deal with any enemy who had broken through to the rear.

Again, the shield wall closed and as the English stepped back for a second time, Owain knew he had to take the opportunity to regain some sort of advantage.

'Prepare to move,' he roared, 'sound the advance.'

The different tone of a Welsh horn echoed through the air and as one, the front lines lifted their shields out of the mud and ran forward ten paces before replanting them in the ground at their feet. The rest of the supporting army followed them forward and within moments, despite having been on the receiving end of a brutal attack, had gained ten paces of territory. It wasn't much but Owain knew it would have a huge effect on the morale of both armies.

Fitzmartin was caught cold and reacted angrily at the enemy's audacity.

'Reform,' he shouted, *'advance.'*

Again, the English charged forward and again managed to breach the Welsh lines in several places, yet it was not enough to break through completely and many of his men fell to the enemy reserves before they could make any difference.

'My lord,' shouted Salisbury, 'we have to commit more men.'

Fitzmartin agreed. He had already lost over a quarter of his force to the longbows and the unsuccessful advances and knew he had to do something drastic. He looked at the remainder of his levies before him, standing ready to advance. To commit his whole army so soon in the battle without a tactical advantage was a huge risk but he had to do something and do it soon.

'Men of England,' he shouted as he rode along the rear of his lines, 'upon my command, every man will advance and when we do, there will be no reorganising or retreating. There is only one direction we are going and that is forward, straight through the Welsh position. I want to see those lines shattered and God help any man who falls short in giving everything he has in achieving that aim.' He turned to his own archers. 'When we charge,' he shouted, 'you have my authority to cut down any of our own men who turns from the fight. I will suffer no cowards in this battle.' He drew his sword and raised it high into the air. *'No retreat,'* he roared, *'no surrender, no quarter, advaaance!'*

The whole English army stepped forward, heading toward the Welsh lines just over fifty paces to their front. The English attackers still fighting at the shield wall heard them coming and slowly backed away from the defensive position leaving hundreds of dead comrades behind them.

'Spears,' shouted Fitzmartin and hundreds of spear men launched their weapons high in the air to land amongst the enemy defenders causing panic and huge casualties.

'Ready,' he shouted as the spears continued to fly, 'sound the charge.'

Several horns blew across the English lines and every man raced forward to engage the enemy, crashing into the shield wall with a furious aggression.

The effect was catastrophic for the Welsh, and this time, there was no possible way they could withstand the assault. Men fell everywhere, and it was moments only before the English were amongst the defending lines. The ranks broke under the pressure and the combatants spread out over the field, fighting desperately for their lives against a rampaging enemy.

Owain fought furiously, his sword smashing through flesh and bone as if they were nothing. His face was covered with blood - his own as well as others - but he was in trouble as he fought off three attackers at the same time. Despite his prowess with a sword the pressure began to tell, and it was only a matter of moments before he would succumb. One of the men bearing down on him suddenly fell to his knees with a sword blade sticking out from his chest and Owain looked up to see Paulus had raced in from the rear, furiously cutting down any attacker standing in his way. Encouraged, Owain delved deep and finding an untapped source of energy, drove his sword straight through the chain mail of the man to his front before turning and slamming the heel of his boot against the remaining attacker's knee causing him to collapse in agony. Owain fell onto the fallen man and drawing his knife, stabbed him over and over again through the face.

'My lord,' shouted Paulus, pulling him up, 'you have to step back from the fray, to lose you now would be a disaster.'

'I cannot turn away, Paulus,' gasped Owain, 'my place is here, amongst my men.'

'Your place is to provide command,' said Paulus, 'and that cannot be achieved from amongst the fight. Step away and lead us from the rear else we will lose this day.'

Owain hesitated, knowing the man was right. From within the lines there was no way he could have an overview of what was happening. He nodded his agreement and joined Paulus as he made his way back to the rear and to the top of a small rise in the ground. The new position afforded him a relatively good view over the battle field and after wiping the blood from his face, he looked around at the devastating brutality unfolding right across the valley.

Men fought everywhere, and it was hard to make out who was who. The lines had been breached and the battle had lost any formal shape or form. Men fought toe to toe as individuals or in small groups as they struggled to stay alive in the carnage and the screaming of the wounded rent the air. Despite the confusion it was obvious that the two armies were evenly matched, and victory was not yet assured for either side but even as he watched, the experience of the English started to take its toll and the Welsh were slowly being forced back up the valley.

Owain looked around, seeing his men fall all around him. He needed to do something, or the day could well be lost. His mind worked furiously as he sought a solution but without extra men, he could see none.

'My lord,' shouted Paulus, pointing his sword toward the ridge on his left, 'look.'

Owain turned toward the ridge line and to his astonishment, saw hundreds of unknown horsemen galloping down the slope to join the battle. For a few moments, his heart raced, fearing they were English forces but when he saw the flag of the standard bearer blowing hard in the wind, he gasped in relief. It bore the colours of Deheubarth and behind it came three hundred riders, led by Tarw himself.

'Who are they?' shouted Fitzmartin from the far side of the field.

'Whoever they are,' responded Salisbury, 'they carry the ancient flag of Deheubarth so will turn this battle in favour of the Welsh. We have to do something.'

Again, Fitzmartin looked around at his available forces. Most were committed on the battlefield but would be torn apart if he allowed the enemy riders to get amongst them without counter. All he had left was his own cavalry and though he was loathe to commit them at this stage, their numbers vastly outnumbered the Welsh horsemen, including those already stationed on the enemy flanks. With no other option, he made the decision.

'Sound the attack,' he shouted, 'send in our cavalry.'

Again, horn signals echoed above the battle raging on the valley floor and two thousand English cavalry kicked their horses into action.

'Paulus,' roared Owain seeing the threat, 'form up the archers. Use everything we have left.'

'My lord, we cannot risk hitting our own men,' replied Paulus, 'the enemy is deep amongst us and the fight is evenly balanced.'

'I don't want you to aim at their infantry,' shouted Owain, 'your targets are there.' He pointed to where the enemy cavalry was thundering down the slopes of Crug Mawr hill.

Paulus immediately saw the risk and shouted his commands to every archer in earshot.

'Load your bows,' he roared, *'aim at the enemy cavalry. Loose when ready.'*

Within moments, hundreds of arrows filled the sky and again the extra power of the longbows meant they could reach far further than anything the enemy expected. A deadly storm of willow and steel fell amongst the riders, thudding into horse and human flesh alike. Many of the mounts fell, bringing down those behind them but despite the devastating casualties, the rest thundered on, determined to cut off the newly arrived Welsh reinforcements.

'My lord,' shouted a voice, 'we are almost out of arrows.'

'Use your last,' ordered Paulus, 'and then draw whatever blades you have. We need every man in the field.'

The final few volleys of heavy arrows smashed into the English cavalry, bringing down even more of their riders but even as Paulus watched, the rain of death fell away as the longbow men finally run out of ammunition.

'That's it,' shouted Paulus to Owain, 'we are out of arrows.'

Owain turned back to face the battle. Despite the enemy cavalry's huge losses, they still came on and were moments away from clashing with Tarw's smaller force. The riders from Deheubarth would have no chance, such was their number and though it meant committing the last of his forces, Owain knew he could not let Tarw and his men get slaughtered by the English lancers.

'Sound the final attack,' he roared, *'send in our own cavalry.'*

Moments later the Welsh cavalry galloped forward from the flanks and led by Cadwaladwr and Hywel, thundered toward the English forces. The ground shook beneath thousands of hooves and as they smashed into each other, the air was torn apart with the sound of steel on steel and the heart wrenching screams of the wounded horses. Tarw's extra three hundred riders finally ploughed into the fight from the flank, and from that moment on, there was only one possible outcome.

On the English side, Fitzmartin stared coldly, numb with shock at the unfolding slaughter. The devastation wrought by the Welsh longbowmen meant that his cavalry were now heavily outnumbered and could not possibly win the day.

'It's no use,' shouted Salisbury, 'the fight is lost. We should sound the retreat.'

'There will be no retreat,' said Fitzmartin as his lancers broke ranks to flee the field, 'we will see this thing through.'

Tarw reined in his horse and stared at the retreating horsemen, knowing that although the initial fight had been won, there was nothing stopping them from reforming and coming back into the fray. He looked around and knowing there was little his men could do to add to the infantry battle without losing many of their own horses, decided to ensure that the English cavalry would no longer be a threat.

'After them,' he roared, *'don't let them escape.'*

Owain watched his cavalry gallop away in pursuit of the defeated English lancers and turned his attention back to the matter in hand. The intensity had eased and both sides retreated to reform their own lines. The dead and dying from both sides lay scattered across the field, but the English army had emerged stronger by far and still outnumbered the Welsh almost two to one.

Fitzmartin also noticed the numerical superiority, and the retreat of his cavalry cut him to the core.

'Reform the infantry,' he roared, *'three lines, present shields!'*

The weary combatants ran back into formation, gasping for breath after the exhausting fight. Most were spattered with blood and many carried wounds of varying severity, but they were still unbowed, knowing they were winning the struggle. Gradually their breathing slowed, and they stared across the field, sizing up the vastly reduced numbers of Welsh that would soon lay dead on the valley floor.

'We still have the advantage,' shouted Fitzmartin, 'one more push and they will fall as easily as did the witch Gwenllian.

On my command we will crush them like the vermin they are and claim this land for the king once and for all.'

Across the valley, the Welsh had also hastily reformed their lines and it soon became apparent that they were far narrower than those of the enemy. Paulus ordered the archers and civilians to pick up whatever weapons they could from the fallen and though it helped, they were still vastly outnumbered.

'What do we do?' asked Paulus to Owain quietly. 'We do not have the strength to defend another assault. Do we withdraw?'

'We cannot,' said Owain, 'for to do so would mean every one of our men would die here on this field. Fitzmartin has been humiliated and would pursue us to Gwynedd if necessary to get his retribution.'

'But we can't just stay here and wait,' said Paulus, 'they will crush us.'

'I agree,' said Owain, 'so we will do the last thing he expects.'

'And that is?'

'We attack,' said Owain turning to his comrade, 'and if we are to die this day, we will do so fighting for what we believe in, not running away as cowards.'

Paulus stared at his commander for a few moments and felt the blood racing through his veins.

'In that case,' he said eventually, drawing his sword, 'let it be me who leads the van.'

'You and I will both share the honour,' said Owain drawing his own sword. 'Lead the way, Paulus for one way or another, this battle is about to change the course of history.'

Both men forced their way through the ranks until they were in front of what remained of their own army.

'Men of Wales,' roared Owain turning to face his own men. 'We have come this far together, many kingdoms fighting as one, each man a brother, irrespective of colours. I am humbled by those I have fought alongside this day and know I could not ask for more. What happens here today will be talked about in the mead halls and taverns across the kingdoms of Wales and beyond for many generations. Story tellers will recount your names and bards will sing songs of the bravery shown on this field of blood.' He paused and looked along the lines, every pair of weary eyes were upon him and he knew he was about to ask that which should not be asked. 'Your bravery is the making of legends but there is yet unfinished business.'

He turned to point his sword at the approaching enemy.

'Those men,' he shouted, 'those *invaders,* those mercenaries who fight for money not freedom, represent the country that has caused your families hardship for many generations. They have raped your women, starved your children and taxed every man until his back breaks from the toil. They covet the soil that warms the bones of our ancestors and as long as I have a single drop of blood left in my veins, I will fight to the last breath to deny them that desecration.' He paused again, and every man hung on his every word. 'This battle will end here today,' he continued, 'and whether I am alone or amongst kinsmen, I intend to stand in their way. If any man wishes to stand at my side, then the only pain I fear is when my heart bursts with pride.'

For a few seconds there was silence until a wounded man limped forward toward Owain. Immediately, the rest followed until every single Welshman on the field, warrior, archer or civilian stood before him shouting out his name. Owain held up his hand for silence.

'There is no prouder man under God's sun this day,' he shouted, 'and if it is his will that we fall short, then we will do so as free men!'

He turned to face the enemy across the field.

'Look to your front and let the generations of hurt flood your veins for though they outnumber us, I would not exchange a hundred of those men for a single one of those already at my side.'

The men cheered again and reformed their lines alongside Owain, the weary look in their eyes replaced with one of steely determination.

Fitzmartin saw the Welsh army prepare and knew the time had come.

'*Men of England,*' he roared, drawing his sword, '*for king and country, advaaance!*'

Once again, the English army marched forward and as they were no longer hindered by the devastating Welsh archers their confidence grew at every step. Their speed increased, dictated by the sergeants so that by the time they reached the enemy lines they would be at full tilt and achieve the maximum impact.

'*Men of Wales,*' roared Owain, raising his sword into the air, '*for Gwenllian and for freedom, chaaarge!*'

The whole of the Welsh army burst into a run, each screaming their battle cries as they raced across the ground to smash into the English with a rage born of generations of subjugation. They slashed their way through, smashing bones and cleaving apart enemy flesh in a blind rage, neither wanting nor expecting to survive.

At first the English soldiers struggled to counter the brutal assault but as their superior numbers came to bear, they slowly regained the advantage.

Owain and Paulus fought like madmen, killing anyone who dared to come close. A sword smashed into Paulus' side and he collapsed to the floor like a felled tree. Owain bent down and hauled him to his feet.

'Stay on your feet,' he shouted, 'the earth is where we lay to die.'

'*I am not dead yet,*' gasped Paulus, as blood oozed through his damaged chainmail, 'a few broken bones, no more.'

Desperately they fought on, but the enemy numbers were overwhelming. Men fell across the whole battlefield and as the Welsh army were slaughtered, those that remained gathered around Owain, less than a few thousand men left alive from the horde that had marched from Gwynedd.

Owain looked around as his remaining men battled furiously with the enemy. Even he could see that the battle was close to being lost and though it went against his very soul, the situation was hopeless, and he knew he would have to ask for quarter.

'We cannot win,' he shouted eventually as he gasped for breath, 'and I cannot ask any more men to die needlessly. This day is over, Paulus, we have to sound the retreat.'

'No,' snarled Paulus, 'you said yourself, we will all be killed if we choose that path and I for one would rather take a few more with us. Let us fight on.'

'I cannot,' said Owain, 'If I agree to surrender, then perhaps Fitzmartin will show mercy and let some of our men go back to Gwynedd. At least that way our people will know what happened this day. Sound the retreat, Paulus, this day is done.'

Before Paulus could answer, the sound of a hunting horn echoed above the valley and though Owain was expecting a signal, it was not one of those practiced or recognised by his army.

'Who is that?' he asked lifting his head, 'have our cavalry returned?'

'Alas no,' said Paulus looking around, 'It is not one I recognise. I can only pray it is not English reinforcements.'

A few hundred paces away, Fitzmartin also looked up, not recognising the signal.

'What's happening?' he said looking around the valley. 'Where is that sound coming from?'

His officers all scanned the horizon in confusion and moments later the horn sounded again. This time their attention was drawn to the slopes of smaller hill a few hundred paces distant and were surprised to see a single man sitting on a horse.

'Who is he?' demanded Fitzmartin, 'somebody tell me what is going on.'

'It looks like a monk,' said Salisbury, 'or a priest.'

'It can't be a priest, said Fitzmartin, 'for if he is,' he turned to stare at Salisbury, 'then why is he holding a sword?'

Chapter Twenty-Nine

Crug Mawr

October 10th AD 1136

Cynwrig the Tall sat upon his horse and stared down at the battlefield in shock. He had seen many such scenes in his life especially in the days when he had fought alongside Gruffydd ap Cynan in his quest to reclaim Gwynedd, but never had he seen such carnage. Thousands of bodies lay scattered as far as the eye could see and even from his position on the hill he could hear the pitiful screams of the mortally wounded.

At the base of Crug Mawr, the last moments of the battle were being played out and though there were still many men still alive on both sides, it was evident that the English were in the ascendancy and he had arrived not a minute too soon.

He looked down at the sword cradled in his arms. Everything he had done in the last few months had been for this very moment and his heart raced with the responsibility. Slowly, almost reverently, he clamped his hands around the blade and held the sword up before him like a crucifix, his eyes filling with tears as it was silhouetted against the early afternoon sun.

'Dear God,' he whispered as his own blood ran down the blade, 'give us strength to carry out your work this day. Grant us the courage to do what has to be done in your name.' He looked down at the battlefield and saw the Welsh lines beginning to break. He had ridden hundreds of miles for this moment and it was time to fulfil his vow.

'It is time,' he shouted and just behind the ridge to his rear, a huntsman from Gwynedd raised a horn to his mouth, sending a haunting signal echoing through the air.

As he continued to stare downward, men started to appear from the rear of the hill, some on horseback but many on foot as they scrambled up the last few feet to join him on the ridge. Many bore no formal weapons, having only the tools and implements they had carried from their homes and farms across Wales. The dozens became hundreds but still they came, a peasant army, five thousand strong seeking retribution from generations of tyranny.

Down below, Fitzmartin's gaze remained frozen as the hill darkened with the silhouettes of hundreds of men pouring over the ridge.

'Who are they?' he shouted, 'our scouts spoke of no other armies.'

'They are not soldiers, my lord,' shouted the young officer struggling to control his own horse, 'they are dressed in the garb of commoners.'

'Commoners or not,' shouted another, 'their numbers are huge and will sweep us away if we don't do something.'

'There is nothing we can do,' shouted the first man, 'we have to withdraw.'

'There will be no withdrawal,' shouted Fitzmartin again, 'they are peasants armed with nothing but farm tools. Our men will swipe them away like the insects that they are.'

'But my lord,' shouted the officer, 'their numbers are overwhelming.'

'*Did you not hear me?*' roared Fitzmartin, his voice shaking in rage, '*I said we will continue this fight.*'

'Aye, my lord,' replied several men but even as they acknowledged the order, a final horn blast echoed from the peasant army above.

Cynwrig dismounted and walked out onto a protruding rock overlooking the battlefield. Every man who had answered his call to crusade looked up in anticipation as the priest once more held up the sword like a giant crucifix before him. Cynwrig looked along the expectant lines and realised he had never felt so humble in his entire life.

'Men of Wales,' he shouted eventually, 'our hands may be dirty, but it is the toil of humility that gave us our callouses and it is a blessing from God himself that we now hold our destiny within them. Use them this day to wrest your freedom from these invaders and drive them back from whence they came. In Gwenllian's name, *advaaance!*'

Down on the battlefield the last few thousand Welshmen were being forced backward by the English, but as the peasant army swept down like a swarm of ants, the roar of their voices reached the combatants and the intensity of the fighting died away. Men looked up in shock, some in relief but most in fear as the sheer number of the reinforcements became apparent. Within moments, some of the English started walking backward, knowing there was no way they could survive such an onslaught and as the terrible realisation sunk in as to what was happening, the trickle became a flood and the English army turned to run.

Owain also stared in shock, exhausted from the brutal fight and though he had no idea where these extra men had come from, he knew their arrival had surely saved the lives of every Welshman still standing on the field.

'*My lord,*' gasped Paulus as he leaned on his sword at Owain's side, 'can you hear it?'

'Hear what?' asked Owain, his gaze still captured by the charging peasant army.

'Their battle cry,' said Paulus standing up straight, 'the name upon their lips is not of God or any king, but she who has risen this country from its slumber.' He looked across at the charging men. 'They roar the name of your sister, my lord,' he said, '*they fight in the name of Gwenllian!*'

Cynwrig's peasant army charged through the exhausted Welsh soldiers in pursuit of the retreating English but though his heart burst with pride at the sight, Owain knew it was a false hope. The enemy were trained fighters and if they were to pause long enough to reorganise, they could easily defeat those who raced after them.

'*We cannot stay here,*' he roared across his own lines, '*and watch our countrymen die. These people have saved our lives but will be surely slaughtered without our help. Pick up your weapons, my friends and join our fellows to wipe this field clean.*'

The remaining soldiers joined the throng racing across the field, adding their strength and experience to the peasant army and as the battle turned, the air filled with the triumphant battle cries of those who only moments earlier, had faced defeat and certain death.

Exhausted Englishmen weighed down by armour and gambesons were soon caught and hundreds fell before they could reach safety, cut down mercilessly by those not interested in giving quarter.

As thousands fled toward Cardigan, Owain's cavalry, headed by Tarw and his men from Deheubarth returned from their successful rout of the English horsemen and as far as the eye could see, Welshmen slaughtered the fleeing English without mercy.

In Cardigan Castle, Stephen Demareis stood at the top of the keep, staring over the rooftops of the town toward Crug Mawr. His face was ashen, and his heart raced with fear as he faced the inevitable. Over the last ten minutes, riders and wounded men had started trickling into the town with reports of a terrible defeat. The trickle soon became a flood and he realised the unthinkable had happened. In the distance, the fields that had shone green in the sun only hours earlier, now swarmed with men from both sides and it was obvious his countrymen were in full blown retreat.

'My lord,' shouted a voice from the gate towers, 'look.'

The castellan's gaze followed the direction of the guard's outstretched arm and saw hundreds of panicking civilians hurrying from the town toward the safety of the castle.

'My lord,' shouted the guard again, 'there are too many for us to take. What are your orders?'

The castellan looked around nervously. He had been very astute by stocking up the fortress in case of a siege but to cram the bailey with hundreds of people incapable of fighting made no sense and it would only be a matter of time before the castle would fall.

'My lord,' shouted the guard again, 'your orders?'

Demareis suddenly realised though it meant committing hundreds of innocent civilians to a probable death, there was only one course of action open to him.

'Lock the gates,' he shouted, 'and man the palisades.'

'You heard him,' roared the guard commander, 'secure the castle.'

The sentries stationed outside the walls raced inside as the giant gates slowly closed and a dozen men lifted the huge locking bar into place.

The crowd reached the castle only moments later, falling upon the giant timbers, and beating them with clenched fists, begging fervently to be let in.

Up above, the remaining men ran along the palisades, taking up their positions. The castle's defensive force was far smaller than the one Demareis had commanded at Aberystwyth, but this fortress was far stronger, and they were well equipped to face any siege or assault.

He raced down the steps of the keep and into the bailey before climbing up onto the palisade and pulling his chain mail hauberk over his head.

'My lord,' shouted one of the men, 'you'll need this.' The soldier threw across a helmet and Demareis secured the leather ties beneath his chin, hoping it would be enough to protect him from the storm he knew was coming.

The retreat from the battlefield at Crug Mawr had turned into a full-scale rout. Any semblance of order had been torn apart and the English army was in total disarray. Everywhere Owain looked he could see the enemy being slaughtered by the overwhelming Welsh forces and the cavalry, headed by Tarw and Cadwaladwr, ran riot, cutting down fleeing soldiers at will. Despite the horrendous number of casualties, thousands still made it to Cardigan town and raced through the streets seeking somewhere safe to hide. Those townsfolk still unaware of what had happened soon realised they were in mortal danger and added to the panic as they fled their homes to seek refuge in the one place they knew they might be safe, the castle.

Fitzmartin and Salisbury battled their way through the throng, using their mounts to knock people out of their way wherever needed. They headed through the town but as they passed through the last of the streets, they reined in their horses in dismay as they saw the thousands of people fleeing toward the castle.

'My lord,' shouted a nearby soldier, 'they've locked down the castle. Where are we to go?'

Fitzmartin looked around, his mind racing. His army had been devastated yet there were still thousands of men alive. He knew there was no way they would all fit into the castle but to keep fleeing like this invited slaughter. What he needed was somewhere he could rally his men and defend a narrow front.

'We need to set up a defensive position,' he shouted to Salisbury, 'perhaps a street.'

'It's pointless,' shouted Salisbury, 'there are too many alleyways and we have no time to block them all.'

'The bridge then,' shouted Fitzmartin looking toward the wooden structure spanning the river Teifi, 'if we can get across that we can defend the far side. No matter how large the Welsh army, they can only cross a few at a time. You head on over and rally those already there. I'll round up however many I can as they come through the town and send them over.'

Salisbury turned his horse away and headed toward the crossing, kicking civilians to one side as he forced his way through the throng. When he reached the other side of the bridge, he tied his horse to a tree and ran back to the river's edge, screaming orders to anyone in earshot as he started to set up the defensive position.

On the other side of the river, the fleeing army poured into the town, desperately seeking refuge from the rampaging Welsh. Fitzmartin's voice rang out above the noise and the men headed through the narrow streets and alleyways towards the bridge. As if this wasn't a big enough problem, the sudden reappearance of those cavalry who had survived the battle added to the confusion and soon the streets were clogged with men and horses alike, hardly able to move in the deafening chaos.

As the enemy neared the outskirts of the town, the pressure increased, and the huge backlog meant that the wooden crossing became dangerously crowded. Riders tried to force their horses through and many of the foot soldiers lashed out in reply as they tried to save their own lives. Fights broke out between countrymen and though the bridge was already overcrowded, even more added to the crush as they tried desperately to escape certain death.

John of Salisbury stared at the ensuing panic and as he saw pieces of wood splinter away from the structure, he realised the whole thing was in danger of collapse.

'Go back,' he screamed over to the far side of the bridge, 'there is too much weight,' but his cries were ignored as every panicking man strove to save his own life.

Within moments the inevitable happened and as Salisbury watched in shock, several of the timber supports snapped under the weight, sending the central span of the bridge crashing into the river. Men screamed in fear as they fell but as if that wasn't enough, the sudden lack of reinforcement from the main timbers meant the rest of the bridge became substantially weaker and both ends, now free from the stabilising centre started to sway in the heavy flow. Those remaining on the bridge desperately tried to escape but the surge of panicking bodies caused more timbers to shatter and as the entire bridge collapsed, the fleeing English army were plunged into the freezing water of the Teifi.

The scene was horrific. Many, weighed down by their chainmail sunk immediately to the bottom while those still able to stay afloat lashed out desperately, grabbing onto whoever or whatever they could to keep their heads above water. Many dragged comrades under in the process and the thrashing legs of terrified horses, weighed down by panicking men added to the pandemonium. The air echoed with the desperate screams of hundreds of men begging for help but there was nothing anyone could do and as many watched in horror from either side of the river, over a thousand men and horses drowned.

Salisbury was numb with shock, standing like a statue as he watched the tragedy unfold. Hundreds of men stood all along the banks watching their comrades die, knowing that only moments earlier they had all been on that same bridge. As they watched in horror, the last of the victims succumbed to their fate, all strength finally depleted as they sank to the dark river bed. Bodies of horses and men floated everywhere as the noise subsided and though a lucky few survivors managed to reach the banks, the majority had perished in the freezing river, breaking the backbone of the English army once and for all.

'Get me my horse,' said Salisbury to a young soldier at his side.

'My lord,' said the young man, 'what are we to do?'

'I said get me my horse,' screamed Salisbury, spinning around to knock him down with the back of his mailed fist.

The young soldier scrambled to his feet and ran over to do as he was bid. Within moments he returned, leading Salisbury's destrier by the reins.

Although he was desperate to get away, Salisbury could hardly tear his eyes away from the carnage as the currents of the river started regurgitating its prey to form large floating rafts of dead men and horses.

His mind raced as he realised the implications. Most of the substantial English forces were either dead or on the far side of the river, still at risk from the attacking Welsh. Already there was smoke rising from the far boundaries of the town as the buildings were being torched and though there were other crossings upstream, he knew the remains of the army would have to fight their way to them.

The situation was dire. It was obvious the battle was lost and with dawning horror he realised that the way was now open for the Welsh army to sweep south into Deheubarth, and it would be only a matter of days before they engulfed his own castle at Pembroke.

He tore his gaze from the river and climbed into the saddle as another soldier ran over to address him.

'My lord,' said, the soldier, 'where are you going? You are the only officer alive on this side of the river, what are your orders?'

'I have no orders,' shouted Salisbury, 'see to yourselves.'

'But what should we do?' shouted the soldier grabbing the bridle of Salisbury's horse, 'there is nowhere to go.'

'I don't care,' roared Salisbury, *'now get out of my way.'*

He kicked out with his boot, striking the soldier across the face and sending him crashing to the floor. Without another word, he turned his horse away and digging his spurs in deep, galloped from the battlefield as fast as his destrier would carry him.

Chapter Thirty

Cardigan

October 10th AD 1136

Fitzmartin stared in disbelief as the bridge collapsed, knowing it ended any hope of turning the battle around. Many of the men still on the eastern side of the river fell silent, momentarily stunned at the sight of their comrades drowning before them but those who were colder to such sights, thought furiously, seeking a way to save their own lives rather than dwell on those who could not be helped.

'The northern bridge,' shouted a voice, 'it's only two leagues upstream.'

The word spread and like the turning of a tide, the throng headed northward, desperately seeking an escape.

Fitzmartin stayed where he was. Whatever happened now, he knew the army could not be reformed so it was pointless becoming just another face in the withdrawal. He turned and looked toward the castle. Hundreds of civilians gathered beneath its walls, begging the defenders to open the gates, but it remained secure and he instantly knew it was his only hope.

Fighting against the human tide he forced his horse south, ordering people from his path or barging them aside as necessary and within a few minutes, cleared the throng to gallop toward the castle. Behind him, in the distance he could hear the feint battle cries of the Welsh as they started to sack the town and he knew that if he could not get into the castle as soon as possible, he was a dead man.

Up on the battlements, Demareis looked down at the crowd begging for entry into the safety the castle. Every fibre of his being screamed at him to open the gates but he knew that if he did, they would be overwhelmed by civilian refugees and that would risk the fortress. Despite this, he was also aware that there were many soldiers amongst the crowd and they would be a definite asset to the garrison when the fight came.

'Bring ropes,' he shouted, 'haul up as many of our own as we can.'

Those on the palisades ran to the task and within moments, were pulling up their comrades one by one as down below, others kept the crowd at bay with drawn swords.

'Bring water and food,' shouted Demareis, seeing the exhaustion on the rescued men's faces. 'Get those with serious wounds to the lesser hall but anyone still capable of wielding a weapon are to remain on the palisades. We need every man we can get.'

Frantically they hauled up the last of the soldiers and started to retrieve the ropes when someone shouted out to the castellan.

'My lord, look.'

Demareis stared over to the river and saw a lone rider galloping amongst the scattered crowds of civilians still escaping the town. His clothing and horse indicated he was an English officer and as he watched, the castellan recognised the commander of the English army himself, Robert Fitzmartin.

'My lord,' shouted a soldier, 'there is no way he can reach the ropes through that crowd. They will tear him apart.'

'Then lower one from the eastern wall there are fewer people there.'

Fitzmartin rode as fast as he was able through the crowd, refusing to give up hope. The crowd became thicker the close he got to the walls and he drew his sword to defend himself against anyone who got too close.

'My lord,' shouted a voice from above and he looked up to see Demareis pointing towards a rope hanging partway down the castle's eastern palisade, 'this way.'

Immediately the commander forced his horse through the refugees until he was at the base of the eastern wall.

'Reach up,' shouted Demareis, 'we'll pull you up.'

The army commander hesitated for his horse had been with him since it was a foal, but he was realistic enough to know he had no choice. He released his feet from the stirrups and climbed up to stand on the saddle before reaching up to grab the rope.

Moments later he was dragged over the battlements while down below, a group of peasant men fought over the horse, each desperate to flee the oncoming battle.

'My lord,' said Demareis as the commander regained his breath, 'are you wounded?'

'My body is intact,' gasped Fitzmartin, 'but my pride has been torn asunder.'

'What happened out there?' asked the castellan.

'I will tell you soon enough,' replied Fitzmartin, 'but before I do, I need to ask is the castle ready to withstand a full-scale assault?'

'We are as ready as we can be,' said the castellan, 'our numbers are relatively few, but the walls are strong and our supplies higher than they have ever been.'

'Good,' said Fitzmartin, dragging himself to his feet, 'because the Welsh are coming, my friend, and when they do, it will be like nothing you have ever seen.'

On the far side of the town, Owain knelt beside Paulus helping the wounded man remove his chain mail. Paulus winced as the prince lifted it over his head, letting out a groan as his cracked ribs sent waves of pain coursing through his body.

'You sound like a woman in childbirth,' scorned Owain, 'surely such a scratch is nothing to a man such as you?'

'If childbirth is as bad as this,' winced Paulus as Owain undid the straps on his bloodstained gambeson, 'then I shall respect every woman undergoing such torment forthwith.'

Owain looked at his friend's wounds. The skin already turning black but luckily the wound from the English blade was shallow.

'There is some metal in there that needs to come out,' he said, 'but you have flesh wounds only.'

'And broken ribs,' grimaced Paulus, 'don't forget the broken ribs.'

Owain used the point of his knife to prize the broken links of chainmail from his friend's skin before pouring fresh water from his flask to wash out the wound.

'That will have to do for now,' he said, handing Paulus a pad of cloth, 'the support wagons are on their way, so we'll leave you here for the women to stitch you up. Speak to them nicely and they may even give you some poppy juice to stop your whining.'

'Just ensure they have ale,' said Paulus with a wince as he pressed the pad against his wound.

'My lord,' said a voice behind them, 'your presence is requested.'

'I have to go,' said Owain, 'but I'll see you later. Don't go drinking all the ale.'

He got to his feet and walked over to where several horsemen were waiting. As he neared, he recognised the man who had been so instrumental uniting the kingdoms.

'Tarw,' he said walking up to grab the prince's wrist, 'your arrival was timely and helped us turn the tide. You have my gratitude.'

'I only wish we had arrived sooner,' said Tarw,' perhaps more of our countrymen would still be breathing god's clean air if we had.'

'On the contrary,' said Owain, 'the impact of your arrival probably had more of an effect than if you had lined up with our own cavalry.' He looked up as several more riders joined them. Amongst them was Cadwaladwr.

'Brother,' said Owain as he walked over carrying the water flask, 'I'm glad you survived. What news do you have?'

'Half the English cavalry are dead,' said Cadwaladwr taking the proffered flask, 'and the other half spread out from here to Deheubarth.' He tipped back his head and poured water over his face before drinking his fill and handing the flask back to Owain. 'We pursued them as far as we could but when it became obvious they were too spread out to present a continued threat, I thought we would be of more use here.' He looked toward the town where dozens of houses were already ablaze, and the sounds of their rampaging countrymen filled the air. 'They will tear that place to the ground,' he said, 'do we rein them in?'

'No, 'said Owain. 'Let this play out as it will and tomorrow we will reform to set our plans.'

'My lord,' said a voice, 'this man begs audience.'

They turned to see two of their own soldiers dragging a half conscious English officer between them. His hands were tied behind his back and he had obviously been the subject of a severe beating.

'Who is he?' asked Owain as they threw him to the floor at Owain's feet.

'We found him coming from the town under a white flag,' said one of the men, 'he said he is one of the commanders and seeks terms of surrender.'

'Surrender?' sneered Tarw. 'Is he blind? Can he not see his army has already been defeated? Why would we offer terms?'

'I want to know why this man is still alive,' growled Cadwaladwr drawing his sword, 'we agreed no quarter.'

'Wait,' said Owain, holding up his hand, 'he was brave enough to offer himself into the custody of our men, at the very least we should hear what he has to say.' He looked down on the prisoner. 'Well?' He said, 'say your piece and make it good else we'll all revel in watching your guts fall in a steaming heap to nourish this Welsh soil.'

'My lord,' gasped the man through a mouthful of broken teeth, 'I appeal to you as a man of honour. The victory is yours and you have defeated us in a battle bloodier than any I have ever seen. Not only were we out-thought and out-fought at every turn, but our cavalry has been scattered to the winds and what remains of our levies are fleeing for their lives. The praise goes to you and you alone and as a military man I salute you.' He paused and spat out a mouthful of blood. 'But surely, with a victory so complete, there is no need to continue to slaughter those who suffer the effects of such a rout. Men already wounded cry in fear as your warriors hunt them down, begging for mercy even as they are impaled on your spears. Surely, this is not the way an honourable man such as yourself would want to be remembered?'

'What?' gasped Cadwaladwr before Owain had chance to answer, 'you expect us to show mercy to those who have killed so many of our own, knowing full well that we have suffered brutality and servitude under the English heel for a generation. How many of our own people, young and old, man or woman also begged for mercy only to be hung from gibbets or starved to death at the whim of an overlord? Where is their voice, my friend, where was their mercy?'

'My lord,' spluttered the man, 'I know there have been such instances but those you now run down like sport had no hand in such things. They are soldiers who only do as they are ordered and have wives and families just like you. Indeed, my own wife and children live in Pembroke and unless I do as I am ordered by my masters, I would not be able to put food on the table. Yes, I have fought and killed Welshmen but only on the field of battle. Surely it is not the lowly soldier who is at fault in such things but the overlords who issue the commands.'

'So where are these lords now?' asked Owain. 'Did they send you here?'

'No, my lord, they have fled the field. My lord Fitzmartin has sought refuge in the castle but the others fled with the cavalry. I also know John Salisbury managed to get across the river before the bridge collapsed and was last seen galloping south to Pembroke.'

'The bridge has collapsed?' asked Owain, his interest suddenly piqued.

'Aye, my lord, and they say over a thousand men and horses drowned in the river. A tragedy surely cast by the devil himself.'

For a few seconds, the Welshmen stared at each other before bursting out in laughter.

'God is truly on our side,' guffawed Cadwaladwr, 'not only has he killed a thousand English in one swoop, but he also denied the remainder an easy escape route. These next few days will see the Teifi turn red with English blood.'

Before he could continue, Tarw barged him out of the way and drawing his knife, knelt down to press it against the prisoner's throat.

'Repeat what you just told us,' he said, his voice heavy with threat.

'I said the bridge has collapsed,' said the man the fear rising in his eyes.

'No, who did you say escaped across the bridge?'

'John of Salisbury,' said the officer, 'the castellan of Pembroke castle.'

The laughter died away and Owain stared at Tarw, just as shocked as the prince at the revelation.

'Tarw,' he said, 'I swear I had no idea Salisbury was involved. If I did, I would have told you.'

Tarw ignored the prince but continued staring into the prisoner's terrified eyes.

'Are you sure it was him?' he asked.

'Aye, I recognised him from the time I was in Kidwelly castle. '

'But his castle is at Pembroke. When did you see him at Kidwelly?'

'I was stationed there several months ago,' said the officer. 'We had been sent by ship to join Maurice de Londres to fight against another Welsh army.'

'The battle outside Kidwelly Castle?' asked Tarw quietly.

'Aye my lord, but you and I are both soldiers and like I said, we only do what we are ordered to do.'

'Did you fight that day?' asked Tarw.

'My lord? '

'I said did you fight that day?' screamed Tarw, his spittle splashing the prisoners face. 'Were you there?'

'Yes, my lord,' cried the man in fear, 'I rode with Maurice de Londres.

Silence fell as Tarw absorbed the information. He lowered his knife and stared at the floor for a few moments, gathering his thoughts.'

'So, you saw her die,' he said eventually.

'Are you talking about that woman who led them?' asked the prisoner, 'for if so, you must know she was a witch. Everyone said so.'

'She was no witch,' said Tarw eventually. 'She was a beautiful woman and a wonderful mother who wanted only for her sons to grow up in a free country. Her name was Gwenllian and she was my wife.' Tarw looked up again at the prisoner. 'Did you see her die?'

'Yes, my lord,' said the man as tears came to his eyes again, 'I saw her executed.'

'And did she beg for mercy?' asked Tarw, 'as you now beg the same?'

'She did,' whispered the man, knowing he was probably sealing his own fate. 'She begged for mercy, not for herself, but for her remaining son.'

'And yet he had them both killed in cold blood.'

'No,' sobbed the man, 'she was beheaded on the field, but her son was taken into captivity. I have heard he is still alive in the dungeons.'

Tarw's eyes opened wide in shock and for a moment he stared at the prisoner in silence, hardly able to comprehend what he had just heard.

'Say that again,' he said.

'The boy,' said the man, realising he may yet have a chance to escape death, 'he is a prisoner in Pembroke Castle. Allow me to live and I will arrange his immediate release, I swear.'

Tarw stood up, his mind racing at the revelation. If what this man was saying was true, his son Maelgwyn was still alive but with John of Salisbury headed back having suffered such a humiliating defeat, it was doubtful that he would remain so for much longer.

'Where are you going?' asked Owain as Tarw turned to walk back to his horse.

'I'm going after him,' said Tarw. 'If I don't stop him, Salisbury will kill both Maelgwyn and Nesta as soon as he gets there.'

'I'll come with you,' said Owain.

'No,' said Tarw, 'there is still fighting to be done here.' He nodded to the castle. 'As soon as that thing is nothing more than a pile of ashes, bring the army into Deheubarth. I will rally the people and if it is God's will, together we will free the south.'

'Consider it done,' said Owain and watched as the prince jumped back into his saddle.

Tarw was about to spur his horse when Cadwaladwr called out behind him.

'Gruffydd ap Rhys,' he shouted using Tarw's formal name.

Tarw turned around to see Cadwaladwr had spun the English officer around and was holding his head back by the hair, exposing his unprotected neck.

'This one is for my sister,' said Cadwaladwr and as Tarw watched, the Gwynedd prince drew the blade slowly across the prisoner's throat.

Chapter Thirty-One

Pembroke Castle

October 11th AD 1136

Nesta lay fast asleep in her quarters, exhausted from the constant turmoil in her mind. The clouded skies outside meant no light crept through the shutters and apart from the feint glow of a single candle, the room was in complete darkness. Dawn was only hours away and apart from the sound of a dog barking somewhere in the backstreets of Pembroke, the castle was a still as the grave.

On the other side of the town a man rode his exhausted horse through the cobbled streets. He had been on the road for hours and carried a shoulder wound from an arrow but despite the fact he was close to death, he was determined to reach his destination.

The horse picked up the pace as it emerged from the town, recognising the fortress looming above it as a place of rest and safety.

On the palisade above, one of the few guards still on duty sat against the wooden wall, his cloak wrapped tightly around him as protection from the cold. Life had been easier these past few weeks for him and his fellows for when the main garrison had been deployed to Cardigan with Salisbury, they had taken the hated sergeants with them and though one remained in charge, discipline was now far more relaxed than he had ever known. He closed his eyes again, silently cursing the dog who had woken him from his slumber and was on the verge of sleeping when a familiar noise forced him awake, the rhythmic sound of a horse's hooves on the wooden bridge spanning the castle's defensive ditch.

'If that is a trader seeking shelter,' he swore under his breath, 'I swear I'll have him horse whipped.' He climbed to his feet and walked over to the palisade to peer down. Below him he could see a horse standing before the gates, its laboured breathing audible even from high on the castle walls. The man in the saddle was slouched forward as if asleep, an irony not lost on the castle guard.

'Who's there?' he asked, his voice carrying in the darkness.

For a moment there was no movement but eventually the rider forced himself upright and looked up at the walls.

'Open the gates,' he said, 'I am wounded and in need of aid.'

'These gates remain closed until dawn,' said the guard, 'and open for no man. How are you wounded?'

'I have a Welsh arrow in my shoulder,' said the rider weakly, 'and need a surgeon. You have to let me in, the castle needs to be prepared.'

'For what?' asked the guard.

'To defend itself from a coming army the likes of which you cannot imagine.'

'You are making no sense,' said the guard. 'Explain yourself.'

'I have come from Cardigan,' said the rider, 'and have ridden the night through. Our forces have been defeated and men lay dead in their thousands. The battle was lost.'

'What?' gasped the soldier, 'How could we possibly lose a battle against an army of peasants and farmers?'

'If you want answers, my friend,' said the rider, 'I suggest you open this gate for I fear I am not long for this world.'

The guard stood upright and suddenly coming to his senses. He ran over to sound the alarm bell.

Nesta heard the bell and jumped from her bed to don a robe. She picked up the candle and walked to the window to peer out at the commotion below. Two men knelt next to a third laying on the floor while across the courtyard, one of the grooms led an exhausted horse away to the stables.

As she watched, a knock came on the door but before she could answer, the handle turned and someone crept in to the darkness.

'Who's there?' she gasped as she turned around, her heart racing.

'It's me,' whispered a voice, 'Rowan.'

'Rowan,' she gasped stepping forward, 'what's happening? Who is that man in the bailey?'

'He is one of our own men,' said Rowan, 'and rode with Salisbury to aid Fitzmartin against Owain. It seems our army was routed in Cardigan and Owain's forces are on the rampage. Even as we speak, the English flee southward in fear for their lives. He walked over to the window and stared down at the bailey. The garrison was now fully roused, and men ran to the battlements carrying their arms.

'We have to move,' said Rowan, 'we have little time.'

'Time for what?' asked Nesta.

'If what he says is true,' said Rowan, 'this place will soon be awash with those seeking refuge and close on their heels will be Owain and his men. We cannot stay here, my lady, for even though you are a Welsh princess, the castle will soon be under siege and fire does not discriminate by nationality.'

'But the plan,' said Nesta, 'tonight we were to spirit Maelgwyn away from this pace.'

'Circumstances have changed,' said Rowan, 'and we have to get you to a place of safety while we still can.'

'No,' said Nesta shaking her head, 'I will not go without Maelgwyn. The only reason I haven't hurled myself from the tower since Gwenllian died is because I thought I could help him. If I flee now, it would all have been for nought.'

'My lady,' said Rowan glancing toward the door. 'We have no time. The plan included hiding him in the cook's cart being sent out for rations but that is no longer possible. The gates are locked and will allow no traffic in or out. Even if there was a slightest chance before, this news will ensure they remain barred until someone in authority returns.'

Nesta's hand flew to her mouth as she realised the implications.

'Oh, sweet Jesus,' she said.

'My lady?'

'If the army has been defeated, I suspect Salisbury will be on his way back here as we speak and if it is as bad as you say, then his temper will be as black as the devil's heart.'

'Then that confirms it,' said Rowan, 'we have to get you away.'

'And Maelgwyn,' said Nesta, 'he comes with us.'

'My lady,' gasped Rowan in desperation, 'you know not what you ask.'

'He comes with us,' snapped Nesta, 'or I go nowhere.'

Rowan's shoulders dropped as he realised there was no arguing with the strong-willed princess.

'So be it,' he said, 'you get dressed and meet me near the stables as soon as you can. I'll see if I can get him out.'

'Get who out?' asked a voice and they both turned to see the lady Anwen standing in the doorway.

'Lady Anwen,' said Nesta thinking quickly, 'you must have heard the noise. This soldier has just come up to inform me of the news.'

'What news is this?'

'That Fitzmartin has been defeated in Cardigan. Apparently, what remains of our army are on their way back and are being pursued by the Welsh forces.'

'Is this true?' asked Anwen, turning to face Rowan.

'It is my lady,' he replied, 'I have few details as yet, but it looks like there was a terrible battle and we came off second best. The castle is being prepared for a siege, so I should be getting back.' He started to walk to the door, but the big woman held out her hand, barring his exit.

'You may be telling the truth,' she said, 'and I will find out soon enough, but my first question has still not been answered. Who is the person you are going to try and set free? Not the witch's son I hope.'

Rowan looked at Nesta, a glance noticed by Anwen.

'I thought so,' said Anwen after a few moments silence. 'This is betrayal of the highest order and I will see you hang for your treachery.'

'Lady Anwen,' started Nesta but before she could continue, Rowan leapt forward and grabbed the woman, dragging her further into the room

'What do you think you're doing?' she shouted, 'get your hands off me.'

'Rowan, do not hurt her,' shouted Nesta.

'Close the door,' shouted Rowan as he wrestled the woman to the floor, 'quickly.'

Nesta pushed the door shut as the woman continued to struggle. Her panic added to her strength and she fought like a wild cat.

Knowing she could scream out at any time to alert any nearby guards, Rowan resorted to violence and as soon as one of his hands were free from her grasp, he punched the woman as hard as he could across the face. Anwen fell back on the floor, momentarily dazed.

'Rowan,' shouted Nesta as the soldier punched her again, 'stop.'

'I'm sorry, my lady,' he said, 'but we could not risk her crying out. She will be fine, but we need to tie her up while we make our escape.'

Nesta looked around the room before producing a sheet of linen. Rowan used his knife to cut it into strips before tying the woman's hands and feet securely together. Anwen started to come around but before she could cry out, he dipped a strip of cloth into a jug of water and placed it in her mouth as a gag.

'I'm sorry, my lady,' he said as he tied the knot around the back of her head, 'but we can't risk you calling for help.'

Anwen glared at him in response, her eyes full of fury.

Nesta walked over to the captive.

'I'm really sorry,' she said, 'please forgive me.'

'My lady,' said Rowan, 'get dressed as quickly as you can and meet me at the stables. Bring a cloak but nothing else as we will have to move quickly.' Without waiting for a reply, he ran from the room, leaving the princess behind him.

Down in the dungeons the jailer picked on the remains of a chicken carcass, sucking the bones dry before throwing them in a corner to be fought over by the resident rats. At the end of the corridor, the door opened and Rowan walked in, closing the door behind him.

'You again,' said the jailer as the soldier approached, 'I hope you've remembered the ale.'

'Alas I have no ale,' said Rowan, causing the jailer to look up in disgust, 'but I do have this.'

Without warning he pounced forward and drove a knife down through the man's throat, cutting off any cry of alarm. The guard's eyes opened in horror and his hands flew to the blade, desperately trying to pull it free but it was too late and as the strong soldier brought all his weight to bear, the knife cut through his victim's spine causing him to collapse backward, already dead as he slipped from the chair.

Rowan froze, waiting in the darkness to see if anyone had heard the commotion but nobody came. They were all too busy running around the castle preparing for the coming fight. He retrieved the key from the dead jailer and opened the cell before ducking inside with the candle.

'Maelgwyn,' he hissed, 'it's Rowan. Get to your feet, we have to go.'

'What do you mean?' said Maelgwyn from his place on a pile of rotten straw. 'You said you would give me fair warning.'

'I know what I said,' replied Rowan, 'but things have changed, and we have to move now. Here, put this on.' He placed the guard's cloak around Maelgwyn's shoulders and helped him to his feet.

'Where are we going?' asked Maelgwyn weakly.

'To the stables,' said Rowan, 'I have horses ready.'

'I don't think I will be able to ride,' said Maelgwyn, 'I have little strength.'

'I'll tie you across my saddle if I have to,' said Rowan, 'but first we have to get out of this place.' He led the young man down the corridor and up the steps to the doorway. 'Wait here,' he said and peered out into the bailey. In the east, the sky was beginning to lighten, and he knew he had to move fast.

'When I say go,' said Rowan, 'follow the wall to the left.' Stay in the shadows until you reach a stable block then hide yourself away. Nesta will meet you there.'

'Where are you going?'

'I need to ensure the gate is opened,' said Rowan, 'and I cannot do that from the stables. I'll be as quick as I can.'

'Wait,' said Maelgwyn, 'I need a knife.'

Rowan stared at Maelgwyn, unsure why he would need such a thing.

'Why do you want a blade?' he asked, 'you are in no fit state to fight a child, yet alone a man.'

'It's not to use on someone else,' said Maelgwyn, 'it's for me.'

'Why?'

'I will not go back to that cell,' said Maelgwyn. 'If they come looking, then I will open my wrists before I let them take me again.'

For a few seconds, Rowan considered denying the young prince his request but realizing that in his place he would do the same thing, reached to his belt and retrieved his knife, the blade still sticky from the jailer's blood.

'Here,' he said, 'and pray to God that you don't need it.'

Maelgwyn nodded silently.

'Right,' said Rowan, 'we have to go while we still have darkness.'

He opened the door and both men stepped out into the bailey, one turning left for the stables while the other turned right and headed for the gates.

Up in the keep, Nesta pulled on her own cloak and after a final glance at Anwen, hurried from her quarters and down the stairs. She exited the keep and walked unchallenged down the motte into the bailey. Dawn was breaking and most of the few dozen men still stationed in the castle were already at their posts up on the palisade or carrying armfuls of spare weapons from the armoury.

'My lady,' called a voice, 'you should go back to the keep. Heaven only knows what will happen here these next few hours.'

'Thank you,' she said, 'I will return shortly,' and continued toward the stables, reaching them without any further interruption. She hurried inside and waited in the shadows, expecting Rowan to appear at any moment.

A weak cough made her freeze to the spot and she turned to stare into one of the stalls.

'Who's there?' she whispered. 'Rowan, is that you?'

For a few moments there was silence but eventually she heard movement and Maelgwyn limped out of the dark.

Nesta stared at her brother's son in shock. His whole body was not much more than a flesh coloured skeleton with a face swollen and blackened from the daily beatings at the hands of his jailers.

'Maelgwyn,' she gasped, 'what have they done to you?' The young prince collapsed into her arms and as she held him tightly, his pathetic body shook with sobs.

'Worry not,' whispered Nesta through her own tears, 'it is all over, Maelgwyn. I'm going to get you out of here and look after you for the rest of our lives.'

Out in the courtyard, Rowan looked around desperately, knowing he had to find a way out. Most of the castle soldiers were up on the palisades but the gate guards remained at their posts and were preparing the extra locking bars to reinforce the entrance. For a few moments he considered his chances of overpowering the three men but soon realised that even if he could, by the time he had the gates open and collected his charges from the stables someone would have noticed. His heart sunk as he realised it was futile but as he was about to return to the stables, a voice rang out across the bailey.

'You men,' shouted the sergeant from the palisade, 'there is no need for four of you to stand there doing nothing. Leave one behind and start bringing more arrows from the armoury. There will be time enough to reinforce the gate when the enemy appears.'

Rowan held his breath and watched as three of the men left, leaving a solitary guard on duty. Despite this he knew the chances of him escaping without help were minimal and he had to do something drastic. Swallowing hard he walked over to the soldier.

'Gethin,' he said, recognising the guard, 'I am glad it is you on the gate. I seek a favour.'

'What sort of favour?' asked the guard. 'I have no money if that's what you want.'

Rowan hesitated, knowing he was about to risk everything.

'Listen,' he said, 'my sister and her son were here yesterday, visiting me from their home in Kidwelly. They were supposed to leave last night but it was dark and I bid them stay. Now they are stuck here but need to get home, especially if war is coming. Can you let them out?'

'I'm sorry, friend,' said the guard, 'you know the standing orders. No man or woman is to leave or enter the castle without the direct command of the castellan.'

'Yes, but he isn't here is he? Can you not just push the gates open a little bit while it is still dark and let them through? Nobody will ever know and I'll give you my ration of ale for the next three months.'

'Three months?' asked the soldier, shocked at the generosity.

'Aye. Six if you promise not to tell anyone about it.'

The guard thought for a moment before nodding his agreement.

'So be it,' he said glancing up at the palisade, 'but make haste for it will be light soon.'

'A few moments are all we need,' said Rowan. 'I'll be straight back.'

He walked as fast as he could without attracting attention to himself before running to the stable.

'Lady Nesta, are you there?' He whispered as he pushed open the door

'Over here,' answered Nesta and she and Maelgwyn appeared from the shadows.

'We have to be quick,' said Rowan, 'the guard is going to let you through the gate, but we have moments only. In the far stall there are three horses ready saddled.' He looked at Maelgwyn. 'You will never stay astride a horse on your own in that state he said, 'come on, you can both share.'

They walked over to the horses and Rowan helped them both up into the saddle. Maelgwyn sat behind Nesta and clamped his hands around her waist.

'Pull up your hoods,' said Rowan taking the reins to lead the horse out through the doors, 'and as soon as you are out of the castle, head for the safety of the Cantref Mawr.'

'Wait,' said Nesta, 'what about you. We agreed you would come too.'

'I cannot,' said Rowan, 'for to do so would give the ruse away. Worry not about me for if this works, there will be no suspicion upon my head.'

'Until they find Anwen and she tells them what happened.'

'This place will be a frenzy of activity by then as the army starts arriving back. When they do, they will have to open the gates to let them in and I can slip away in the confusion.'

'Rowan …' started Nesta.

'My lady,' snapped Rowan, 'enough argument. This is the best I can do so it is either this or stay here until Salisbury returns. Make your choice for I am all out of ideas.

'So be it,' said Nesta eventually, 'but you make sure you get out, Rowan. You are too good a man to die in the service of such a tyrant.'

Rowan nodded and led the horses out of the stable, keeping to the shadows as best he could. Within moments they were at the gates and he stared at the guard, knowing this was the crucial moment that everything hinged upon.

The guard looked over his shoulder and saw them waiting in the shadows. Nervously he walked over to speak to Rowan.

'I'm not sure about this,' he said, 'if we are caught I will be whipped.'

'We will not be caught,' said Rowan, 'and we had a deal. Now open the gates.'

'I don't know,' said the guard, 'your offer of ale is good but who's to say I will even be alive to drink it at the end of today.'

'I have nothing else,' said Rowan. 'Please, my sister and her son have to get home before the fighting starts.'

The man still hesitated but looked up as Nesta spoke.

'Will this help,' she said and removed a jewelled ring from her finger, handing it down to Rowan.

'My sister's husband is a wealthy man,' lied Rowan as he handed the ring to the guard. 'Open the gate and this is yours.'

The man stared at the beautiful ring, knowing it was worth more than he could ever hope to earn in a lifetime. He swallowed loudly and looked up.

'I agree,' he said. 'Just be quick.'

He turned to walk back to the gates but as Rowan looked up at Nesta with renewed hope, a gravelled voice called out from the watchtower.

'Open the gates, riders are approaching.'

Nesta looked down at Rowan in confusion. The fact that the gates were about to be opened anyway was good but with people coming in, there was no way they could slip out unnoticed.

'What are we to do?' she gasped.

'We have no choice,' said Rowan. 'Get ready to go as soon as the riders are in. It will take a few seconds before the gates close again so use that time to affect your escape. Worry not about subterfuge, just spur your horse and ride like the wind.'

'But won't they follow?'

'If they have ridden from Cardigan their horses will be exhausted. All you need to do is reach the forests and you will be safe. Now get ready.'

'Who ordered the gates to be opened,' shouted a voice from the palisade over to the gate tower, 'our orders are we open the gates for no man.'

'We do for this one, my lord,' answered the gravelly voice, 'it is the castellan himself, John of Salisbury.'

Chapter Thirty-Two

Pembroke

October 11th AD 1136

Tarw rode as hard as he dared through the darkness. He had stopped neither for food or rest, pausing only long enough at the streams to allow his exhausted horse to drink. Even then he lingered no longer than was necessary before spurring it on to reach Pembroke Castle before it was too late.

In the East the sun was just rising and as the morning mist cleared, he could see the fortress towering above Pembroke town.

'Nearly there, boy,' he said and kicked his horse to one last effort.

In the castle the gates swung open and a group of ten men rode their own exhausted horses into the bailey. At their head was the unmistakable figure of John Salisbury, his face etched with tiredness after his long ride from Cardigan. A groom ran forward to take the reins as the castellan slid from his horse to stand in the mud.

'Someone give me a flask,' he growled and moments later, caught a leather water bottle tossed from the ramparts. He removed the stopper and drank deeply before throwing it to one side.

'My lord,' said the sergeant, walking across the bailey to greet him, 'it is good to have you back. What news from the battle?'

'There is no battle,' spat Salisbury, 'not anymore. Those peasants fooled us with trickery unbecoming of any decent man. As we speak they are murdering the innocent women and children of Pembroke and we must take measures that the same does not happen here.' He looked around the palisade at the men already on station.

'I see you have called the garrison to arms,' he said, 'good. What state are we in?'

'My lord,' said the sergeant, 'we are few in number, but every man is well armed and ready to fight. Our food stores are adequate, and we have plenty of water. What we need most is men.'

'There will be plenty headed this way soon enough,' said Salisbury, removing his gauntlets. 'In the meantime, get me some food.'

The sergeant turned away as Salisbury looked around the bailey. His gaze passed the stable block but quickly returned as he saw someone hiding in the shadows.

'Who's there?' he called, 'show yourself.' Every eye in the castle turned to see who he was shouting at.

For a few seconds nobody moved until finally, a horse appeared carrying two riders, their faces hidden by the hoods of their cloaks.

'Who are they?' demanded Salisbury to the sergeant.

'I have no idea, my lord,' he replied, 'I did not know they were there.'

'Come closer,' demanded Salisbury, 'and remove your hood.'

Nesta walked the horse closer, knowing the game was up. She lifted her hand to her head and pulled back the hood, revealing her face to the castellan.

Salisbury stared in silence, until suddenly, contrary to all expectations, he burst into laughter, Genuine, uncontrolled mirth that caused him to bend, such was the pain.

Nesta stared at the man, knowing he was truly mad. She had expected him to drag her from her horse or have her cut down but not this, not the unbridled hysterics that echoed around the castle.

'What's wrong with you?' she asked as his laughter eased. 'Are you possessed of some sort of demon?'

'Oh no, sweet Nesta,' replied the castellan, wiping away the tears of laughter on his face. 'I am as sane as I always was.'

'A matter of judgement,' spat Nesta, 'and I, my lord, would beg to differ.'

'What is wrong with you people?' shouted Salisbury, opening his arms and turning on the spot to address the garrison. 'Do you not find it amusing that I escaped an enemy over ten thousand strong and a ride that would have scared the devil himself only to find that upon my safe arrival home, the woman I was going to make my wife is hell bent on fleeing this place with another man? Is it not funny that God himself saw fit to spare me long enough that it is I that foiled her flight?'

A few men on the palisade feigned laughter but it died away as quickly as it started.

The smile faded on the castellan's face as he turned to the figure sitting directly behind Nesta on her horse.

'And who is this suitor?' he said, walking over to the horse. 'Is it some noble with riches untold or a handsome prince with a line of castles strung out across a beautiful kingdom?' He reached up and pulled Maelgwyn from the horse to land in the mud at his feet.

'Ah,' said Salisbury, 'I should have known. It is indeed a prince, or at least it was. Now it is a filthy animal not fit to feed my pigs.' He spat on Maelgwyn as the young man moaned on the floor,

'Stop mocking us,' shouted Nesta, 'and do what you will. Kill us if you must but know this, you will send me to my grave knowing that these men were witness to my last words. They and their comrades will know you are a tyrant in name and nature. A so-called noble who has lied and cheated his way to the top table, betraying those who called him comrade in return for favour or coin. A pitiful man whose cruelty hides his cowardice and even in the bed chamber, uses his strength to hide the fact he is a useless lover.'

Salisbury's face winced at the taunt, but he maintained his calm.

'Yes, that's right,' shouted Nesta, realising she had struck a nerve. 'Your castellan is so useless when it comes to satisfying a woman, he uses his fists in frustration at his incompetence. Perhaps boys are more to his taste.'

'*Enough,*' roared Salisbury, '*get her down,*'

Two of the soldiers pulled her from her horse and dragged her across the bailey to throw her at his feet. She looked up in contempt.

'What's the matter, my lord,' she said sarcastically, 'does it hurt to have your secrets unveiled?'

Without warning, the castellan lashed out with his boot and kicked Nesta across the face sending her sprawling into the mud. A shout of dismay echoed around the walls at the brutality, but Salisbury shouted back in anger.

'*Shut your mouths,*' he roared, '*and look to your fronts. This is the business of nobility, not peasants.*' He turned to deliver another kick but spun in surprise as a roar rang out and Rowan ran at him from the shadows, sword in hand.

With seconds to spare, Salisbury ducked out of the way and drew his own sword as the soldier slipped in the mud. Rowan fell to the floor but as he struggled to get to his feet, Salisbury stepped forward to thrust his sword straight through the soldier's throat. Rowan fell back into the mud and Salisbury slammed his boot onto the dying man's face as leverage to withdraw his blade.

'*Treachery everywhere I look,*' roared Salisbury, looking to the men on the ramparts. 'I have been gone days only and this is what I return to. An escaped prisoner, a treacherous wife and a would-be assassin from amongst your own ranks. You are all supposed to be soldiers but all I see before me is incompetence.'

He walked over to Nesta and grabbing her by the hair, dragged her up to her knees.

'This woman,' he continued, 'this so-called princess has had more men than the cheapest whores in the taverns of Pembroke, yet half of you revere her like a goddess. Why? Because she was lucky enough to be born to the right family. She and others like her had their lives made from the time they were born while people like me had to fight for everything we have, scraping a living to even get noticed amongst the nobles. Where is the fairness in that?' He looked down at Nesta and grimaced as he slapped her hard across the face sending her sprawling again.

'My lord,' shouted a soldier on the ramparts, 'enough.'

'Why?' shouted Salisbury, 'she is my woman so I will treat her as I will.' He turned again and lashed out with his boot, kicking Nesta in the ribs.

More voices joined the first, but Salisbury just laughed, ignoring their concerns.

'I am castellan of this place,' he roared circling Nesta's prone body, '*and I will do as I please.*' He returned to Nesta and stamped on her ankle, snapping it in two. Her scream echoed around the castle and her sobs of pain were pitiful as everyone realised he was going to beat her to death.

'Well,' shouted the castellan, 'are there any more dissenters. Are there none amongst you who would challenge me or are you all too afraid of your own shadows?'

'I thought not,' he said eventually as all the men fell quiet. 'You just do what you are paid to do and leave the governance of this place to your betters for it is people like me who were born to rule, not the likes of her.'

He turned and stepped toward Nesta, lining up another kick but stopped as a shout echoed across the bailey, stopping him in his tracks.

'Salisbury!'

The castellan turned and looked at the man walking through the open gates. For a few seconds he stared, trying to work out where he had seen him before and then the evil smile returned as he recognised who it was.

'Well if it isn't Gruffydd ap Rhys,' he said slowly, 'delivered into my hands right here in my own castle. God certainly works in mysterious ways.'

'Leave her alone, Salisbury,' snarled Tarw, 'she is a woman who has never raised a fist in anger her entire life.'

'You are right,' said Salisbury, 'for there is little sport in someone so weak. I would much prefer a stronger opponent, someone like your wife perhaps. Oh, I forgot, I've already killed her. Where is Gwenllian, Tarw? Oh yes, I remember, rotting somewhere on a Welsh field minus her head.' He pressed his foot on Nesta's broken ankle, causing her to scream out again.

'Enough,' shouted Tarw, taking a few steps forward. 'It is me you want, not her. Let her go or I swear I will kill you like the dog you are.'

'Really,' said Salisbury. 'Take a look around, Tarw, you are surrounded by my men and as far as I can see, you are alone. Your wife was stupid, but you, sir, are truly an imbecile if you believe you can march in here and expect me to do your whim just because of your reputation. Now be a good boy and stay there while I cut her throat.'

'You touch one more hair on her head and I will kill you where you stand,' shouted Tarw drawing his sword.

Salisbury stared at Tarw and though his arrogance meant he thought he was a better man, he was not stupid and knew the prince could easily better him in a fight.

'Enough of this nonsense,' he sighed, 'archers, cut him down.'

For a few seconds there was silence around the walls as all the men stared down into the bailey.

'I said cut him down,' said Salisbury again. 'Now.'

Again, nobody moved, and Salisbury looked up at the men on the ramparts.

'Are you deaf?' he roared. 'I ordered you kill him so do it.'

One by one the archers lowered their bows.

'You,' he shouted to the guards by the gate, 'kill this man.'

The guards each sheathed their swords and stepped back from Tarw.

All around the bailey, men lowered their weapons, each at the end of their tether at the brutality of the castellan.

'Traitors,' roared Salisbury, 'all of you. Every man will hang for this.'

Tarw walked slowly forward, brandishing his own sword.

'It's over, Salisbury,' he said, 'let her go and I'll allow you to ride out of here.'

Salisbury's eyes were glaring with madness and he looked down at the moaning Nesta, still laying in the mud. He drew his knife and before Tarw could react, dropped to his knees to press the blade against the princess' exposed neck.

'You will not have the last word, Tarw,' he spat, 'I am castellan of this place and her life is mine to do with as I will.'

'Do that and you are a dead man,' said Tarw.

'Perhaps so, but I will die knowing I had a hand in killing your wife, your eldest son and your sister. That's not a bad tally for any man.'

'Don't do it, Salisbury,' pleaded Tarw, realising there was nothing he could do, 'don't do this.'

Salisbury smiled at Tarw, revelling in the power he had regained so quickly.

'It's too late, Tarw,' he said coldly, 'we are done here.' He took a deep breath and looked down to watch the blade slice through Nesta's flesh but just as he was about to drag the blade, his body arched backward in agony as a knife was plunged deep into his back. He staggered to his feet and turned to face his attacker.

'You,' he gasped.

Before him was Maelgwyn, kneeling on the floor exhausted, having spent the last few minutes crawling through the mud of the bailey, armed with the knife Rowan had given him in the stable.

'You are a dead man,' gasped Salisbury.

'As are you,' said Maelgwyn weakly from the mud, 'but I know I can meet God with a clear conscience while you will surely roast in the fires of eternal hell.'

With a scream of rage Salisbury fell onto Maelgwyn and drove his own knife deep into Maelgwyn's stomach, causing the young man to gasp in pain.

'Nooo,' roared Tarw and he raced across the bailey to pull Salisbury off his son. The castellan groaned in pain and crawled away through the mud.

Tarw fell to his knees and picked up his mortally wounded son, cradling him in his arms as blood poured from the boy's mouth.

'Maelgwyn,' he said, brushing the boy's matted hair from his face, 'I am here, my son. Your father is here.'

'I knew you would come,' said Maelgwyn weakly, 'I prayed every night for your return and here you are.'

'I didn't know,' whispered Tarw as his tears started to flow, 'I thought you were already dead. If I had known you were alive I swear I would have come sooner.'

'It's alright, father,' said Maelgwyn, 'I will soon be with mother again and all this pain will be gone.'

'Maelgwyn,' sobbed Tarw as he felt the boy's body weaken, 'please don't go.'

'It is time, father,' whispered Maelgwyn, 'I love you.'

'And I love you, my son,' he replied and as his own tears fell on the boy's face, Maelgwyn died in his father's arms.

For what seemed an age he knelt in the mud, cradling his dead son as the garrison watched silently from the palisades. Nobody spoke and for a few moments the bailey was as still as any graveyard. Finally, a quiet plea for help broke the spell and everyone turned to see Salisbury sitting against a water trough, his face ashen and screwed up in agony.

'Help me,' he said again, his voice laden with pain, 'please, somebody.'

For a moment nobody moved but a murmur of surprise rippled through the watching men as Nesta started to inch her way through the mud towards him.

'Nesta,' gasped Salisbury as she neared, 'I need the physician. They'll listen to you, tell them to send for him.'

Nesta paused for breath and looked down into the mud. Rowan's sword lay beside her and she picked it up before turning her cold stare back to Salisbury.

Another murmur came from the ramparts as the men realised her intention.

'Somebody help her,' cried Tarw, 'in the name of God!'

'No,' hissed Nesta through her tears of pain, 'everyone stay where you are!'

The castle fell silent again as Nesta dragged herself through the last patch of mud towards the man responsible for causing her and her family so much heartache.

'Nesta,' gasped the castellan, seeing the blade, 'you don't have to do this. Help me and I promise I'll do whatever it is you want. Your lands, your family castle, even Deheubarth itself, I'll hand them all over to you, I swear.'

Nesta struggled to her knees. Her whole body was covered in mud and her face smeared from the tears of pain that had flooded down her face. For a few moments she caught her breath, staring down at the sword now laying across her lap.

Finally, she looked up and Salisbury gasped at the sight of so much hatred in her face.

'I curse you, John of Salisbury,' she said quietly, 'I curse your soul with every ounce of my being.'

'No,' gasped Salisbury as she lifted the sword to rest the point against his chest. 'Please, I beg you…'

Nesta took a few deep breaths and summoning the last of her remaining strength, drove the blade between the castellan's ribs, cutting his heart in half.

His gasp of pain echoed around the bailey and as Nesta watched on coldly, John of Salisbury died in the stinking mud of Pembroke castle.

'Somebody send for the physician,' said one of the sergeants eventually, 'and get the lady Nesta up to her quarters. The rest of you, back to your posts.'

The men turned back to face out over the palisades, knowing that their fight was still to come. The sergeant walked over to Tarw.

'My lord Tarw,' he said, 'you can't stay here, this place will be crawling with my countrymen in a matter of hours. You need to leave.'

'You are letting us go?' asked Tarw looking up at the sergeant.

'What happened here today is dishonourable to everyone who witnessed it. Take your son and bury him in the soil of his forefathers.'

'And Nesta?'

'We will look after her. Her injuries are bad but will heal. Now, you should be gone before it is too late.'

Tarw stood up and waited as two of the soldiers wrapped Maelgwyn's body in a blanket before placing him over the saddle of the Welsh prince's horse.

'I will never forget this,' said Tarw, 'you are an honourable man.'

'We may be enemies,' said the sergeant, 'but in the eyes of God we are still nothing but simple men. Now be gone.'

Tarw stared at the sergeant for a few moments, all thoughts of hostility and hatred fading until finally, he nodded his head in respect.

'I pray you survive the coming storm, my friend,' he said eventually, 'this world needs men such as you.'

Without another word he took the reins of his horse and as the doomed garrison watched from the palisade walls, walked out through the gates of Pembroke Castle.

Chapter Thirty-Three

Kidwelly

Four years later

The spring sun shone warmly down on the peasants tilling the land outside Kidwelly town. Children played freely amongst the hedgerows and the people worked hard, knowing that even after paying their taxes to the new castellan of Kidwelly castle, there would be plenty left over to feed their families, a luxury they had not enjoyed for many years.

Up on the battlements, the castle steward looked out over the town, his heart gladdened at the way it was recovering after the devastating war that had engulfed Deheubarth after the battle of Crug Mawr.

Many had died in those dark few months following the fight but buoyed by their success in Cardigan, the Welsh armies had consolidated and marched across the south of the country, fulfilling their promises to Gruffydd in memory of his daughter.

The English had fought back hard but with the support of the people, fed up of the terrible tyranny imposed upon them for so many years, the tide finally turned and with King Stephen's attention focused elsewhere, Tarw and his allies eventually wrested full control of Ceredigion, Deheubarth and Gwent from the grip of the English crown. Indeed, all across the country, the people rose from their slumber and for the first time since the arrival of William the Conqueror, Wales was mostly back in the governance of those who had been born there, and would remain so for many, many years to come.

In Cardigan, the one castellan who managed to withstand the rampant Welsh army during the bloody war, Stephen Demareis, eventually surrendered his castle peacefully and was allowed to leave Wales unharmed along with his men and their families.

In Gwynedd, Owain and Cadwaladwr returned to Aberffraw as heroes and after retelling their tales of glory to any man who would listen, turned their attentions to governing their father's kingdom in his name. Gruffydd's illness eased and though he was an old man, he and Angharad settled down to enjoy their last few years in peace.

Back in Kidwelly, a single covered wagon trundled slowly along the muddy road, pulled by a pair of oxen. Eventually it came to a halt a few hundred paces in front of the castle and the cart master climbed down to open the tail gate.

'Father, we are here,' he said and helped an old priest down from the cart.

Cynwrig looked around, his head spinning from the emotions running through his body. For a few moments he stared out at the field before him, knowing full well that this was where the greatest cost of Wales' new-found freedom had been paid. After a few moment's contemplation he turned to the cart.

'Come,' he said, 'this is the place we talked about.'

As he waited, Gwenllian's two remaining sons climbed from the cart, eight-year-old Rhys ap Gruffydd and his brother, Maredudd ap Gruffydd, two years older.

'You'll be needing this,' said the cart master handing the priest his staff, 'the ground is wet and uneven.'

Cynwrig took the staff and led the way out onto the field, followed closely by the two young princes and the cart master.

'Is this the place?' asked Maredudd when they finally stopped.

'It is,' said Cynwrig, 'this is where your mother died but by doing so, sent a cry across this country that awoke us all from our slumber.' He turned to the cart master. 'Do you have it?'

The cart master stepped forward and held out a wrapped package.

Cynwrig discarded his staff and carefully unfolded the hessian to reveal Gwenllian's sword. Holding it reverently across two hands, he held it out gently to the boys and each took it in turn to kiss the blade before Cynwrig placed the tip into the soil where she had been killed.

'Her body may be gone,' he said as Maredudd and Rhys each took a grip on the hilt, 'but her soul is already with God.' His two hands covered the tiny hands of the boys and he looked lovingly between them. 'Ready?'

Both princes nodded and Cynwrig looked up to the cloudless sky.

'Dear Lord,' he said, 'bless the memory of your daughter and may heaven be big enough to hold her heart. In her name and for evermore, I name this place Gwenllian's Field, let her name live forever upon the lips of every soul born in Wales forthwith.'

He nodded at the boys and with a concerted effort, all three drove the sword deep into the soil where the famed warrior princess had lost her life.

'It is done,' said Cynwrig. 'May your mother rest in peace.'

He made the sign of the cross before turning away to return to the wagons. Beside him, each of Gwenllian's sons held one of his hands, helping him across the field where so many men had lost their lives in the pursuit of freedom.

'Father,' said the cart master behind him, 'you forgot your staff.'

Cynwrig paused for a moment and looked down at each of the boys

'I need no staff,' he said gently, 'I have all the support I need.'

Epilogue

Kidwelly

The fields were quiet now, the sun sending tired but free workers back to the safety and warmth of their humble homes. Several leagues away, a wagon trundled westward, heading for the Cathedral of Saint David, carrying two sleeping boys and a very tired priest back to the place where he knew he would shortly die.

In the fields below the towers of Kidwelly Castle, Gwenllian's blade swayed slowly in the soil that had once accepted her life blood.

The silence was all encompassing, the country enjoying the sleep that only peace and freedom could bring and as the darkness deepened, something moved at the point where Gwenllian's sword had pierced the earth.

There, from the soil there appeared a tiny welling of water, a mere teardrop as if the earth was crying for the memory of Gwenllian.

The teardrop became two and then three as more water appeared, wrapping itself around the blade. Soon there was a trickle and as the moon arose, the natural underground spring finally breached the soil to pour out onto the land, and as the growing flow trickled away to find its route to the sea, it was as if it the wind itself was whispering her name in the darkness...

'Remember Gwenllian!'

The End

The English

In this book, as indeed in the others, the enemy forces from the Welsh perspective are usually referred to as English. This of course is not entirely correct as after the invasion of William the Conqueror in AD 1066, many of those occupying the armies of the crown were of French, Flemish, English and even Welsh descent along with mercenaries from all sorts of places. The use of the term 'English' is purely used to ease the understanding of those readers who may be confused with the many nationalities involved.

Gwenllian Ferch Gruffydd.

For those who may not have read the previous four books, Gwenllian Ferch Gruffydd was indeed a true-life warrior princess who lived a wonderful life of romance and excitement. She eloped when she was about sixteen with a handsome prince and spent the next twenty years or so fighting the Normans and English who had overrun the southern kingdom of Deheubarth (modern-day south Wales.)

She had four sons with Gruffydd ap Rhys (Tarw) but her life was cut tragically short when, while Gruffydd was away seeking reinforcements from her father in the north, she led a Welsh army against the English at Kidwelly castle. Alas she was betrayed by a fellow Welshman and she lost the battle but despite surrendering, she was beheaded on the battlefield by men under the command of Maurice de Londres. Her name went on to become the battle cry of the Welsh for hundreds of years.

Gruffydd ap Rhys.

Known as Tarw in our tale, he spent a lifetime trying to regain the kingdom of Deheubarth from the control of the English. When he met Gwenllian, they fell in love, married, and raised their family together whilst living amongst the manors and safe houses of Deheubarth. When Gwenllian died, he raised an army and joined with her brothers to drive the English out of Deheubarth after a spectacular and unexpected victory over them at the battle of Crug Mawr. He died in mysterious circumstances the following year after finally achieving what he had dreamed of all his adult life, the reunification of Deheubarth under Welsh rule.

Gruffydd ap Cynan

Gruffydd was a successful king who ruled Gwynedd in the north after many, many years of struggle, including being exiled to Ireland several times and being thrown into a dungeon for over 12 years by an English earl called Hugh the Fat. During his fight to reclaim Gwynedd, he fought anyone who stood in his way, be they English, Welsh or any other nationality. He even once hired a Viking army to help his cause. He never gave up and eventually managed to gain full and complete control over the land he claimed was his birthright. When his daughter, Gwenllian was killed, he was too old and weak to retaliate but his sons united to march south and join with other armies against the English and Normans. Gruffydd died in his bed at the age of 82, a blind old man, but undisputed king of Gwynedd.

Cynwrig The Tall

Unlikely as it may seem, Cynwrig was a real person and saved Gruffydd ap Cynan from captivity when the king had spent over twelve years as a prisoner of Huw the Fat. Little is known of his subsequent life but suffice to say, history would not have been the same if he had not stumbled upon a wretch of a man tied up outside a tavern in the market place of Chester, who eventually went on to become one of the country's greatest kings.

The Ill Way of Coed Grano

One of the first actions leading up to the battle of Crug Mawr was the killing of an important English noble, Robert Fitzgilbert. While returning home to Ceredigion after visiting the English king in AD 1136, he was ambushed on the path known as 'The Ill Way of Coed Grano,' by the grandsons of the infamous king of Gwent, Caradog ap Gruffydd.

The success of the attack prompted Gruffydd ap Cynan's sons, Cadwaladwr and Owain to launch attacks on several castles in Ceredigion, returning to Gwynedd victorious and laden with the spoils of war. Encouraged by their success, the two brothers then led their armies south to Crug Mawr and joined with the army of Gruffydd ap Rhys (Tarw) to fight a strong English army.

The Battle of Crug Mawr

The battle was a real event in history and changed the political landscape of Wales for hundreds of years. Depending on the sources, the make-up of the combatants vary as does the actual tactics employed by both sides but in general, the following information seems to be somewhere near the truth.

With the combined Welsh army approaching Cardigan, a strong English force assembled at Crug Mawr and occupied the advantageous high ground.

The English were led by several English nobles, namely Robert Fitzmartin, the lord of Cemais, Maurice Fitzgerald, lord of Llanstephan and Stephen Demareis the constable of Cardigan castle.

Their forces were made up of over a thousand Flemish mercenaries in the vanguard, seven thousand Norman levies in the main body of the army and over two thousand horsemen. In all, their number was in excess of ten thousand combatants.

The Welsh were led by the brothers, Owain and Cadwaladwr ap Gruffydd from Gwynedd and an alliance of men from across the kingdoms of Wales including Hywel ap Maredudd, Madoc ap Idnerth and of course, Gruffydd ap Rhys. They had several thousand archers armed with longbows, a main army of over six thousand men and a thousand cavalry.

When the battle started, the Welsh archers devastated the Flemish vanguard with the accuracy and the power of their longbows, causing them to turn aside and flee from the field of battle. Seeing the catastrophic effect of the enemy arrows, the English committed their cavalry early but again, the longbows took their toll and they were easily countered by Owain's cavalry. The Welsh bowmen then turned their attention on the main English army, wreaking havoc before withdrawing behind the Welsh lines as the main battle commenced.

With Owain's cavalry now dominating the field, the English hopes of victory were shattered and their ranks eventually broke to flee back to Cardigan, harried at every step by the triumphant Welsh.

There is no doubt that the longbows were the main factor in the surprising victory for the Welsh, and it has been suggested that this was one of the first times they were used seriously in warfare. History shows that they went on to become a very important weapon for hundreds of years.

Many survivors fled back to Cardigan, but the triumphant Welsh pursued them and sacked the town. When the fleeing English reached the river Teifi, the main bridge collapsed under the weight and many hundreds of men and horses drowned in the river. Some chroniclers of the time reported that a man could cross the river without getting his feet wet, such was the quantity of dead bodies. Every castle in Ceredigion subsequently fell to the Welsh except one, the small castle of Cardigan commanded by Stephen Demareis and as the uprising spread, Deheubarth eventually came back under the control of Gruffydd ap Rhys.

Fact or Fiction

The 'Brut y Tywysogion' (The Chronicle of the Princes), is one of the most important primary sources for Welsh history, probably written by Geoffrey of Monmouth in the 12th century AD. In it, he records the following:

'After that Owain and Cadwaladr, sons of Gruffudd ap Cynan, moved a mightly, fierce host into Ceredigion - the men who were the splendour of all the Britons, and their security and their strength and their freedom and were jointly upholding together the whole kingdom of the Britons. Those in the first attack burned Walter's Castle. And thereupon, with their wings stirred, they laid siege to the castle of Aberystwyth and burned it. And along with Hywel ap Maredudd and Madoc ab Idnerth and the two sons of Hywel, namely Maredudd and Rhys, they burned the castle of Caerwedros. And thence they returned home.

At the close of that year they came a second time to Ceredigion, and along with them a numerous force of picked warriors, about six thousand fine foot-soldiers and two thousand mailed horsemen most brave and ready for battle. And to their aid came Gruffudd ap Rhys and Hywel ap Maredudd from Brycheiniog and Madoc ab Idnerth and the two sons of Hywel ap Maredudd. And all those united together directed their forces to Cardigan.'

Gwenllian's Field

The place where Gwenllian died is well known in the shadows of Kidwelly Castle and it is indeed called Gwenllian's Field.

Legend has it that where she was killed, a spring miraculously appeared from the ground and has remained flowing from that day to this. That may or not be true, but even so, what a way to be remembered!

Summary

And so, we come to an end of the fascinating tales of Gruffydd ap Cynan and his wife Angharad. Of Gwenllian Ferch Gruffydd and her husband Gruffydd ap Rhys (known as Tarw in our tale) and of course the wonderful, colourful life of his sister, Nesta ferch Rhys.

Over the past five books it has been my privilege to look back into the past, glimpsing into their extraordinary lives and using whatever limited information is available to bring them to life between the pages.

As is usual in these types of books, the story is made up of a lot of research and a heavy dose of artistic license. Many of the events actually happened and are easily found on the internet but where information was sparse or indeed, needed some tweaking to make the story work, then it is down to the imagination of the author to tie it all together.

Hopefully the right balance has been struck for your maximum enjoyment and if I have remotely succeeded in providing just the smallest of windows into what were undoubtedly fascinating, yet cruel times, then it was all worth it.

I hope you enjoyed reading them as much as I enjoyed writing them.

Thank you
Kevin

For more books by the same author, go to:

KMAshman.com

Made in the USA
Lexington, KY
12 July 2018